TERMINAL BLACK

A selection of recent titles by Adrian Magson

The Marc Portman thrillers

THE WATCHMAN *
CLOSE QUARTERS *
HARD COVER *
DARK ASSET *

The Harry Tate thrillers

RED STATION *
TRACERS *
DECEPTION *
RETRIBUTION *
EXECUTION *
TERMINAL BLACK *

The Riley Gavin and Frank Palmer series

NO PEACE FOR THE WICKED
NO HELP FOR THE DYING
NO SLEEP FOR THE DEAD
NO TEARS FOR THE LOST
NO KISS FOR THE DEVIL

* available from Severn House

To Ann. Essential to everything.

ACKNOWLEDGEMENTS

To David Headley of DHH Literary Agency, for his continued support and belief in my writing.

To Kate Lyall Grant (who writes the best reviews of a manuscript EVER), for her continued belief in and support for Harry Tate and others; to her colleagues at Severn House and Black Thorn Books, Natasha Bell and Loma Halden, for the truly excellent editing work; to Holly Domney, cheerleader and production coordinator; to designer Jem Butcher, who keeps turning out those great cover images; to Canongate Books for keeping it all going.

ONE

'*Target on the move. Repeat, target on the move.*' The voice came from a phone on the van's dashboard, startling the driver.

As he reached for the gear lever the woman in the passenger seat said, 'Not yet. She's on the sixth floor. We go when she leaves the hotel.'

'Whatever you say. But I really do not like this.' The driver's accent was, like the woman's, Russian, with a faint American twang. He checked his mirrors repeatedly and scratched at a recent tattoo on the side of his neck where the skin was red and puffy. It was meant to be a phoenix but bore only a faint resemblance.

He had good reason to be concerned. At a mere spit away from the Houses of Parliament in central London, one wrong move would bring a firearms team to the area within minutes. If they managed to get away, their actions would be captured by the extensive array of cameras on every street and they'd be tracked through the capital like watching a bug on a tabletop.

'What you like is not important.' The woman, whose name was Irina, was stocky, with wild, curly hair, and the way it bounced when she was agitated gave her the appearance of a caged animal. Dark clothing and black jump boots rendered her almost invisible in the gloom of the van.

'Why do we have to speak English?' the driver queried.

'Because English with accents is common here – you know that. If anybody hears us, we're just a couple of dumb foreigners working crazy hours.'

He shrugged. 'Dumb and crazy is right.'

Her voice took on a hard edge. 'Don't let Kraush hear you talking like that.'

He shook his head and turned up the radio. A news announcer was talking, the mellow tones flowing around the interior of the van like treacle.

'*Amid shifting reports of the on-off relationship between Minsk and Moscow, Belarusian President Alexander Lukashenko has voiced characteristically blunt concerns about the supposed union between the two countries, telling a press gathering that the reality was of a proposed take-over by Moscow, undermining and destroying Belarus sovereignty. Russian Minister of Foreign Affairs Sergey Lavrov reacted—'*

Irina reached out and hit the off button. 'More lies,' she said briefly. 'We don't listen to that—'

She was interrupted by the voice from the phone. *'Target approaching exit. Repeat, target approaching.'*

'Once only!' she snapped. 'You think we're in a freaking movie?'

Silence. When the voice came back on it was deliberately and dryly British. *'Target to exit . . . five, four, three, two . . . one and out . . . and turning left. Over to you.'*

Irina nodded. They had checked out the area around the hotel after hacking the target's phone. They knew where she was going. All they had to do was choose their moment.

'Now,' she said, grabbing the door latch. *'Go!'*

The driver stamped on the accelerator, jumping the boxy delivery van away from the kerb. The sudden movement rattled the boxes in the back and pitched the phone on the dashboard into the woman's lap.

'Slower,' she muttered, flat-handing a signal for him to ease off the pedal. Getting spotted by a keen-eyed cop wasn't part of the plan. In the meantime, the watcher on the hotel would follow the target to ensure they didn't lose her.

The plan of attack had been decided as soon as they had learned their target's location. They had been down here three times the previous day, the first on foot and twice in the van. On the last two occasions they had stopped at the kerb feigning delivery drops, scoping the buildings and streets around them, then checked the intersections and alleyways, the routes in and out and the likely presence of police and traffic wardens. Nobody had given them a second look. And why should they? Delivery vans were a common sight in these streets, part of the patchwork of city life.

The driver, who knew the area a little, had pointed out that a fast exit wasn't going to be easy. But Irina had accepted no argument, saying time was against them. With luck they'd be gone and far away before anybody could react.

'Target turning left.'

The disposition of street lights cast patches of heavy shadow, while light refraction from elsewhere combined to create the false impression of movement.

'We need a description!' Up against the windscreen, Irina was searching for a sight of the target. 'Clothing, bags – anything.'

'Short hair, medium height, knee-length coat, collar up, black boots, a bag on the left shoulder. Padded laptop bag in her right hand. The street is clear. No traffic or pedestrians. Am now pulling back.'

'Good. Go back in and clear out her room.'

'Got it. Over and out.'

The driver increased speed towards the corner, which he knew would take them into a narrow street with double yellows either side. A movement in the shadows showed the watcher making his way in the opposite direction, his task complete.

Once round the corner they would have a clear pavement on a darkened street, with no obstacles save for an occasional rubbish bag or wheelie bin. Two of the street lights had been deactivated in readiness by the watcher less than an hour ago.

'Slow as you turn,' said Irina. 'We don't want her spooked.'

'Got it.' The driver hauled on the wheel, the headlights flaring off glass on each side, illuminating the rich gloss-painted iron railings and the polished brass of door furniture.

Irina jabbed at the windscreen. A solitary figure was walking away from them on the left-hand side of the street. 'There!'

She released the door latch. They had rehearsed the manoeuvre many times, tracking, spotting and moving in. The vehicle type had been similar and the tactics transferable. Only the scout in the hotel was different, a local contractor with no connections to them and no knowledge of what was about to take place.

Stop. Snatch. Go.

The driver was humming again, working the simple mantra in his head, seeing it unfold just as they'd practised. He waited until they were thirty metres behind the target before lifting his foot a fraction, ready for a quick stop.

Then the mantra was ripped apart. Without warning Irina grabbed the wheel, yanking it downwards and out of his hands.

TWO

'*What the hell—?*'

The van swerved sharply, tilting under the sudden torque. The driver tried correcting the direction but it was too late. There was a teeth-shaking bump as they hit the kerb, then they were on the target before she knew it. The headlights blasted the scene with a flood of clarity, highlighting the white blob of the woman's face turned in alarm, mouth open.

It was her. Irina hissed in triumph. The short, cropped hair framed a pale face over a long, dark coat and boots, the style fashionable, almost Goth-like, couldn't be mistaken. Probably pretty once, but no longer.

Terror has a habit of draining prettiness like a pulled plug.

The driver braked but it was too late; the van a relentless and deadly 7,000-lb weapon. A sickening bump signalled the collision and the figure was gone, snatched out of the glare of the headlights with brutal finality and the briefest ghost of a scream.

'*What have you done?*' he protested. This hadn't been part of the scenario. Stop and snatch was what he'd been told, nothing more. This was insanity.

No answer. Kicking the door back Irina was gone, hitting the pavement with ease and sprinting on rubber soles towards the figure lying against the railings of a house with a shiny front door and a potted bay tree.

The driver rode the clutch, unable to believe what had just happened. He checked his mirrors and the nearby windows for signs of observers. Nothing yet, but it wouldn't stay that way. The collision would have been heard. Ahead of them was an intersection, and fifty metres from there was an underground station the target had probably been heading for. All it would need was for one person to turn the corner and come this way—

Then she was back, breathing heavily and eyes staring with the adrenalin-rush of action. She tossed two bags on the floor and slammed the door, then opened her mouth.

'I know!' said the driver, cutting her off. He felt sick. He took the van off the pavement and down the street, making another turn and heading south, forcing himself to reduce speed. The downside to a sudden burst of adrenalin was an unwanted loss of control.

'Is she dead?' he asked. He didn't really want to know, but all he could think of was the woman lying on the pavement. Killing a person in battle was one thing; it was you or the enemy. But this was different. More personal.

Irina snarled, 'I wasn't about to check her pulse, was I? Concentrate on driving and get us away from here. I have to check something.' Saying that she reached for one of the bags and took out a slim laptop computer and switched it on, the screen light making a witch's mask of her face.

The driver shook his head. The crazy bitch had lost it. But caution clamped his mouth shut. After what she'd just done he wouldn't put it past her to sign him off if she got the idea he was surplus to requirements.

'What?' she demanded, sensing his disapproval. This time she was speaking in her mother tongue: Russian. 'You have something to say?' She tapped furiously at the keyboard. 'Drive more slowly – I'm trying to do something here.'

He shook his head but slowed down. 'I meant no offence.' The language switch made her seem suddenly all the more threatening, and he wondered how much longer he could take her overbearing attitude. He'd been given this job because it demanded little and he could do the tasks expected of him with his eyes shut. As long as he didn't have to handle weapons he'd be fine. But this vile creature had changed all that. As soon as they completed the mission, he was going to ask for a re-assignment.

She finished typing, then took out her phone and dialled a number. When it answered, she said, 'As we thought, the target's contact's name is Rik Ferris. I've sent him a message from her laptop.' She waited, then nodded. 'Yes, the place in Stepyanka.'

THREE

Clare Jardine watched as a line of passengers from the latest inbound flight made their way into the terminal building. They looked by turn tired, impatient, rushed and even robotic under the bright lights, as if disconnected from the real world. The steel, glass and aluminium structure of Minsk International airport was impressive, but like a giant greenhouse its glaring light exposed every flaw and furrow, especially in travellers who'd been cooped up in a recycled-air capsule for hours, cheek by shoulder with people they didn't know and probably wouldn't want to.

Most looked like business types in suits, heavy coats and carrying briefcases. Among them was the occasional figure fitting none of the expected norms, looking instead like an oddball member of somebody's family turning up for a surprise visit. And a few Russians, she noted. Returning home and in transit, or here on some other business to further tighten Moscow's grip on their small neighbour.

Not that she could criticize; she had her own Russian here in the form of her partner, Katya Balenkova. An officer with the Russian Federal Protection Service or FSO, Katya wasn't here to undermine Belarus but to improve their equivalent organisation. After her failed participation in a honey-trap mission against MI6, the posting had been a slap in the face but better than the bleaker alternative.

Clare checked faces and body profiles out of habit while trawling through her memory for the face of the passenger she had come to meet. Heinrick Debsen, a Danish businessman on a one-city, two-day visit, was seeking commercial premises to set up a major distribution centre. Her job was simple: collect and ferry him around as and where needed, keeping him safe until it was time for his return flight. Debsen, a high-profile millionaire in his home country, didn't seem overly concerned but, as Clare had been advised by her employers, the rest of the board and his investors were, which was why she had been retained to look after him.

It was the kind of job she was used to, undemanding unless one of her charges turned out to be a sworn enemy of the local mafiya or he decided to get a little too hands-on, which sometimes happened. Then it was down to using tact to dissuade the suggestive comments or the wandering mitts. If that didn't work she was capable of snapping a finger or a wrist if it got too persistent, although she'd resisted that so far. Good-quality security work wasn't that easy to get here in Belarus, and she didn't want to find herself barred because of what the industry might regard as an over-enthusiastic display of *#MeToo* solidarity.

She couldn't see Debsen so she made her way to the security office overlooking the baggage carousels for a better view. She flashed her security pass, which Katya had arranged some time ago. It wasn't her first time in here to check on a client; having established a degree of bona fides when escorting two important state visitors from China a couple of months ago, she was accepted without question. But she didn't want to push her or Katya's luck. Even a member of the Russian FSO on assignment was subject to certain restrictions.

The crowd below was growing from a straggle into a mass. She waited, wondering if Debsen had gone to the bathroom. Then she spotted him, walking casually towards a carousel with flashing lights. The photo sent by his assistant was current and accurate. Debsen was fifty-three, according to the job file, coiffed, brushed and smartly dressed, married with three mini-Debsens and in the upper income bracket among his countrymen. A client to take care of and deliver back unsullied and with a smile on his face, business successfully completed. Just as long as he didn't turn out to be a serial groper. Then Daddy Debsen might be going home with his arm in a sling.

As he bent to pull a leather holdall from the belt, she turned and headed towards the arrivals point where she would impress him, not by holding up a grungy piece of cardboard with his name scrawled on it, but by recognition. First there would be a brief check of his itinerary to make sure he hadn't made any last-minute changes, before making the 40-km drive into the Belarus capital.

As she stepped aside to avoid a group of students being led at break-neck speed by a woman with a flag and a serious display of attitude, she felt a jolt go through her and stopped dead.

A face had jumped out of the mêlée, unexpected and out of place. Not Debsen, but someone else. Someone she knew well. She stood still, stomach cold, scanning the crowd, her VIP client momentarily forgotten.

Rik Ferris? It couldn't be. A trick of the light, perhaps, or someone with a similar look. Ferris wasn't the only deluded type who thought eye-wateringly bad Nirvana t-shirts and hair like a wire brush were cool. He might manage to blend in among a bunch of political activists or extreme gaming nerds, but down there among the ordinary and business classes, not a chance.

There. It was him, one of a number of people she was in no hurry to see again. She automatically scanned the faces around him. Ferris worked with a man named Harry Tate. Both former MI5 officers, they'd been thrown into the same snake-pit punishment posting as herself, guilty of mistakes and judged to be best hustled out of the way where the media couldn't find them. Had their masters' plans gone right, she reflected soberly, that's how they – and she – would have stayed.

Because dead makes you the most unfindable of all.

Tate had been blamed for the death of two so-called innocents during a drugs bust, while Ferris had been caught snooping in classified MI6 archives. Her own mistake had been the opposite side of Katya's honey-trap failure. You don't fall for your target, ever. It's one of the great unwritten rules of the entrapment game.

There was no sign of Tate. Maybe they'd gone their separate ways and Ferris was operating solo. But doing what – and why here?

She felt unsettled at having the memories stirred up after all this time. Ferris belonged to the past, along with Tate and all the others. Yet here he was, in the flesh. She reminded herself that she had no reason to fear him or to avoid him; their knowledge of each other had been brief and remarkable only because of the dangers they'd shared. But he was no threat. She studied his face, reading signs the way she'd been trained. He looked stressed, she thought, unlike the bumbling, no-worries IT-nerd he normally portrayed. Moving with the flow, he had a rigidity to his walk as if he was treading through a minefield, rather than the loose-limbed gait she remembered. A bit older since she'd last seen him and leaner, perhaps. Maybe he simply wasn't ageing well.

She followed his progress through the glass, keeping well back in case he looked up and recognized her. Not that he'd find it easy. Her brown hair was shorter than it used to be, she was thinner in the face and body, partly because of the new diet forced on her by a gunshot injury more than – what, five years ago now. The regular gym sessions and judo classes had helped keep her weight below its level before the shooting by a Bosnian gunman, but she wasn't complaining.

And, she reflected, Katya liked her new look so that was good enough for her.

Apart from that, getting shot had reminded her that being fit and ready to meet whatever challenges might crop up was a vital and necessary habit.

She checked her watch. Debsen still had a way to go, unless he ran into a passport problem or was carrying a couple of kilos of sniffing dust in his bag, in which case the dogs would have him.

She stayed back from the windows and made her way through to a spot overlooking the escalators. All passengers would have to funnel through this point leading to the exit, giving her a chance to see if he was accompanied or being met. A couple of security guards armed with KBP 9A-91 assault rifles gave her a familiar nod. They had seen her on numerous occasions collecting or delivering clients, and she nodded back. They wouldn't be any trouble. The only direction that might come from was whoever Ferris was here to see, especially if they were past or current members of the British Intelligence community. One look from someone who knew her face and her goose would be cooked.

She scanned the crowd of greeters, using a pillar as cover. Drivers, family members, work colleagues and unnameable others, but no face springing out at her from years ago. Nobody with that look of a Security Service or embassy-attached watcher who would see her and ping the news to the bulletin board geeks in Thames House, London.

The tension began to drain away as the passengers flooded out, heading at speed for the main exit. Debsen appeared, looking unruffled and smooth. He'd made the transition faster than expected. Probably the aura of money and importance that surrounded men like him. Ferris must still be making his way through, his t-shirt alone enough to have him hauled aside for a chat and, if the gods were feeling playful, a full body-search.

But Ferris would have to keep for later. She wondered if she should mention it to Katya. No doubt her partner would be concerned at his re-appearance and what it might mean, but she felt an instinct

to downplay the news. One thing was certain: there was no way
she would rest easy until she found out where he was going and
what he was doing here.

As she greeted Debsen and gestured towards the exit, where a
smart BMW 5 series was parked just outside in the restricted zone,
she caught a glimpse of Ferris coming through the arrivals exit. He
was looking the other way and didn't see her. Then her gaze skipped
across two passengers walking not far behind him. A man and a
woman, casually dressed in jeans and warm-weather jackets and
carrying sports bags. Fit-looking, like athletes; not business types
or family members waiting to be greeted with flowers by a loving
Aunt Polina or Uncle Konstantin and hustled away to a crowded
apartment in the city centre.

She did a double-take to be sure. There was something in their
demeanour that rang bells. They were pretending not to watch Ferris
but keeping their eyes firmly fixed on him. Clare had seen that body
language too many times before to be mistaken.

And Ferris didn't seem to have a clue they were there.

FOUR

'I sense that you're not happy, Iain. Care to tell me why?'

The speaker was one of two men seated in a small and exclusive meeting room off Whitehall, which had been swept electronically just minutes before to ensure absolute confidentiality.

Sir Geoffrey Bull, current head of the Joint Intelligence Organisation or JIO, was accustomed to secrecy, as he had been all his working life. When you spend your days dealing with matters of the utmost sensitivity to the nation, it becomes ingrained in your very soul.

'Bloody right I'm not happy, Bull,' came the reply. 'I read my file as you suggested and I'm definitely not happy.'

'Actually,' Bull replied coolly, 'it was your request and my agreement, Colmyer. I did say you might not like it.' He reached out for his tea, his hand showing a slight tremor. It was due to his body giving out on him with increasing rapidity rather than the status of the man seated across from him. Sir Iain Colmyer, Government Chief Whip whose official title was Parliamentary Secretary to the Treasury, was not a man to cross. But Bull had seen and met far worse, and while his physical self was diminishing for reasons he preferred not to divulge to anyone save his physician, his mental defences were not.

Colmyer flushed at the correction but said nothing. He had the smooth appearance of a US senator rather than a British cabinet member, with an expensive tan, neat hair and the glaring confidence that dared anyone to challenge him. It was in stark contrast to Bull, whose skin looked paper-thin and grey and his silvery hair lay lank around his head as if he'd just emerged from a steam room. Rumour had it that he wasn't long for this world, but Bull had so far done nothing to confirm or deny it. Colmyer didn't care one way or another: he knew that he was a frontrunner to occupy Bull's chair and was prepared to give up his post as a politician to fill it.

'You told me that nobody would ever see my file,' he said, his voice low. 'Yet now I see someone *has* seen it. Ferris or whatever his fucking name is. A low-level mouse of an IT worker in MI5, no less. I thought those archives were beyond restricted.'

Bull winced, although whether at the obscenity or the inaccurate level of secrecy was unclear. 'Ferris is no longer in play. He was canned years ago and last heard of doing private security work. Besides,' he looked up and said with near silky slyness, 'what's your worry? Is there something you haven't told me?'

Colmyer leaned forward, jogging the table. 'There's nothing else – you know that! My business interests in Moscow are all in the past, over and done.'

'Indeed, you've been very frank about your connections there. And I've spent a lot of time speaking up for you on that subject, as did Sir Anthony Bellingham for your father before me.' He gave the faintest of smiles, adding, 'But friends in high places can only do so much.'

'What the hell does that mean?'

'It means, Colmyer, that you're running out of reasons to be cheerful. You benefitted from your father's business acumen in Russia and elsewhere, but you've also – what's the term . . . oh, yes, you've also played off two suitors, one against the other.'

Colmyer stared at him, his tan fading slightly. 'What?'

'It's true, you've explained fully your past financial interests over in the east, and apart from one or two small matters remaining, it's done and dusted. But did you honestly think you could use the Americans for the same purposes . . . and nobody would find out?'

'Rubbish,' Colmyer snapped. 'Those were strictly social meetings.'

Bull pulled a buff-coloured folder towards him and flipped it open. It seemed to require a great effort and he took a deep breath. 'Yes, they were,' he agreed. 'Very social. But will your friends in Moscow think so?' He flicked a photo out of the folder. It skidded across the cloth and made a *tink* sound as it hit the side of Colmyer's saucer. 'That's you at a meeting three years ago with Jameson Skinner, currently National Security Advisor to the White House. Back then he was Director of the Central Intelligence Agency. In the background is his then Operations Director, Barney Pressley, and alongside him the head of the NSA, the National Security Agency.'

Colmyer's face had turned red and he began to get up. 'Where did you get this?'

'Please sit down,' Bull murmured. 'This is for your own good, not mine. And where we got it makes no difference. It came to light, that's all you need to know.' He passed across another photo. This one was a little grainy but clearly showed five men seated at a restaurant table. The atmosphere seemed to be one of good humour with full glasses and empty bottles.

Colmyer waved an angry hand, trying to brush it off. 'That was taken in Moscow years ago . . . a private function. So what?'

'At least three of the faces around that particular table have since been suborned by the CIA, using information that could only have come from someone close to them. Further, following your meetings in Washington with Skinner and Pressley, your business interests in the States were subsequently given an unexplained easy passage.' Bull closed the folder. 'These photos are on your file, the first one a recent addition. You evidently didn't see it . . . and neither would Ferris who, it appears, has suddenly disappeared for no apparent reason.'

'So there's no problem.'

'There shouldn't be . . . until you learn that the "low-level mouse", as you called him, has recently been in communication with a hacker known to have Russian connections. See where I'm going with this?'

'I'm not stupid!' Colmyer retorted angrily. 'How did he get to see the file in the first place?'

'An error of judgement? Trusting someone who couldn't resist poking his nose where he shouldn't? The thing is, it doesn't matter now – it's done. I don't care what you did in the name of financial expediency, but I'm here to warn you that your dinner contacts in Moscow probably won't feel the same way if they hear you've been cosying up to the Americans. They have nasty, suspicious minds when it comes to "friends" talking to the CIA. Malicious, even.'

Colmyer's eyes went wide for a moment, then he recovered. 'I don't understand what you're getting at.'

'This is my last attempt at watching your back. You've done very well in the past, having Bellingham and me behind you, heading off enquiries and attacks. But no more. If you want this job after me, you had better make sure that nobody – *nobody* – can use any of this against you. There's too much riding on it.'

Colmyer said nothing for a long time, and Bull allowed him to stew. He had long ago lost all patience with the man, whom he had come to see as an overambitious, devious and ruthlessly astute power-player who used people for his own ends. But his private attempts at steering the selection panel away from this man's candidature as head of the JIO had been foiled. So the best he could do was hope that Colmyer would clean up his own mess.

'I'll deal with it.' Colmyer stood this time, his face rigid. 'I take it I can use some resources?'

'To find Ferris? Yes, you can. But limited. We don't want to broadcast it. Someone will be in touch later today.'

'You can trust me.'

'I hope so, Iain.' That quiet voice again, faint but with an edge of steel. 'If Ferris decides to chat a little too loosely to his contact, who knows what he might reveal?'

Fifteen minutes later, Colmyer barged into his office and barked at his secretary to hold all calls. He closed the door and took an encrypted mobile phone from his desk drawer. He hesitated momentarily over dialling the number from memory. He'd used it sparingly over the years, but there had never been an imperative like this one. He was so close to being able to exert some control over events that had long gone too much the other way. Now, on the brink of the next step in his career, he needed to dictate terms rather than being subjected to them. Anything else was unthinkable. He took a deep breath and dialled the number.

The voice that answered was smoothly cosmopolitan with the faintest of accents. 'Sir Iain,' it said. 'How pleasing to hear from you.'

'Hello, Michael,' he said, and winced. He'd so nearly said Mikhail, the man's original name, but stopped himself. Encryption notwithstanding, slips like that could be fatal. 'I need your assistance.'

'Of course. Is it urgent?'

'Yes. A personal matter.'

'Go ahead.'

Colmyer kept it brief. He knew his words would be relayed all the way back from Michael's base outside London to an office in the heart of Moscow. The thought gave him both a tremor of apprehension and a tight rush of excitement.

When he was done Michael's only response was, 'Thank you. You did well to call me.'

The call was disconnected before Colmyer could reply.

FIVE

Harry Tate wanted coffee and chocolate cake, and not necessarily in that order. He'd settle on the sugar rush and the caffeine hit as they came and be happy at the start of another new day.

Idle thoughts for a happily idle mind. He was sitting in a first-floor restaurant in west London, where Chelsea bleeds into Fulham. It had a hard-wood floor, walls painted blue-grey and glass tables with comfortable chairs and bench seats with buttoned backs. The furniture and lighting were designed to make a leisurely meal easily bearable, with dome lights over each setting and sufficient space between the tables to provide privacy.

It was Harry's current favourite for taking coffee whenever he had the opportunity. Right now it was nearly ten a.m. and the place was empty, which suited him fine. The staff didn't mind early customers, especially the easy-to-serve ones who knew what they wanted and possessed good manners.

Their normal business clientele leaned towards loud start-up wannabes with venture capital money and a firm belief that the bubble couldn't burst without warning because they were the new gods of the here and now and could foretell the future. Some were known to throw their weight around with anyone regarded as a menial, and probably spent more on tight pants and designer shirts than most of the restaurant staff could imagine. They also liked to use their smart phones as loud hailers calling up contacts in San Francisco, Munich or Rome to show how connected they were.

The staff had also observed that Harry had a face that spoke of experience and the kind of build that didn't look as if it would budge if one of the start-ups got carried away with his own sense of self-importance. He was occasionally joined by a woman, a slim red-head with a throaty laugh that got the waiters all of a buzz because it was as sexy as hell. Even the female staff envied her poise and would have paid good money for that laugh. One of the waitresses said she'd seen the red-head running an up-market flower shop in Fulham, the kind of place that had a celebrity client list and charged the earth for elaborate arrangements.

As for smart phones, Harry was enjoying a rest from his; it had died several days ago and he hadn't yet felt the need to get it fixed. His few close friends knew where he was and had his landline number. And he was enjoying the silence.

As usual he'd had taken a corner window table where he could study the traffic below, pausing only to give his order to a hovering waitress. Pot of coffee one, cups two, slices of chocolate cake two, no cream. She didn't need to write it down; his order was always the same, although occasionally for a single cup, slice ditto.

'You always have that,' the waitress said with a faint smile and time to waste. 'Chocolate cake.'

'It's my favourite,' he replied. 'Too good to miss.' The restaurant was known for coffee and cake, the former excellent, the latter in Harry's opinion, simply the best.

'What would you say if I told you we were out of it?'

'I'd throw myself in the river and die hungry.'

She feigned shock at the thought. 'Well, we can't have that. Should I bring it right away?'

He glanced at his watch. Jean was always on time, one of the many things he loved about her. 'Give it a couple of minutes, would you? I think I can hold out until then.'

'Of course.' She smiled and moved away with a swing of her hips, disappearing through a pair of batwing doors with twin glazed portholes.

As the doors finished slapping together, two men entered the room. They looked around for a moment, scoping the place, then the one in the lead walked towards Harry. The second man stayed by the door, hands clasped in front of him.

A minder, Harry knew instinctively, the hairs on his arms bristling. Capable looking, fit, watchful but not hostile. Hostile would have approached first, feigning innocence and circling around to the side, winding up and ready to jump.

'Harry Tate?' The first man also looked capable but was better dressed and sleeker. He walked with the slightest lift of one hip, as if he'd picked up a bruise in a weekend game of squash. Leader of the gang, thought Harry. 'Mind if I sit?'

'Actually, I do.' Harry wondered which secret government agency these two worked for. Definitely not cops, though. There were so many off-shoots now, all employing people with similar back-grounds; hunters and catchers and seekers of information. The good ones were easy to miss if you didn't know what to look for, the not-so-good like actors in a bad spook show. The furrowed brows and open mouths were the usual giveaway. But these two were different. Maybe they were from one of the shadowy departments operating between the cracks; the really clever dicks who'd been out there and done it all and didn't need to show off. Either way, right here and now, it was an inconvenience.

'It won't take long. Better here than dragging you into an office down by the river.'

That narrowed it down. MI6 or MI5, the River Boys and Girls. Spies or spy-catchers, take your pick.

'What do you want?'

'My name's Ben Cramer. I tried calling but your phone's not working.'

'How would you know that?'

'I checked. You might be missing some excellent work opportunities.'

'I doubt it.'

Cramer grunted. 'In any case, we can still track it, broken or not. Maybe you didn't know that.'

'Thanks for the tip.' Harry had left the phone at home, so any tracking would have involved feet on the ground, not signals in the atmosphere. It meant he was the focus of a Security Services or SIS field operation and they'd known where to find him. 'What do you want?'

'A quick chat, if you don't mind.'

'I do, but I doubt that will put you off. Which particular cubbyhole did you spring out of?'

'Let's say I straddle the two main agencies with a bit of overlap. Mostly Five, if I'm honest, but one has to be a multi-tasker these days.' He moved the cutlery around to make room for his elbows. He had the remains of a suntan on strong hands, and short fingernails. The kind of hands accustomed to gripping things that went bang.

Ex-army, thought Harry; a bit like Kevin Costner on a bad day. Officer grade, maybe a captain, scooped up after a decent stint in an infantry regiment, too good to let go to industry or the private contract sector.

'Be careful you don't fall down the crack in the middle. Can you get to the point?'

Cramer didn't even blink. 'I was warned you might be a little cranky.' He adjusted one leg to a more comfortable position. 'You've got quite a record, you and Red Station's little band of stuff-ups. Between you, you left a few bodies lying around along the way. Messy.'

'It was a messy situation. Have you come here to spoil my appetite?'

'Nothing like that. It's by way of a preamble, letting you know what I know about your background, so to speak. So what happened to the girl – Jardine, wasn't it? The one who gutted Six's esteemed controller, Sir Anthony Bellingham on the Embankment. Nasty way to go. What was that about?'

'If you know about Red Station, you shouldn't have to ask.'

'Actually, I was elsewhere at the time, otherwise engaged. I'm having to play catch-up. Where is she now, by the way, Jardine?'

'No idea. She moved on, left the game.' A game that had nearly killed her, Harry reflected. Himself, too, at one point. Luckily for him, Jardine, MI6-trained and run and hating the world after they'd canned her to the dustbin outpost known as Red Station in Georgia for getting stung in a reverse honey-trap, had been close enough to save his bacon. He'd been able to repay the favour in due course, but it hadn't made her any friendlier towards him or anyone else. Like others caught up in situations beyond their control she'd become damaged goods. Wherever she was now, she was better off out of it.

A flicker of something in Cramer's eyes might have been scepticism. 'Pity. She's got a permanent spot on Six's finders-keepers bulletin board. Whoever tracks her down will earn himself a lot of brownie points.'

'Him? Bit sexist, isn't it? The agencies were equal opportunity employers last time I looked.'

'You're right. My bad. I'll have to apply for a spot of retraining.'

'And all that is history now, anyway. Years old. Why bother?'

'Because we can't have rogue officers knocking off the top execs and getting away with it. It looks bad for our rep. Let it go and there'd be a queue along the Embankment with guns out, looking for targets.'

'Even though said top exec was a traitor?'

'Even though. Them's the rules.'

'Is this about Clare Jardine?'

Before he could answer, the door at the end of the room opened and a slim figure stepped through. The minder tensed, then relaxed; his thought processes almost visible. Anyone wishing to harm his boss wouldn't come armed with a drop-dead smile or dressed with such understated elegance. Harry didn't need to look to see who it was; he could tell by the footsteps. He kept his eyes on Cramer's face. As the click of heels approached, the minder detached himself from the wall and followed the woman slowly down the room.

Harry picked up a fork and waggled it back and forth. As the woman continued past the table his peripheral vision caught a soft sway of auburn hair brushing her shoulders. She left by the door to the washrooms at the far end. The minder relaxed, rolling his shoulders to show that he'd had her covered all along.

'Your man's looking the wrong way,' Harry said softly. He was holding the fork a hair's breadth above the back of Cramer's hand. 'It's crazy people with sharp cutlery he needs to watch out for.'

Cramer blinked and looked down. He looked desperate to pull his hand away, but didn't, displaying impressive cool.

'Point taken. Although I'd heard you were dangerous, not crazy.' Cramer sounded calm but his eyes gave him away. He hadn't expected this. 'Was that the other coffee and cake who just walked by? If so it was smooth, her picking up your signal like that.' He looked towards the minder and opened his mouth as if to issue an order, but Harry interrupted him before the man could move.

'Don't. Seriously, don't.'

Cramer relaxed with a fleeting look of surprise. 'By God, you're serious.' He inclined his head towards his man. 'You know he'd be on you in a second if you tried anything.'

'But not before this fork got used on something other than cake.'

SIX

Cramer gave a signal for the minder to return to his post. 'OK. Bigger dick session's over. What do I need to say to convince you I'm serious?'

'What you want might be a start. But remember I'm old hat. I have no interest or value to whoever employs you.'

'Not according to your file.'

'What file?'

'Everyone's got a file, Harry – may I call you Harry? Past, present . . . in some cases future. Files are the in thing these days – only digital, of course. Lots of bytes about lots of hats, old and new.'

'Sounds like things got even more bureaucratic since I got canned.'

'Bitter?'

'It was a set-up.'

'I suppose. And?'

'You don't look like a Thames House recruit.' It was a punt; you never knew what you could learn about people without seeming to try. It worked more often than not.

'I was army for a few years, like you. Then I got picked up by Six. Things didn't work out so I transferred again.'

'What happened? Did you use the wrong cutlery?'

Cramer responded by straightening his left leg away from the table and hitching his trousers to reveal a shoe fitted to a prosthetic leg made of a shiny construction, some sort of poly-fibre mix. 'I was attached to a Six Basement team. We were sent after a bomb-maker and local warlord in Kandahar. The information on him was crap but we didn't know that. We were told he was ready to change sides so I was given the all-clear to meet him. He wasn't anything of the sort. On the way in I trod on an IED he'd left for us. I don't remember much but they said it misfired.' He shrugged. 'It bloody hurt, that's all I know. Goodbye, Afghanistan.'

Harry knew about the Basement. They were the specialists MI6 kept for when they needed something doing that they didn't like to admit to. Drawn from the ranks of special forces, they were mobile and 24-hour RTG – ready to go. Where the CIA had the Special Activities Division, Six had their pursuit team controlled from their headquarters in the lower levels of the ziggurat at Vauxhall Cross. But they hadn't always been the only ones they'd used.

'What happened to the Hit?' he asked.

'The what?'

'You heard.' He was sure Cramer was being coy. The Hit, so called, had been led by a man named Latham. They'd been sent to deal with the potential embarrassments that were the members of Red Station once it became clear that the Russians were about to roll across the border into Georgia in support of South Ossetia's demand for independence. The exposure of such a place was a likely career-ender for the two men who had conceived the idea: George Paulton, from Five, and Sir Anthony Bellingham, from Six, and having a bunch of quarantined and highly resentful foul-ups, so called, scooped up by the Russians and potentially liable to talk their hind legs off was unthinkable. Thus, the Hit.

'It never was official, as I understand it,' Cramer replied. 'They were unsanctioned.'

'Try being pinned down by them in a hostile zone and shot in the arm and you wouldn't see the distinction.'

Cramer pursed his lips. 'I guess. Sorry. What can I say? It shouldn't have happened.' He smiled. 'Anyway, I hear you coped well enough, you and the others. I take it Latham's dead and buried?'

'No idea what you mean,' said Harry. It was time to move on. 'You didn't get an offer of a desk job, then?'

Cramer took the switch in his stride. 'Hardly. While under medication I apparently said some very uncomplimentary things about my bosses' incompetence, planning and parenthood.'

'Good for you.' Harry knew all about talking out of turn. He was a past master at it.

'A trawling newshound overheard and blew the op wide open. They suggested I wasn't playing by the rules and relegated me to the side-lines, crewing a desk and a phone. Then I got a call from a joint services panel who wanted to build a dual-agency team and . . . well, here I am.'

'And knowing my background you're still ready to talk about all that?'

'Sure, why not? It's all out there in the spyosphere if you know where to look. Nothing's secret for long in our game, right? Besides, a point in your favour says you're not given to blabbing.'

'Who told you that?'

'Richard Ballatyne.'

Ballatyne was MI6. One of their controllers responsible for field operatives and agents, and one of the few men Harry trusted. 'What is "our game" exactly? Mine's free enterprise.'

Cramer sniffed. 'Come off it. You're grubbing around at the lower end of the security industry doing odd jobs for whoever needs a former spook.'

Harry recognized the tactic: unsettle the target and get him to lower his guard. Anger was always a good way in. But he wasn't about to play ball. He put the fork down and got to his feet. 'I'll see you around.'

He'd taken two steps when Cramer called out. 'Wait. Sorry. That was rude of me. Please . . . sit down.'

'Do I need this? No.' Harry was conscious of the minder moving to block his way. He looked relaxed and ready; accustomed to a spot of rough-house and probably very good at it.

'Maybe not. But an old friend of yours needs your help.' Cramer waved the minder away and gestured at the chair, waiting while Harry sat down.

'Old friend?'

'One of the other Red Station residents. Rik Ferris.'

'Go on.'

'You see much of him?'

'Not recently.'

'But you've worked with him.'

'Off and on.'

'When was the last time?'

'I don't know. About a year ago. Why?'

'We think he's become a problem.'

Harry waited but Cramer didn't elucidate. 'How?'

'He's disappeared. Dropped off the radar.'

'So he's on holiday somewhere. He doesn't have travel restrictions on him, does he? Anyway, how would you know he's gone?'

'Pure fluke, the way these things often are. He was on a random surveillance list . . . like a lot of former spooks. But that wasn't what triggered the search. He was recently picked up in communication with a known hacker who's done work for Moscow. That's bad enough.' He hesitated before adding, 'Now I'm told he's in possession of some highly confidential information. If he's meeting with a Russian contact, that makes him a potential traitor.'

Harry counted to ten, wondering what Cramer or his bosses were really after. How had Red Station reared its ugly head again, an echo of recurring charges and accusations? He couldn't see why, since that had all been cleared up and disposed of. Or had it? A clatter of pots and pans in the background and a voice calling for clean aprons jarred his focus. Maybe this story was an elaborate stitch-up, a ruse to get him on-side for one of Six's nefarious double-dealing jobs.

'Rik wouldn't jump ship. His mother wouldn't let him.'

'Is that a joke?'

'If you knew her you wouldn't need to ask. She knows he was with Five and would skin him alive if she thought he'd gone over the fence. A pity the country hasn't got more like her.'

'Past tense, I'm afraid. Ferris's mother died four months ago. Breast cancer. Word is he went to pieces and hit the bottle, along with some other stuff. He must have thought a lot of her.'

Harry experienced a sense of shock. Rik had a flat in Paddington but kept in close contact with his mother south of the river and had made no secret of his closeness to her. But would her death have been enough to send him off the rails? He didn't want to believe it but grief has many outlets, affects people in different and subtle ways.

'It doesn't sound like him,' he said at last. 'And how would he have got hold of anything in Six's files? He was with Five. Last I heard they weren't good at exchanging their little secrets with each other.'

'That's not totally accurate – his level of access, I mean. Before he got himself dumped Ferris was on loan to Vauxhall Cross in an IT support role while Six was getting some new systems up-do-date.' He lifted an eyebrow. 'He never mentioned it?'

'No.'

'I'm surprised, you two being such good buddies and all.'

'We didn't live in each other's pockets and the past was the past. Some things weren't for sharing.'

'But you worked together. No little chit-chats over the campfire about old times?'

'That's past tense, too. Like I said, I haven't seen him for a year.'

'Did you fall out?'

'No. We went different ways. He stayed in IT. I'm more your blunt instrument kind of person. Some jobs don't require both skills. It happens.'

'True enough.' Cramer flicked at something on the tablecloth. 'And he never gave any indication that he might change sides?'

'No. It wasn't in him. Why would you assume otherwise?'

'Because someone caught snooping in restricted files even once shows form. It's why he got canned, remember, delving into the nation's electronic underpants. Perhaps we now know why. A bit of long-term planning coming home to roost, perhaps.'

'Balls. Being nosey is a long stretch from spying for the opposition and you know it.'

'I might agree with you . . . if he hadn't bunked off with some sensitive data.'

'How sensitive?'

'I haven't been given that information. My job's to get him found.'

This doesn't sound good, Harry thought. To play for time he said, 'But why would it matter? Anything pre-Red Station would be out of date, so why the panic? And why right now? It's – what, ten years ago.'

'Information is never truly old, you know that. Even the long-term, locked up, covered in dust stuff nobody wants to talk about has the power to haunt.' Cramer studied his fingernails. 'All I know is there are restricted files with his mucky fingerprints all over them – or, should I say, footprints.'

'What kind of files?'

'I'm not at liberty to say.'

'Bollocks. You don't know, do you?'

Cramer coloured slightly and Harry knew he'd scored a hit. Cramer was a messenger and hadn't got more than the few details he'd been told to help him do the job.

'Before you jump to conclusions,' Cramer continued, 'I don't mean he's been seen with men in long leather coats or extremist jihadis with bombs in their backpacks. I'm talking about hackers with links to Moscow.'

'Right. Next you'll be telling me he helped get Trump into the White House.'

'Not quite. That began way before Ferris disappeared.'

'OK, so he knows some hackers. Didn't it occur to anyone that it was an extension of his work with Five? He was expected to penetrate groups to expose them; why wouldn't he have got friendly with some of them since?'

Cramer blinked, and for a second Harry wondered if he'd scored another point. Logic was useful in intelligence work, but some people preferred looking at cold, hard facts to the exclusion of common sense.

But Cramer scotched that immediately. 'There's been a lot of unusual cyber activity recently. Something's in the wind and we think it's related to some recent attacks – and we're not talking about a DoS against a single target but serious stuff.'

As Harry knew from Rik, a DoS – or denial of service attack – involved flooding a target's computer system with messages from a vast number of computers, causing it to crash and become unavailable. He knew that just wasn't Rik's style. He might be nosey but he wasn't malicious.

'This has the hallmarks of something much bigger,' Cramer continued. 'The National Cyber Security Centre have their work cut out just keeping up. But these aren't grubby little nerds with nothing better to do than make a nuisance of themselves; it's organized at hostile state level.'

'So send comrade Vladimir an email and ask him to stop. It still doesn't implicate Rik.'

'Why not? We've had word over the past few weeks that a number of known activist hackers have gone silent, mostly across Germany and eastern Europe, and a few here, too . . . experts like Ferris. It's usually a sign that they're being coordinated and trained up for some kind of offensive. As for Ferris, he's on record as having been in contact with a hacker named Nebulus. We picked that name up a while back in connection with some hacks we believe were initiated by a Moscow-affiliated group, and we've been following it. Ferris and Nebulus exchanged messages recently about a meeting in London.'

'It could be harmless.'

'I agree. But it's a hell of a coincidence.'

'What do you expect me to do?'

Cramer's response was blunt. 'Find him and bring him in. Clip his wings before he takes a stupid pill. I want to know what he's been up to recently and who this Nebulus is. As you know the government's recruiting a number of extra experts to boost our cyber-defensive capability, but they'll take time to get into position. It would help if you can find Ferris and give us a heads-up on what's likely to happen.'

'Why should I help you?'

'Well, there's always Queen and country. On the other hand, if you don't help, Six will send someone else after Ferris. And you know how that's likely to turn out.'

Harry stared at him, chilled by the brutal statement. 'You're talking about a state-sponsored execution of a former employee. That'll run well in the tabloids. I thought Five and Six were supposed to be recruiting people, not knocking them off.'

'I'm saying nothing of the sort. You've drawn the wrong conclusion. Maybe I was a little . . . dramatic in tone. Still, accidents happen, you know that.'

'You really don't know where he is, do you?' Harry resisted a smile at the idea of Rik pulling one over on the might of the security services. In simple terms he'd gone to ground and they hadn't a clue how to find him. The rise of the techies.

'Not yet,' Cramer admitted, looking a little sore. 'But whose fault is that?'

'Mine? You're kidding.'

'Of course yours. He was a pinhead IT geek until Red Station. Then you got your hands on him and turned him into Junior fucking Action Man.' He stood up in a smooth movement and flexed his false leg. 'You trained him, Harry, so it's up to you to find him. Before somebody else does.'

Harry wanted to tell him to sod off but thought that unwise under the circumstances. Beneath the seemingly calm exterior, Cramer seemed to be under some pressure. All it needed was for him to overreact and push a go-button and sooner or later Rik would pop up somewhere in the world in the gunsights of a professional cleaner. 'What's my motivation?'

Cramer tapped the table with a blunt finger. 'Your freedom and his life. How's that for starters? Play dumb on this and we can tie you up on holding charges as an accessory for years. It'll make Guantanamo look like play-school.' He smiled without humour. 'That's not me talking, but there are people out there who will make it so, given a push.' He dropped a card on the table. All it held was a phone number. 'That's where to find me. But make it quick because time's a-wasting. Enjoy your coffee and cake.'

'What did the spookies want?' Jean reappeared through the door at the end of the room, where she had been waiting for the two men to leave. As the widow of a former army officer, she had learned long ago to recognize government men when she saw them. She also knew Harry's background and what he now did for a living.

Harry stood up to greet her and murmured an apology. The waitress appeared as if by magic and tilted her head in the direction of the exit where Cramer and his minder had gone.

'Sorry, but I got the impression you weren't ready to share.'

'I wasn't,' Harry said with a smile. 'Thank you.'

As soon as she left to bring their order, Harry gave Jean a quick run-down on the reason for Cramer's visit. He figured he wasn't breaking the Official Secrets Act by telling her that a friend was in trouble, although he doubted a prosecution lawyer would see it that way. But he trusted Jean implicitly. Certainly more than he trusted Cramer. And the fact that Cramer had known what his movements were meant he'd been under observation for a while. The thought was unsettling but too late to worry about now.

Jean listened in silence and waited while the waitress served them and departed, then scooped up a forkful of chocolate cake and ate it with an appreciative roll of her eyes which made his heart flutter. But she also looked concerned. 'You're going to look for him, aren't you?'

'You know it and so do they. It's what they're counting on.'

'Do they think you know where Rik is?'

'I doubt it. But they're hoping I can draw him in.'

'Couldn't that be dangerous?'

'Not for me. I don't think Cramer's the sort to carry out terminations.'

'I was thinking about who else might be looking for him; people behind Cramer.'

'Yeah, there is that.'

'Would Rik really have done what they say?'

'I doubt it.' As he knew well, it wouldn't be the first time either agency had made mistakes in pinning guilt on someone. 'But it looks as if I'm going to have to find out.'

They concentrated on their coffee and cake, enjoying the silence and each other's company, albeit with an unwanted hint of tension in the air. All the while Harry was faced with a burning question: if he didn't track down Rik very soon, what was he going to do if Cramer's people got impatient and sent a team out into the field to take what some euphemistically called 'executive action'?

More importantly, what the hell could Rik have picked up ten years ago that would merit the threat of a kill order?

SEVEN

Rik Ferris was cold. Not skin-chilled, the way you get in the open air on a brisk afternoon, but deep-in-the-bone numb, the way sitting in a freezer for an extended period would work its way into your soul. He lifted his head, awareness making him shiver uncontrollably as the air moved around him, and began building a picture of his surroundings.

He was sitting on a hard-backed chair. He could feel that much. It was uncomfortable. A quick scan of his surroundings showed he was in a large, empty shell of a structure, with grey concrete flooring, rough cinder-block walls and, high above, a latticework of rusting metal beams and struts holding up a weather-beaten corrugated roof. Holes in the puddled floor by his feet showed where unknown machinery had once been bolted, the surface heavily stained with oil and the accumulated dirt and labour of many years. The air smelled musty and dead.

His chair was the only item of furniture, placed in the centre of the floor. He looked for and found window spaces, which were few and high up and blanked out with black paint. It was enough to tell him that he was as much a prisoner as if the place had iron bars and unscalable walls.

He dropped his head, trying to take it all in. His face and neck hurt and he had no idea how he'd got here. Wherever 'here' was.

A rumbling sound rolled around the space like subdued thunder, and he looked towards a growing patch of light, where a heavy steel door was sliding back on runners. The clank of a chain gave flight to a group of small birds in the roof, and when he lifted a hand to rub at his eyes, he was surprised to find he was free of any form of restraint.

Dressed as he was in a t-shirt and jeans, he tried to control his shivers, waiting as the thin light washing through the doorway swept over two figures. They advanced towards him, footsteps echoing around the empty space, and stopped twenty feet away, moving apart. Backlit by the open door, their faces were in shadow. Two silhouettes, he could see that much. One on the left, smallish, stocky, the other tall. But that was all.

He shook his head, trying to clear his thinking, and made as if to stand up. But the taller figure put out a hand to stop him.

'Stay where you are.' The voice was authoritative. Sharp. Male. It sounded flat in the large space, with surprisingly little echo, as if the concrete was absorbing the human sound like a sponge.

He stayed still. Focussed instead on breathing and trying to calm the noises in his head. He'd been drugged, he knew that much. There was no other way he could account for the headache or the bitter taste in his mouth, or the feeling that he'd gone a couple of rounds with a heavyweight boxer. But he didn't know why. Or who these people were. Then a memory surfaced: a feeling of pain, the sting of a needle in his arm back at the . . . the apartment block, that was it. But why had he gone there?

'What's this about? Why have you brought me here?' His voice came out as a dry rasp, a little shaky because talking was something he hadn't done in a while . . . maybe as long ago as yesterday, he couldn't tell. Couldn't remember much. Drinking, yes, he'd done some of that, along with others who were sinking pints as fast as they could. Strangers, though, not friends, people he'd met in a pub or club where your presence was dictated by how much you could put away. He didn't normally do that because it didn't interest him. But he must have overdone it this time.

He un-gummed his tongue from the roof of his mouth. It was a reminder that he hadn't had any liquid for what seemed like several hours. Not that time was an issue. He checked his wrist but his watch was gone, as were his iPod and his phone, which he last remembered using in a car. Not a taxi, though; he'd caught a bus from the airport then took a cab to . . . wherever the place was. He'd been texting someone, he remembered that, but the name was drifting on the edge of his memory. Harry? Why would he have texted Harry? They hadn't spoken in months. He was sure he'd pressed 'send', before someone had leaned over from the front seat and snatched his phone away.

He gave up the struggle to remember more and wondered how long he'd been here. And where 'here' was.

'You don't know why you're here, Mr Ferris?' The tall figure on the right again. The man's accent was foreign, maybe German or further east. But not heavy. Someone at ease with speaking English, the contractions and intonation correct.

'How do you mean? I don't understand—' He stopped. *How did they know his name?*

'You help us, and everything will be good.' This was the person on the left. A woman. She had a faint American twang; her tone sharp and loaded with menace. Oh, shit. Was this an interrogation?

'I don't know what you mean. Who are you?' Then another flicker came back, surfacing slowly out of a toffee-like depth. 'I came to see a friend of mine.'

'At the apartment block?'

Rik hesitated and counted to three. He wasn't sure about the apartment block, although there was a vague image floating about in his brain. Some place old and unwelcoming. It was all a haze and his head felt full of cotton wool. Instinct told him to keep his replies simple. Keep them happy. 'Yes. There.'

'What friend?'

A count of five this time. Spread it out but not too much: a distant instruction from a training course a long time ago. 'Nebulus. I was trying to contact Nebulus.' It sounded dramatic saying that name out loud in this cold room. As if he'd been aiming for a distant planet. But he didn't want to say her real name. Nebulus was just a pseudonym, a tag. A handle. No threat to anyone, with no more significance to outsiders than a smiley-face emoji.

'We don't know that name.'

'In that case I'll be going.' He got to his feet and winced, his knees cramped through having sat still for too long. He flexed them and made to move forward. 'Sorry to have troubled you, but this kind of crap is really out of order. I'm going to complain to your tourist authority—'

'Stop.' The man moved forward as he spoke, revealing something in one hand. A mobile phone? 'What does she do, this Nebulus?' the man asked.

'If you don't know her, what difference does it make?'

'I said, what does she do?' The voice came colder, harder, the enunciation scarily deliberate. This time there was another movement of the hand, lifting slightly to the horizontal. It made the object in his hand clear to see, even in the poor light.

A taser? Jesus.

Rik swallowed and sat back down. Why did his legs feel so tired? What had they done to him? They wanted some kind of information, that was obvious. Checking facts. The training-day memory surfaced again with vivid clarity. He hadn't given it a thought in years. There had been an assault course, brutal and pointless but survivable, followed by weapons familiarity and a few other things he couldn't be bothered to recall, all under the relentless gaze of a bunch of stone-faced instructors whose default mode seemed to be contempt for their charges. He'd managed to wipe most of the pseudo-shouty bullshit from his mind since then. It was part of the conditioning and meaningless thereafter.

But not the taser. One of the instructors had used it on him to see how he'd react, and to demonstrate its effectiveness to the other recruits. He'd expected a brief jolt like you'd get from an electric cattle fence. Instead the bloody thing had knocked him on his arse. He'd also peed himself. The others in the group had laughed . . . until it became their turn.

'She's a researcher.' When answering questions tell them only what you can afford to and keep it plausible. The training had also included deflecting interrogation. Not that he'd ever expected to have to use it, not after all this time. Not now. He was out of all that.

'In what field?'

'Information. Data.'

'Public domain data?'

'Sure. Trends, outcomes, simulations – market research stuff.'

'So how would you happen to be a friend of hers?'

'Because I used to work in a similar field.'

'So you're here to do that same work?'

'No. I'm on a vacation.'

A lengthy pause, then, 'I don't believe you.'

The silence was heavy save for a scrape of fabric on concrete as the figure on the left, the woman, shifted her weight. She stepped forward, bringing herself out of the darkness and said, 'We know all about you, Ferris. Your background, your . . . fall from grace, I think you would call it. We also know why and what you were doing that cost you your job.'

'I don't know what you're talking about. I'm in IT, pure, boring and simple.'

She ignored that. 'What we would like is for you to tell us what you saw that got you fired.' She lifted her shoulders. 'That's not so hard, is it? After all, what loyalty do you owe them, your bosses in Thames House.'

Rik let his breath out in a long, slow stream, fighting a rising sense of panic. This wasn't good. Nobody like these bloody munch-kins should know he'd once worked for MI5.

'The problem is, can we persuade you to tell us a few truths?'

'Truths? What kind of truths? You want market research data, get your own. And like I said, I'm on vac—'

The man stepped forward and pointed the taser at his face, a bare inch or so from his eyes. It made Rik rear back, which was when he realized the chair he was sitting on was bolted to the concrete floor and he had nowhere to go.

The shock seemed to clear his vision a little. Up this close he saw that the man and woman were their late thirties, maybe older. Fit looking. Fitter than him, anyway. Dressed in dark clothes; heavy shoes, black jeans and fleece jackets with no logos. Activist *chic*, as if they were about to go out and break a few windows, lob bricks at some cops and torch a few cars. Up the revolution, down with capitalism. All they needed was the Guy Fawkes mask and a couple of banners and they'd be ready to rumble.

But this was no rumble, where the figures would fade into the background and disappear as soon as their job was done or the opposition got serious. The man had the face of a boxer, lightly bearded, with short dark hair, high cheekbones and a crumpled nose. But it was his eyes that held Rik's attention. Light blue, with unusually large irises, they seemed to drill right into him as if reading Rik's very thought processes.

And the taser didn't help.

He looked at the woman. At a distance she might have been described as ordinary. But the hard face and down-turned mouth negated that, with an air of aggression coming off her in waves. She had gingery hair, wild and curly like a crazy halo, and eyes that might have been dark brown. Medium height and stocky, like a gymnast. Princess Merida, he decided, only a long way short of pretty.

He wasn't sure which one to be most afraid of. His instinct was veering towards the man, mainly because of the taser. But there was something decidedly off about the woman's vibe. And off vibes were the worst of all.

'What happened to Nebulus?' he said at last, to unlock the sense of fear growing in him. An image of a grungy apartment block was emerging slowly in his head, with the memory of large balconies, dirty windows and the fumes of burnt cooking fats rising up the cold stairway like an invisible miasma. The place had had the feel of somewhere he didn't want to be, but it was too late to turn round.

He'd knocked on the door but there had been no response. Knocked again, louder this time. But all he got was the dead sound of an unoccupied space inside. Then he'd heard the scrape of footsteps behind him and . . . nothing.

'What have you done to her?' he demanded, because letting this staring match go on was too scary to contemplate.

'We? We haven't done anything,' the man said. 'She wasn't there.'

'Why?' Rik muttered, trying to make sense of it.

'Why what?'

'Why were you there?'

'Ah, I understand.' The man smiled. 'Let's say we were acting on information from your friend Nebulus.'

'What information?' Keep them talking, he thought furiously. Shake this bloody fog out of your brain but keep them talking. Maybe then there might be a way out of this nightmare.

'She was assisting us on a project we are working on. She has certain skills, has she not? Skills not available to everyone. We needed some of her expertise.'

Christ, no, Rik told himself. She wouldn't. Not her. Nebulus was a hacker – and a bloody good one. But she wouldn't trade her skills to people like this.

'However,' the man continued quietly, interrupting his thoughts, 'she decided to disappear without fulfilling our agreement. So we put a watch on her communications and . . . your name came up.' He gave a massive shrug. 'What else could we conclude but that you were in the same line of work? Which, as we have already discovered from a background check, is very . . . fortuitous. Is that the correct word – fortuitous?'

'It'll do. But I don't see how that involves me. I'm a friend, that's all. Passing through.' He was thinking fast; not quite on his feet but close. There was something that didn't ring true in this man's voice, as if he was reading from a script. 'I know she was into IT in a specialized way, but that's all. She didn't talk much about what she did. She liked to play it close to her chest.'

The man sniffed. 'That's a pity.' He turned away and took three steps in a tight circular movement, returning to stand close to Rik, leaning over him. 'Let me cut to the chase, Mr Ferris – or may I call you Rik? I'm Kraush, by the way. We're likely to get to know each other a lot better in the next few days, so let's do away with all that formality. See, if you don't cooperate with us instead of stalling, we will hunt down your absent friend, this Nebulus, and see how long she can stand this little toy of mine.' He held up the taser. 'I should tell you that this is no ordinary device but can be ramped up much higher than others if the target requires a little more . . . persuasion. Do you understand?'

Rik nodded. There was really nothing else he could do in the face of this nut-job and his helper. He'd come across people with hair-trigger responses before, and wasn't about to deliberately antagonize these two without having at least a tiny attempt at getting out in one piece.

'We have some time,' Kraush continued, 'but not unlimited. So it would be good to reach an agreement as soon as you are able.' He reached inside his fleece jacket and took out a notepad and pencil, which he placed on Rik's lap. 'Write down whatever you remember seeing in the files and archives.'

'What?' Rik stared at him. 'What archives? I don't understand.'

'Intelligence archives in MI6, your Secret Intelligence Service. You did some work there and looked in some files, for which you were dismissed.'

'But that was years ago! How do you expect me to remember anything?' It was a feeble statement and Kraush probably knew that. Experience in IT usually relied a great deal on recall. If a user didn't have it to begin with, repetition and demand created it. The pattern of words and numbers, the layout of code which was meaningless to most people, eventually became, if not second nature, then familiar.

Once he began writing he knew he'd find the digits and letter groups spiralling relentlessly out of the recesses of his mind, no matter how far back they came from – especially those last days, which were imprinted on his memory like a bad dream. Some things you never forgot completely, even if they were only vague snatches of something seen in passing.

Kraush was unmoved. 'I think we both know better than that. Start simple, with headings, file names and folders, and build from there. It will come to you.' He leaned closer, his face serious. 'I am not like you – an expert in IT. But I know enough to know this is true.'

Rik wondered whether Kraush was telling the truth or stringing him along as a means of retrieving the information he wanted. He took a gamble on the former and said, 'But you won't know what's relevant, will you?'

Kraush hesitated then said, 'Show me what you can and I will tell you which ones you can ignore.'

Rik felt a tiny thrill of victory. Kraush was just a middle man. He'd been told enough to recognize what was needed, but he'd have to show the details to someone further up the line for confirmation.

'What if I can't remember anything?'

Kraush blinked as if at the absurdity of the idea. 'Then we have a problem. If you will not – or do not – cooperate . . . and your friend Nebulus cannot, we will return you to London, to your MI5, your Security Service, in a wooden box. Think about it.'

With that he turned and walked out of the room, handing the taser to the woman as he passed.

She made no sign in return but slipped the device into her back pocket. As soon as Kraush's footsteps had faded, she stepped forward, and before Rik could react, slapped him hard, knocking him off the chair. Multi-coloured fairy lights sparked about in front of him and a feeling of nausea swept through him at the sour, oily smell of old concrete. He felt a coldness down his cheek followed by a trickle of warmth, and realized she must have cut him. Through a veil of dizziness, he looked up and saw her rubbing her hand, where a large metal ring sat glinting in the dull light.

'You really should consider this, Mr Ferris,' she said softly, watching him climb back on the chair. 'Time might be shorter than you know. The clock is ticking. You really don't want to die here, do you?' She gestured over to one corner, where he saw the vague shape of what looked like a mattress and a blanket. 'In the meantime, make yourself comfortable.'

Then she was gone, sliding the door closed and leaving him to the silence and the dark.

'*You haven't told me what you're looking for!*' he shouted. But the words sounded futile, bouncing back off the walls, dulled and flattened by the cold air and rotting brickwork around him.

EIGHT

'This Ferris thing,' said Sir Iain Colmyer. 'What's the situation so far?' The question was aimed with a degree of impatience at long-time MI5 officer, Richard Hough.

The two men were in Colmyer's private office just outside the Westminster bubble, to which Hough had been summoned. It wasn't on the list of approved sites, but Colmyer evidently had sufficient clout to have temporarily overridden any concerns from Whitehall's internal security watchdogs.

Hough was feeling puzzled. Off-campus meetings were fine in the intelligence world, even accepted as part of the ducking and diving necessary to do the job. Back-street meets in faraway places were his norm – had been his norm – for a long time. Unless you were one of the techno-masters at GCHQ, wired into the electronic pulse that was now the new world order, you simply couldn't do the kind of work he'd been doing all his life stuck behind a desk. But politicians engaging in the practice made him nervous. For a start he wondered how long it had been since this office had been swept for electronic devices.

Colmyer – pronounced, he liked to demonstrate, with emphasis on the second half – Col-*myah* – claimed a family lineage going back to somewhere in the nineteenth century, before petering out altogether. As Hough was aware, Colmyer was a cabinet member with the title of Parliamentary Secretary to the Treasury and Chief Whip. He was on the right side of fifty – just – for such an energetic and important post, but after hovering over two shock cabinet resignations like an opportunistic buzzard over a road-kill, one male MP due to a sex scandal and a female colleague on medical grounds, Colmyer had been in a position to make sure there were no other serious candidates in the running for the post.

He also made no secret that he considered his next move to be the natural progression and reward of many years' hard work. Along with this arrogance and a natural sense of entitlement was a complete absence of tact, evidenced by his enjoyment for strong-arming any MP who looked like stepping out of line at crucial moments.

For Hough, having this man as the incoming head of the JIO was surely a joke being played on the establishment. And God help us all, he thought. Bullying and hectoring were the more polite words he'd heard associated with Colmyer's style, but the skin of a political rhino had made him immune to any barbs of criticism. In fact he appeared to enjoy knowing his presence sowed disharmony and had been heard to boast that it gave him an accurate finger on the pulse of the party.

'Well? Speak up.'

'Our man has been briefed. He should be up and running as we speak.' Hough's reply was instinctively reluctant. As a long-time career intelligence officer, he didn't like hard-nosed politicos who appeared to think the intelligence services were there for their own amusement. Even less did he enjoy discussing operational matters with people who appeared to have sailed through the rigorous vetting procedures applied to everyone else – even intelligence professionals – with casual ease. It went against every instinct in his being. But his orders had been made very clear by the current head of JIO, Sir Geoffrey Bull: '*I want you to provide full assistance to the Chief Whip, because short of falling under a bus or being assassinated, he will one day be taking over as your boss.*'

'Why me?' he'd queried. 'Can't someone else handle it? I'm not ready to put my feet up yet and there's plenty more important work I could be doing.'

'No, there isn't.' Bull had fixed him with tired eyes. 'It won't be for long, Richard. And frankly, you could do without getting deeply wired into another project at this point; you're not long for this place after me, are you? Just get him briefed and keep him happy.'

'To what level?'

'I'll let you be the judge of that. He's been asking lots of questions already. I've given him a briefing about current activities and access to the archives for background at his request. But there's no way I can realistically put him off much longer, otherwise I'll have the PM on my back preaching a lack of cooperation. I don't care for the man, but as the chosen incumbent he needs to know what's going on in the world. And you're the one best able to handle him.'

Hough wasn't so sure. The word around the office was that he'd copped an unpleasant undertaking from which no good would come – especially for him. Being steamrollered by a politician on the up was impossible to resist for someone in his position, and after a

lifetime serving the country in the shadows and trying to avoid the
bear-pit that was the political hunting ground of Whitehall, Hough
recognized a poisoned chalice when he saw one. But he wasn't
going to go down like a cheap whore just because this incomer
demanded it.

The problem was, Colmyer was sounding more up-to-date than
Bull had suggested. The old man must have given away quite a full
briefing, he thought shrewdly. Perhaps he was closer to giving up
the job than anyone had realized.

'By up and running, what do you mean?' Colmyer demanded,
bringing him back to the present.

'He's started work on a plan of action.' It wasn't strictly correct,
but it would do for now. A delaying tactic could only work as long
as the opposite party couldn't check. And there was no way Colmyer
would be able to do that just yet.

'I hope you're right.' Colmyer eased back in his chair, making
it creak with the effort. He'd made no secret of his views that the
intelligence world needed shaking up, and intended to see that it
happened. If that meant treading on a few toes, he was more than
up to the job. 'How long before we hear something?'

'That's a little hard to say,' Hough replied. 'He needs to get up
to speed from a standing start, which isn't easy in his position.'

'What the hell does that mean? Why do you spooks always talk
in riddles?'

'He's what we call unattached. Outside the agencies, which I
believe was requested, although I'm not sure why.' He shrugged as
if to convey his puzzlement about this issue, which he was sure
would irritate Colmyer no end.

Colmyer fixed him with a cold stare. 'I'm well aware of the status.
What's his name – or are you going to resist telling me that, too?'

Every instinct in Hough's professional life had been trained
against giving out such information, short of having bamboo splin-
ters stuffed under his fingernails and being water-boarded to within
a millilitre of his life. That applied equally to non-agency personnel
– or former serving personnel in this case. But again he had no
choice. If he didn't cough it up here and now, Colmyer would find
out another way, and whatever was left of Hough's own career,
which was winding down fast, would end even more abruptly in
some backwater office filling out electronic databases. 'His name's
Tate,' he said. 'Harry Tate.'

'What the fuck?' The expletive was as much a surprise as Colmyer's stunned expression. 'I've heard of him.'

'Have you? I wouldn't know.' Hough was glad he'd been trained to keep a straight face. *How did you hear?* he wanted to ask but didn't.

Colmyer scowled. 'Wasn't he the idiot sanctioned years ago for a shooting during a terrorist operation? I thought he was finished and gone.'

Hough experienced a small measure of satisfaction. So much for a finger on the pulse. But at the same time he wondered how much Colmyer really did know. The detail surrounding Harry Tate's expulsion from MI5 was hardly common knowledge outside the agency, and the entire Red Station fiasco had been consigned to a deep vault in the archives where the agency's more embarrassing episodes could be left to fade and die, safe from the eyes of the press and those who would like to bring down that particular establishment in a pile of rubble. A bit like Tate's intended fate had been mooted at one time, he thought. And look how that had ended.

He'd heard relatively little about Tate since then, save for the occasional intriguing echoes whispered around the corridors of Five. He'd done some work for Five and Six, it had been rumoured, doing pretty much the same job he'd been doing before but no doubt paid more appropriately. It was only when Hough had been handed this latest task by Sir Geoffrey Bull that the name had cropped up and he'd been briefed more fully.

'It was a drugs bust, actually,' he corrected smoothly. 'One of Five's side-line responsibilities helping the Met. And he's very much active, albeit not in an official position. In fact,' he continued ignoring Colmyer's raised hand meant to silence him, 'Tate's quite the survivor.'

'Christ, you sound as if you admire the man!'

'Merely stating facts.'

'But he got two people shot – one of them a girl!'

And there it was, Hough thought sombrely. Confirmation that Tate's file history wasn't as secure as he'd been led to believe. He wondered who else knew about it. More importantly, who had briefed this idiot?

'The young woman,' he said, to cover his thoughts, 'was in a relationship with a member of the international drugs gang they were intercepting.'

'That doesn't make Tate blameless. As control on the ground, the outcome rested with him.'

Hough considered his response to that and thought to hell with it; he hadn't got long to go. 'If we took that attitude across the board, we'd find a lot of senior police, security controllers and army officers without jobs. Politicians, too.'

Colmyer leaned forward over his desk like a toad about to jump. 'Well, I'm not bothered about them. Let's hope Tate doesn't stuff things up this time, otherwise he – and you – will be in the shit. Are you saying he's the only option we have in locating this Rik Ferris person?'

'Only and best. Ferris has been monitored on and off since he was fired; it's common for most personnel with his background. But he dropped out of sight recently without warning. If anyone can find him, Tate can.'

'I hope you're right for your sake. What about a fail-safe?'

'Fail-safe?'

'What if he can't locate him?'

Hough hesitated. The term fail-safe was laughable, unless you were talking about taking sharp instruments away from three-year-olds. Hough hadn't been briefed on precisely what Ferris was supposed to have seen, save that it was archived material. In spite of having been thoroughly debriefed following the discovery, someone must have raised the suspicion that he might now sell whatever he'd seen to an 'unfriendly' buyer. With the current state of the world, that made Ferris the holder of the Willy Wonka Golden Ticket of tradeable secrets. But that was all Hough knew. Judging by the excited reaction of this over-fed fool, who seemed to know more about it than he did, the information was potentially damaging enough to haul Ferris back in. If they could find him.

'The only fall-back situation,' he corrected the other man, 'would be used only in extremis.' He was sure Colmyer knew what that was; every minister at cabinet level was briefed on the government's various resources, soft and hard. But he didn't want to encourage Colmyer to start salivating at the idea and demanding the attack hounds be sent after Ferris.

'Go on.' Colmyer's eyebrows lifted expectantly.

'If Tate comes up dry, we'll have to consider spreading the load. The problem there is that the wider you spread the information, keeping it under wraps becomes tenuous.'

'You mean the press?'

'Yes. They'd get very excited if they heard we'd got a team out looking for a specific individual. It makes them visualize big headlines, huge sales and world-wide scoops.'

'So tell them it's terrorist-related. We do it all the time and the public never questions it.'

And nobody in authority pays much attention, Hough wanted to say, until some bugger with a body-belt or a holdall loaded with explosives and a pile of nuts and bolts from B&Q gets shot trying to kill innocent kids at a pop concert. Then the shit hits the fan and there are more Independent Police Complaint Commission enquiries than ticks on a dog.

'This is different. Jump too early on a suspected terrorist and we get the anti-racist bodies on our necks. That sells newspapers. But go after an unnamed former member of the security or intelligence services and that's like lighting the blue touch-paper for every spy-obsessed nut-job in the country.'

'Well, clamp down on the editors. Hit them with a D-notice. That should make them pull their heads in.'

Hough counted to five. If Colmyer really believed that, he was seriously deluded. He was tempted to correct the misuse of the term D-Notice but decided against it. The original D or Defence Notice, used as a means to prevent the media reporting on sensitive issues, was now called a Defence and Security Media Advisory Notice (DSMA), and split into five categories. No doubt some wonk must have thought using more letters gave the issue greater gravitas. He wasn't sure which category applied to a former spook who'd reportedly gone off the rails with some rib-tickling information which nobody was talking about, but issuing any one of them would have media bosses wetting themselves with anticipation. And something told Hough that there must be a story in there somewhere, if this man was showing such an interest. He might, of course, merely be playing what he considered a responsible hands-on position before taking up the lead chair in the JIO, but somehow he doubted it. Colmyer wasn't that kind of politician.

He told Colmyer what the reaction to DSMAs would be and how counter-productive it would turn out, but he could tell by his sour expression that he wasn't convinced, merely momentarily assuaged.

'We have to allow Tate time to do his job,' he concluded. 'I'll keep you advised of progress.' He got to his feet and scooped up the buff folder that was his briefing document. 'Of course,' he suggested, turning at the door, 'we could get GCHQ onto it. They might be able to track Ferris by following his past cyber contacts and activities.'

'No.' Like the three-second rule of falling food, Colmyer barely allowed the suggestion to hit the floor. 'I don't want them involved.'

Hough nodded and closed the door behind him.

He returned to his office with a serious sense of unease. In the world of intelligence operations, it was as important to look for what you weren't being told as much as what you were. Everybody had something to trade and nobody laid out all their knowledge like fish on a slab; invariably something was held back for later, a teaser saved for appeasement or encouragement.

There was something he wasn't being told about this business. He'd spent years in various parts of the world as a spy hunter digging under stones for intelligence titbits and listening to expert liars pretend they knew nothing while displaying just a glimmer of anxiety or desperation. It had given him an ear for a bad echo and he was hearing one now. Still, it wasn't his job to second-guess the vested interests or agendas of politicians; that was a quick way to get his fingers burned. Right now it was time to get out of here before this idiot called for a rapid reaction force and air cover to begin spraying the planet with gunfire.

NINE

'You should eat. Being hungry will not help you.'

At the sound of the woman's voice Rik Ferris lifted his head and felt the skin of his face stretch where the blood had dried. He had no idea how much he'd bled, but he could feel the stiffness of a crust around the neck of his t-shirt. *How long had it been since she'd hit him?* It felt like he'd been out for a few hours, but he put that down to his sense of disorientation. He sat up, remembering that he'd had enough energy after her last visit to leave the chair and kip down on the mattress, dragging the blanket around him against the cold. After that, darkness and lights out, and the enveloping silence of a prison.

He sniffed and detected a faint burnt smell in the air. He looked around but could see nothing to give him a sense of time. Hours or days, he had no clue. The windows looked slightly darker, the gloom thicker, but that might be his vision playing tricks.

The woman, whose name he still didn't know, was standing by the chair. She beckoned him over. He levered himself upright, his legs rigid with cold, and walked to the chair and sat down. She was close enough for him to have tried something, but he felt too weak. He didn't need the added humiliation of her beating him to a pulp with one hand behind her back.

'A bit of warmth would help,' he said, a shiver beginning to build up in his shoulders. 'You don't want me to die of hypothermia, do you? I'm sure your bosses wouldn't like that.'

The woman sneered. 'You think this is cold? Is nothing. Where I come from, is so cold people freeze to death in their homes.'

'What, no double-glazing in the Urals? I thought things in the *Rodina* were much better since Uncle Vladimir took over.'

She looked as if she was about to respond but didn't. Instead she gestured to a spot behind her, where an electric heater now stood, buzzing quietly. It explained the burnt smell. 'See how we are looking after you? We don't want you to get cold. But don't try using it for anything else.'

Rik shrugged. 'What am I going to do – build a hover-board and fly out of here?'

She stepped closer and pushed a plastic plate under his nose, the kind his mother used on picnics when he was a kid; soft enough to resist childish clumsiness but just rigid enough to keep its shape in the hurly-burly of holiday packing. Not much good as a weapon, though.

He felt surprised at the thought, wondering at what point he'd begun to think strategically about getting out of here. Not that he was going to be able to do much. But still.

He looked down at the plate. It held a few thick slices of sausage, grey and unappetising, and a pile of bean mix and three boiled potatoes. The aroma of garlic from the sausage made him want to throw up. He shook his head.

'No thanks.'

'Is no matter. More will be arriving soon.' She dropped the plate on the floor, the slap on the concrete echoing around the room. The food, a semi-congealed mess, didn't even bounce. She bent and put a hand to his face, the one with the ring knuckle-duster, fingertips ghosting along the open skin of his cheek. 'Perhaps you would like one like this on the other side? You think the girls like a man with a scar? Find it sexy?'

'Whatever turns you on, sister.'

She cuffed him with her other hand, the blow coming out of nowhere. She put hardly any effort into it but it was vicious enough to make his head ring.

'Great forehand,' he muttered, and instinctively pulled his head away as she lifted her hand again. But it was a feint. She stopped and gave him a cool smile. 'I did, once. I wanted to play in your Wimbledon and . . .' she hesitated, snapping her fingers as she searched for the name, '. . . Arthur Ashe Stadium in New York. But they would not let me do it.'

'They? Your family?' Get them talking, find out as much as you could, he thought. Information was key.

'My work. I was in the military.' She said it with a degree of pride, and he wondered what part of the military and who for. Before he could ask she continued, 'In any case I did not make the grade.' She waved a hand to dismiss the past. 'That was long ago. But now I suggest you tell us what you know. It will make things easier for you.'

'Really? I don't know who you think I am or what I can tell you. You're making a mistake.'

She put a fingernail against his septum and forced his nose upwards. The pain was excruciating and made his eyes water.

'Don't insult our intelligence,' she hissed. 'We know you work for MI5, the British Security Services.' She took her finger away, allowing his head to drop.

Rik hesitated. *Give a little, hold back a lot.* 'I used to. They fired me.'

She nodded and her eyelids dropped momentarily, a sign of satisfaction at the response. 'We know that, too. We also know why.'

He shrugged. 'Then you know they won't want me back. So if it's a ransom demand you're planning, you might as well shoot me now and save us both a lot of time. They won't give a bugger.'

She frowned. 'Ransom? We don't want a ransom. What was that, that last word?'

'Bugger. It's the same as damn. They won't give one.' Before he could stop himself he added, 'They already tried knocking me off once after my debrief, so if you're expecting any help from that quarter, forget it. I'm no longer relevant. In their eyes I'm damaged goods.' He sounded bitter, even to himself. 'They must have taken lessons from Mr Putin on how to deal with failures. Is that the next step, a dose of something from the poison cabinet?'

Her head cocked to one side, bird-like. There was no reaction to the name of the Russian president. 'Doesn't that make you angry? Your own side turning against you?'

'A bit. Believe me, if I had anything they hadn't already screwed out of me and sanitized the hell out of, I'd tell you about it. But I don't.'

She nodded. 'So what will you do when . . . you leave here? Will you go back?'

'Not me. They'd likely arrest me on arrival just for the fun of it.'

'Why should they do that? It's been a long time since your . . . debrief.'

'Because someone with my record who drops off the planet with no explanation causes a mild panic. They'll already be wondering where I am and what I'm up to. God knows why, though.'

'Even though you know nothing?'

'It's standard procedure. They're a bunch of control freaks who get their tits in a twist when someone does the unexpected.'

The woman scowled, heavier this time. 'What does that mean? Are you being discourteous to women?'

Rik stared at her. Christ, was she serious? He'd got himself a feminist interrogator. 'Calm down, lady. It's just an expression. Anyway, men have tits, too. And most of the pen-pushers at the top of Five are the biggest tits going.'

She appeared to accept that. 'I see. Of course. English idiom. So you say if you had anything to tell us, you would do so?'

He nodded. 'Why not? I've got nothing to hide, not after the way I've been treated. And since we're putting cards on the table and all that, what are you, KGB – sorry, FSB?'

She shook her head, the halo of hair moving like a live thing. 'You British are so obsessed by FSB. Why?'

Rik smiled. Information at last. A fragment, but useful. So, if not FSB – who? Before he could reply the metal door rattled and a figure entered. Rik expected to see the tall bruiser, but it was another man, shorter and more thickset. He was carrying a tray covered in a cloth and moved hesitantly, as if unsteady on his feet. Rik wondered what was on the tray and felt his bowels shrink at the thought. Probably a selection of dentistry tools. Had to be. First the slap, then the food, now for the rough stuff.

'More food,' the woman said, as if reading his mind. 'Although I doubt you will want it. We don't have a varied menu.' She gestured for the man to come forward and place the tray on the floor, which he did.

'Thanks,' Rik said to the man. 'I don't suppose you have a little Merlot to go with that, do you?'

The newcomer glanced uncertainly at Rik, then at the woman, before picking up the plate holding the uneaten food and backing away. He had a large tattoo of a bird across the side of his throat. A phoenix . . . or was it a bad drawing of an eagle? It was hard to tell.

'Leave us,' the woman said, without turning her head. The man turned and walked out without looking back.

'Have you spoken to him before?' The woman bent forward, placing her face directly in front of his, her breath warm and coffee-stale in his face. This close up, he could see she had bad skin and eyes like holes in the snow. If there was any warmth in their depths it was a long, long way down.

'How could I?' he replied. 'I've never seen him before.'

She nodded, seemingly satisfied. 'Good. Do not speak to him again. Me or my colleague only, but nobody else. Understand?' The last word came out with a touch of ice.

'Whatever you say, Helga.'

'That is not my name. Why do you call me that?'

He shrugged. 'It's a just a name. I know your friend's name is Kraush, but you haven't told me yours.' He decided not to tell her where the name came from. She probably wouldn't react well to being compared to a fun German figure in a British wartime comedy series.

'I am called Irina.' The admission came suddenly, and he wondered if this was part of a softening-up process. Get friendly with the prisoner and he'll blab like a parrot on steroids.

'You should eat,' she said, and looked down at the notepad on the floor at his feet. It was still blank. 'You have not written anything.'

'I don't have anything to write,' he replied. 'You pumped me full of some shitty drug, remember? It's scrambled my brains, along with the cold in this shithole. Drugs impair memory, in case you didn't know.' Then, because he didn't want more beatings or taser treatment, he added, 'You'll have to be patient. How about Nebulus – has she eaten?'

Irina's face moved, but it wasn't a smile. The expression, whatever it meant, didn't look good. 'She is no longer of importance.'

'Why? Your friend said you had some kind of agreement with her.'

'It is true. We did. She brought you here. That was her job . . . in a way.'

'What does that mean?'

This time the smile almost reached up her face to her eyes. 'Is no matter. Now we have you, and this is your job.'

She turned and walked to the door. It made him think of getting on the outside away from this shitty place. Even for half an hour would be good. There was only one way to do that. 'I need exercise,' he shouted, just before the door closed. 'I need to walk, or run. And some music. I need my iPod.'

The metal door closed firmly behind her, cutting off any reply. He didn't know if she'd heard or even cared.

Christ. Sense of humour failure. But it had left him with a deep sense of unease. The stuff about Nebulus sounded bad. What the hell had happened there? Worse was the fact that they knew he'd worked for Five. How? He racked his brain, trying to recall if he'd ever mentioned it to Nebulus, the only common factor between them. It was a possibility; they'd messaged back and forth for a while after meeting in an online forum for hackers. He'd been trying to impress her and she'd asked what he'd been doing, where he worked. She'd even expressed admiration for some of the things he'd talked about. How idiotic was that? For all he knew she could have really been a hairy male welder from Vladivostok . . . or an FSB agent. Harry Tate would have blown a gasket at the thought.

He bent and picked up the tray, trying not to think about him. That was a no-go area, if only because Harry wouldn't have a clue about where he was, even had he been interested. He and Harry hadn't so much fallen out as drifted apart, each busy following their own line of work after years of working together on and off. He wondered what the older fella was doing now. Probably close protection work for some big mover and shaker or running a security team in one of the world's minor hot spots. He doubted it would be a war zone, though; Harry had done enough of that for three lifetimes, and now he'd hooked up with Jean he wasn't going to be in a hurry to have that fall apart due to long absences.

He pulled the cloth to one side and saw the tray held more sausage, bean salad, and a hunk of bread this time instead of potatoes. The food hadn't congealed yet so he picked up the single plastic spoon provided and began to eat. Another lesson from long ago: eat and sleep whenever the opportunity presents itself because hunger and exhaustion make you vulnerable. If they'd drugged the food with a truth drug to make him blab, they'd be wasting their time. All they'd get was meaningless rubbish.

While he ate he found himself thinking about Jean the flower-shop lady. She was nice. He hoped she and Harry were still together. The old fella was very different around her; somehow lighter and more laid-back for one, although he'd never admit it.

He ate some more and looked down at the notepad. God, he hated garlic. But he was hungry. And he couldn't deal with this weird shit on an empty stomach.

He put the plate down and stared at the blank page as if it might conjure up something useful by magic. But all it did was give him a headache. He closed his eyes and let his head loll back, allowing the memory of the stuffy office he'd been assigned to in MI6 emerge. Might as well try to dredge up something useful, even if only to keep them happy. It was vague at first, like the image of an old school you didn't want to think about. It began to build, along with even vaguer faces and the disappointingly mundane surroundings of the rest of the floor he was on. For MI6, he reflected, the world-renowned Secret Intelligence Service of fact, fiction and film, it was no more exciting than a trip to his local job centre, with no tough-looking agents strolling along the corridors with guns or boffins blowing up mannequins in underground workshops.

Instead it was cubicles, phones, drab lighting and drabber people. An ant factory with secrets.

He took a series of deep breaths. He had to come up with something, even if only to delay the inevitable. Delay it for what, he hadn't a clue, but he recalled Harry once saying that if you gave up trying to find a way out of sticky situations, you might as well roll over and die.

Screw that. He thought instead of some familiar words; something to get the brain working, made up of remembered passwords, networks, encryption codes and firewalls.

He and a handful of other high-clearance IT personnel on loan to MI6, had been given administrator access to a set number of archives on the database. The material was too sensitive to be handed to outsiders, the female supervisor had explained, as if trying to convince them how special they were. But they all knew different: it was because budgets had become overstretched and bringing in outsiders from Five was cheaper.

Unfortunately, Rik was soon outpacing the supply of material. The supervisor monitoring him had soon got into the habit of sneaking off for regular cigarette breaks with a male colleague down the corridor. By her flushed demeanour when she did return, he concluded that the 'break' involved more than sharing a smoke, and boredom began creeping up on him like a siren call.

Intrigued by references to special forces support team assignments going back years, he began reading further. The teams were usually two to four strong, depending on the posting, and operating on a rota basis providing security and back-up for intelligence personnel in British embassies around the world. From a few dips into the files he saw a pattern emerge. Most of the reports were mundane, little more than form-filling to satisfy some pinhead in headquarters that everyone was doing their job. But occasionally he stumbled on one that was different, where an assignment had turned 'hot', requiring a rapid evacuation of an individual across a border into a friendly or less-hostile environment. Rik had soon begun to recognize these by the file size and zero in on SAS, SBS or other special force assignments.

Unfortunately for him, the canoodling supervisor was replaced one day by a humourless buzz-kill who made it his duty to run an audit trail and install some hidden alarm systems among the files Rik and the others were working on.

Although Rik had taken early precautions not to leave any evidence of his illicit dips into the archives, he'd become careless. Within days he was called in and presented with the evidence of his misdemeanours.

The nightmare scenario of being escorted out of the building and quarantined under guard were scenes he didn't like to dwell on. Instead he forced himself to think about the files themselves and examine what Kraush and his bosses could possibly get from them.

The result was a blank. What the hell would they get from a few reports of intelligence-gathering missions that had gone wrong? Or details of MI6 heavies dragging a compromised officer or agent out of hostile territory and bundling them across a border to safety? By now it was all old news. After a while fatigue took over and he rolled onto his mattress and went to sleep.

TEN

Forty kilometres away, on the outskirts of the city, Clare Jardine had drawn another blank. On leaving her charge, the well-behaved if enigmatic Heinrick Debsen, back at the airport after he cut short his trip by a full day due to a family crisis, she had been unable to drop the sighting of Rik Ferris from her mind. Ferris was somewhere he shouldn't be, she told herself. Belarus was foreign and therefore hostile territory to the former MI5 IT geek. The fact that she herself was in some danger here was something she chose to ignore; she had a free pass under Katya's protective wing. The situation might change one day, and they had both prepared for it with a plan to decamp fast if needed. For now, though, they were living below the Belarus security forces' radar by silent agreement of an influential friend of Katya's. The authorities here had more than enough to worry about already with their giant neighbour to the east. Relations with Moscow had deteriorated recently, with both sides taking opposing positions and the Belarus President Lukashenko making ominous sounds about Moscow's plans to absorb the smaller country into a greater Russia. If that happened, all bets would be off and she would have to decide where to go next.

As for Ferris, she had drawn a blank. Airports were usually a fund of information about lone travellers, who often left details of themselves in their wake like scattered confetti. Talking to bored cafeteria staff while in transit elsewhere with too many hours to spare; discarded or lost boarding passes; purchase receipts at the duty-free kiosks; lost luggage; hotel, cab and rail bookings for onwards journeys.

Nothing.

Although, that wasn't entirely correct. A trawl through the line of cab drivers outside the main terminal had found one man who recalled speaking to an Englishman.

'He dressed like a Russian pop star,' the man had said disapprovingly, and mentioned a rock band Clare had heard of. 'I don't think he had much money.'

'Sounds like him,' Clare agreed, hiding her cynicism. Some of the cab drivers operating at the airport were known to charge extortionate fares from gullible foreigners, and if you looked as if you couldn't hand over a huge tip as well, they'd lose interest fast. 'Where did you take him?'

'I didn't. I had a pre-booked fare, so I told him to get the bus from gates five and six.'

She knew the airport bus dropped passengers at the main terminal in the city. From there Ferris could walk in any direction or catch a cab. It would be like hunting a ghost. But she had to try or risk it bugging her for days.

She drove into the city and parked near the *Tsentralny* – the bus terminal. She found a few bored looking cab drivers gathered at a refreshment stand nearby and began asking questions. One by one they shook their heads. No Englishman. Not for a long time. Then one man walked in and overheard her question.

'I remember him,' he said. 'Wild hair and great T-shirt. I wanted to buy it but I don't think he understood. He asked to go to some place near Stepyanka.'

'Do you remember the address?' She slipped him a couple of notes which vanished in an instant.

'Some shitty apartment block beyond the Beltway,' the man replied. 'The only one left. I dropped him outside. I told him it wasn't a good place to go but he ignored me – or maybe he didn't understand that, either. He gave me a good tip, though.' He showed his teeth and turned away, the limit of his help reached.

Stepyanka. She'd been there a couple of times, but always within the Minsk Beltway, the M9 encircling the city. According to eager house-hunters, inside the Beltway was good, outside not so much. Inside was part of the new revitalized city, an area of smart, tree-lined streets and high-rise residential buildings where the newly wealthy middle classes could live the dream. But just a short distance away on the other side of the motorway lay a small, desolate area still largely untouched by the hands of construction workers.

She went back to her car and drove east until she found a narrow road leading from the new area and dipping beneath the motorway towards the old. The mouth of the tunnel was partially blocked by makeshift barriers, but she threaded her way through them and entered a darkened space filled with a light mist. There were no lights, and when she rolled down her window, she caught the acrid smell of wood smoke. Further on she saw the flicker of flames and a trail of what she at first thought was rubbish bunched up against the curved side walls. But when she switched on her headlights she saw a face appear from beneath a fold of cardboard followed by another, and a brazier with several figures gathered around it, heads wreathed in smoke. More figures appeared, no doubt drawn from beneath their make-shift shelters by the sound of the car's engine and the glare of lights. She heard voices raised in protest and the bang of something hitting the side door of the car.

A squatter camp.

She put her foot down and closed her window, checking all the doors were locked. Stopping here would be tantamount to committing suicide. She reached instinctively towards the glovebox in the door panel in case she needed to take drastic action. This was the unadvertised side of a modern Minsk, where the unfortunates and outsiders gathered, where drugs and arms were rumoured to be traded and only those with a known reputation or a back-up squad dared to step outside their vehicles.

She emerged into the open air into a desolate patch of mean, ancient housing and crumbling buildings. In the middle sat a single apartment block, solid and ugly, like an obstinate reminder of the old days. Weather-worn and scarred by years of neglect, with grimy windows behind large balconies, it rose seven floors up, towering over the few surrounding buildings. The area in front of the block showed signs of having been cleared, the brutal scrape trails of bulldozers plain to see. But that was all, as if having laid down their first markers, the planners had departed to allow things to settle before they returned in force.

She stopped the car and turned to look back across the Beltway, where the smart new high-rises seemed to gleam deliberately in the weak light as if taunting the residents here with their new, modern look.

Half an hour later she was no wiser. She'd parked behind the block out of sight of the people in the tunnel, and knocked on many doors. But so far she'd spoken to just three people, all elderly women in big coats and colourful scarves. They were pleasant enough, if wary, but it was clear that if Ferris had been here, nobody had seen him.

Or if they had they weren't saying.

ELEVEN

After leaving the Englishman Irina walked through the complex to a nearby room where they had a few stores set aside for the prisoner. The man who had delivered the tray was there, splashing water over the plastic plate he'd picked off the floor.

He hadn't heard her, and seemed focussed on the simple task. She knew him only as Alex and had never really taken to him. A former FSB man who'd suffered some kind of trauma, he'd been foisted on them by Control for low-level duties, such as being the wheel-man for the London operation, a city he apparently knew well. But since completing that task and coming to this place where he'd been posted as a perimeter guard and general runner, he'd been making noises about wanting to go back to see his girlfriend in the UK where he'd worked as a security guard on Russian facilities in and around London. In Irina's opinion he'd become soft, grown too fond of the British capital and the easy-going lifestyle, and saw himself as a bit of playboy. And that meant he was a risk.

'Why did you look at the prisoner?' she demanded, grabbing his arm and spinning him round, causing a bottle of drinking water to crash to the floor and smash. 'What were you trying to do – send him a message?'

'What?' He looked startled by her approach. 'No. I wasn't doing anything.'

'We told you, do not even make eye contact. You know the rules.'

'I looked up when he spoke but not at him – I swear. Anyway, what's the problem?'

For an answer, she reached behind her and pulled out an automatic pistol. She thumbed off the safety and pointed it at his head. He went white and shrank away, reminding her that they'd been told he should not be given any action-service roles other than driving due to his nerves. It made her wonder what possible use he could be to them if he was frightened of his own shadow. Why the hell they had been told to use him was a mystery. FSB and GRU didn't often mix, but when she'd been called into the GRU site off Komsomolsky

Prospekt in Moscow, her mind had been too filled with excitement at the new mission to question who else was in the team.

'The problem is, you cretin, you disobeyed an order.' Her knuckles went white as her finger tightened on the trigger.

'What is happening?' The voice came from behind her. It was Kraush, his presence filling the room. She turned. He was holding a mobile phone and frowning. 'Irina?'

She lowered the gun and re-engaged the safety. 'This idiot got too close to the prisoner,' she explained. 'I'd told him not to have any contact.'

Kraush looked at the driver and shook his head. But it was to Irina that he spoke. 'You need to calm down,' he said. 'You think a gunshot here would go unnoticed?' He looked at the driver. 'You, go about your business and clean up this mess later. First check the perimeter and make sure there are no snoopers.'

'I was dealing with him,' Irina hissed, after the man had gone. 'I don't need talking to like a school kid in front of the hired help.'

'I know perfectly well what you were doing. You were about to blow his brains out.' He waved his phone to forestall further discussion. 'No matter. I've had a call from headquarters. They have received information from London that the intelligence authorities have begun tracking Ferris out of the country. An operative has also been following Tate to see where he goes.'

Irina frowned, instantly pushing the disagreement aside. This news was far more urgent. She could press the matter of Alex later. MI5 being on the case was only to be expected, but was a worrying development this soon into the project. They had been counting on Ferris not being missed for a while yet. 'Perhaps we should get rid of him,' she said.

'Him, too?' Kraush snorted. 'Is that your solution to every problem? If we do that we will never find out what he knows.'

'Maybe that's the point: he might not know anything. He was clearly a low-level operative in their IT section.'

'That's not for you to decide. We have to keep questioning him, increasing the pressure but being careful. Sooner or later, he'll crack. It could be that he did see something, but doesn't realize it.'

'If that's the case he would not have said anything when he was debriefed by the British. If we get rid of him now it will go no further. Win, win.'

Kraush studied her in a way she had come to dread. They were not equals, she knew that, and standing up to him was a high-risk tactic with little chance of success. But she was determined to show that she wasn't merely a camp-follower just because she was a woman. His eyes held an almost translucent, dreamy quality that she knew some women would find distracting, even seductive. What they didn't realize was that behind the eyes was nothing but a well-trained and highly focussed operative who didn't know the first meaning of the word seduction. All he knew was following orders.

'Perhaps I should talk to him,' he said at last. 'Nicely to begin with. Now we know they are after him, time is shorter than we thought.'

'I doubt the British will find us here. How would they know where to begin?'

'Because they're not stupid. One picture from a CCTV camera, one airport watcher who spots a familiar face or name and they'll come running. We cannot take the risk.'

'What will you tell Ferris to get him to cooperate?'

'As much as I think is necessary.' The smile didn't reach his eyes. 'Who knows, I might even appeal to his better nature.' It was as if he were talking to himself, a facet of his nature she was finding hard to accept. Almost as if she weren't there, a piece of furniture.

'He does want to go outside,' she said, to fill the void. 'He says he needs exercise. And his music player.'

'Not an unreasonable request, I think. It might convince him to help us. We will have to limit his movements, of course.'

'How? We would have to be with him every step of the way.'

'Not necessarily.' He smiled. 'I brought a little something with me for this very possibility.'

'What – a Dragunov?' She grinned at the idea. She'd used the sniper rifle herself, but never on a human. She fancied the idea of bringing down a running man to see the reaction.

'Something much more efficient. Don't worry – I'll show you.'

'And him?' She nodded towards the door where the driver had disappeared. 'He's a weak link and I don't trust him. We should get rid of him before he lets us down.'

'Why do you say that?'

She hesitated. Suggesting dumping a team member was tanta-mount to disloyalty, even a distrust of the superiors who had given them this assignment. But she'd gone too far now to pull back.

'He's battle-damaged,' she said, choosing the term with care. 'In

London he was very jumpy and showed a lack of moral fibre. When the time came to approach the target he nearly lost control . . . and even questioned our mission orders.'

'Well, you did kill the woman. It was messy.'

'It was a risk worth taking – and we couldn't leave her to talk to the British.'

He nodded. 'I understand.'

Emboldened, she said, 'I think he's a liability. I don't trust him.'

Kraush pursed his lips, eyes on her as he reflected on what she'd said. Eventually he said, 'How do you propose we deal with him? We can't simply send him back; he was assigned to this mission by Control and they would assume we were questioning their judgement.' He turned and began flicking through a box of mixed foodstuffs.

'I realize that,' Irina said, and felt a shiver go through her as she realized what Kraush was doing. He was expecting her to make a decision; that whatever happened from here on with Alex, it would be her responsibility. Out of desperation, she said, 'But we can't risk him talking. They always do.'

'They?'

'People like him. The broken ones. Head cases.'

'You know this as a fact, do you?' He appeared to be only half listening, his attention on the rations. But she knew better.

'I do. My Uncle Yaroslav was wounded in Afghanistan. Bullet to the head from some stinking tribesman five hundred metres away. A lucky shot, they said, although not for my uncle. All he could talk about when they medevac'd him home and released him from hospital was the war. Didn't matter that he shouldn't – he couldn't remember the rules, only the war. We would find him in the local bar telling anyone who would listen about the things they used to do.'

'Who?'

'Our troops.'

'Like what?' Kraush's eyes were now drilling into hers. It was unsettling enough to make her mouth go dry. But at least she had his full attention.

'They'd take a captured Mujahideen five-hundred metres up in a gunship over his village, and when the villagers came out to see what was happening, they'd toss him out . . . with a grenade inside his kameez. Minimum resources, maximum psychological damage, Uncle Yaroslav used to say.'

Kraush looked at her as if studying an unusual kind of insect. 'Now I can see why they suggested you should be on this programme. However, we cannot go terminating the man because he looked at the prisoner. Who would be next? Me? You?'

'That's not what I meant.'

'I hope not.' He placed a hand on her shoulder, making her flinch. 'We're under stress at the moment, in danger of seeing shadows where there are none. Keep an eye on him for now and we'll talk about it another time. For now I have to get Ferris to open up, otherwise we will both be on a return trip to headquarters – a prospect neither of us wants.'

TWELVE

After leaving Jean, Harry went back to his flat and collected his dead phone. If he was going operational again he had to get this one kicked into life or buy a replacement.

There was a phone boutique just down the street. A young man behind the counter was fiddling with two phones at the same time, like Rick Wakeman on keyboards. He looked up. 'Can I help?'

Harry explained the problem, and the man began tapping buttons. Less than a minute later he handed it back. 'There you are. It's all good.' The phone immediately began pinging repeatedly and the assistant smiled. 'Been out of action for a bit, has it?'

'A week, maybe two. Why?'

'Sounds like you've got some catching up to do.'

'What's the charge?' Harry said.

'No need. Just remember me next time you want to buy a new one.'

Harry thought about it. 'In that case I'll take a back-up now.' There was nothing worse than being in the field with no way of making contact with anyone.

'Sure. Pay-as-you-go?'

Three minutes later Harry left carrying a spare mobile loaded and ready to go. He stopped in the doorway of an abandoned shop and used it to dial Rik's number. No answer. He cut the call and checked his old phone directory, then dialled again.

'Maloney.' The voice was the same growl he recalled from a long time ago, and he gave a sigh of relief. Bill Maloney had been with him on the bust that had led to Harry's posting to Red Station. He had no idea if Bill was still with the agency, but it had been worth a try.

'Ben Cramer,' he said without preamble, because he didn't know where Maloney was or who he might be with.

'Fuck me sideways, Harry,' Maloney breathed. 'You trying to get me into trouble? What do you want?'

'I love you, too,' Harry replied, surprised at the less than genial reception. 'How are you?

'I was fine until now. And I'm still in the job, if that's what you're asking. Why are you asking about Cramer?'

'I've had a visit from him.'

'Count yourself privileged. So?'

'Rik Ferris. He wants my help to bring him in.'

'Wait one.' There was a pause, then the sound of Maloney's breathing and the rustle of cloth, and a door closing. 'Sorry, pal. You took me by surprise. I work in a fucking cubicle, would you believe, surrounded by other cubicles. We sell double-glazing and life insurance on the side. Did you say Ferris – the tech bod you worked with?'

'That's him. I haven't seen him in a while and Cramer says he's gone rogue. He wants him found before the Basement get sent out to bring him back.'

'Good luck with that. Although if it's true he's jumped the fence I doubt they'll bother. They're preaching the cut-it-off-before-it-spreads approach these days. And it won't be an in-house job like the Basement.'

'Contractors?'

'Positive. For that kind of op they won't want any mud to stick.'

Harry sighed. Things hadn't changed. Send out non-attributable or black ops personnel and the official line if things went bad was to deny all knowledge. Clean hands at any cost.

'Good to know,' he said. 'What about Cramer? Anything I need to know?'

'He's ex-army, lost a leg in Afghan working with Six on some poxy-arsed contact mission and got side-lined even though it was their planning foul-up. Word is, to cover themselves he was assigned a post hopping between the two agencies. No pun intended. He's now a fixer, I hear it said, arranging jobs between the cracks.'

'You know him?'

'Not really. Met him a couple of times, but never worked with him. Seems nice enough. Did he play nice?'

'You mean did he use threats?'

'Like that.'

'Obliquely, yes. But more towards Rik.'

'Ah. Like find Ferris or the heavies will nobble him. We know how that'll end.'

'Yes.' Harry felt a sinking feeling. He was no further forward. If Cramer was a blunt tool of Five and Six, he'd do whatever they ordered him to do, no question.

'It's unusual, though,' Maloney said quietly. 'Getting a rag-and-bone man like you involved.'

'Cheers, Bill. Appreciate the image.'

Maloney chuckled. 'Only kidding. You know what I mean. If they hear someone's gone over the fence, the last thing they do is let their mates in on it. Too much chance of it going wrong and the target getting a friendly tip-off, like Burgess and MacLean. I'm not saying you would or wouldn't, but they must know your history with him.'

'So why would they disregard it this time?'

'Dunno. Could be because we're all fighting bush fires at the moment. The moment we crap on one threat another one pops up. There's a shortage of personnel and the budget's never big enough.'

'Is that what you're on? Anti-terror?'

'We all are, one way or another. But I'm guessing this business is different.'

'Like what?'

There was a long pause. Maloney was processing the question, thought Harry. Trying to figure out how much he could safely say. Finally he said, 'I'm being kept out of the loop as far as your name's concerned. But I did hear the Russia desk has put Ferris on the bulletin board for action. But that's all I know. You need to watch your tail.'

In other words, he was probably being followed as part of their suspicions about Rik. It wasn't news but the idea gave him a ticklish feeling on the back of his neck. They'd be checking whether he, too, was suspect, tainted by association and saving manpower until they had reasonable cause. He wondered what Cramer would do if he also dropped out of sight without warning. Probably have kittens and call out the heavies.

'Thanks, Bill. I'll do that.'

'No worries. Stay loose.'

Harry cut the call and dropped the new phone into an inside pocket, then continued to the last address for Rik's mother. He didn't bother looking over his shoulder; if Cramer's people were doing their job they would have already covered all the addresses associated with Rik and himself. The time to check his tail was when he wasn't going somewhere that obvious.

It made him think about Rik's chances if he didn't manage to get to him first. When he'd first met him, the young IT geek had been unversed in all but the most basic level of security training, with limited trade craft and a vague notion of which way to point a gun. It wasn't that he'd been unwilling to learn; computers were his thing, and his idea of a hot zone was an overheated computer room in the bowels of Thames House.

Thrown together in Red Station, the two of them had been chalk and cheese. To them and the other inmates it was a punishment posting until the day they would be forgiven and welcomed back into the fold and re-assigned, all sins forgiven.

What none of them had known was that there was to be no re-assignment nor a welcome home. They were tainted by the dust-cloud of failure and under a no-contact rule, a tighter version of radio silence, monitored and enforced by watchers who knew their every move.

Once Harry had learned what was really going on, he'd begun the fight back. Not for him the dull prison-like existence or the sour taste of acquiescence. He'd wanted to go home and find out who was behind this desolate confinement. Fortunately, Rik had been a quick learner. With an elimination squad on their heels to obliterate all trace of them, and half the Russian army about to roll over their tiny outpost, there had been no time for classroom lectures, slide shows of escape-and-evasion tactics or battlefield scenarios with grizzled instructors. There was just Harry, a former soldier voted in as leader to get them out of the mess they were facing and giving them the kind of instruction which said fight or die.

Now, of course, in the brave new world of the intelligence and security services health-and-safety manuals, before anyone so much as picked up a gun there would be suitability evaluations, psychological profiles and enough paperwork to sink a small freighter.

They had come through it, however, with a little help from a couple of the other drop-outs, equally damaged and bruised but still standing who'd chosen fight-and-flight. It had been a close-run thing, and there had been a few bodies left in their wake. They hadn't been welcomed back with open arms and a photo-op outside the shiny black door of No 10, but at least they were still alive and not cooped up in a Russian prison being fed Pentothal or whatever Moscow Centre was currently using to get hard truth out of reluctant captives.

One of their number, an MI6 operative named Clare Jardine who, according to Stuart Mace, the outpost's station chief, 'didn't do fluffy', had gutted Sir Anthony Bellingham, her former boss, on the Embankment with a nasty little knife in retaliation for sending her to Red Station in the first place. But since Bellingham, along with MI5 rogue officer George Paulton, had broken more rules than anyone had cared to list or have broadcast to the wider world, the search for her had been scaled back after a while for fear that a hungry media would eventually stumble over the details. In the end, after a couple of scuffles alongside Harry and Rik, Jardine had quietly slipped away to who-knew-where, to everyone's relief, including Harry's. The memory of having once had her favoured razor-sharp little blade hovering over his inner thigh and his femoral artery was still enough the make his blood freeze.

Now he had to catch up with the skinny, badly dressed and coiffed IT drop-out, who could be anywhere in the world. Cramer had been right, albeit probably by accident: Harry had indeed trained Rik, starting by getting them out of Georgia, then by hooking up and pairing Rik's talents with his own in a fledgling security business. With the Red Station fiasco forgotten by the intelligence establishment, but not allowed back inside even if they'd wanted it, they were forced to use their talents in a growing market for security specialists, all the while hunting for and finding George Paulton, one of the two architects of their downfall.

However, even good partnerships can begin to drift. Or maybe it was because they'd tracked down Paulton, although they'd had nothing to do with his eventual demise on a late-evening Eurostar to Paris. That had been due to a sliced femoral artery, for which there was only one suspect in Harry's book. But Clare had disappeared into the vast night of Europe and wasn't likely to be coming back to face that particular piece of music.

He and Rik had eventually been drawn apart to separate graft. The world was changing fast and becoming less free, less predictable and far more dangerous. And while there was plenty of freelance work on offer, much of it went to a man of Rik's talents, while Harry found offers of placement in Iraq, Afghanistan and other hot-spots, where military experience counted for a lot.

Harry left the underground at Southwark and walked to where Rik's mother had lived. He doubted there would be anything to find, but overlooking the blindingly obvious would be a mistake. A neighbour, maybe, a curtain-twitcher who might just know something he could use.

THIRTEEN

Bright netting showed behind the glass door panel, and the letterbox was shiny with polish. A few seconds after knocking the door opened to reveal a tiny black lady with thick spectacles staring up at him.

'You from the council?' she asked in a sing-song voice. 'If you are I gotta bone to pick, y'know? It's about the drains – I wrote in two weeks ago and heard not a thing. Nothing. It's pretty rank, let me tell you.'

'Sorry, I'm not,' said Harry and told her his name. 'I'm looking for information about the lady who used to live here – a Mrs Ferris.'

'Sure. I remember.' She considered him for a moment, then pointed a slim finger down the street. 'I used to share a room with me sister along the river, then I got the chance at this place. I felt bad, you know, taking over from the old lady, but it's what we all do, right? We have to move on and trust in the Good Lord.'

'She died, I believe?'

The woman agreed that she had. 'I attended her funeral, but from a respectful distance, you understand. Nobody deserves to go to their final resting place unobserved, as if they never mattered in this life. There were a few others, but an extra person takes up no room at all.' She gave him a look. 'You weren't there, though – I'd have remembered. I got a good memory for faces.'

'I was out of the country. Did you know Rik, her son?'

'Not personally. Just to say hello, the way you do. The poor lamb was very upset, though. I felt for him.' Her face creased in sorrow. 'It's always hard on those left behind, especially those who were close. Death is like a desertion over which we have no control, did you know that?'

'I know what you mean. I take it there was nothing she left behind?'

Her head cocked to one side. 'Now why would you be asking such a question, Mr Harry Tate? Are you the po-lice?' The word came drawn out with a hint of distrust, and her eyes drilled into his as if checking the back of his head for deep, dark thoughts. 'You have the bearing, if I may say so.'

Harry stared right back at her, suspecting she would pounce on any attempt at defence. 'I'm not, actually. I never fancied the uniform or the hours. Rik's a friend. He's gone missing and I'm trying to track him down. I thought maybe there might be some indication here as to why he's gone and where.'

'Grief, I expect.' She nodded with certainty, her voice softening. 'That's most likely the reason. We all react in different ways, y'know. Some cry, some shout, some sing. Some go inside themselves. Maybe the boy just wanted to get away somewhere quiet, to reflect. But to answer your question, no. There was nothing she left behind save memories in the air and echoes in the breeze. Sorry.'

Harry quite liked the poetry in her words. He thanked her and headed back to the other side of the river, playing dodgems in the underground and emerging at Oxford Circus. He started walking at a steady pace along Oxford Street, not looking left or right, a man on a journey with no measure of haste. His target destination was the area around Paddington station, but he wanted to travel in the open and, if possible, get there without company.

He'd picked up a couple of possible 'ticks' after leaving the old lady. Nothing concrete at first, more a feeling on the back of his neck when he saw the same two faces more than once. One was a man, fair-haired, mid-thirties, wearing a suit and heavy spectacles. The other was a woman, fifty-ish, carrying a shopping bag and rolling slightly as if her feet were hurting.

He didn't try to lose them, but let them follow if that was their purpose. Shaking a possible tick wasn't as simple as some made out, especially if you were only a train carriage apart and in a crush of people in close proximity. It made identifying any one follower almost impossible unless he or she made a mistake.

By the time he entered the underground at Marble Arch, the man had dropped out of sight but the woman was still on his tail, chatting on a mobile phone. He did a tour of the underground passageways, stopping to check his Oyster card and drop a coin in a violin case on the way, but she was still there, stuck like glue.

Just for the hell of it Harry drew the chase out to see what happened. His army days had left him with the ability to cover a lot of ground at a deceptively slow pace. He arrived at Paddington station, stopping once for a take-away coffee, and a glance in the mirror behind the counter showed a familiar figure loitering down the street.

The station was an ants' nest of commuters, travellers, sightseers and those with simply nowhere else pressing to be. Just how he liked it. He made a tour of the interior, checking the train departures board before buying a ticket to Didcot. When he was sure the woman was checking the ticket machine to see if his destination was showing, he headed for the exit behind a group of backpackers and out into the street.

Just to be sure he took a circuitous route to where Rik lived, checking for followers on the way. Nobody obvious showed up, no one dodging back looking out of place or pretending to be studying a street map. But if they were any good they wouldn't do that anyway.

Rik's place was in a brick-built, four-storey block perched over a line of shops comprising a small supermarket, a fabrics store and a betting shop. The street was littered with the remains of a market Harry recalled from previous visits. Other shops lined the far side, colourful and busy, a close community in the heart of the city.

He entered the foyer and climbed the stairs, his footsteps echoing on the tiles. Except for a small child wailing indistinctly in the background, the building was quiet, the outside noise dulled to a faint murmur. He tried Rik's door. Locked. Then he knocked, a gentle rattle of knuckles, more friend than official if anyone else was listening. No point disturbing the other tenants unless he had to.

'Can I help you?' The voice was soft, and came from the door to his left. The speaker was a man, tall, rail-thin and with a brush of untidy grey hair and sallow skin with a few liver spots. He was wearing shorts and a vivid Hawaiian shirt over flip-flops and was watching Harry with a steady gaze.

'I'm here to see Rik,' said Harry. He stepped closer and smiled, friendly, reassuring.

'Haven't seen the young fella in a while,' the man replied easily. 'You a friend?'

'We used to work together. I was looking to catch up. It can wait.'

'Ah. You local?'

'No. Warwick. Down for the day.' Anything to throw off Cramer's men if they came calling. A friend from Warwick? Cramer would probably see through it but his men might not.

'I never been to Warwick,' the man said. 'Good cricket team. Keep telling myself I should get up there.'

'You should.' Harry turned away.

'Wait.' The man held up a hand. 'What's your name?'

'Harry,' he said. 'You?'

The man almost cracked a smile. 'I'm Adam. He said you might come round. He said to ask the name of the place where you first met.'

Harry hesitated. Was this Rik playing silly buggers or was he being careful for once? 'Red Station.'

'He told me just before he left to ask whoever came calling two questions.'

'Did I pass the test?'

'You did. Lucky for you I was in, right? I'm not always here, see; I move around a bit, seeing friends, doing odd jobs here and there.' He glanced back inside the flat. 'Hang on a moment.' He disappeared inside, and re-emerged holding a plain white envelope. 'It's none of my business, but if you don't mind me asking, what do you two do for a living? I know Rik works with computers – he helped me sort out mine when it froze on me. Never seen anyone work so fast. Like magic.'

'We're in cyber security,' Harry told him. 'Corporate protection, mostly. Anti-hacking and computer theft, that sort of thing.'

'Ah, right.' Adam nodded slowly, his eyes losing interest. 'So not the guns and dark glasses type, then, with the squiggly wire thing?' He pointed at his ear, referencing a bodyguard's comms earpiece.

'Not really,' Harry replied. 'Everybody asks that. We're more high-tech.'

'I should have guessed, him being the way he is. But those t-shirts – and the hair.' He gave a bark of laughter. 'Sticky-uppy.' He flicked his fingers up either side of his head and laughed again.

'It's a lost cause,' Harry agreed. 'I'm trying to get him to drop the t-shirts. It's not really good for the corporate image. But he's a tough one to break.'

The man appeared to relax and handed over the envelope. Harry felt the shape of a key through the paper.

'He said to give you this. I hope he's OK, you know? Be nice to see him again.' With that the man turned and went back inside, closing the door.

Harry opened the envelope and extracted the key. It was standard Yale, silver. What else could he do but use it? He walked back to Rik's door and inserted it in the lock. A smooth number of clicks and the door opened.

FOURTEEN

A rush of stale air washed over him, but no smell to signal bad news. He closed the door behind him and tuned in to the silence. He was standing in a small lobby, bare save for a single hook on the wall holding an umbrella and a long scarf, and a small battered camel seat stool holding a phone, a pencil and a virginal pad of sticky notes. On the floor nearby was a small pile of post, mostly junk mail with assorted dross; a couple of pizza menus from a takeaway down the street, an invitation to join a spa near King's Cross and a variety of leaflets for various insurance plans, a funeral service company (too late but no doubt trawling for future custom) and several carpet offers. Also a fitness boot camp, the idea of which would have frightened Rik stiff. Rik didn't do fit; if he'd had a religion it would have been against it.

Harry checked the phone for messages. Empty. Two steps across the lobby placed him in a living room. Nothing had changed since his last visit. But then, Rik wasn't big on staying on-trend, furniture-wise. The same L-shaped sofa, a glass-topped table with four steel-and-plastic folding chairs, a space-age steel-and-glass coffee table, a flat-screen television and music centre, but not much else. IKEA, Harry thought. Patron saint of singles who don't get home much.

Brushed aluminium spotlights featured freely, and he flicked them on. The floor here was woodblock, covered like everything else with a layer of dust. Except, he noted, for some faint scuff marks, just visible under the glare of the spotlights.

He wondered how much dust could accumulate in a place like this after a few days of inactivity. Enough to leave a few marks, obviously.

He did a rough-and-ready scout of the place first, gaining impressions, looking for obvious signs of something wrong. When that produced nothing he settled down to a room-by-room trawl. The bedroom was the easiest, proving Rik did nothing there but sleep. There were few clothes, all Rik's, with no signs of double occupancy, occasional or regular, nothing remotely feminine or temporary. The bathroom was just that: taps, shower, bath and cabinet, an untidy collection of shampoos, deodorants, shaving creams and hair gels, as if Rik had never settled on a single brand. A place to visit when necessary but not for idling.

The kitchen showed Rik was a keen user of local takeaways, with an empty fridge and a cooker that had never been used in anger. He checked the freezer section just in case, but there were no bags or boxes holding anything remotely useful that might tell him where Rik had gone or why.

A corkboard on the wall held a few photos of Rik with his mother. Tucked into the edge of the board, they looked as if they had been taken not long ago. On impulse he took one of Rik grinning inanely into the camera. He was wearing a Deep Purple t-shirt and his hair looked even wilder than usual. Probably taken by his mother. Harry tucked it into his pocket.

Other than the IKEA collection the living room held an ancient bureau with the gleam of highly-polished care over many years. He figured it must have belonged to Rik's mother. It held an assortment of papers, some photos, invoices and guarantees, along with all the other paper dross people keep because they didn't know what else to do with it. No helpful travel tickets, though; no brochures showing that he'd simply bunked off on a break to Ibiza or one of those other favoured hotspots of the young, single and blissfully uncaring.

It took Harry a while to realize that there was something else missing.

No computer.

Every time he'd been here before it had been sitting on the table, a high-end laptop with the power light winking. But not now. It suggested Rik had taken it with him, unless Cramer's people had snaffled it. It was probably them who'd left the footprints in the dust, too; no way would he have left Rik's flat unchecked. It would have been the first place they'd call, like a dog heading for its favourite lamp-post.

He went through the place again, this time looking for computer peripherals, like a power lead or memory sticks. But there was nothing. He tried to recall if Rik had ever referred to using the cloud, and remembered him saying it wasn't as secure as people thought, a bit like putting all your private correspondence out on the pavement and allowing people to browse through it at their leisure. So that was a no.

He sat down on the sofa and stared around. How the hell did he move forward on this? Rik wasn't a seasoned field operative, but he knew how to vanish and cover his tracks if he had to, a skill Harry had drummed into him.

Passport. He hadn't found a passport. He stood up and searched the bureau again. Nothing. That wasn't a good sign; it suggested he'd gone overseas.

Come on, brain, he growled softly. Engage. There must be something. Why else would he have left the key to his flat and no clues about what he was doing?

He did another trawl, his concern growing, a fingertip search in and under every item of furniture, checking for panels, behind heating ducts and lifting the only carpet, in the bedroom. He came up empty. The place was a clue desert, save for the scuff marks on the woodblock floor in the living room. That in itself was something. Was that what had happened – that all traces of any recent activities had been erased after his departure?

He was heading for the door when his old phone pinged. He took it out and checked the screen. A Netflix email. He deleted it, then saw a number of accumulated messages he hadn't had a chance to go through. Most of them were unimportant or could wait.

Except for a WhatsApp message.

It was from Rik.

He returned to the sofa and sat down.

It was dated from last week, when his phone was out of action. *Nathalie Baier. Westminster Inn. Frid.* The words were insignificant in their normalness, a few keystrokes which told him nothing. But which Friday? And no explanation of why Rik had sent it or who Nathalie Baier might be. He knew the hotel vaguely, located a short stroll from Westminster Abbey and Big Ben. Tourist territory . . . but for those with money rather than budget trippers, like members of parliament and staff caught short by a late sitting. He pictured it in his mind, dragging an image from memory. Glass and white stone-block was the overall impression, intimidating, almost, with a don't-touch-me look about it. It was hardly Rik's kind of haunt, but who knew; he hadn't seen him in a long time so maybe his tastes had changed.

There was another message, dated a couple of days later, with a photo of an old apartment building. Grey and uninviting, a fifties-era

Soviet concrete monster. He'd seen many like it over the years and recognized the style. The text below it read: *Building 1, Apt 24. 4th floor. Stepyanka District, Minsk, Belarus.*

Harry left the flat and made his way back to his own place in Islington. His mind was buzzing. Were these messages significant, and if so, why? And if it was important, why hadn't Rik called him on his landline? Along the way he picked up a familiar figure: the man in the suit. He ignored him. If Cramer wanted to waste time and manpower keeping an eye on his movements that was his problem. He would have made it a priority to cover all the expected locations, including Rik's mother's place, his flat and now Harry's own address.

As soon as he was inside he switched on his PC and called up his emails. While waiting, he dialled Rik's mobile number. No signal.

He was trying to think of anyone who might know Rik's recent movements. With his mother gone, it was a short and unproductive exercise. In between work Rik had kept to his own narrow circle of contacts, usually referred to vaguely as 'a mate' or 'a guy' – and once even 'a girl'. That last reference had sent a flush to his face, Harry recalled, and he'd moved on quickly. Some of the contacts Harry knew were in the hacking community, about which he'd known little and preferred to leave that way. They were a small, secrecy-obsessed group who kept a low profile and operated under a variety of tags, numbers or even graphics, none of which pointed towards a real identity. It would be a waste of time asking them, he decided, even if he could reach out to them. Without Rik's lead, he'd never get anywhere.

He walked over to the window, chewing over a course of action, and checked the street. There was no sign of the woman with the bad feet, but the man in the suit was standing in the shade of a doorway further down, chewing on a roll.

Harry took out the card with Cramer's number and rang him. It was picked up immediately.

'Are you having me followed?'

There was a slight pause. 'Not my decision. I'm afraid my superiors insisted on it.'

'Just the one?'

'Come again?'

'I've counted two tails. One suit, male, in his thirties, with specs. He's still hanging around. The other is a woman. Older. Rolls when she walks.'

'The woman's mine. Former Czech intelligence from years back. Her name's Alicia. Are you sure about the man?'

'I know a tail when I see one.' He didn't bother asking how Six came to be employing former foreign intel members for surveillance work in London. Instead he told him where the sightings had been, that the woman was no longer visible but the man was eating his lunch.

Cramer swore quietly, then said, 'Alicia's mine, but not the male. Sounds like someone on a rush job. Leave it with me. I'll have someone check the CCTV coverage.'

'You do that – and call Alicia off. I'll work better knowing I'm not being watched. On the subject of CCTV, have you had anybody check departures at ports and airports?'

'Some, yes. But we're stretched at the moment. Have you got a lead?'

'Not yet. Did you check his flat?'

'Of course. It was the first port of call.'

'Did you take his laptop?'

'Hang on.' There was an empty air sound and voices in the background, then Cramer said, 'No. There wasn't one. Why?'

'I think he might have gone travelling.'

'That's what we thought. On the CCTV thing, you'll have to help. I can supply one tech to access and run the footage but you'll have to assist with scanning it yourself. You know Ferris's physical profile better than anyone so that'll save time. I'll text you details of where and when. It will be a satellite location.'

'Why not Thames House? Isn't that where all your techs live?' Actually the last thing Harry wanted was to set foot inside the MI5 headquarters; he was merely having a quiet dig to see if Cramer rose to the bait.

'Nice try.' The chuckle was devoid of humour. 'You and I both know that there'll be another ice age before you're allowed back inside that particular building.'

FIFTEEN

'Which is your favourite leg, Rik?' Kraush was standing in front of him, holding a small cardboard package in one hand and the taser in the other. On the floor nearby was what Rik guessed was a small transmitter device with an aerial. There was also another chair, a twin of the one he was sitting on.

Rik shook himself. It felt late in the day and he'd been nodding off, exhaustion and the tension of his situation having got to him. He hadn't heard Kraush come in. 'Why do you want to know that? And who are you people?' The questions were automatic, hoping for a response that might offer a chink of light in this nightmare.

But Kraush didn't play ball. Instead he lifted the taser. 'Do we really have to go through this again?' His face was blank, the voice bored.

'Left,' Rik said. 'My left leg.'

'Good. Please lift up that trouser leg for me.' As he spoke he dragged the other chair forward and sat down in front of Rik, placing the taser on the floor. Irina appeared in the doorway. She was holding a pistol and watching Rik with an expectant smile on her face. Something told Rik she wouldn't worry for a split second about using it on him if he tried anything as crazy as having a go at her colleague.

Kraush opened the package and took something from it. It was green plastic and looked like a bracelet with a small box attached to one side.

Rik stared. 'You're putting a tracker on me?'

'It's more than a tracking device.' Kraush placed the bracelet around Rik's ankle and fastened the buckle with a series of clicks, securing it with a screwdriver. Then he turned and picked up the transmitter. He pressed a button and waited, before nodding. 'This device sends out and receives signals to and from your tracker every twentieth of a second. While the signals are being sent and received, confirming that the tracker has not been tampered with, you are perfectly safe.'

'Safe?' Rik felt his groin recoil at the thoughts pounding through his head. What was this maniac talking about?

'Remember this carefully, because it's important. If you move beyond a five-hundred-metre radius of this transmitter, the signal will be interrupted. If you try to undo the buckle or cut the bracelet off, contact will be lost and the same thing happens. If you try to cut the box unit off, also the same.' He smiled without humour. 'I advise you not to do any of these things.'

Rick didn't want to ask, but he was caught up in a circular conversation he'd had no part in devising. 'What would happen?'

'The box on the bracelet contains a small charge of explosive—'

'*What? That's nuts!*'

'— so do any of the things I have advised you not to do, and you will certainly lose a leg, possibly both. We're a long way from the nearest medical facility and neither Irina nor I know about treating serious wounds.' He stepped closer and picked up the notepad he'd left for Rik. 'In other words you will die. Not immediately, I confess, and in great pain.'

'But that's insane! A stray radio signal might set it off!'

'No. It won't. The technology is very advanced. Only the absence of a signal will do that.' He smiled. 'I advise you not to test it out.' He leafed through the notepad, stopping to check something, then handed it back. 'You have not given this much thought. You have written lines of meaningless code, but that is not what we want.'

Rik said nothing. His mind was in a whirl trying to cope with what was happening. These people had considered all the moves, including using advanced military technology to hobble him.

And that meant they weren't simply random hackers working for financial gain. This was a lot more serious.

'I'm trying, all right? As I said to Helga over there, you've buggered up my brain and I'm cold. None of that helps me think back ten years.'

Kraush almost smiled, his mouth moving slightly but the rest of his face immobile. 'First of all,' he said, getting up and walking over to Irina and whispering something in her ear, after which she left, 'you should know that upsetting Irina is not a good idea. She does not have a nice temper. Secondly, I need to explain what we are here for. There are two projects which I am concerned with. The one you know about concerns you personally, the other is . . . not your immediate concern. But I'm going to tell you about it anyway because the success or not of the first project impacts on the other.' He rubbed his hands together. 'Is it cold in here? I feel cold. Still, down to business. Let me remind you about the first one, in case the cold has affected your short-term memory also. You were discovered a few years ago to have delved into the archives of MI6, we know that much. Agreed?'

Rik shrugged. 'What about it?'

'Well, during your search through the files, you saw various things. Give me an example.'

'Specifically?'

'Specifically.'

He'd thought about this and what to tell them, and had come to the conclusion that they knew enough already to make any reserve futile. 'Mostly database headings, files, folders and sometimes video and audio files.'

'About what?' Kraush's tone was genial, as if he were talking a child through their homework assignment. But Rik wasn't fooled; he was being genial because he had to be. But it was simply his surface manner, and would change in a flicker.

'About special forces operations in support of SIS. I was interested in special ops, but only for me – nobody else.'

'Of course. I believe you – as, I think, did your superiors and the debriefing team who interviewed you at great length. That was why you were fired and sent to the place known as Red Station. Is that not correct?'

Rik wondered what else this man knew. The details about Red Station were hardly general knowledge, even along the corridors of SIS and MI5. The entire episode had been an embarrassment for both agencies and quickly nipped in the bud. As far as he'd been told it was best forgotten, the files closed and never to be spoken of again.

'Isn't that so?' Kraush reminded him.

'Yes.'

'Good. Now we're getting somewhere. So most of what you saw in the archives concerned special operations. What else?'

'Nothing else.'

'Come now. There must have been other items.' Kraush looked directly at him. 'I've done a bit of surfing in files and archives myself, so I know how tempting it is to stray from the path into areas that look a little more interesting . . . a little juicy. In fact, the very presence of all that material is a lure, isn't it? Lure – is that the correct word?'

'It'll do,' Rik confirmed. He'd figured Kraush more as a blunt-force trauma kind of operative than archive-hacking. 'But I still don't know what you mean.' He stopped as Kraush took something from his pocket and saw the black shape of the taser in his hand.

'Look, I'm telling you the truth! I was only looking at specific special ops files – nothing else.'

'I understand that. But are you saying you didn't *ever* look at other file headings or maybe *stumble* into archives or summaries by mistake? Not once? I don't believe you. All that mind-blowing information about agents and spies and you didn't feel the slightest temptation to have a little peek?'

'No. Yes.' Rik felt a line of perspiration around his neck, high-lighted by the cold air. 'I told you. There wasn't much time – we were closely supervised. I did look but I was in and out very quickly. I shouldn't have done it but I did.'

Kraush nodded slowly, turning the taser in his hands. 'Well, the bad news is, I don't believe you. You saw something, I know you did. In reality I know you tripped over a record which to an outsider – you – appeared to be about special ops, as you call them. But in reality it was there because it had a cross-reference to something else entirely . . . maybe a field report picked up on another operation.'

'Like what?'

Kraush shrugged. 'Who knows? These things happen in our work, do they not? An agent goes out, meets an asset to discuss some material he requires which the asset has access to, and suddenly he learns something entirely different . . . yet incredibly important. It's like finding gold in a coal mine; unexpected and ground-breaking.'

Rik hesitated, a vague memory stirring, but not solid enough to see clearly. *God almighty, what if there was something after all?*

'Well?' Kraush was closer, staring down at him.

'I still don't know what you're talking about.'

Without warning Kraush reached out and touched Rik's hand with the taser. There was a spit followed by a fierce crackling sound and that was the last Rik knew until moments later, when he woke up on the floor. His hand hurt like hell and he felt as if his tongue had been fried.

He pulled himself to and sat up, his head spinning. All the while Kraush watched him carefully as if studying the focus of a scientific experiment.

'That was just a little zap, I think you call it,' he said. 'Oh, and before you ask, that will not have affected the tracking device, which has been insulated against outside electrical interference as a precau-tion. The next one will not be so mild and will likely cause you more serious physical and mental damage. In fact, if I turn it up a notch it will probably cause you long-lasting cognitive impairment.' He bent to catch Rik's eye. 'You understand what that means, yes?'

Rik nodded. It took an extreme effort of will to move his head even slightly but he managed. 'Yes.'

'Good. So perhaps you will put more effort into remembering what I know is in there somewhere.' He tapped Rik's head just above his ear. 'I saw it in your eyes, so please do not treat me like a fool.' He straightened up. 'Before we move on, you told Irina you wanted exercise. Well, I agree. We don't want you to go stale, do we? That would be counter-productive.' He waited a heartbeat before adding, 'Of course if you don't want to—'

'Yes.' Rik forced himself to speak, before the moment was lost. Any information, especially visual, about their surroundings would be useful. And getting out of this room, even for a few minutes, would be brilliant. Whether he could even break into a trot was something else, but better than nothing. 'Yes, please.'

'Good. We will go just before dark. You may wish to do some gentle stretching first, to warm up your muscles. Oh, and I almost forgot: we understand that your former employers have issued a search-and-detain order on you.'

Rik looked up. 'What?'

'They seem to think that you are a security risk and possess strategic information vital to an enemy. Those are not my words, but theirs. How painfully British.' He smirked. 'I'm telling you this in case you were harbouring any thoughts of returning home. So why not throw in your lot – is that the right expression – with us?' He turned and walked out of the room, leaving Rik wondering if this wasn't part of some cruel kind of mind game intended to wear him down.

He slept without meaning to, time sliding by with no way of measuring its progress. When the door slid open with a rattle, jerking him out of a headache-like dream, he found he'd got a headache.

Kraush appeared and waited by the door, silent and unemotional. More psychological treatment, Rik decided. Good-guy, bad-guy scene to show what was on offer. Do what we want, good; play the idiot, bad.

Twenty minutes later they were walking into a small, shabby park at the end of an avenue between the large outlines of factory buildings. The air of abandonment was total, the windows broken and the concrete and fabric rotting, the skeletal remains of a past era. It looked like a war zone, the dying light of day adding an even sadder air of decay. Grass grew unrestrained from the cracks in the concrete between the lots and there was no sign of life; no vehicles, no people, no sounds of machinery.

Rik looked around, storing up information and finding it depressing. He might as well have been on the moon. Kraush did nothing to prevent him doing so, and he realized that was intentional: it was a clear indication that there was nothing and nobody here that could help him. He was on his own in a wasteland and this apparent indulgence he'd been allowed was strictly limited.

The park itself was a sad left-over from a time when this area was probably a buzzing workers' paradise of joyful faces on propaganda posters, exhorting everyone to work hard for the motherland. A circular cinder pathway and a scattering of rusting iron benches were the main feature, the area surrounded by trees and bushes blocking out any view of the world beyond. He saw some tubular steel exercise bars off to one side, and realized that this must have been the workers' paradise idea of an outdoor gym.

He shivered uncontrollably. It was cold and damp, but after his cell, a taste of freedom. They hadn't blindfolded him before leaving the building, which surprised him at first; but in this shitty area and with the device on his leg, what did they have to worry about? Where was he going to run before the bang he would probably never hear?

Kraush was on one side and Irina on the other. Bizarrely, he thought, they were both dressed in running gear. The man who'd brought his food one time, the one with a tattoo on his neck, was following a few yards behind with a backpack over one shoulder. Rik wondered if it was the transmitter. It would serve them right if something went wrong with the signal and they all got caught in the blast. Fat lot of good their fancy Spandex would do them then. He plugged in the buds of his iPod which Kraush had returned to him before leaving the warehouse, and took a few deep breaths before breaking into a slow trot. It hurt like hell after days of hardly moving, but he wanted to see how Kraush and Irina would react.

He hadn't gone three paces before they were right alongside him, moving with the kind of easy jog that spoke of more-than-average fitness levels.

Bugger, he thought. Why couldn't they be military rejects with fallen arches and bad knees? He turned up the music to blot them out and allowed himself to sink into the beat.

SIXTEEN

'He's what?' Richard Hough's jaw dropped at what he'd just heard. Sir Geoffrey Bull was out of the picture, maybe for good. He wondered with a flash of guilt why this had to happen right now. 'Was it a heart attack?'

Colmyer nodded. He'd called Hough to his office a few minutes ago and told him the news. 'Or a stroke,' he confirmed blandly. 'Not that there's much difference at his age. I doubt we'll be seeing him back here, anyway.'

Hough was shocked by the Chief Whip's obvious indifference. He sat down without being invited, etiquette forgotten. This was devastating news. Sir Geoffrey had been one of the more successful heads of the Joint Intelligence Organisation, with a keen interest in operational matters and the well-being of its staff, both internal and in the field. He had also been a staunch defender of the intelligence community against the criticisms aimed by politicians and the media when something went amiss, an eventuality in all organisations, he'd said often, usually transfixing the critic with a gaze that could pierce concrete. Sadly, of late his health had seemed to be on the wane, and he had deferred more and more to others, most recently to Colmyer.

'Never mind,' Colmyer said, shifting a few papers around on his desk. 'Sad as it is, we must carry on regardless. I've been given special dispensation to stand in for the time being until,' he paused and looked towards the window with an important jut of his jaw, 'the next head is appointed.'

Which means you, you scheming, cold-hearted bastard, thought Hough darkly, and wondered if he could apply for a transfer. Anywhere would do as long as it was away from here. Kew Gardens would be nice. Or Kabul.

But Colmyer's next words killed the thought stone dead. 'You're dealing with the Ferris-stroke-Tate thing through Cramer, is that correct?'

'That's right.'

'Good. I've decided to bring forward some activity on that front.'

Hough swallowed. Hell, no. 'Really?'

'I've ordered a team on stand-by. They will be putting every effort into helping locate Ferris as quickly as possible.'

Hough wondered if he'd heard right. Did Colmyer even have the authority to do that? He wasn't even in the chair yet and here he was arranging an op.

'A team.'

'Correct. Problem?'

'If Ferris is overseas there will be jurisdictional problems.'

'That's a risk we'll have to take. I spoke to the Germans and the French as soon as I got word of Bull's situation, and they've declared no interest. Ferris is not relevant to anything as far as they're concerned. Neither does it concern Europol.'

'Even if he turns out to be on their territory?'

'Doesn't matter. They've given me – us – clearance to use limited means to settle the issue as quickly as possible. It comes,' he said, raising a hand to cut off Hough's objections, 'with some conditions, as we would expect in these changing times. But we can deal with those later. For now the priority is find him, bring him in . . . or neutralize him to prevent the information he possesses from reaching other hands.'

Neutralize? Dear God, he didn't like the sound of that. As for conditions, they were usually political and too far above his pay grade to worry about. He was more concerned about Colmyer having taken over with regard to the hunt for Ferris. It was an outrageous and blatant abuse of power. Why hadn't Ben Cramer warned him? He'd rung the former soldier barely an hour ago for an update and he'd said nothing. Surely Six, the most obvious agency, wouldn't have agreed to it so readily. Unless they didn't know anything about it.

He said as much to Colmyer.

'It's nothing to do with Six,' Colmyer said abruptly. 'This is too sensitive a matter for an in-house operation. We need to preserve some distance and that's what I intend to do.' He fixed Hough with a cool stare. 'Don't look so disapproving, Hough – it's been done before and you know it. I'm merely taking a lead to get this matter dealt with quickly and cleanly.'

Hough couldn't believe his ears. This idiot had just admitted to setting in motion a black op. He guessed it would involve inde-pendent contractors with more than a passing familiarity with agency methodology but none of the accountability. It had happened before, but in extreme circumstances due to operational overstretch. But this wasn't that kind of circumstance . . . not unless someone told him the real reasons why Ferris was being hunted.

'What about Tate?'

'What about him?' Colmyer looked surprised, and Hough wondered whether he'd even given Tate a thought.

'If you're sending out a contract team it raises issues of accountability and control. It could come back to haunt us if anything goes wrong.'

'Only if we allow it.' Colmyer sat forward and gathered up the papers on his desk, a clear signal that he was done talking. 'Leave Tate out there. The team can follow his progress. If he finds Ferris before they do, they will take over.'

'Am I allowed to know who the team consists of?'

'Why would that help? You have your brief.'

'Because if the shit hits the fan and this team of yours gets into trouble, as the lead person tasked with looking for Ferris I'm the first person who will have to answer questions. Or are you happy to take that role?'

Colmyer looked surprised by the tone of Hough's voice, but Hough was past caring. This operation was going seriously off-track thanks to this man's involvement, and he could already hear the repercussions coming down the line if Colmyer's team went over the top and upset the French or Germans.

Colmyer said grudgingly, 'Very well. His name's Garth Perry. Former Military Intelligence with a lot of experience. He's a hunter, which is what we need right now. You'd better brief Cramer and remind him of the need for absolute discretion. And I mean absolute.' He tapped the desk with a blunt finger. 'This must not reach the outside, understand? If Cramer objects, let me know.'

Hough nodded and left the office. He was going to have to speak to Cramer all right, so that he could let Tate know that he was about to get some competition in the field. If he were in Tate's shoes he wouldn't like that one bit.

SEVENTEEN

Harry called Cramer twice before getting a response. His request for technical help checking departures' CCTV footage was too long in being granted. Obstruction or a lack of willingness to throw bodies at the problem?

'Sorry I was off-line,' Cramer replied. 'Bureaucracy, I'm afraid. On the tech footage help I'm pushing as hard as I can.'

'Then push harder. I need a start point to know where we go next.'

'Of course. But do you think searching Heathrow departures will give you that? It's a mammoth job. It can't be done without a big team effort, and—'

'I know – you're stretched.' Harry bit back on his impatience. No doubt a lot of form-filling was being called for and argued over between Five and Border Control, to name two lots of bureaucracy. 'But you do this all the time. There's that thing called facial recognition technology, remember? Why else do you have all those techies tucked away in mouse-runs in the basement checking videos and passenger lists?'

'It's not exactly universal yet. Anyway, it won't help.' Cramer sounded tired, and Harry realized why: they had already checked, running Rik's face through the system, looking for enough points of reference that would light up the board like a Christmas tree. It had evidently come up empty.

'Just how long have you had him under surveillance?' he asked bluntly.

'Who said we have?' Cramer's voice echoed in his ear, too smooth and lacking conviction.

'Because it would have been careless not to. I didn't come down with the last rain.'

Harry regretted his anger immediately. It wasn't Cramer's fault; he was just a cog in the machine. This thing involving Rik wasn't a recent decision; it couldn't be. The security and intelligence services were often forced to play catch-up, especially with threats appearing out of nowhere, whether newcomers from overseas, or clean skins, the home-grown variety of lunatic you'd pass in the street without a second glance because they looked like the kid next door. No agency on earth could predict every source of danger, every appearance of weakness in the system. But whatever they thought Rik was doing, it would have been impacted by the knowledge of his previous service and his punishment posting to Red Station. Any whiff of suspicion would have sounded alarm bells because in the narrow, hot-house atmosphere thinking of the security world, once a suspect always a bad bet. And a trawl through the archives for a known name would have led quickly to a former member of staff with a questionable record. But for that to have happened, something must have set off the search in the first place. But what?

'Sorry,' he said. 'Let me know when you've got a desk and a location for me.' He cut the connection before the other man could respond. Cramer would have already tried the most obvious avenues open to him to locate Rik, but had so far failed to turn up a single lead. That would have been enough to shred anybody's nerves if they were under pressure to get the job done.

His phone beeped thirty minutes later. It was a text from Cramer. *Waterloo Court, Theed Street. Imminent. Name Davis. Call me on arrival. C.*

Harry texted him back. *Got it. But 'C'? Seriously?* He left that for Cramer to take whichever way he felt able, and went in search of the nearest cruising taxi.

Theed Street was a narrow street of homes, converted warehouses and neat lock-ups behind Waterloo Station. The overall colour of the brickwork was tan, and it was easy to detect the area's history. It seemed too gentrified now for a location used by Five, with their desire to blend in, but he allowed them credit for finding somewhere out of the way. He found Waterloo Court at one end of the street, with a brick archway leading through to a courtyard. He dialled Cramer's number and waited.

'Go through the door in front of you,' Cramer told him, 'and up the stairs to the second floor. Davis will be waiting on the landing. I suggest you don't get too pally; he's just a tech body for punching buttons and I need him for other duties.'

EIGHTEEN

'It's getting complicated.' Hough was trying to rein in his anger at the decision Colmyer had made and wasn't doing a very good job. The walk back to his office hadn't done anything to cool him down, any more than his subsequent quick and dirty search of the records into one Garth Perry, late of the Intelligence Corps. Launching in to Cramer with a negative wasn't the best way to brief someone, but he wasn't feeling too rational. Not now.

'Whassup?' Cramer replied. 'Trouble in the kitchen?'

'Tate's going to have company.' Hough explained about Perry and the likely outcome if his suspicions about Colmyer's plan were correct.

'Ah, Jesus,' Cramer muttered. 'That's not good. Do you know anything about Perry?'

'Enough to know it doesn't promise anything good. He's former Intel Corps, saw service in various trouble spots including Kosovo, Iraq and Afghanistan among others. He was cashiered out after discipline problems and an inability to abide by the rules of the Geneva Convention regarding detainees. That was in Helmand Province. It's a neat way of saying he's a nasty bugger who likes throwing his weight around. He was saved from a prison sentence because of a diagnosis of PTSD. I won't bore you with the details, but he's thought to have been responsible for the deaths of two insurgents while being interrogated and has what one expert referred to as psychopathic tendencies.'

'Great. Just what we want to help with the tricky problem of bringing in someone like Ferris.'

'That's the bit I don't like,' Hough commented. 'If I read this man right, bringing Ferris in isn't part of his remit.'

'Do you think Colmyer knows that?'

'I'm bloody certain he must. He chose the man. What worries me more is how it will impact on Tate.'

'I'll tell him to watch his back. Can we track Perry's movements?'

'I doubt it. He's already been briefed, and with his experience and head start, he'll have gone dark. My guess is he'll be plugged into the system somewhere and be watching Tate to see where he goes. We'll have to wait for him to pop up and make his move. That reminds me, how is Tate doing?'

'He's on the case but it's early days. He's pretty certain Ferris is out of the country by now.' He explained about Tate's request for technical back-up to search airline routes and the provision of Davis to help.

'He doesn't hang about, does he? Whose buttons did you push to get him his own personal techie?'

'I went over to army rules,' Cramer replied. 'Do it first and fight the bureaucrats afterwards. Best you don't know the sordid details.'

Hough chuckled, and felt considerably lighter, although he knew it wouldn't last. These things had a habit of snowballing out of control if the wind was in the wrong quarter. 'Dare I say it, but good work. You're developing some seriously bad habits.'

'Thanks. Will you be able to find out what Perry's doing? It would help us keep Tate out of trouble.'

'If I can, but don't hold your breath. I might have been Colmyer's first go-to person but I think I've probably slipped onto his don't-tell list.'

NINETEEN

Harry climbed the stairs, his footsteps echoing ahead of him. It reminded him of the main stairway at his old school, which he recalled being perpetually cold and unwelcoming, a gloomy trap for unwary boys at the hands of others with malice on their minds.

He found a figure standing at the top.

'Davis?'

The man nodded. He was in his forties, rail-thin with a brush cut and rimless glasses. Dressed in chinos and a thick shirt with pockets on the upper sleeves, he seemed neither pleased nor sorry to see Harry. He gestured towards an open door and led the way inside.

The air in the office had an overcooked quality of heat and machinery, and was being blown around by two large fans, one on either side of the room. A constant humming sound was coming from two sets of double monitors turned in on each other, and a stack of electronic boxes under a trestle table.

Davis didn't waste any time on small-talk, but sat down in front of a keyboard and a set of monitors. He gestured at a second chair before tapping on his keyboard and lighting up the screens.

'I hear you're looking for a face,' he said without apparent interest.

'That's right,' said Harry. 'And a name from passenger lists. Rik Ferris.'

'I got that.'

'You have a match already?'

'Three, actually. Heathrow, Stansted and Bristol. Is your Ferris Irish?'

'Not that I know of. Why?'

'Because it's an Irish name, originally. Could he be going there – to family or friends? Easy to reach from any of these airports. Narrows the search field quite a bit.' His voice was a monotone, the sound of an expert speaking to the unknowing. His fingers moved and a list of names filled the screen on the left. He filled a search box and hit Enter, and the name Ferris was highlighted in green.

'No,' said Harry. The screen was headed Stansted and the initial was H.

Davis nodded. 'You sure he doesn't use another initial? People do all the time, but not for buying tickets; for that they have to match their passport.'

'He doesn't.'

'Good to know.' Davis attacked his keyboard again and Harry sat back to wait. He didn't even pretend to understand what the man was doing, and Davis didn't seem inclined to explain. The screens were changing faster than Harry could read but he guessed Davis was inside a series of databases of flight times and numbers, and no doubt doing it in a way that most people wouldn't even know how to begin.

Davis finally tapped a button and sat back. Another list appeared, this one longer than the previous one. The name Ferris R was high-lighted.

Harry moved closer, picking up a hint of body odour from the technician and a smell of cheese and onion crisps. 'Can you run passport details?'

'Got it.' A rattle of keys and the second screen opened up showing Ferris Rodney, a passport number, which meant nothing to Harry, save for the age, 53, and an address in Dartford, Kent.

'Wrong one. Where's this from?'

'Heathrow. Two down, one to go. Bristol. After this it's going to take a long time and I'm not sure Cramer will be happy if we spend too long at it. We're under a bit of pressure since the Salisbury poisoning.'

Harry nodded and sat back. He wanted to move the nearest fan to direct the air away from blowing in his face, but he had a feeling the techie would take umbrage. And right now he didn't feel like beating him up until he played ball.

Finding Rik Ferris, if he didn't want to be found, wasn't going to be a quick job, and Cramer knew that. But Cramer was under pressure and there would be a limit to how long other forces were prepared to wait. Throw in a recent brazen assassination attempt by the Russian Main Intelligence Directorate or GRU, on a former Russian officer, Sergei Skripal and his daughter Yulia, in the heart of the Wiltshire city, and separately, a number of cyber attacks across the world, and it must have been sufficient to send the intelligence and security services into a frenzy. The poisoning alone had highlighted, along with other similar incidents, just how far Moscow was prepared to go in the targeting of dissidents.

Davis dragged his monitor round for Harry to see the screen.

'Bristol airport,' he said. 'It's a smaller structure and their systems are limited. My little daughter could run around inside this from her Micro.'

Harry guessed he was expected to ask, so he said, 'Her what?'

'Micro. A kit for introducing kids to the joys of coding.' He looked at Harry with a smile, although the proud dad moment was spoiled due to a fragment of crisp stuck to the far side of his face. 'I upgraded it for her so she can do more stuff.'

'I could have done with a dad like you,' Harry said. 'Mine was more into bricks and mortar.'

'Estate agent?'

'Brickie.'

Davis said nothing and went back to the keyboard. Ferris R was revealed, and the familiar address in Paddington.

Harry eyed the flight details at the top of the screen but Davis beat him to it. 'Nineteen-ten hours flight with Stobart Air,' he read off. 'Landed Dublin twenty-twenty-five hours. Commuters, mostly, at that time. Easy to blend in, especially with his name. Does he do accents?'

Harry looked at him, then realized he was serious. Davis had undoubtedly been chasing people this way for a long time, quite apart from all the other complex jobs he performed, so would know the score when it came to fugitives and targets and the tricks they used to avoid detection.

'If he has to.' Harry was developing a strange feeling in the pit of his stomach. Rik could have flown out from any of the London regional airports, including London City. Easier to reach than Bristol, already familiar with the layouts and more choice of destinations. So why Bristol and why fly to Dublin?

'He's dog-legging,' said Davis, reading his mind. The man seemed to be warming up, getting involved in the chase. 'Dublin's a great hub for that kind of thing. Lots of outlets all over Europe and further, and easy to drop a tail if you grab whatever flight's available. Means he can go anywhere he wants to as long as he uses cash.' He looked round at Harry. 'The passport might be a problem unless he's got a spare, but no credit card trail to follow makes it that little bit harder for us to track him through his spending activity.'

Davis was right. From Dublin he could leap off into the unknown, transiting through any number of airports and ending up anywhere on the globe, especially if he used railways or sea ports along the way to break his trail. It would take more than Davis and his dual screens to find him, especially if he chose not to be tracked.

Whatever else Harry had taught Rik, not leaving a trail had been close to the top of the list. But why would he have gone using his own name? He was pretty sure Rik still had a couple of alternative passports, acquired when they were working under cover, so why not use one of them? No way would Five or Six have known of their existence. Rik wouldn't have been careless enough to leave them lying around, and if Cramer's men had found them he'd have said so.

Davis nodded and hit the keyboard, opening a Dublin flight map showing destinations. It opened to a schematic of coloured curves shooting out of Dublin across Europe like a fibre optic lamp.

'Christ,' Harry muttered. 'That's a serious amount of dog-legging.'

'Is he a friend?' Davis queried.

'What makes you ask?'

'Just guessing. You're concerned rather than desperate. Looking for rather than hunting.' He grinned. 'It usually shows.'

'Do you get many of the desperate kind?'

The techie scratched his face. 'Quite often. Mostly, in fact. They're usually scrambling to close the door after the horse has buggered off and are scared shitless they'll lose their job. Anything else?'

'How long would it take to extend the search further afield?'

'Hours, probably. Longer. There's no guarantee that the passenger records are available from foreign hubs, and if they don't feel like cooperating it won't even get started. I can begin with Dublin easily enough but the trail might run out at the next stop.'

Harry thought about it. It had to be done; without following the trail they had no way of knowing where Rik had gone. But in the meantime the Westminster Inn kept popping back into his head. It was a link, he was certain. But how useful was it?

'Can you access hotel security systems from here?'

Davis gave him an owlish look. 'If you mean CCTV, then yes. But I'd need authorisation. I can't just go round nosing into private data—'

'Bollocks,' Harry said mildly. 'Who would know?'

'The good ones have alarms and firewalls if they know what

they're doing, which they don't always. But if they're happy to
allow people to steal their client data, that's their look-out.' He
paused, stretched his neck as if about to take a dive off a high board,
then said, 'Which one?'

Harry gave him the Westminster details and Davis bent back to
his keyboard, saying, 'You wouldn't like to go out and get a couple
of decent coffees, would you? There's a good place just round the
corner. I need to stay wide awake for this.'

Harry nodded. He could do with a caffeine kick himself. 'Will
do.'

He walked back downstairs, leaving Davis to his box of tricks.
He'd been prepared for a lengthy search but this had already moved
further forward than he'd expected. If Davis could turn up something
at the Westminster, he'd be even more grateful.

He bought coffees and two slabs of cake from a boutique coffee
shop the size of a small garden shed, and headed back to Waterloo
Court. By the time he stepped through the door, Davis was sitting
back staring at a screen. It showed the front lobby of a smart hotel,
with clients, a luggage trolley and a receptionist handing out key
cards.

'This is from twelve hours ago,' Davis explained, taking one of
the coffees and giving a vigorous nod of thanks for the cake. 'I just
wanted to get a feel for the image quality. Some hotel footage is
rubbish; you wouldn't be able to recognize your own mother in
most of them. But this stuff's quite good.' He took a sip of coffee
and bit a large piece out of his cake. 'What are we looking for –
Ferris or someone else?'

'Ferris. Can you go back several days?' He remembered Adam,
Rik's neighbour, saying he hadn't seen Rik for a week. If he was
right, that was when the journey would have started.

'Sure. This is a good system, so they probably have plenty of
storage space.' He worked fast and before long had a screen full of
client data; time and date checked in, room number, package deal,
home address and phone number.

But no Ferris.

'Are you certain?' Harry asked.

'Absolutely. I did an alphabetical search. No name anywhere near
it. Sometimes you get a typo error, maybe a couple of letters out,
but not this time. I checked for credit card use, too, but nobody by
the name of Ferris. Sorry.'

Harry swore softly. A dead end. But why had Rik written down the hotel name if he wasn't staying there? Unless he was meeting someone.

'How about Nathalie Baier?' He spelled the name.

It took two minutes. She was a registered guest. 'Can you print off the details for me? And run footage of the reception lobby from the same time?'

Davis nodded. 'No problem. Shout if you see something. I just need a while to set it up.' He worked away for a few minutes, then sat back. 'This is a week ago. It'll take a while to run through it, so don't get your hopes up. The good bit is that the lobby's not that big, so faces will funnel through like fish into a barrel.' He hit a button and the screen jumped to reveal a moving image of the lobby, with figures moving back and forth. 'I can't use FRS on this system because it's not compatible, so I'm afraid it's eyeball-dependent only. I hope you don't suffer from migraine too easily.'

Harry began studying images of faces. Anyone who looked like Rik and anyone who looked like . . . a Nathalie. God he was getting desperate. After thirty minutes he was feeling the pressure on his eyes. After an hour his head felt like it had been in the drum of a spin-dryer.

'Is it always this hard?' he asked.

'Not once you get used to it,' Davis replied. 'Without more information about times there's no way round it.'

Harry turned away from the screen. There had to be an easier way than this. 'Will you be here later?'

'I'm always here. Where else would I go?'

'I was told you were on loan.'

'I am. But this is my place of work. There's usually a couple of others here, too.' He switched off the screen. 'What do you want to do?'

'I want to go to that hotel and show a photo around, but Cramer said you wouldn't be able to spare much time on this.'

Davis smiled. 'Cramer? He doesn't know what I do. I'm just a resource as far as he's concerned. He reckons we just sit here and press a few keys and a face pops up like magic. Frankly, if we'd found your man I'd have been amazed.' He looked at the dead screen and said, 'Come back with anything before seven this evening and I'll still be here. I'll start checking flight lists from Dublin.'

'Don't you have to check with Cramer first?' Harry was hoping the man would say no. His wishes were granted.

'Only if he asks.' The light flashed off his glasses as he looked up and grinned. 'And he said you were somebody not to upset.'

'He's a real joker, that Cramer.'

'Maybe. But I want to see this through before they put me onto some other work.'

Harry stood up. 'In that case I might get to owe you more cake.'

He left Davis and took a cab round to the Westminster Inn.

TWENTY

'So. Here we are again. I hope you are feeling better after your exercise?' Kraush was standing in front of Rik and pulling up the other chair. 'We can do it again if you wish. But now we must move forward.' He sat down and crossed his legs as if about to engage Rik in an interview.

Rik wasn't feeling quite so relaxed. The outing to the park had been a welcome break from this ghastly cell, but it had confirmed that getting out of here wasn't going to be easy. The man with the transmitter had stayed within easy range, and neither Irina nor Kraush had given him the impression that they were anything but highly capable and that he'd never outrun them.

'Go ahead.'

'Perhaps I should give you a little detail about the other project going on here. It is relevant because your failure to provide me with the information I want will result in the most serious cyber attack on your country that has ever been launched.'

Rik stared at him. 'Why?'

'Shall I explain? Good. But first, I want you to give me a chance to avoid the second project.'

'How do I do that?'

'Simple. Tell me everything you know about Cicada.'

'The bug?'

'Not bug, no. Cicada. Is a word. A name.'

'I . . . I don't recognize it. Where's it from?' He closed his eyes, trying to think. For a millisecond after Kraush said the word something had sparked deep in his memory, like a flash of light. Then it was gone.

'No matter.' Kraush waved it aside. 'We can come back to that. Let me enlarge on the project I spoke about.' He brushed something imaginary off his knee as if gathering his thoughts. 'We can engage on three levels. One is relatively simple. It's troublesome for the target but not deadly, a mere inconvenience. We call it random cyber disruption or RCD. Of course I'm translating the initials to make it easy for you.'

'Neat,' Rik muttered, trying to stop shivering but failing. 'RCD – sounds like a transmittable disease.'

Kraush said, 'Well, we like acronyms, too; they save so much time. The second level is strategic or SCD, and more than a little inconvenient. Then there's the very worst – from your point of view, not ours. We call it TCD.' He smiled, his eyes like empty spots in an unmoving face. 'Can you guess what it stands for?'

'Troublesome?' said Rik.

'We prefer the word terminal.' He clapped his hands together, making Rik jump. 'Terminal. Cyber. Disruption.' He spaced the words out. 'Everything stops. Can you imagine that? Total blackness. Every utility, the infrastructure, transport, banking, communications – even the military.' He leaned forward and tapped Rik's knee. 'And all because of you.'

'Me.' Rik wondered if this idiot had a white cat tucked away somewhere. He'd met people like Kraush before. If they were more dangerous than others it was because they thought they were invulnerable and therefore were unpredictable.

'Yes. In an adjacent building we are setting up one of the most intensive hacking projects we have ever undertaken. We have gathered some of the foremost cyber warriors we can find, and they will be tasked with building first, the random attacks, then the strategic level, followed, if we do not get the information we need, the total shut-down of everything you can think of in your home country.' He snapped his fingers. '*Poof.* Impressive, no?'

'You're fucking nuts,' Rik said. 'What do you think this is – a Bond movie?'

'Please. Bond is entertainment for fools and fantasists. This is for real.' His eyes glittered. 'We like to think of this as a revolutionary first strike in modern electronic warfare.'

Rik couldn't even begin to frame a response, the concept was so crazy. It would bring the country to its knees. Instead he said, 'Was Nebulus in on this?'

'Of course. At first, anyway.' He shrugged. 'But then she lost her nerve and refused to play. She ran away to London, we think because she knew a certain former officer in the Security Service whom she must have believed could help her. And we couldn't have that.'

Rik felt a cold spear go through his chest. The unimaginable must have happened. Nathalie had died trying to see him. There was no other explanation. Somehow Kraush and his helpers had intercepted her messages to him, and from that point on she had been doomed.

He hung his head, wanting to scream and rage at the cruel injustice of just how close they had come to meeting. She had first suggested a hotel address where they could meet, then changed her mind to a club near Leicester Square. He'd been OK with that; he wasn't sure how he'd recognize her or she him, but she said she would know him. And that had been enough.

She hadn't arrived, but two days later he'd got a message to go to an address in Minsk, Belarus. It had turned out to be a rotting and deserted apartment block due for demolition. Nathalie wasn't there but this bastard was.

The suggestion to come to Minsk had been a set-up. Somehow they'd read enough into the messages to realize that Nathalie was going to speak to the authorities, something they had to stop at all costs. And he was sufficiently familiar with the Russian intelligence system to know that his name and prior service with MI5 would have been easy to find. That had sealed her death sentence.

'You killed her.'

'Actually, no. She was involved in a traffic accident. But the effect was the same.'

'You bastards.' Rik felt sickened. He didn't know whether to believe a word this man was saying and wanted to jump on him and pound him into the floor. Anything to wipe that humourless expression off his face. But he knew he wouldn't get more than halfway off his chair.

Kraush ignored the insult. 'All you have to do to prevent the cyber attack is to tell me what you saw in those files. A reference to Cicada – a person, I think. Someone of minor importance at the time . . . maybe it didn't seem relevant to you.'

'So it's a code name.'

'It doesn't matter what it is. Tell me what the file said and who it related to and we can do without all the unpleasantness that I, with the tools I have at my disposal, can bring to bear on you . . . and ultimately on your country's infrastructure.'

'*I told you I don't know!*' Rik shouted. 'I've never heard of anyone called Cicada. Why don't you believe me?'

Kraush leaned forward again, placing himself with unnerving lack of concern within easy reach. 'Because we know from the digital traces you left behind when you went into those files and what you saw. That is how they caught you, is it not?'

Rik stared at him. *How the hell did he know this much?* Whatever had been discovered about his penetration of the files would have been locked away and buried, the lessons learned and used to prevent anyone else following the route he'd taken. This was getting crazier by the minute. Was this Cicada a British agent in a strategic position inside the Russian system? Because suddenly it didn't take rocket science to know that this had all the hallmarks of a Moscow operation to uncover a mole.

'Oh, there is one proviso,' Kraush added, twisting the knife. 'And you must consider it equally. Our threats do not stop at a cyber attack. No. They become more personal than that. You're not the first person to say they will cooperate with us and change their mind. Nebulus did that. If we find you are trying to be . . . difficult, then be sure we – I – will respond appropriately.' He gave a thinly-veiled smile. 'It's only fair to warn you.'

'What does that mean?' Rik muttered. 'You can't hurt my family – I don't have any.'

'We know that. But there are alternatives in everybody's life.' He took out a phone and pressed the keys. Then he turned it to Rik. The screen showed a street scene, with a few vehicles and pedestrians. The area looked prosperous, the buildings smart and well-kept, with black iron railings and steps leading up to smart front door. It was also disturbingly familiar.

London, Rik realized. It was a street in London . . . maybe Chelsea or Fulham.

'What's this?'

'Everyone has at least one person they value,' Kraush replied. 'I believe yours was your mother. But now she is gone, I think it is this man. Am I right?' He was pointing at a figure in the background. A man with a purposeful stance and solid build, dressed in casual slacks and a coat.

'I don't know him.'

'Really? We pulled his name from your computer. His name is Harry Tate and he's a former MI5 officer . . . like you.' He pulled a second mobile from his pocket. It was Rik's own phone. 'You used this to send a text to him just after we met you at the apartment block. Remember?'

'No.'

'This isn't your phone?' Kraush frowned dramatically at the screen as if he'd made a mistake. 'Let me see . . . yes, there it is – the WhatsApp text you sent to him. The one which reads, Building One, Apartment twenty-four. Fourth floor. Stepyanka District, Minsk, Belarus. You didn't send this?'

Rik didn't answer. There was no point.

Kraush continued. 'You've worked together many times on private projects.' He turned off the phones and leaned back. 'You think we don't keep track of people from your intelligence community – just as they do with us?'

'So?'

'So my question is, if we send people to this Building Number One, to apartment twenty-four on the fourth floor, to wait for Mr Harry Tate, what should we do with him? Should we bring him here to keep you company? Or should we treat him as an enemy of the state?' He tilted his head to one side. 'Personally, I think we should just shoot him and dump him in the gutter. And then ask our colleagues in London to deal with *his* friends . . . and so on. You see where I am going with this? Put simply, if you don't cooperate, we won't simply punish you; we'll reach out to Mr Harry Tate and everyone he holds dear.'

TWENTY-ONE

After his talk with Ferris, Kraush went in search of Irina. He had a lot to do and time was getting short. He was already under pressure to get Ferris to remember what he'd seen, but pushing him too far and fast might result in brain shut-down. For now he had to focus on the other part of the operation.

'Anything?' Irina asked. She was waiting in one of the anterooms, checking and cleaning the working parts of a Serdyukov SPS semi-automatic pistol. A box she was using as a table held a small can of oil, rags, brushes, a magazine and several rounds of 9mm ammunition. Her movements were fluid and competent.

'Not yet. But he will talk eventually. For now we have other tasks to complete.'

'The other project?'

'Yes. The group responsible will be arriving shortly after dark. I estimate an hour from now. They will be housed in the warehouse next door where the electricity supply is good. There will be a coach bringing them and their equipment. We need to get them settled in and operational as quickly as possible.'

'What is their purpose?'

'That does not concern us,' Kraush lied easily. It had been made very clear to him that Irina was not on the need-to-know list, for reasons he didn't fully understand but could hardly object to. The need for cut-outs was usually the best explanation; a result of the level of paranoia among those who commanded him and his colleagues in the GRU. He didn't think it necessary, knowing Irina as he did, but he would abide by it. The people arriving on the coach were recruited hackers from various locations around Europe. It was not normal GRU policy to use outsiders, but the nature of the operation meant they were expendable. Something else Irina didn't need to know. 'They will be here for a couple of days, then moved to another location for security purposes.'

'Why here? Won't the extra activity expose us to risk?'

'No. The opposite, in fact. If their operation is compromised by foreign intelligence services it will provide excellent cover for us, with time enough to leave here and find another base. In fact I already have another building in mind.'

'Clever. But a waste of talent if they get scooped up, surely.'

'There are plenty more out there,' Kraush muttered curtly. His tone cut off any argument, but he knew she was angry at being kept in the dark. She had probably guessed what was being planned when Kraush had told her he was searching for a suitably remote building with an electricity supply, close to the city and its internet infrastructure. But she would also know that showing too much curiosity in details she hadn't been informed about was a fast way to be side-tracked and relegated to dog duties like Alex. Even so, she countered by asking, 'Is it a high-level operation?'

Kraush looked at her with those cold eyes. She was probably jealous of the fact that he had the confidence of people higher up the GRU ladder than she did. 'Do you really want to know?'

She shook her head. Annoyed, jealous, but subservient.

'Good.' He checked his watch. 'I need to look over the building they will be using, in case there are any two-legged vermin to eject.' They had already discouraged a handful of local drunks and addicts who had been using the deserted factories as squats, but some of them were too far gone to get the message first time round and needed a sharp reminder.

'What about Alex?'

He decided to throw her a bone. 'Deal with it as you see fit. You're right – he's a complication we don't need. But no noise, understand? Our presence here only extends so far.'

He was referring to the fact that the real reason for them being in Minsk would have been kept deliberately vague from the wider Belarus authorities. While the government could undoubtedly guess what was being planned by the use of the group of hackers, they had chosen to turn a blind eye and not ask too many questions. Had that been known by the foreign media, it would have been viewed as a not-so-subtle form of bullying by the larger country, symptom-atic of the generally shaky relationship existing between the two nations.

'Fine,' Irina said. 'Can we get a replacement?'

'You think we need one?'

'If the British get lucky in their search for Ferris it would be useful to have some support. Just in case.'

'Already done,' he replied. 'I've asked for two extra bodies, but they must be our own people. They will be arriving with the hacking group later today.'

He could see by her face that she was pleased at the prospect of dealing with the FSB man. Her final words confirmed it. 'You won't hear a thing.'

While Irina was enjoying the satisfaction of having convinced Kraush that Alex was a problem, she would have been even more pleased with her views if she had seen what the guard was currently doing.

The door to Rik's prison opened and Alex stepped inside carrying a bottle of water.

'I come to check the tracker,' he said, placing the bottle to one side. 'Put your leg out, please.'

Rik did so. 'What's your name?' he asked. He was wondering if he could get this man to talk. He was obviously lower on the pecking order than the other two, probably a gofer. But gofers were sometimes eager to show they were better informed than outsiders might think, especially if they had a sense of resentment against those higher up the ladder. 'I know Irina and Kraush.'

'They call me Alex,' the man replied.

'You speak good English. Did you learn it in the FSB . . . or SVR?' The SVR was the Russian foreign intelligence service.

Alex scowled and didn't respond at first, busy checking the bracelet on Rik's ankle was secure. Then he looked up with his chin thrust out. 'I am FSB,' he said proudly. 'We have excellent language training facilities. Also I was stationed in London for two years.' He gave a half smile. 'My girlfriend is Sonia, from Billericay. You know Billericay?'

Rik nodded. 'Sure. Everyone knows Billericay. So Sonia's an Essex girl?'

'Yes. Essex.' Alex gave a soft chuckle. 'Essex girls are fun. I hope to go back there soon. I was stationed in London for two years. Her name is Sonia. From Billericay.' He paused with a frown, 'Did I say that already?'

'Yes, you did.'

Alex touched the side of his head, and Rik saw where a line of scar tissue had cut a vivid swath through his scalp. 'Sometimes I forget.' He stopped speaking as a metallic clatter echoed through the building door. A door had closed in the distance. He stood up quickly and pushed the bottle of water closer to Rik with his foot.

'Wait,' said Rik softly. 'Is there any way of getting this thing off?' He nodded at the bracelet.

Alex shook his head, his expression almost regretful. 'I cannot help you. It's too dangerous,' he murmured. 'You must do what they say otherwise they will hurt you. Me also.'

'What? You're colleagues, aren't you?'

'No. FSB would not have brought you here. These two are GRU, Directorate Six – part of their direct action unit.' He pulled a face. 'They are not good people.'

Damn. It confirmed what he'd suspected. The Sixth Directorate was a branch of Russian Military Intelligence responsible for cyber ops. They were highly specialized with support units for protection and heavy lifting. Now everything Kraush had said about a cyber attack made sense. They weren't the only cyber unit Moscow had up its sleeve, but the GRU had the muscle and the know-how. But why were they so interested in what he might have seen in MI6's archives files? And why bring him to this god-forsaken place when they had fully-equipped bases in and around Moscow? Unless it was a ploy to use Belarus as cover.

'Good luck,' whispered Alex. Then he turned and walked out of the room, closing the door behind him.

TWENTY-TWO

The Westminster Inn was smart, designer-cool and anonymous, a modern edifice of glass, marble, polished aluminium and white stone. Inside the lobby was an atmosphere of subdued lighting and two check-in console pillars for the busy client with little time to spare.

It reminded Harry of the deck of the Starship *Enterprise*, minus the tight suits and pointy ears. The warm, gently scented air was humming with the soft sound of a busy establishment, with an undeniable sense of activity held discreetly in check behind sound-proofed walls so as not to upset its up-market clientele.

Harry asked a hovering receptionist if they'd had a Mr R. Ferris registered any time over the past ten days.

The man, tall and slim as a male model on a photo-shoot, sported a badge proclaiming his name to be Paolo. He fluttered his fingers over an on-screen keyboard with the dexterity of a concert musician, then shook his head. 'I am sorry, sir, but we haven't had anyone of that name.'

Harry showed the man his ID card. The next question might be a little tricky. 'How about a Miss Nathalie Baier? Same time-frame.'

'Of course, sir. One moment, please.' Paolo repeated the exercise, pursing his lips, then looked at Harry in surprise. 'Sorry, sir – for a moment I forgot that name. Are you not with them?' He nodded across the reception area to where two uniformed police officers had appeared from a side door, followed by a woman in a smart suit and a hair-do like tightly-coiled fine copper wire. She looked almost distressed as she shook hands with them in turn, before disappearing back through the door without a backward look.

Instinctively Harry said, 'They're uniformed division. Why are they here?'

The receptionist looked puzzled. 'They are here about a car accident in this area a few days ago. A woman was killed. Hit and run. So tragic.' His eyes moved sideways as if he were looking for a way out of the conversation.

Harry had a horrible presentiment 'Are you talking about Miss Baier?'

'I'm sorry, sir . . . you should speak to the manager about that.'

Harry passed him a folded note. 'Let's agree a short-cut.'

Paolo took the note with a weak smile. He did the dancing thing with his fingers and confirmed, 'She was a guest, from Geneva, Switzerland.' He looked around cautiously and his voice dropped. 'She was found not far from here with no identification, so they thought she was passing by. Then someone discovered one of our guest key-cards lying near where the body was found, and returned it. That's when we found she had left the hotel a few days ago without checking out, but had not returned.' He sighed and shook his head. 'So sad, do you not think? That nobody knew she was gone?'

Harry wasn't sure if he meant in the physical or terminal sense, but nodded and said, 'Have you seen this man recently?' He showed him the photo from Rik's flat.

Paolo studied it and shook his head. 'I'm not sure, sir. We have so many people passing through . . .' He shrugged. 'I cannot be certain. Sorry.' His liquid eyes slid past Harry's shoulder as a luggage trolley rolled towards the lifts. A small queue had formed up at the adjacent check-in console. Harry got the message and stepped away, then turned back. 'Just one more thing. When was this accident?'

Paolo touched his console screen. 'Last Friday thirteenth was the last time she used her key-card, when exiting her room. At twenty-two hundred hours and three minutes.' He made a sad sound. 'Friday 13th is considered not lucky, I think.'

Harry thanked him and moved away. He wondered where Miss Baier would have been going so late at night. Was it to meet Rik? If the WhatsApp message meant anything there was evidently a connection, but why? He walked over to the door where the woman had gone and knocked. A voice called what he took to be an invitation to enter and he stepped inside. He was in a small office suite, and the woman with the coiled hair was sitting behind a desk bearing a triangular brushed-steel *Manager* sign. She was brushing at her eyes with a tissue.

'Can I help you?' she asked. Her voice sounded shaky as she dropped the tissue to one side.

Harry waved his ID card again, careful not to let her see his name. 'I'm sorry to double up here,' he said. 'I know you've already spoken to the other officers, and I don't want to upset you further. But I wanted to check something about the dead woman, Miss Baier.'

The manager looked at him vaguely as if her mind was elsewhere, then stirred herself back to the moment. 'Of course. Excuse me . . . we have a lot going on at the moment. Even so, it's a tragic accident and we always do whatever we can to assist the police.'

Harry didn't correct her misunderstanding but said, 'Has her room been cleared?'

'Yes. It was done a few days ago.' She frowned. 'I was off sick at the time, otherwise I would have queried it. The stand-in manager didn't appear to know anything about it and presumed the guest had skipped. I suppose he wasn't to know about the accident, but he'd no idea what that does to our figures; we don't have defaulters in this establishment.'

'So this was before she was identified by the key-card turning up?'

'That's correct. By the time I did a double-check of the room everything was gone.' She tapped irritably on her desk. 'I told those two policemen about it just now, but they didn't seem to know anything. And now you come along asking more questions. I thought we had joined-up policing these days. Which station are you from?'

'Different departments,' he said smoothly, avoiding the question. 'It's tough keeping track of everything – probably a lot like your job, I imagine.'

She looked slightly mollified by the sympathetic comparison. 'Tell me about it. It's like herding cats – most of them foreign.' She stood up, 'Now, I'm afraid I must get on, Detective . . .? I'm sorry, I didn't catch your name.'

'Cramer,' Harry said. 'Ben Cramer. Don't worry, I'll see myself out.'

Harry left the office wondering about the connection between the dead woman and Rik. And who had cleared her room? He was certain it wasn't the local cops, otherwise they'd have left their footprints all over it. He wondered if he was grasping at straws, hoping that Rik's whereabouts would pop out of the woodwork.

He stepped into the bar off the lobby, where it was quiet, and dialled Cramer's number. It was picked up after two rings. He told him what he'd learned at the hotel, and that there had to be a connection between the dead woman and Rik.

Cramer sounded sceptical. 'She's not Russian, is she?'

'You tell me. Can you find out if her possessions are in a local evidence room? I'd like to take a look.'

'I'll get back to you. Stay close.' The connection went dead.

Harry went out for a walk. In the absence of direct action he needed time to think. Needles in haystacks didn't bother him; at least you could always set light to a pile of hay and see what was revealed. But this was a puzzle of another kind. Rik could be anywhere in the world by now, and the dead woman merely a chance encounter of time, date and location.

His phone rang. It was Cramer. His voice was tight.

'Who did the manager say collected the woman's effects?'

'She didn't. Just that the room had been cleared and she assumed it was police. What's going on?'

'The local cops have no record of it. The first they knew about the woman was when she was picked up and pronounced dead at the scene. When a key-card was found nearby they made the connection. No property has been recovered or registered.'

Harry thanked him and cut the call. A dead end. What the hell was going on? The Security Service chasing down a former officer who'd gone missing, purportedly in possession of information he shouldn't have; an empty flat with no clues to speak of; a dead woman who might or might not be connected; and someone – not the cops – having cleared her effects from the hotel.

That pointed to someone knowing she was dead before the cops did and making sure nothing was left behind.

He rang Davis. When the tech answered he said, 'Can you check if everything about Nathalie Baier at the Westminster was printed off? I'm thinking bar bills, restaurant, phone calls – anything you think is useful.'

'Got it,' Davis said, and disconnected.

Harry took a cab back to Rik's flat and let himself in. Back to square one sometimes helped focus the mind. And while he wasn't in a position to go running off round the globe in search of a man who might still be in London, it was the only thing he could do. One thing working for Five had told him was, never assume you'd covered every angle. Life wasn't like that.

He'd barely set about going through the flat again when his phone pinged. An incoming message. It was Davis.

Got something.

TWENTY-THREE

'I checked the hotel files as you asked,' said Davis, when Harry got back to Waterloo Court, 'but there was nothing else on Baier. However, I was trawling the hotel's interior footage and noticed some suits talking to staff members not long after you were there. I took a closer look.' He tapped a key and showed footage of two men talking to hotel workers and taking notes. In the background was the hotel manager, looking agitated.

'Pity we can't hear what they're saying,' Davis said. 'I thought there might be a connection with your problem.' He worked the keyboard and brought up some footage of the exterior of the hotel, showing a dark and shiny saloon car parked at the kerb. 'This vehicle was outside.' He pointed at the screen to a pale patch of something behind the windscreen. 'See that square? It's a government-issue I.D to warn off cops and parking wardens.'

'Security Service?'

Davis shook his head. 'No. I checked. They stopped issuing the passes six months ago; they were being copied and used for private business in the west end. Whoever these two were, they weren't authorized.'

'Is there anything about Baier on the hotel database?'

'Only the standard: home address, passport and Visa card details. I haven't had time to run footage of her actually in the hotel, but I can do that later if you like.'

'Do it,' Harry said. 'What about the RTA?'

'What about it?'

'She was killed near the hotel. And yes, I'm grasping at straws, but it's all I've got.'

Davis looked at him without expression. Then he nodded and sat back. 'I can do that. But I'm going to need some privacy.'

'For what?'

'I need to get help on the next bit, to save time. A mate of mine works with the monitoring division of the Met's Roads & Transport Policing Command. If there's been an RTA he'll have it listed. But I never told you that or my balls are fried.'

'Got it,' said Harry. He knew when to recognize a special offer when it was made. 'Can you do it without your mate talking?'

Davis nodded. 'Guaranteed. He's playing away from home – with my sister. If he doesn't do as I ask, I'll tell his wife.'

'That's harsh.'

'It is, but I love my sister more than my mate. I'll call you as soon as I've got something.'

'Make it a text,' Harry said. 'More secure.'

Davis gave him a lop-sided grin. 'That's what I meant.'

Harry left him to it and went for a walk. He didn't want to but he was too impatient for progress to sit still and wait. He made his way to the river and turned east. It was easier going than heading into the centre, and less wearing on the nerves while waiting for Davis to call.

Just over an hour later, after circling back towards Waterloo, he got a beep. *You shld see this. D.*

Harry acknowledged receipt and hurried back to Waterloo Court.

'My mate the philanderer has his uses,' Davis told him dryly. His face was bland but his words were loaded with excitement, as if he'd discovered a winning lottery number but didn't want to let on. 'He's setting up a track of the van, but that might take a while. In the meantime, he showed me the RTA details. Also, I found something else.'

'Show me.'

Davis tapped his keyboard and the nearest screen lit up. It showed an internal scene of a long corridor with doors off to each side. The carpet was dark with a vague pattern, and wall sconces glowed dully as if more decorative than functional.

'Is this the hotel?'

'Yes. I guess you won't have seen this part. It's on the sixth floor, rooms three-hundred to three-twenty. I've edited it down to save time and saved the original if you need it.' He stabbed at the screen with a finger. 'Watch this door. This is where it all begins.'

The door in question moved, then opened. A woman stepped out. She was slim, in a knee-length coat open down the front and what looked like heavy boots. Her hair was cut short but she was moving too quickly to get a clear fix on her features. She walked away down the corridor. Davis worked the keyboard, catching her again as she exited the lift into the lobby. The light was better and it was clear that the woman was carrying what looked like a laptop bag in one hand with another smaller bag over one shoulder. She walked through the reception area and out through the main entrance, turning left and out of sight.

'Watch this,' said Davis. He tapped the keys and this time showed a street scene, taken from high up. The street lights were on and the area beyond lay in darkness. 'This is the area back from the hotel, and there's the Baier woman walking away along the street.' He pointed to a female figure moving away. Her pace was brisk and purposeful, and she was staying close to the buildings, her collar around her face and shoulders hunched against the cold. 'See that?' The screen froze and Davis looked up at Harry in expectation.

'See what?' said Harry. 'She's walking down the street.'

'Not her. That.' Davis tapped the screen again, this time on one corner. 'I was tooling back and forth between street cams to see if the cops had called at the hotel before. Might be a regular thing what with Parliament being so close. Anyway, I got this segment from ten minutes earlier, before she left the hotel.' He tapped the keyboard and the screen began running again, showing pedestrians in the background, a car pulling out of a narrow street and the square shape of a van at the kerb. Harry could just make out a logo behind the driver's door but it was just out of reach of the lights. 'Now watch this.' Davis switched to another camera, this time in daylight. 'This was the day before. Same van.' He switched again. 'And this was earlier that day. Same again.'

Harry's heart was hammering as he realized Davis had stitched together a near-complete record of events in and around the hotel, leaving out anything not immediately relevant.

'Can we trace the van?'

'I tried that. The logo's a fake . . . at least, no longer used. It was a delivery company and it went bust several months ago. The van probably got sold off at a winding-up auction.'

Harry watched as Davis re-ran the three segments, completing the moving jigsaw puzzle. He checked the registration plate each time. It was the same.

'Three times – is that likely?' he said. He wanted it to be too much of a stretch, the same van used on three days in the same area. But he knew nothing about deliveries. Maybe it was common-place and he was beginning to snatch at anything that looked good.

'No idea.' Davis shook his head. 'Watch this. It's taken from a different angle and further back along the street. It shows Baier leaving the hotel the night she was killed. The van's on the right of the screen.'

'Keeping watch.'

'Yes.'

Night-time, with the flare and movement of vehicle lights confusing against the picture. A lone figure in the distance was walking away from the hotel entrance. Nathalie Baier. Harry switched his look to the other side of the screen, and sure enough the nose of the van was just visible. He couldn't see the driver, but a puff of exhaust smoke was drifting into view, curling around the wing and dispersing into the night.

He glanced back towards Baier just in time to see her turn the corner.

'Where's she going?'

'Wait one,' said Davis. His voice sounded tense. The van jumped, moving sharply away from the kerb. Baier was no longer visible.

Davis cut the screen and moved to another camera shot. This showed another street with a turning to one side.

'This is looking back towards the corner where Baier turned. She's just walked off-camera. Now watch.'

A vehicle swung round the corner, the headlights flaring against the lens and flooding the screen with white light. Then the light dimmed as the vehicle moved by beneath, and Harry caught a snatch of the registration plate.

The same van.

Davis nodded and moved his fingers on the keyboard. 'This is from the RTA footage. I don't think they've had time to analyse it yet, but they're starting further back than we are – and we know where the woman came from.' This time the screen showed a familiar figure turning the corner towards them, a bag in one hand and another slung over her shoulder, coat collar turned up.

The next footage was a jumble of conflicting lights throwing shadows everywhere. Headlights came round the corner after the woman, but this time the camera must have been mounted higher on the building because the light wasn't so invasive. It was the same van, this time moving fast.

Harry felt an awful prescience as the vehicle moved towards the camera. It was a common-enough scene, a pedestrian and a vehicle on a city street, repeated a million times every day. Then everything changed.

The woman had moved closer to the buildings as if seeking the shadows. The van came closer, then swerved violently, jumping the kerb. Was the driver trying to avoid an obstacle in the road? Had they lost control for a second? The van continued along the pavement, then stopped sharply.

The woman on the pavement had disappeared.

A fleeting figure jumped out of the van and ran into the shadows. Woman or man, Harry couldn't tell. Then the figure returned carrying something: a bag – no, two bags. The way the figure moved looked like . . . *a woman?* Seconds later the van was on the move again and disappearing from sight.

The street was now clear except for an indistinct shape in the background, where a leg stretched out into a patch of light. A woman's leg, coat rucked up. Still.

Harry almost didn't dare speak, his throat dry and stunned by what he'd just seen.

'Where's the van?' he said at last, his voice unnaturally calm. 'Find that van.'

Davis began toggling from one set of screens to another. He widened the search, but the van had gone. Eventually the screen was filled with other vehicles as he flicked from one camera view to another. Lots of cars, pedestrians and the square shapes of London cabs. Eventually he stopped and sat back.

'Sorry,' he said. 'This is going to take longer.'

'Keep looking,' Harry told him. 'It must be there somewhere.'

'I agree.' Davis tapped the keys and closed his screen. 'But that's all I've got so far. I'll need to ask for more.'

'How do you do that? Can't you access the other cameras in the area?'

Davis nodded but without conviction. 'It's possible but it would need a team on it. It would take a while, covering all the routes away from there. It's a big area to check.'

'South or west,' Harry told him.

'What?'

'They'd have been in a hurry to get away. Going north into the city would double the risk of an accident or being stopped in a random road block. That leaves south across the river or west along the embankment.'

'Would that happen?'

'Of course it would. The current level of alert is Substantial. Anything that looks out of the ordinary stands a high chance of being spotted and reported city-wide. They will have gone for the least risky route away from there. Tell your philandering mate to check for similar vans heading away from Westminster. If he argues the toss, tell him I'll track him down and hang him by his balls from a lamp-post.'

Davis laughed. 'I'd buy tickets to see that.' He nodded at the phone and said, 'You want to call Mr Cramer, tell him what we found? He'll be getting edgy.'

Harry nodded. Davis was right. He seemed to be enjoying this. By nature, most of his tech work would be close-ended, with little information about end results. But this was a chase, albeit a frustrating one. Talking to Cramer was something that might be better done in confidence.

He found a quiet corner table at a nearby café and called him. He ran quickly through what Davis had found in the hotel and on the street cameras.

'Wait,' Cramer said, after he'd digested the information. 'You think the suits were mine?'

'You tell me.'

'They weren't. There's nobody else on this. Just Alicia, the woman you saw before. But she's been called off as you asked. Did you get the registration of the van?'

'Davis has. He's very good.'

'Glad you think so. Talking of which, the sandwich eater who was following you has left the country. One of our Russia desk observers recognized him from the street cameras.'

A pity Alicia hadn't done so, Harry thought. But he knew how close surveillance occasionally threw up a loss of all-round perception, focussing too much on what lay in front. 'Who was he?'

'A fly-in from Moscow. He's been to London twice recently, two-day stops only. He's probably a courier and low-level surveillance operative.'

'Is that all?'

'No. His passport number is just three away from a batch used by the Skripal poisoners.'

Harry felt a chill breeze touch his neck. 'So this was a GRU operation.'

'It seems so. A number of others from the same batch went to Russian mercenaries working in Africa, all issued by the same desk in Moscow.'

'Not exactly subtle.'

'That's one description. Thing is, why would a Moscow GRU operative be interested in you? It must be connected with Ferris.'

'Search me. I'll think about it and let you know. What about the suits at the hotel?'

'I'll ask around. If I come up with anything I'll let you know.'

The connection was cut and Harry pulled a face. He was about to leave the café when his phone rang. It was Davis.

'I got a ping on a face from a few days ago. Ferris flew from Dublin to Amsterdam with KLM-stroke-Belavia, then on to Minsk. His ticket ended there. He might have bought an onward flight but I don't have that information. For somebody being hunted, I have to say he didn't look like he was trying to hide.'

Harry grinned. Davis was right. It told him a lot about Rik's disappearance: if he wasn't trying to hide it was because he probably didn't know he had any reason to do so.

'There's something else, too,' Davis continued. 'You might want to see it.'

Harry disconnected and walked back round to the office. Davis let him in and opened a screen.

'This was not long after the woman was knocked over,' he explained. 'I decided to trawl back to see if anything jumped out at me.' He changed screens and showed the corridor which Harry recognized as the one containing the dead woman's room. A man was walking under the camera. He was dressed in smart-casual clothes, his face obscured by a peaked cap. He stopped at a doorway and knocked.

'That's her room,' said Davis.

The man looked around, then did something with the door handle. 'He's using a key-card device,' Davis explained. 'It goes through every permutation until it gets to the right one and . . . bingo.'

The door opened and the man disappeared inside. Less than three minutes later by the on-screen clock, he emerged and walked away. He was carrying a holdall.

'I bet he's not one of ours,' Davis concluded.

Harry was impressed by the speed with which the man had moved. He'd entered, checked the room and walked out with whatever he'd found in there. No evidence left, and no clues to help tell them why the woman had been there.

Or why anyone would want her dead.

He stood up. 'Davis, if that daughter of yours wants another upgrade for her Micro, it's on me.'

Ten minutes later Harry was on his way back to his flat. He'd managed to snag a last-minute cancellation on a direct flight to Minsk. He hadn't got time to dog-leg the journey to lose any possible followers because it would take too long. Instead he'd have to rely on luck and trade craft. As for Cramer he'd tell him where he was going when he was ready. If he did it now there was a risk the information would leak out and somebody else would be on their way over there.

For now the chase was on.

TWENTY-FOUR

L eaving Kraush to do whatever he was planning with the prisoner, Irina went in search of Alex. She'd checked on Ferris
earlier and seen the bottle of water by his chair. She hadn't
left it there and was certain Kraush hadn't. That left Alex. It was
confirmation to her that the man was a weakness and a liability and
had to be dealt with.

She had waited for darkness to fall, checking the windows to
make sure there were no intruders nearby, even scouting the outside
perimeter for signs of scavengers collecting wood. For what she
was about to do she needed to make sure that nobody heard anything
and raised the alarm.

She found the former FSB man checking the outside perimeter
through the windows of one of the warehouses. She waited until he
had finished, then beckoned him to follow her to a side room. It
had probably been an office once, with the remains of an ancient
pin-board on one wall, although it contained no furniture now and
was fighting a losing battle against the ravages of time. The walls
had once been plastered and painted and where the plaster remained,
still showed a faint sheen of lime green colour. A pile of mouldy
cloth lay in one corner, and she saw something skitter away beneath
it. A rat.

'Wait here,' she told him. 'I have a job for you.'

She returned to the storeroom where she went to a cardboard
box in one corner. She took out an empty plastic bottle that had
once held engine oil. She had earlier discarded the screw top and
used a kitchen knife to cut a hole in the base, then sliced up a coarse
blanket into strips, which she'd wrapped around the bottle and
secured in place with some string.

Humming to herself, she left the storeroom, closing the door
softly behind her. When she got back to the former office, Alex was
standing by the door, picking at his nails, an almost dreamy look
of unconcern on his face.

She put a hand on his shoulder and steered him backwards into
the room, kicking the door shut behind her. Alex moved without

resistance and thrust his hands into his pockets, no doubt waiting for instructions.

'You gave the prisoner water,' she said.

His mouth opened to deny it, the colour draining from his face. But no words came out.

'Are you armed?' He wasn't supposed to be but you could never tell with trauma victims; some of them thought they were still fighting a war, even when at home. And former FSB men, and she'd known a few, were in the habit of thinking they could carry a gun even when ordered not to. It was ingrained into their daily thinking, like putting on a favourite belt or a pair of boots.

'No.' He frowned and held out his hands. 'I was told not to. Why would I?'

'Turn round. Let me see.'

He did so, raising his arms to show her he wasn't hiding a weapon. 'See?'

Irina lifted the oil bottle, and with her other hand reached round behind her and slid the semi-automatic out of her waistband. She thrust the snout of the gun into the neck of the bottle and waited for Alex to turn round. When he saw the gun he made to step back and stumbled, one of his shoes coming off and a look of shock on his face. Before he could recover Irina pointed the base of the bottle at his face and pulled the trigger. He was thrown back against the wall by the bullet's impact, dead before he hit the floor.

Irina nodded slowly, satisfied with the result. The shot had still been loud in the confines of the room, although reduced by the make-shift suppressor. But no worse than the slamming of a door.

She dropped the bottle on the floor and stamped on it, killing a few sparks in the fabric caused by powder burn, then dragged the dead body across to the corner, before throwing some of the mouldy cloth over it and leaving the room, closing the door behind her.

TWENTY-FIVE

Night time. Other than an occasional scraping noise from the darker corners of the vast structure Rik was in, the rest of the natural world appeared to have been switched off.

With his head clearing after the exercise, Rik was able to appreciate the serenity of nightfall. But not the cold. He shivered as it reached deep into his body. Something had woken him, but he couldn't identify the cause. A late-night vehicle; someone nearby, perhaps, and a bang . . . but that might have been the tail-end of a dream brought on by whatever drug they'd been feeding him.

He stood up and stretched cautiously, wishing he had a source of light to give him a sense of perspective. The darkness was messing with his balance and his head was spinning like the aftermath of too much deep breathing. His leg muscles were tight but a few high steps and careful stretches on the spot loosened them up a little. He felt around for the water bottle and took a sip. His throat was dry but he was beginning to feel better than he had in a while; less fuzzy and more alert.

It was time to take a sneaky peek at his surroundings.

If what Kraush had told him was true, and not merely a bunch of lies to scare him into staying where he was, he wouldn't be able to go further than the main fabric of the building. But that left him some leeway. He made his way to the door and slid it back on its runners, wincing at the rumble that seemed to echo through the building. So what if they caught him? What could they do but lose whatever source of information they were keen to exploit?

He stood outside the door and listened. Nothing. No sounds of voices, nobody rushing out of the dark to beat him senseless and kick him back into his cell. But there had definitely been a noise. He tracked his way by feel along the wall, his eyes growing accustomed to the dark. Not enough, though, for getting out of here and losing this thing on his leg.

He heard the sound of an engine and stopped. It was coming closer and definitely beyond the brick walls. A truck by the sound. A big one. Then he saw through minute holes in the metal part of the walls a wash of light moving past and a hiss of air brakes, followed by the slam of doors and the low hum of voices.

He kept moving, finding more doors. Some were locked or jammed shut, others opened into empty rooms, some big with echoes, others small and claustrophobic, the scrape of his footsteps flat and dull. All contained the smell of damp and decay, of a place long unused and deserted. The skittering of small animal sounds slid past him in the dark at ground level, and he hoped none of them were feeling hungry. He didn't like rats, not unless one of them had a degree in electronics and was skilled at bomb-disposal.

He smelled the familiar aroma of garlic. He pushed at a door opening off a corridor and the smell became stronger still. He saw the vague shadows of boxes on the floor and a sink against the wall, and heard the drip-drip of water against metal. He checked the boxes by feel, testing the contents. Tins. Probably the bean mix they were feeding him on. And packets of something wrapped in grease-proof paper. Sausages . . . the smell was enough. He turned to the sink and ran his hands across the metal drainer. Bits of plastic wrapping, greasy paper and . . . something metallic which rolled as soon as he touched it. He grabbed for it before it could roll onto the floor, his gut heaving with nerves, and felt for the shape.

A torch. He'd found a torch! Metallic and cold with a ribbed case. He crouched and felt for the glass lens, then turned it against his stomach and switched it on. The relief he felt when it worked was all-consuming, as if he'd won a major victory against his imprisonment. He turned it off and continued his exploration, but that was the end of his fun for the night so far. If they had any tools for preparing his food, they had been very careful not to leave them lying around.

He used the torch sparingly, catching snatches of items as he moved. He was almost ready to give up when he spotted a familiar outline on the floor. It was a laptop with a smiley face on the lid bearing a penned-in moustache.

Damn. It was *his*. But there was no sign of his phone.

He knelt down and opened the lid. He'd had it with him on the journey over; they must have taken it from him when they caught up with him at the apartment block. He pressed the power button. Maybe he could get a message out to Harry.

He swore. Dead as a doughnut. And no sign of the power cable.

He put it back where he'd found it and scratched at his leg. The skin around his ankle was itching. His instinct was to blame the plastic bracelet but reason told him it had more to do with the lack of a shower. It made him realize that he'd been here three days now – or was it four . . . he couldn't tell. He shrugged it off; he'd got more to worry about than personal hygiene, like *how many more steps before this thing decides to go bang*?

A rattle of distant laughter reached his ears and he stopped. There were voices and the hum of an engine in the distance. The sounds seemed unconnected with this building, and he wondered if a rescue attempt had been mounted. But why would they take a chance on being heard? He took a few cautious steps forward, expecting at any moment to see the glare of lights and find himself on the wrong end of Kraush's taser. But everything remained dark and silent. He eventually arrived in a large space with windows very high up. These were not blocked by plywood, and he could see a faint glow of light moving through the dirty glass. He needed to get up there and see what was going on. On one wall was a heavy-duty pipe running from floor to rafters and disappearing through the roof. One of the windows was close by.

He pocketed the torch and tested the pipe. It rattled but seemed solid enough. If the only way he was going to see out was up here, he'd better get to it.

He began to climb, bracing his feet against the brickwork and leaning out to gain purchase. It was hard going, and by the time he was halfway up his shoulder and leg muscles were screaming and his feet threatening to slip on the damp wall. He gritted his teeth and dug hard, eventually reaching the window level where he hugged the pipe and peered through the filthy glass.

At first he couldn't make out anything through the film of dirt and the darkness outside. He didn't dare scrape at the glass in case Kraush or Irina spotted the movement. Then he realized what he was looking at: it was a large passenger coach parked outside the next building. It had blanked-out windows but he could see people climbing out and moving into the structure where someone was directing them with a flashlight. Some of the arrivals were carrying bags, others had boxes. They were moving in concert, a line of worker ants, as if this was a practised procedure they had gone through before.

Then he noticed two familiar figures standing watching them. It was Kraush and Irina. Standing alongside them were two others, taller, clearly male and heavily built. They were carrying holdalls and dressed in dark clothing.

Rik felt a rush of unease. He'd seen men like this before, similarly equipped and dressed, usually about to go on an operation. The holdalls were canvas and usually carried a minimal change of clothing, basic supplies and an assortment of weapons. Whatever they were here for, they weren't a cheer-leading team.

He was desperate to see more but his energy levels were diminishing fast and his breathing was becoming forced and harsh. His legs were trembling in protest at holding this position, threatening his precarious grip on the pipe. If he fell from this height he wouldn't be getting up anytime soon. He slid back down, his feet dragging against the brickwork, and dropped to the floor with a groan. He crouched still for a moment, stress pains burning through his legs, shoulders and arms, and listened for some sign that he'd been heard.

Voices. More like muted chatter than a call for action. He took a deep breath and stood upright. He had to get back to the room before they returned. If Irina caught him wandering around there was no telling what she would do.

He made his way back towards his cell, but got disorientated in the darkness and turned the wrong way. Where the hell was the big door? He risked flicking on the torch, a hand over the lens to restrict the glare, and saw a single door in front of him. He pressed his hand against it and was surprised when it moved.

He pushed it further, wincing as the bottom scraped on the concrete floor. A rush of colder, damper air came in and his breath ghosted in front of his face. He saw a glint of night sky where a heavy cloud had shifted to reveal a lighter patch of colour. He couldn't see much at ground level but he was guessing he was at the rear of the building. The idea of perspective gave him a lift, and he hoped he could soon use this and get away from here. Miracles, he told himself, did sometimes happen.

More voices and a burst of laughter. They were distant sounds muffled by the walls but a reminder of the gravity of his situation.

He pulled the door to and moved back into the dark. He flicked on the torch and saw another door. It opened into a small space with no windows and the same pervasive, dead atmosphere of every other room he'd been in. Yet there was something else: the acrid smell of burned plastic.

He moved the torch, hoping for another way out. No furniture or fittings, but a pile of cloth in one corner. And a shoe? It looked heavy with a thick rubber sole. Almost new.

With a sense of foreboding he crossed the room. He knew he should be out of here and getting back to his cell but something drew him on. He bent down and flicked back the nearest handful of cloth, and gagged.

A body.

It was the man who had brought his food on a tray. The FSB man – Alex. He wondered why he hadn't seen him after their last talk, but things had been so unstructured, so crazy, his entire perception of time and what was happening had been thrown off course.

Alex was lying on his back, the tattoo of the phoenix standing out clearly on the side of his neck. His head was thrown back exposing the paleness of his skin, his eyes half-closed.

He'd been shot once in the forehead.

Irina. Instinct told him this was her handiwork.

Rik felt the hairs bristle on the back of his neck. He dropped the cloth back into place. Alex had been right to believe they would hurt him. But why? He was on their side, albeit FSB, if he'd been telling the truth, rather than GRU. Had they had a falling-out about something and he'd paid the price?

He wondered why he hadn't heard anything. This room wasn't far from where he was being kept and sound travelled easily enough through the building. The movement of metal doors was fairly audible, so a gunshot would have been perfectly clear, unless . . . He recalled the bang he'd heard earlier, waking him up. He'd assumed it to be a door slamming. Maybe not.

As he turned to leave his foot brushed against something which skittered away across the concrete floor. A flick of the torch showed a plastic bottle, partially wrapped in cloth. A hole had been cut in the base. The bottle had been crushed and part of the wrapping showed signs of scorch marks. He picked it up and immediately the bitter tang of burned plastic became stronger. The inside of the bottle from the neck down had been melted and fused by intense heat.

He'd seen something like this once before on another training demo. It was a makeshift suppressor.

He put it back where he'd found it and walked out of the room, his gut turning over. Was this the beginning of a clean-up operation? Had they aborted their mission and were reducing their numbers prior to clearing out? If so, what was the coach next door all about?

He heard the distant clang of a door and a rattle of chains. He dodged down the corridor and finally found his way back to his cell. He still had no viable weapon against two fit opponents. If they had been joined by the two heavies he'd just seen outside it was pointless worrying about it. Fighting back against such odds was ludicrous.

He closed the door and dropped onto the mattress, pulling the blanket around him just as he heard a rumble of approaching voices and the door slid open.

The hairs on the back of his neck moved. There was silence, although he could hear the sound of someone breathing. He coughed deliberately and moaned. Eventually the door slid shut and he was alone again.

He rolled over and stared into the darkness, thinking about what he'd just seen. The people who'd arrived on the coach must be the hacking group Kraush had boasted about. Ferried in under cover of darkness to a desolate, abandoned spot, it reeked of an operation unsanctioned by the authorities. But then, who was going to protest against the might of the people behind the GRU?

So much for Kraush's threat to launch a cyber attack only if Rik didn't provide him with the information in his head. He was familiar enough with hacking operations to know that a team like this would have been briefed and trained before arriving here, ready to go on the offensive the moment they set up their equipment. Hackers worked best when they all knew what they had to do and had the means to go into action for a limited but intensive period. Hackers preferred to live in the shadows, aware that their activities would be traced if they made even a simple error. The risk of discovery was always there in every key-stroke and each newly-won connection. The moment their work was done they would be up and away, taking every trace of their presence with them.

He felt cold and huddled inside the blanket. He was trying not to give into a sense of panic, but getting out of here with this thing round his leg was not an option. The best thing he could do was play along and hope he got some kind of break.

TWENTY-SIX

'I'm on the subject. He's done exactly what we expected.'

Colmyer signalled for his secretary to leave the room, and waited until the door closed behind her before saying, 'Go ahead.'

The voice on the other end belonged to Garth Perry. A twenty-year veteran of undercover work in Military Intelligence, a failure to respect the rules of the Geneva Convention while on deployment in Afghanistan had led to his dismissal. Diagnosed as a case of PTSD, Perry had narrowly escaped a jail sentence. It hadn't stopped him registering with a company sourcing experienced staff for military contracts overseas.

As a sleeping but not always silent partner, as he was with several businesses he was involved with, Colmyer had come across Perry's details by chance. He'd noted the man's past record and had quietly put him into a file of potential assets, disposable and otherwise.

'Tate called at Ferris's mother's address in Southwark, stayed five minutes on the doorstep, then moved to Ferris's address in Paddington where he spoke to a neighbour, before entering Ferris's flat.'

'Does that suggest recent contact?'

'Possibly not. I heard part of the conversation down the stairwell. The neighbour handed him something, probably a key. He was inside for thirty-three minutes, easily time to toss the place.'

'Toss?'

'Search. I was going to follow him in for a look but a neighbour was hanging around cleaning her front door.'

'Forget it. If Tate's any good he'll have found anything useful. What then?'

'He went home to Islington then to an office address behind Waterloo Station. I'm pretty sure it's an outlier unit for Thames House. He visited a hotel in Westminster, too. There's been some activity there over the death of a guest.'

'I know about that. It's nothing to worry about.' Colmyer wanted to swear; anything to relieve the tension he was feeling. This bloody Tate was turning into a nuisance. The decision to put a freelancer on finding Ferris was a mistake. He'd picked up on a bulletin about the death in a traffic incident of a guest registered at the Westminster hotel, but it hadn't revealed anything useful. So what the hell had Tate found that had dragged him there? The office unit near Waterloo was a potential problem. The Intelligence and Security Services used cover offices all over the capital, most, he suspected, serving to blanket some of their more dubious activities and something he was determined to change. But he'd have to be careful asking questions about its function and why Tate had been there. 'Where is he now?'

'At home. I'm standing by to see where he goes next.'

'Very well. Stay on him at all costs – wherever he goes.'

'Wherever?'

'You heard. But no contact, understand? He mustn't know anybody's interested in him.'

'Got it. What about Ferris?'

'If they meet up that's for you to deal with. In any case I'll make a decision once Ferris is located. Keep me informed.'

Colmyer cut the call and sat back, fighting off a rising surge of near-panic. He needed this matter dealt with, and fast. Having to wait for others to make their moves was something to which he wasn't accustomed. And all the while he had a feeling of time and opportunity ticking away.

TWENTY-SEVEN

Clare Jardine felt sick. Her stomach was tight with nerves and she was nursing a strong desire to be anywhere but here. It was an unwelcome reminder of the job she used to do and the regular flutters that would invade her system every time she had to go on a mission. She'd never confessed it to anybody else but she knew others, more open than her, who'd suffered the same way.

She was standing once again within sight of the arrivals door from the planes, watching passengers, workers and security personnel merge and part like schools of fish, the first group on their own individual journeys and, for the most part eager to be through immigration and out of here. Outside it was dark save for the security lights flooding the aircraft parking spots.

She shivered in spite of the warm air from the ventilation ducts overhead, and wished she could turn around and go home. Three hours ago she had received a text message that had turned her day upside down.

Passenger Tate H arriving 18.00 BEL 852. Sorry, no pic. K. x.

She hadn't wanted to believe it, not after all this time – and especially after seeing Ferris here, too. Was it already five years ago since they had last met? Seeing the message had been enough to get her into her car and heading for the airport as fast as possible, grabbing her security pass on the way. One eye on her rear-view mirror and a map unreeling in her head showing exit routes and places where she could disappear if she had to, was a measure of how time had not diminished the ingrained training that followed her everywhere like a bad dream to which she was forever chained.

She caught sight of her reflection in a polished metal screen. She looked pale and drawn after a late night ferrying two visiting Ukrainian army officers and their minder around the city, neither of them troublesome save for an insistence on getting mortally drunk. But at least she looked very different to what former MI5 officer Harry Tate – if it was him – would remember.

She tried to conjure up Tate's face and found it unclear; a shifting mirage. But she'd know him if she saw him. If it wasn't him on the plane it would doubtlessly be some engineering salesman from Sheffield touting for business in the brave new world that included large swathes of Eastern Europe.

Using her security position, Katya had put in place a daily scan of passenger lists not long after Clare had arrived here, largely so that she could rest easy in knowing that her past wasn't about to come back to haunt her. The murder of her MI6 boss, Sir Anthony Bellingham, had been a just retribution in her view. Bellingham had been one of the architects of her eventual dismissal from SIS and the cause of more than one death. Unfortunately not everyone shared that opinion, and she had lived under a cloud for the past few years expecting to find herself the subject of a snatch squad or worse.

But now a specific name, one of several Katya had fed into the system, had popped up. It might be a duplicate, some innocent Tate H on normal business because there was only so much specific data that could be fed into a system without arousing the interests of the eagle-eyed wonks who watched for bugs, malware, hacks and other anomalies. And if Tate was here as an instrument of the state, would he really travel under his own name? Time would tell. There were ways of making a definite identification, including seeing a passport, although documents could be falsified, stolen or replicated. The most reliable method was surveillance. Seeing a face, the body outline, the walk, even the voice if she got close enough to hear it, were no-brainers.

Out of habit she kept an eye on her surroundings. Watching her back took time but it was another habit she hadn't been able to cast off completely. And while she was reasonably certain that none of the local security agencies had any interest in her, and the tag around her neck would keep anyone from asking awkward questions, only a fool took the passing of time for a dimming of memory. In the minds and annals of security departments the world over, time was a fluid concept that had no run-out point or statute of limitations.

She resumed her study of the arrivals, a slow-moving snake with a gradually diminishing tail, only to be added to and swollen as another flight of eager incomers caught up with them. She wondered if Tate H had already gone by, an unknown face with a similar name, or he'd stopped to make a phone call.

Or maybe he'd hung back to merge with the next group, a trade-craft move to confuse any watchers.

Then she felt a jolt go through her chest. A glimpse, that was all she had. A brief snatch of a face behind a group of four bulky men in suits and carrying briefcases. Then the face was gone as the group flexed to allow a cleaning trolley go by. She stayed absolutely still. Up here she was fairly sure she was invisible, but caution made her freeze all the same. If it was him, he'd be alert for any movement that looked suspicious because that was the kind of man he was.

She got another glimpse, first of the face, then the walk. Shit. It was Tate! She almost thought *her Tate* but denied the term. There was nothing possessive or matey about their knowing each other. They'd been fellow-travellers, that was all, along with Rik Ferris and a handful of others; not in any ideological or collaborative sense, but trapped in a nightmare that three of them at least, had been fortunate enough to get out of in one piece.

She searched for him again as the crowd shifted and a luggage tractor went by. There he was, drifting along as if he hadn't a care in the world, blending in without conscious thought, using others as cover against cameras with the insulting ease born of instinct. She ticked off the familiar list: sturdy build, somewhere in his forties, brown hair in a brush cut peppered with hints of grey. Looking older of course, because he was, but then weren't they all? Harry bloody Tate in the bloody flesh. Former soldier, MI5 spy hunter, bulldog, general boy-scout and, the last she'd heard, security gun for hire. And now he was here.

He began to turn his head and she eased back behind a pillar. He'd have been scouting the place all the way through from the plane, she told herself. Eyes on invisible stalks, noting cameras, personnel, doorways and choke points, the way he'd been trained – the way they'd all been trained. That kind of skill, once ingrained, never left you, not entirely. It might dim a little through lack of use, as it had with her, the same way soldiers lost the ease with which they handled weapons after a while. But bits still stuck like barnacles on a boat's hull.

She kept her eyes on him, just as she had watched Ferris earlier. She took out her phone and dialled a number.

'Balenkova.' The voice of her partner was clear, authoritative, yet to Clare, the most welcome and comforting sound in the world.

'It's him,' Clare said. 'Tate. He's just arrived.'

'Coincidence?'

'I don't know. First Ferris, now him. I doubt it. There must be something going on.'

'Could they have joined up for an assignment?' Katya being logical, reasonable in the face of concern. 'You said they were working security together, no?'

'Maybe. But why not arrive on the same flight?' The only reason she could think of was if Tate had called Ferris in to help on an assignment he was undertaking, or if they had travelled days apart to avoid being noticed. It made a kind of sense. Seeing one former MI5 man going through here was unlikely to cause a second look, even given the paranoia towards the west. That's if anyone even recognized him. It might be viewed as odd, even unlikely, but not a cause for alarm. Seeing two together would, in some eyes, smack of an operation in progress.

'What are you going to do?' Katya's voice sounded calm enough but there was an underlying hint of concern that made Clare feel a warmth run through her. She still hadn't got used to someone being worried about her, especially someone who was a former member of the Russian FSO.

'I'm not sure. Find out why he's here, probably.'

'How?'

'I could ask him.'

'Don't. Milaya, you don't know what you might be getting into. If he's on an official assignment he won't be pleased to know you have seen him.'

Clare hesitated, the use of the endearment a confusion, albeit welcome. She wasn't sure why she felt that way until it came to her with a start: she was in operational mode. Without fully realizing it, she had slipped from normal – in other words a life not actively pursuing someone because that was no longer her job – to a status level she had long left behind.

Bloody Tate, she thought. What the hell does he want? Am I just being paranoid? Anyway, she reminded herself, how the hell would he know I was here? She had dropped off the radar completely after their last meeting, partly to recover from her wounds but also to draw a thick curtain over her previous life.

She cut the call with a brief goodbye. She had to find out, otherwise she'd never rest. If Harry Tate was here for her, it could only be that he'd been sent by London, most probably SIS. And he wouldn't be bringing chocolates. No matter that she'd once saved his life and stopped a bullet in the process, some dues were automatically cancelled the moment you jumped the fence and disappeared, the way she had. In the world of secret intelligence, once you were no longer part of the same game, all bets were off.

She followed Tate's progress, using stairways and corridors as cover, the ID tag swinging from her neck. She was surprised by how quickly he appeared to move, a fish among other fishes, only faster than most, yet without obvious effort. She waited while the queue entered and was processed through passport control, then moved onto a mezzanine overlooking the main concourse, where she could watch him moving to the meet-and-greet exit.

She moved around a German couple who were arguing volubly over a mislaid passport, then got back on track. And stopped.

Tate was gone.

Just like that.

She swore to herself and felt a hint of panic. She'd had her eye on him! How the hell—

Then he was walking up a moving stairway towards her. He looked relaxed and mildly interested, as if this encounter hadn't been totally unsurprising. But then the Harry Tate she had known very rarely looked surprised by anything.

She watched as he stepped to one side to allow other passengers to spill off the stairway and move past. He was wearing a heavy topcoat and plain slacks and carrying a holdall. Enough, she figured, for a couple of nights stopover. Visas for UK nationals now lasted for thirty days rather than the original five or ten. If Tate was here for any longer than a couple, he was travelling very light. Dark clothing, dark holdall, dark shoes – all of it anonymous, she reflected, just like him. She'd seen Tate disappear before, like smoke on the wind. It was a rare skill not available to everyone, and although she could do it herself, she wasn't as good as him.

'For a moment, there,' he murmured, 'I thought you were trying to avoid me.'

Clare wanted to hit him, to demand why he was here, to insist he leave her alone and go back to wherever he'd come from, to forget he'd seen her and never think of or speak of her again. But the words wouldn't come.

'Coffee,' he said finally. 'I could really do with a large coffee.'

There was no way out. The best she could do was to go along with him, find out why he was here and move on. Trying to lose him would be like shaking off a piece of lint.

TWENTY-EIGHT

'I lost Tate.' It was Perry, delivering news Colmyer didn't want to hear. He stood up from his desk as if given an electric shock, causing a tray of files to slide off the edge and scatter its contents across the floor. His secretary, busy pouring coffee, rushed to gather them together, but he waved a hand at her and shouted, 'Leave them! Get out.'

When he regained his temper, he said to Perry, 'How? Where?'

'He bagged a stand-by seat on a flight to Minsk. But at least I know that's where he got off.'

Colmyer ground his teeth together. 'Why are you telling me this? Find him!'

'You asked for reports,' Perry replied calmly. 'I'm keeping you updated.'

'Are you sure you can handle this?' Colmyer muttered savagely. 'I had every confidence in you; you'd better not let me down.'

'Don't worry, I'm on it. I know people in Minsk; associates who can find Tate before he knows it.'

Colmyer experienced a momentary buzz of concern and wondered just what kind of 'people' Perry knew in Belarus. He was supposed to be a loner, a man ill-suited to be associated with anyone, least of all in a place like Minsk. There had certainly been no indication of any in his background data, and he wondered if it might become a problem in the future. Using off-the-books talent was a double-edged sword, especially if they responded to a more tempting offer from elsewhere or used others from God alone knew what kind of dodgy milieu.

Perry interrupted his thoughts. 'Are you talking executive action?'

'Of course executive bloody action,' Colmyer snarled. 'Both of them. Do it!'

He cut the connection and sat down. He had the beginnings of a headache inching across his forehead and snatched at his coffee. It was already lukewarm and he was tempted to hurl it across the room. Minsk? Why the bloody hell had Ferris gone to Minsk? But deep down he knew why: if anyone was digging into areas of the

UK's intelligence files, Belarus would be one place where cyber operations were set up with carefully concealed lines to Moscow. And a man like Ferris, with all manner of information stored in his brain, would have been drawn there to be scalped, drained and emptied of every little thing he knew.

He was about to reach for the phone to contact Hough when he had second thoughts. This wasn't a disaster, not yet. If Perry did his job properly, his dealings in the US following his visits to Moscow would never see the light of day and Ferris and Tate would be history. The archives would remain closed, just as Sir Geoffrey Bull, and Sir Anthony Bellingham before him, had promised. As for his financial records and the extent of his undeclared involvement in banking and energy stakes in that region, that could be explained away. Being dragged before the Parliamentary Commissioner for Standards Office and subjected to an investigation would be an embarrassment, but ultimately negotiable. What might be less easy to explain was the considerable and hidden wealth of shares and investments through a network of holding companies and shadow accounts, spread across more than a dozen tax havens and jurisdictions. It was this that would be the finish of him. Making money out of astute and permissible investments was easy to dismiss; being found to be elbow deep in Russian, Ukrainian and Chinese companies, all sanction-busting with some of the world's most hostile states across the Middle East, was not.

He called his secretary for more coffee and told her to postpone the next meeting for thirty minutes. He needed to think. The knowledge that he could be suborned had meant little when he was starting out as an MP. The kind of information he was privy to then was unimportant and therefore unhelpful to a foreign power. But that was then. Now the reality of his situation had struck home with a vengeance. He'd been careless; he should have seen this coming.

The thought brought a chill of fear deep in his chest. He'd thought himself a friend of men in suits with close ties to the Kremlin, and used that for his own gain, playing up his contacts to the Americans. Those same men in suits had even given him a nickname he'd actually thought funny at the time.

Cicada.

TWENTY-NINE

Harry was surprised by the change in Clare Jardine's appearance. Whether the result of a different lifestyle or the physical impact of having been shot, the transformation was considerable. In fact he doubted if most people who'd once worked with her in MI6 would recognize her now. But he did. Share close enough ties even for a short while with someone under stressful circumstances, and you get to know the way they move, the way they hold themselves. That kind of closeness tends to imprint a person on the psyche more than a shared cubicle or a regular chat over coffee and cake.

That he'd spotted her at all was pure luck. She'd moved against the backdrop of an overhead walkway just as he'd looked up, subconsciously checking for cameras or watchers. It was obvious that she was scanning the crowd of passengers around him, and while he might have expected that of security officials at any major international airport, seeing a face he recognized doing the same had been a surprise. His initial thought was that she might be there to meet an incoming traveller. But when he realized she was keeping up with him as he progressed through the airport, he realized that he was the subject of interest.

She led him to a cafeteria area, now largely deserted after the recent flush-through of meeters-and-greeters, and ordered coffee. The woman behind the counter seemed to know her and gave a friendly smile, and he wondered if Minsk was where Clare now lived. In truth he hadn't given a thought to where she had gone, save that he'd hoped she stayed lucky and safe. That was the least he could wish for her.

'You look well,' he said, which wasn't his best opener, but he had to start somewhere.

'You look older,' she countered bluntly. 'What are you doing here?'

Still the same old Clare, thought Harry. He wondered if she was still carrying her deadly little blade, the one concealed in a powder compact which could be unleashed in a moment. He shook a sugar bag and dumped the contents in his coffee. A few stray grains scattered across the table, and he gathered them together with a sweep of his hand. He was playing for time, still trying to get over the surprise of seeing her standing there at the top of the elevator, a blast from the past. 'Sorry. I gave up sugar a while ago, but every now and then I feel the need.'

'I'm not interested in your dietary habits.' Clare's voice took on a hard edge, and her hand nudged her cup aside, spilling a few drops of black coffee. 'You didn't answer my question: why are you here? Is it me you're after?'

Harry said, 'Why would I be after you?'

She didn't believe him, it was written in every line of her face. In addition she looked stubborn, angry, concerned and, unusually, ready to bolt. That was unlike her. The Clare Jardine he'd known had been naturally assertive and ready to face up to anything. But this version was different somehow. He studied her face, trying to gauge what she had gone through since he'd last seen her. She was thinner, but not unhealthily so, her hands strong and unhesitating in their movements. Her hair was neat, short and as an indicator of a person's health, she looked fine. But there was something under her skin that told another story.

'All right,' he said, and placed both hands on the table. What could he lose by telling her the truth? 'I'm looking for Rik Ferris.'

'Christ, is that geek still around?' She tried to make the question casual, but there was something in her expression that didn't look right. 'I'm surprised he didn't shoot himself in the foot a long time ago.'

He was about to suggest she should give Rik a break, but under the circumstances it didn't seem appropriate, not if Rik had really got himself into something messy. Instead he said, 'How come you were here? I didn't imagine you for a plane-spotter.'

She chewed her lip for a moment, then surprised him. 'I live in the city – not that you'd know that. I've been keeping a low profile. I heard you were flying in and wanted to see if it was really you.' She hesitated, then said, 'And now you want to know how I knew?'

'You got it.'

'A friend placed a search programme in the arrivals data program with a list of names red-tagged.'

'Names?'

'People I thought might come looking for me. Six personnel, including you. When your name popped up I came to check it out.'

'I hope the wait was worth it.'

'Don't kid yourself,' she said, but there was now a trace of something else in her eyes: a slight softening of the hard shell he knew so well. It was a tiny sign, but an improvement on the protective expression she'd been wearing earlier. 'I didn't want any surprises after what I'd been through, and the easiest way to check was to have some warning.'

'Warning of what? That I might come for you? Why would you think I'd have any part of that?'

'I don't know.' She shrugged. 'I didn't know what to think after London. Whether they'd want to settle scores or not. It wasn't as if I'd left with a pat on the back and a letter of recommendation, not after what I did.'

'Is that Bellingham or Paulton?' It was risky bringing up Paulton's name, another traitor who'd met an unexplained death. But since cards were being laid on the table, why not?

'I've no idea what you're talking about.' The response was like a bear-trap closing. 'Paulton was your problem, not mine.' Her expression went cold again and he decided to leave it. There was nothing to gain by apportioning responsibility – he couldn't think of it as blame.

'If it hadn't been you it would have been me,' he said, and felt surprised that he'd never voiced that before. He'd thought it plenty of times while tracking Paulton across Europe; what he would do if and when he caught up with him. But he'd never put it into words. Probably because he knew that getting Paulton into any form of custody and facing justice was unlikely to happen.

'God, get you, Tate. You going all Rambo now?'

'Actually,' he said, 'I like to think I could be a member of the Justice League. They have more colourful outfits.' He paused. 'Anyway, why the interest? Did you really think I'd be the one to come after you?'

'Why not? You went freelance but stayed in the same game. Anyway, you have a habit of attracting trouble, remember?'

'Fair point.' He'd got her shot the last time they'd met. Well, he hadn't, not directly. She'd been in the wrong place at the wrong time. But arguing semantics wasn't going to get them anywhere.

'And,' she added, 'you turning up here as well was a surprise I could do without.'

'As well?'

'Ferris came through here a few days ago.'

Harry didn't say anything for a moment. How much could he tell her? He knew of her partnership with Katya, an FSO officer, but that didn't mean she might feel inclined to blab to the authorities.

'Did you follow him to see where he went?' he said finally.

'I was working at the time so I couldn't. He headed into the city but I've no idea where. I know one thing, though: he had company.'

'Who?'

'A man and a woman. They looked like a surveillance crew.'

'You sure?'

'Yes. They were on him like limpets but he didn't know it. Off in one of his own little bubbles, I expect. Why are you looking for him?'

'Before I answer that, is one of your watcher friends Katya?'

'I'm not going to tell you that.' Her face shut down and she looked wary, but it told him all he needed to know.

'You just did.'

She glared at him and he wondered if being out of Six had allowed her to forget about basic interrogation techniques. Never give away more than you have to; it could cost you your life.

'She helped,' she admitted eventually. 'She has contacts all over. I don't know who they are but they're close enough to do as she asks without question. She wanted to protect both our backs.'

'She works here, too?'

'She's on assignment, training up the Belarus government's protection team. And before you ask, Moscow relaxed the career block they had on her since our episode, and they don't seem bothered by me being with her.'

'Glad to hear it.' It was quite a shift in attitudes for any Moscow agency, Harry thought. At one time a Russian security officer becoming and staying involved with a former member of MI6 would have suffered a career-ending with no way back. 'They must think highly of her.'

'And less of me, you mean?' Her eyes flickered. 'Maybe you're right. But we're not taking it for granted. That's why it bothers me when you two turn up unexpectedly within days of each other. Are you saying you're not working together?'

'Absolutely.' Harry explained about their gradual drift apart due to work, about Rik losing his mother and, subsequently, the Security Service's interest in his activities.

Clare stared at him. 'That's a bit desperate, isn't it? No way is Ferris spy material. He probably likes to think he's Jason Bourne when he looks in the mirror, but not in a million.'

'You're being too harsh. I'd trust him any day.' To get back on course he explained briefly what he knew about Rik's recent movements, including the CCTV street footage, and the death of Nathalie Baier.

'Were they a thing?' Clare looked cynical.

'I don't know. Could be, but I doubt it.'

He took out his phone and showed her the WhatsApp message from Rik. 'That's all I've got. And the address in Stepyanka, wherever that is.'

'You don't want to know.'

'Why do you say that?'

'He's not there, that's all.'

'How do you know that?'

'Because I've already been there looking for him.'

'Why? He's not your favourite person, and chasing SIS delinquents isn't his kind of work.'

'Doesn't matter. I just don't like the idea of him being in my back yard. You either, come to that. I wanted to know what he was doing here.'

'Did you find him?'

'No. That bit of Stepyanka is a deserted shit-hole for addicts and people with nowhere else to go. It's due for clearance any day. When they get round to it it'll simply shift the problems elsewhere – probably across the Beltway to where all the "nice" people live.' She made rabbit's ears around the word.

'The Beltway?'

'The circular road around Minsk.' She explained how she had got there by asking around and had struck lucky. 'For all I know he ran into trouble. It's the kind of dumping ground where things happen, people disappear and nobody knows anything.'

'I want to see it.'

'You really don't.'

'I really do. He wouldn't have sent me the address if it wasn't important.'

'You think he was laying a trail?'

He shrugged. 'Maybe. I won't know until I look.'

'In that case be my guest. But don't blame me if you don't come out again.'

'You could always take me.'

'Not a chance. Certainly not at this time of night. Anyway I can't risk being seen with you or Ferris.'

'Why not?'

'Because I'm here under sufferance. If anyone catches on to who you are I'll be out on my ear and Katya will be recalled to Moscow.'

'Fine.' Harry stood up. 'I'll go myself.' He gestured at the coffees. 'It was good to see you again. I hope everything goes well for you and Katya.'

He'd taken three paces away from the table when she called out. 'Wait.' Then she was standing by his side, her breathing light but fast, as if she'd raced up a flight of stairs. Her eyes were glittering but he couldn't decide if it was anger, frustration . . . or excitement. 'You're like a dog with a frigging bone,' she muttered.

'Woof. Are you in?'

'Maybe. Have you booked a hotel?'

'Not yet.'

'I know a decent one. I'll take you there. But we're not going anywhere near Stepyanka until morning. It's too dangerous. My car's out front. Give me two minutes head start before you follow.'

'Am I that toxic?'

'Damn right.' She paused. 'This had better be worth it.' Then she walked away towards the front of the terminal leaving Harry to finish his coffee.

'So why have you been handed the job?' Clare asked, as she took the car out of the airport and headed towards the distant lights of the city. Traffic was light but she kept to a respectable speed to avoid drawing the attention of cameras or patrolling cops. 'If he's suspected of spying, which is beyond absurd, I'd have thought bringing you in would be the last thing they'd do.'

'I was their first option, apparently. They think I'm the one most likely to track him down.'

She glanced across at him, the reflected lights of other vehicles highlighting shadows on her face. 'And if you don't?'

'They'll send a team after him.'

'They must want him really bad. What sort of team?'

Harry shrugged. 'The kind that doesn't have to bring him back.'

'I don't want to rain on your parade,' she said, 'but from what I saw they're already here.'

'Couldn't be,' said Harry. If that was true, it suggested Cramer's bosses must have known Rik was on the move days ago, in which case they'd had him under surveillance.

'Fact. As I told you, when I saw him he was being tailed through the airport by a man and woman. They looked like they knew what they were doing.'

'Locals?'

'No. They were carrying bags so they must have come off the same flight.'

'What did they look like?' It could have been a team from Six, put on him the moment he started moving. Or, given Cramer's suggestion that he'd jumped ship, was it a Russian security team making sure he travelled safely?

'A man; tall, slim . . . I thought an athlete, but I don't know. There was something military about him. And a woman: stocky, shorter, big ginger hair. A Rottweiler type.'

Harry didn't say anything, but stared out into the darkness. Had Rik picked up his tails from London, or were they watching him for some other reason?

Clare picked him up at eight the following morning. He was feeling edgy and exhausted from a restless night's sleep. Itching to get up and take a cab out to this Stepyanka place before she arrived, reason had prevailed; he was in potentially hostile territory with no language skills here and no knowledge of the people or the area. It wasn't an unusual situation for him, but putting himself in extreme danger for no good reason wouldn't do anything to help Rik.

Clare spoke little, concentrating on the traffic which seemed to consist of heavy trucks and a darting accompaniment of cars like pilot fish, good at changing direction without warning or signals and blasting their horns at anyone who failed to move quickly enough.

The area around the hotel sported a number of large, highly-polished Mercedes military-style G Wagen 4WDs, some on the move with others parked outside the fancier hotels and shops. The vehicles all had men in suits standing by them, but they didn't look like business types.

'Are they what I think they are?' Harry asked.

She nodded. 'Prestige vehicles for those who can afford them. There are a lot of new millionaires here and they're scared of losing what they've got. Don't mess with them; the drivers are mostly former special forces and they're always armed.'

'And the government doesn't mind?'

'Of course. But most of their clients *are* the government. It's all part of the new détente in this neck of the woods.'

Eventually they joined the Beltway, where Clare switched to the section heading east before it curved north on its way round the city. On the left Harry saw a number of factory units and what looked like energy plants, and beyond that a grey stretch of housing and, further over, the beginnings of high-rises signalling the progress of a modernized city. On the right lay a thick belt of trees, with glimpses of industrial rooftops in the distance.

Ten minutes later Clare turned off the Beltway and headed east again, this time taking a narrow road through the trees until they reached a junction, where she switched onto a well-used forest track.

'Stepyanka's up ahead by the Beltway,' she told him. 'I'm taking the long way round instead of the tunnel. This brings us in by the apartment block. You'll see it in a minute.'

Sure enough Harry saw the top of the block poking up from the surrounding trees. It didn't look prepossessing from a distance, and closer inspection didn't help much. Clare drove through a scattering of ancient housing, most of it derelict, and parked at the rear of the block.

'It's safer here,' she told Harry, then reached into the glovebox and took out a small semi-automatic pistol, which she placed in her jacket pocket. 'Just in case,' she said. 'Come on.'

She got out of the car and walked over to a rear entrance, which was partially blocked open by broken bed frames, kitchen equipment and other rubbish. She threaded her way through the tangle and led Harry to the front of the building where she peered through the grimy glass of the lobby towards the mouth of a tunnel under the motorway three hundred yards away.

Harry joined her and saw figures moving in and around the tunnel entrance, and a thin pall of smoke drifting into the air.

'That's where we don't want to go,' Clare said. 'Once was enough for me.'

Harry nodded. 'Are they likely to come over here?'

'I don't think so. They've tried to set up squats here but a private security team hired by the developers comes along within minutes and turfs them out. When they start work they don't want any holdups due to protesters.'

'But there are people living here?'

'A handful. Mostly old women. They've been promised help to move when the time comes, and act as wardens for the developers in return. Two of the women I spoke to were holding mobile phones, so I reckon they must have been provided by the developers to call for help. Come on. I hope you're feeling fit because the lift doesn't work.' She ignored the lift and led the way up the stairs at a steady rate. There was no sign that she lacked fitness, and he noticed that she kept her hand in her pocket where she had placed the pistol.

The stairs on the first two floors were crumbling with age, stained a dull brown by rust leaking out of the metal cores, and littered with rotten wood, smashed glass and puddled water. The third floor was a stark contrast. The floor, although pitted with holes, was clean and free of rubbish, and showed signs of having been swept regularly.

Clare continued up to the fourth floor, where she pointed at a door facing the stairs. 'That's twenty-four,' she said softly. 'Before we try knocking I want to let them know who we are.'

She walked along to the next apartment door and knocked, and moments later a woman appeared. She had a deeply lined face and sharp eyes, and could have been any age from sixty onwards. She was dressed in several layers of clothing under a heavy coat, and carrying a mobile phone. She nodded at Clare in recognition and held up a finger for them to wait. She pressed a button on the phone, and when it was answered, spoke briefly before turning it off.

'She's just told one of the other residents who I am,' said Clare.

'Why would she do that?'

'It's the neighbourhood network. She recognized me from before and told them not to call the cops.'

Clare turned to the woman and gestured towards Harry, then pointed towards the door of number twenty-four. The woman rummaged in her pocket and handed over a key, before stepping back into her apartment and closing the door.

The apartment was empty, save for rat droppings and a pool of filthy water on the floor. Harry checked out each room before returning to the front door where Clare was waiting.

'Nobody's been here in years,' he said. 'I don't get it.'

'Maybe it was bait,' Clare said. 'He was told someone would be here just to get him where they could take him without fuss.'

Harry nodded. It made sense. Had Rik been led to believe that Nathalie was here waiting for him? Entirely possible if she hadn't turned up for their meeting. Maybe she'd sent him a message about this place. Or someone else had done it instead.

Clare locked the door behind them and went back to the next apartment and tapped gently on the door. The woman appeared again and took the key.

Harry said, 'Can you ask her if anyone else has been here recently?'

Clare nodded and asked the question. The woman pursed her lips and shook her head, then used her phone again, rattling off a question to the person on the other end.

'She's asking one of the other women,' Clare explained.

The woman gave the semblance of a smile before cutting the connection. She spoke at length to Clare and held up two fingers, then pointed towards the south, away from the city. Harry didn't understand much but he did catch a familiar sounding term: '*Industrial'naya*'.

Clare turned to him and explained. 'Her friend downstairs saw a man arrive in a taxi, which left immediately. It sounds like Rik. He entered the building and was followed upstairs by two men she thought were security police. After a few minutes all three went back out and got into a big car – probably a four-wheel-drive – and drove south towards an old industrial zone.'

'Do you know it?'

'I've driven past it. It's huge. Nothing but empty factories and a few squatters living off the land, too poor to move anywhere better.'

Harry nodded. It sounded as if Rik had been lured into a trap. 'Will you thank her for her help?'

'Of course. It would be polite to offer payment. They're proud but it wouldn't hurt.'

Harry handed over some money which the woman refused before relenting. As she closed the door she said something to Clare.

'What was that?' Harry asked.

Clare looked at him and pulled a face. 'You don't want to know.'

'Humour me.'

'She said you'd got a face like a bulldog.' She shrugged expansively and walked towards the stairs. 'Don't shoot the messenger.'

Harry followed her downstairs. It was the first time he'd ever heard her make anything approximating a joke.

As they stepped outside and started back towards the car, they found four men standing in their way. They were dressed in heavy coats and beanie hats, and holding lengths of steel pipe. They didn't look friendly.

Clare spoke to them but they didn't move. The one who appeared to be the leader stepped forward and gestured towards the car, holding out a grubby hand.

'He wants the car keys,' said Clare, putting her hand into her jacket pocket. 'And our money.'

'Tough,' said Harry. 'We do that and we're dead. Shoot him in the foot. I find that works a treat.'

Clare gave him a look. 'That might bring a load of trouble down on us. If the cops get involved I could lose everything. Amend that – *we* could lose everything.' He realized she was talking about her and Katya.

'You've never heard of shoot and run?'

She huffed for a moment, but when she took her hand out of her pocket she was holding the gun.

The lead man grunted and looked at Clare with contempt, as if she wouldn't dare. He muttered something to his colleagues and spat to one side. The other three looked less sure of themselves, but with the required machismo at stake, they shuffled up to stand alongside their leader.

'Don't call my bluff,' Clare warned the man. But if he understood he took no notice and reached for her gun.

She shot him in the foot. The sound echoed in the immediate area but was largely lost in the cold air. The man howled and dropped his weapon, and fell over clutching his wounded foot and staring up at Clare in disbelief. The other three looked stunned before backing away fast, losing their steel bars in the process.

'Nice shot,' said Harry. 'That'll smart for a bit.' He stepped past the wounded man and led the way to the car while Clare followed, the gun covering the other three men who showed no signs of going to help their colleague.

She drove the car out of the area at a steady pace and regained the track leading back to the Beltway. 'I don't believe this,' she said, wrenching the wheel round as they hit a junction, scattering a welter of gravel, slush and mud in their wake. 'You've screwed it for me, Tate! Why did I ever listen to you?'

Harry said nothing. It was better if she vented. She would know as well as he that if they'd stayed there and tried talking their way out they'd be rat food by now.

'I need a drink,' she said after a while. 'And I'm not talking coffee. I hope you haven't turned teetotal.'

'Not recently.' Harry glanced across at her, trying to gauge whether she was losing it. Being out of the game for a few years would do that to a person. It changes the response mechanisms conditioned by years of training and experience so that suddenly being faced with a stressful situation could trip the whole world out of kilter. And for some drink was a quick way to counter the shock. For others it was the beginning of a form of disintegration.

She must have read his mind. 'Don't worry, I'm not falling apart. I just need a kick.'

He said nothing while she followed the Beltway to the next junction and found a bar where she parked and led the way inside. There were a few customers, mostly travellers or truck drivers who barely gave them a glance. That suited Harry just fine. Clare placed their order without asking Harry what he wanted, and moments later they were sinking shots of vodka.

'God, I needed that,' she said at last, draining her glass and calling for refills. 'This is almost like old times.'

Harry said, 'You don't normally drink?'

She gave him another look. This one almost human. 'Who said I was talking about the vodka?' Then she laughed, a harsh sound that gave Harry a nervous tingle up the back of his neck.

THIRTY

The weather was beginning to close in when Clare pulled up near the gated entrance to a vast collection of factory buildings that had seen better days. They were several miles south of the city in an area surrounded by a thick growth of trees, their dark stalks pointing towards the heavy sky as if sucking out all the available light.

'Nice spot for a picnic,' said Harry.

'It's part of the forgotten landscape here,' Clare replied. 'An old industrial area that some say was easier to leave behind than pull down and rebuild.'

Harry spotted an old metal road sign that had come adrift of its moorings at one end and was pointing down at the ground. Rust had eaten away the original name and someone had scrawled another word on top in white paint. *Revolyutsiya!*

'Does that mean what I think it does?'

Clare nodded. 'Revolution. There are some old diehards here, too, same as in Russia. Most of them are dreamers; they'd never make it anywhere near the government offices in Independence Square because they don't have the muscle.'

Two figures were moving in the distance, made indistinct by a fading light. They looked old, walking slowly and bundled up heavily against the cold.

'Do people live here?' Harry asked.

'Some. Not so much in the zone, but in the forest. They're probably scavenging for building materials and wood to burn. There are small cottages – more like shacks, really – where some older residents have refused to move out. Others have pushed their way in from the outside. Katya told me about it. She said it's lawless; even the cops don't come down here unless they have to. That's why I'm not taking the car in.'

A great place if you wanted to pursue illegal activities without being bothered, Harry thought. He climbed out and surveyed the area, which was marginally less depressing than a giant scrap yard, and shivered now he was out of the warmth of the car. A flurry of

cold needles slapped his face, adding to the depressing landscape
before them.

The buildings were aligned either side of a central access road
several hundred yards long and arrow-straight. The word boulevard
might have been one description, but it didn't quite fit here, lacking
any form of elegance and connecting a shambolic collection of
typical Soviet-era blocks; solid, ugly and uninspiring, everything
built for function over style. The materials were grim, mostly
concrete, brick and corrugated steel, dark in composition and stained
by time, rust and neglect. It was an old story; the production mono-
liths of a former age had been superseded by modern industry,
leaving the ancient shells to moulder into the landscape, no longer
required but too costly to pull down.

'Let's go lookee,' said Harry.

Clare looked at him as if about to argue, then shrugged. 'If we
must.'

She led the way through the rusting iron gates onto the sweeping
concrete avenue that had probably once been impressive, but was
now peppered with rubble, rubbish and large potholes where the
fabric of the surface had cracked and broken away. The buildings
on either side were huge; vast shells with sagging roofs, deteriorating
walls and stretches of cracked or broken glass. Each one had a
fenced compound in varying states of disrepair, overgrown with
weeds and small trees, some with abandoned metal cargo cages and
bits of large, nameless metal structures like some modern artist's
impression of Jurassic Park.

Clare read off the few factory signs that remained, rusted and
battered by the elements. 'Aluminium,' she said, pointing in turn.
'Trucks. Tractors. Cement.' It was a depressing list of activities that
had been here and gone, carried away by progress or change. On
the opposite side of the road was a large collection of buildings like
small aircraft hangars. 'Military vehicles.'

Armoured cars, Harry thought, spotting the remains of a half-
track vehicle rusting into a patch of weeds. The access doors of the
building were too small to have allowed anything bigger.

There was little sign of life save for a dog sniffing at a fence a
hundred yards away, and one elderly woman dragging a three-
wheeled barrow loaded with planks of wood.

Clare took the photo from Harry and approached the old woman,
holding it up for her to see. Harry waited in the background.

Whatever she said he'd be none the wiser and he didn't want to spook the old lady.

She shook her head and gestured briefly at the buildings as if suggesting Clare should take her pick. Then she walked away with a show of speed, dragging the barrow.

'She said people come and go. Mostly vagrants, some immigrants from the south, and others are people of bad character. She doesn't ask questions and didn't want to be seen talking to us.'

'I'm not surprised.' Harry was looking down at the ground, where a glaze of mud had coated the surface like brown icing on a cake. It highlighted several sets of tyre tracks. Off-road rubbers, he guessed, like those on heavy SUVs. And either side of these were the deeper imprints of a larger vehicle. 'These look recent.'

Clare studied the marks. 'You're right. But who?'

Harry was uneasy. It was a feeling he'd learned not to ignore. Some places carried their own aura that weighed heavily on the atmosphere like a lead cloak. He could think of some cemeteries and a couple of former concentration camps he'd visited that had the permanence of a dark cloud overhead as if unable to escape their history.

They were only halfway down the road between the buildings but he decided they'd gone far enough.

'Let's go,' he said, and turned back towards the gates.

Clare said, 'I thought you were going to look around.'

'No need. This is the place. I can feel it.'

'Really? Your hunter's sixth sense?' She might have been teasing but he didn't think so. She had a look about her; a look he'd seen before.

'You got it, too.'

She nodded. 'Something. Where to now?'

'Back to the hotel,' he said. 'I need to get some kit.'

'Then what?'

'I'm coming back later, before dark. I'll get a cab.'

She glanced at him and he sensed an immediate antagonism. 'So you're done with the little woman now? I'm no longer needed by the great and magnificent Harry Tate?' The breath hissed between her teeth. The old Clare, he remembered; quick to anger and busting for a fight.

'If I've thought of you as anything,' he replied evenly, 'it's never as a little woman. I need to check out these buildings but I can't do it with you and a big shiny car sitting outside. I'll pick up more if I'm alone. Besides, you were right earlier: me coming here is a threat to you and Katya. I owe you more than that.'

Her breathing eased, ruffled feathers calmed by the logic of field-craft. Conducting a search for someone – and it was nearly always a someone – was best done without distractions, where listening to the atmosphere was of prime importance. And in a place like this dead zone, with its jungle of shadows and creaks and groans, picking out the presence of people needed absolute focus.

'Fair enough. But what if you bump into some opposition?'

'I'll have to use my old-world charm.'

'Like that'll work.' She reached across and tapped the button to the glove box. Inside was a leather washbag with a zip. 'In there,' she said. 'Take it. I meant what I said about this area – it's not a safe place.'

Harry lifted the bag out. It was heavy and he knew instinctively what it contained. The pistol was clean and shiny but showed signs of use, with a faint pattern of abrasions in the frame and grip.

'It's Katya's personal back-up piece,' Clare explained. 'For someone in her job Stepyanka's not the only place in this city to go without one. It's not registered but I'd rather you didn't lose it.'

Harry checked the safety and placed it in his coat pocket. 'Count on it,' he promised.

'And call me when you're done. You won't get a cab coming out here to pick you up.'

'But will they bring me here?'

'If you pay them up front, yes. But don't expect them to wait.'

Harry was looking into the glove box. Moving the leather bag had revealed something else.

It was a plastic powder compact in a shocking shade of pink.

Clare didn't do pink, he knew that much about her. He also knew that the compact had been a gift from Rik Ferris, delivered to her hospital bed back in London.

'Don't say it,' she muttered, and leaned across to slam the glove box shut. 'Not a word.'

Harry didn't. But he was smiling.

When Harry returned to the zone, it was in a cab which dropped him off a quarter of a mile back from the entrance. Daylight was bleeding away, leaving a mist of cold air hanging over the buildings and trees, and the feeling that snow wasn't far away. If the driver was curious about the Englishman's presence in this remote and unwelcoming spot, he didn't ask before turning and heading back towards the city.

Harry stepped into the cover of some trees by the gates and waited, eyes on the exhaust residue from the disappearing cab. He was fairly sure he'd left London without being tagged, but he wasn't about to get complacent. There were too many variables at play here, and if Cramer wasn't keeping an eye on his progress, someone else might be. Someone he hadn't yet spotted.

He gave it twenty minutes before making a move, then made a final check that he was ready. He was wearing a grubby coat and a tattered ski hat, and a pair of boots that had seen their fair share of wear and tear. A scarf completed the outfit. A new mobile phone was concealed in the lining of the coat, just in case he ran into trouble. A visit to a re-cycled clothing store pointed out by Clare had equipped him for merging into this particular landscape more than his own clothes ever would. The absence of any local language skills was something he couldn't disguise, but he wasn't planning on chatting with anyone. A head-down, unreceptive manner and a visible lack of anywhere better to be would suffice. He'd used the tactic before and providing he didn't run into any cops or security forces looking for papers, he'd get by.

He flicked on a torch in his coat pocket and caught a brief glow through the fabric. In his other pocket was the semi-automatic belonging to Katya. He was hoping he wouldn't have to use it.

The buildings looked ghostly and forbidding in the grey light, but he could just make out the far end of the access road. There was maybe another hour to go before darkness. He scouted around inside the entrance until he saw part of an old hand-trolley lying in a heap of discarded rubbish. The frame was rusted and twisted out of shape, useless for bearing any load, but the wheels, with hard rubber tyres eaten away in parts by the elements, still worked. In an area where reason didn't necessarily make sense to anyone from the outside, it would be perfect cover.

He started walking, unsteadily and veering off-course occasion-ally, listening to the clank and rumble of the wheels bumping along the concrete road and echoing off the buildings either side. Anyone inside would have to be deaf not to notice, which was what he was counting on. If they had no interest they would leave him alone, too intent on their own dire situation to do anything. If they were here for other reasons, and therefore on the lookout, they would watch and wait. Hopefully they would see his shambling figure pushing a pile of rubbish and not give him a second look.

He was halfway down the road, hugging the verge and stopping to pick up some random piece of detritus while listening for any faint sounds going on around him, when he saw a drab figure appear out of a building on the left-hand side. It was an old man, heavily bearded and dressed in bundled layers of clothing. He was half-dragging a large sack, grunting at the effort. As he reached the middle of the road, two figures stepped out from the side of a building on the right-hand side and stopped him.

Harry left the trolley and stepped off the road, his heartbeat ratcheting up a few notches. The two men were dressed in heavy winter clothing and balaclavas, and moved with the easy precision of guards on duty. They didn't look like cops. One of them pointed at the sack and said something, his chin lifting in query. The old man shook his head and muttered a hoarse reply, and tried to walk past them, using his shoulder to block them from getting at his sack.

The next few seconds were brutal; the first guard lashed out with a backhander, sending the old man spinning away, while the second guard stepped in fast and kicked the sack from his hand. Both then used their fists until he dropped to the ground and huddled protectively into a ball.

Their fun over, the two men walked away laughing, and disappeared between two buildings.

Harry debated moving away, but he couldn't leave the old man out there. He pushed the trolley ahead of him and stopped alongside him. He was conscious but clearly terrified. Harry held out a hand and helped him to his feet. With a muttered thank you, the old man picked up his sack and scurried away along the road, casting backwards glances towards the building where the two guards had gone.

Harry was about to move on when a voice spoke. It was one of the guards, no doubt come back for a bit more fun. He was standing a few feet away, his colleague just behind him, and gestured at the trolley.

Harry halted and played dumb. His gamble on them being too bored to repeat their cruel game hadn't paid off. Up close he saw that the man had his hand on the butt of a weapon just visible inside his coat. An assault rifle, he guessed, on a sling. Something short.

The other man stayed back, eyes flicking from Harry to the approach road and back. But what were they doing here?

The first man spoke again, harsher, more threatening. Harry ducked his head to hide his face and tipped the trolley, spilling the rubbish he'd collected onto the road. They were messing with him to pass the time but he didn't want to give them an excuse to prolong the agony.

The first man kicked through the bits and pieces, then said something to his colleague. They both laughed and gestured for him to get going.

Harry gathered up the rubbish and hurried away. He was no more than thirty yards further on when three more figures emerged from a second building. They were bunched together and heading away towards the far end of the road. Two men and a woman.

Harry shuffled to a stop, pretending to adjust the load on his trolley. A glance back down the road showed that the two armed men were watching, but showed no signs of joining in. When one of them nodded before disappearing between the two buildings, he realized they were part of the same group.

One of the three had turned and was watching him. Tall, broad-shouldered and lithe, he was too upright to be part of the destitute community. The other man and the woman continued walking.

Harry bent and picked at something on the road surface, openly sniffing at it before secreting it with deliberate care inside his coat. He left the barrow and walked to the fence at the side of the road, pulling at his fly and coughing repeatedly. Leaning on the fence with one hand, he peered under his arm and saw the man shake his head and turn to follow the other two.

He breathed deeply. The last thing on his mind was relieving himself. But where he was standing he was looking through the fence at the building the three figures had just left. It looked no different to any of the other dilapidated structures along here, save for one thing: it had a large shiny padlock on the front door.

This was the place. He knew it. And the two guards were a security patrol. They must have established a perimeter around this and the buildings on either side to keep unwelcome visitors away.

The temptation to take a closer look inside the fence was pulling at him, but he resisted it. At least one of those three was jumpy enough to turn back without warning.

They were turning off the road between two concrete pillars with a rusted archway overhead. Harry's eyes were drawn to the person in the lead. Dressed in a hoodie and jeans, the figure was fiddling with something, his attention focussed as if not part of the group. Then it became clear. He pulled back his hoodie and plugged a pair of headset buds into his ears, before flicking the fabric back around his head.

It was Rik Ferris.

THIRTY-ONE

Harry stopped near the spot where the three figures had turned off and leaned on the barrow, playing an old man by breathing heavily with one hand in the small of his back. He made sure the scarf was covering the lower half of his face.

Through the entrance lay a small park bordered by a gravel path. It looked dismal and unkempt in the fading light, no doubt a distant memory of what might once have been a gathering point for workers. The three figures had broken into a trot, with Rik in the lead, their feet throwing up spurts of gravel. Rik was clearly dictating the pace, which wasn't fast, while his two companions looked as if they could run all day.

Harry heard voices raised in anger and moved closer to a hedge surrounding the park. Two drunks were arguing on the other side, with one of them trying to snatch a bottle from his companion. They were dressed in layers of ragged clothing and seated on a bench, the ground around them littered with discarded bottles and other trash.

The three runners paid them no attention. Drunks like these were part of the landscape and unlikely to be any threat. If they were driven off now they'd be back again later.

Harry watched Rik. He seemed relaxed although he doubted he was enjoying himself. He'd never known Rik volunteer for any kind of exercise, but he realized that there was possibly a lot he didn't know about his friend. Such as why, if he wasn't here voluntarily, he didn't simply run away? He may have been a techie but he was no fool. Rik knew how to move quietly if he had to, and find a way of disappearing. The only logical explanation was that the two people with him had some control over his movements.

The three runners were beginning to turn at the top of the park before coming back towards the road. Harry went back to the trolley and trudged back the way he'd come, stopping occasionally to pick at something on the ground or scoop up some discarded piece of junk.

By the time he reached the entrance to the zone and turned for a quick look, he saw the three figures walking back to the building they had left. Once he was out of sight he took out his mobile phone and called Clare. He needed a lift back to the city.

He was back again early the following morning. This time he was carrying some extra pieces of equipment: a military grade cold-weather sleeping bag and a groundsheet, and enough basic rations to keep him going for a while. One thing he'd learned in the army was that however much thought went into an operation, it inevitably took longer than planned. And if he wanted to get Rik out of here in one piece, it had to be done carefully.

He made for the park, pushing the barrow which he'd retrieved from the bushes by the entrance, stopping occasionally to root about in the long grass by the roadside until he had enough junk to conceal his survival kit. He ambled through the gate and sat on one of the benches beside the path, where he had a good all-round view, especially of the approach. He'd seen few people out this early; a man dragging two lengths of timber behind him on a pair of old pram wheels, and the two loud drunks from before on the far side of the green, locked once more in their own world of bad booze and discord.

But no sign of the two armed guards.

A flicker of movement showed near the entrance to the park and he glanced across briefly. One figure – no, three. Damn. Rik had company again. It was a complication he didn't need. He recognized his friend instantly, out in front and jogging slowly, twin wires trailing from his ears. Wired for sound, Harry wondered, or in touch with the two behind him, an electronic leash with no escape?

He studied the two others. A man and a woman, around thirty years of age. The man had the face of a bruiser. Military, he guessed, or used to be. The woman was chunky, with gingery hair.

The two Clare had seen at the airport?

They were similarly dressed and looked far more at ease in their movements than Rik, who looked unsteady on his legs, his feet scuffing along the gravel as if unwilling to commit. They, however, looked as if they would win a foot chase backwards and still have plenty in reserve. Guards and watchers, he decided. Trying to talk to Rik was going to be more difficult than he'd thought.

He didn't look up as the rapid slap of feet on the path approached and sped by, the three shadows now bunched closer together. The man and woman had moved up alongside Rik as they approached, forming a blocking manoeuvre as they became aware of Harry's presence. It was an obvious ploy to anyone versed in close protection work; stay close but be ready to react. He wondered if the move was designed to protect Rik or to stop him talking to anyone.

That was when Harry realized these two were armed. As the woman, who was nearest, passed by, her top shifted to reveal the bulk of a webbing holster in the small of her back. Harry couldn't see the man's weapon, but there was the outline of a harness stretched across his shoulders.

They did three tours of the park. Each time they reached open ground between the benches, the guards dropped back, shortening their stride and moving closer together. The woman glanced towards Harry a couple of times, and he saw her mouth moving, although whether in commentary to her companion or over comms to tell Rik to keep going he had no way of knowing.

As they were approaching the entrance to the park on the third tour, the woman turned to Rik and signalled with her open hand twice in the air. Was that a ten? Then she and the man jogged out of the entrance and back down the road.

Harry stayed where he was. Moving now would draw attention to himself, and these two might be replaced any second by the two armed guards. Besides, homeless people didn't have agendas or appointments; they were captives of a non-routine day save for eating when and where they could, finding somewhere to sleep, maybe looking for handouts or an undemanding job of work.

He waited for Rik to come round again. So far he'd showed no signs of recognition, his eyes mostly hidden in the shadow of his hoodie. Harry was hoping he'd signal something, anything, to show it might be possible to talk. The way they'd played it, Rik had been steered into the park and his guards had stayed with him long enough to make sure there was no threat before leaving him to a solo break. But that didn't mean they wouldn't come back at any time. It didn't leave him enough time to manoeuvre a meeting. Prisoner or protectee, Rik was off-limits.

He watched as Rik approached. There was a powerful temptation to speak, but he resisted it. Rik would know if it was safe or not, and he'd have to rely on him to make the first move. Then Harry tensed. As Rik drew close he dropped his hand to his side, the fingers flicked out and held the position. Then he was gone and rubbing at his shoulder as if to ease a touch of cramp.

Harry held his breath. Was that a signal? Five what? Minutes? Hours? Five p.m.?

Moments later the two guards were back at the entrance and waving at Rik that his time was up. The woman stared at Harry, who by now had taken a lounging position of a man sleeping off too much drink, one arm hanging down, his hand trailing unaware in a puddle. Moments later the trio were gone.

Harry gave it ten minutes before making a move. Pushing to his feet he walked with exaggerated sluggishness across the centre of the park in a seemingly haphazard fashion. He stopped and picked up a couple of cigarette butts, tucking them inside his coat, all the time keeping the entrance in sight and the road beyond. Nothing much to do and nowhere important to be, his actions said, and all day to do it.

Rik clearly wasn't able or willing to talk to him freely, so he'd have to initiate the first move. He hadn't yet figured out how to do that, but it would come to him. It might simply take longer than he'd thought. He'd spent years making covert approaches to some-times reluctant contacts; all it needed was a cool nerve and a seemingly innocent reason for being in the right place at just the right time, with just the right amount of cover.

The only question was, would Rik be reluctant to stop and talk or would he shout for back-up from his two guards?

Harry stopped just inside the park entrance. Rik and his two companions were about to turn into their base. He waited until they disappeared inside before heading back towards the main gates. The first order of business was to find somewhere to sleep until it was time to make the next move.

Four o'clock came round painfully slow, bringing a further drop in temperature and a brief flurry of sleet. He'd found a small loft space in one of the structures from where he could see the road and the building where Rik was being held. It had been sheltered enough to keep him out of the worst of the weather but sleep had not come easily. In between the bouts of uneasy shut-eye he'd made a brief sortie to check his surroundings and had spotted the two armed guards. They'd appeared from the shadows and eyed the area care-fully before slipping back between the buildings.

As soon as they'd gone he circled the buildings to check for points of access, weaving his way cautiously through piles of rusted metal on the back lots behind the structures and staying away from the long grass which would leave tracks.

It proved fruitless except for one thing: he was moving past the rear of the building next to the one where Rik was being held when his foot kicked against something solid, hidden by what appeared to be random pieces of wood and metal sheeting. It was a thick cable which snaked away from the building towards a fenced-off area near the trees. He followed it out of curiosity.

It was an electrical sub-station. The area inside the wire mesh contained a number of grey metal boxes with rusted warning signs still visible, and the ground which had been gravelled over was now a profusion of weeds and wind-blown rubbish. But the cable he'd followed looked new and had been fed through the wire fence and connected up to the boxes.

He looked back along its length and wondered why a power supply had been hooked up to an abandoned building in this out-of-the-way spot.

These two buildings were the more robust on the site, with no obvious weak points, and the one with the direct power supply was the most interesting. The fabric of the structure was concrete up to waist level, then metal cladding. The few windows were all dark and had been painted over on the inside. He edged up close and listened. There was nothing at first. Then he detected a low buzz of several voices fading rapidly followed by a door closing. He moved around the outside, using the overgrown weeds for cover, aware that this was dangerously double-edged. If he could see in, the people inside would see him moving against the light.

When he picked up the tang of strong tobacco drifting in the air and heard voices coming from outside the building, he slid back into cover and made his way by a circuitous route back to the loft across the road.

Returning to the park after another bout of sleep, he saw an old man picking up scraps of paper and studying them closely before throwing them away, as if hoping to find a winning lotto ticket.

Harry made for a bench which was best concealed from the road and sat down. He took a bottle of cheap brandy from inside his coat and took a sip. It burned like fire on the way down, but he hadn't dared bring anything better in case the guards searched him. Drunks didn't buy good booze.

Forty-five minutes drifted by before he heard footsteps and voices approaching along the road. He adopted a half-prone position on the bench, clutching the brandy bottle to his chest, and waited for Rik and the guards to enter the park. But when he heard only a single set of footsteps and looked up, he was surprised to see the guards had stopped at the entrance and were watching Rik running solo. After a couple of minutes they turned and disappeared without giving Harry a second look.

Sloppy, he thought. But handy.

THIRTY-TWO

'What are you doing here, Harry?' The words came out in a hiss as Rik shuffled past the bench on his second lap. He was gone before Harry could respond. His hoodie had slipped back a little, revealing his spiky hair looking wilder than usual. He looked pale and drawn, and Harry noted the nervousness in his voice. He was clearly wary of being seen talking to anyone.

The next time round he stopped a few feet away to adjust his laces. 'You trying to get yourself killed?' he whispered, and glanced back at the entrance. 'You need to get out of here.'

'And hello to you, too,' Harry said. 'I was betting you hadn't spotted me.'

'You'd have lost. I clocked you yesterday. I was just too out of it to realize.'

'But not the day before? You're slipping.'

'Right. Great time to be clever. What do you want? You know the guards are armed, right? Two patrolling the outside and the two inside – a man and a woman.'

'I saw them. Ugly looking bunch. As to why I'm here, there's an all-agencies order out on you. Apparently you're hotter than a Kardashian, whatever that is.'

'It's bullshit; I haven't done anything.' Rik didn't sound surprised. 'You knew?'

'Kraush told me. He's the main man here. Russian. I don't know his first name.' His voice was tight and resentful, still with a faint Midlands regional accent, but a long way from when Harry had first met him in Red Station. Back then, even faced with isolation and a no-return-no-contact order on them all, Rik had been casual and chipper, a light-hearted presence in an otherwise dark and unwelcoming environment.

Rik stood up and flexed his legs, then set off for another circuit. When he stopped next time round he sat on the bench and reached for Harry's bottle. 'Give us a taste.'

'I'm not sure you're old enough for this,' Harry warned him. 'I think it's what passes for class grog in this neck of the woods.'

'I need a bit of pain to stop me getting complacent.' He touched the bottle to his lips to test it, but returned it without drinking. 'Bloody Ada, that's bad.'

'Yeah, sorry. I should have called in at Duty Free for some Remy.' He capped the bottle and said, 'Why is everyone after your head all of a sudden?' In spite of Cramer's claims he wanted to hear Rik's version of events. If it produced nothing save for injured innocence, he'd let him have both barrels in the hope that it would shock him into some kind of reality.

Rik ignored the question. 'Is that why you're here – to take me back?'

'Should I be?'

'Well, it's a fair bet. You know me better than anyone and you're a freelancer; always up for a job. It's right up your street.' He looked away. 'Sorry. That was uncalled for. I'm bloody glad to see you, Harry. Who've you got out there as back-up? Anyone I know?'

'There is no back-up. It's just me for now. I was asked to find you but I'm not going to turn you in without listening to what you've got to say. And,' he added, 'you sent me the message with the address of the place in Stepyanka.'

Rik frowned and rubbed his face. 'I did that? I thought I'd dreamed it. They took my phone away immediately afterwards, and my head's been a bit scrambled ever since. I reckon they drugged me.' He rolled up his sleeve and revealed a dark bruise in the crease of his elbow.

Harry looked closely at it. It looked like a clumsy injection bruise. 'Who did it – the local horse doctor?'

'No idea. I was face down in the back of a car at the time. It was probably the woman – Irina. I think she likes hurting people.' He looked tired. 'It's been a while, hasn't it, since we talked.'

'So it has,' Harry agreed. 'I kept meaning to write, send a post-card or a text, but you know how it is. I'm here now, though. Who are these people?'

'GRU. One was FSB, but he's dead.'

'How?'

'I think Irina shot him. I don't know why. Maybe she needed the kick.' He paused and looked around. When he turned back his face was animated, as if thoughts of the dead man had given him a wake-up call. 'You have to get word out, Harry. These people are planning a cyber hit on the UK. They've got a team in the next building all set up to go. You've got to warn someone.'

That explained the power supply from the sub-station. 'How serious a hit?'

'Top-level bad.' He relayed the details of what Kraush had told him, adding, 'Even level one would cause problems. If they find that works, who knows what they'll do next? It wouldn't take long for some nut-job in the Kremlin to suggest going to level two, then . . .'

'I get the picture. Do you believe this Kraush?'

'Yes! I told him he was crazy but it didn't seem to register. He's just a thug with a job to do.'

Harry thought it over. 'Dumb question, but *could* they do it? I mean, is it technically possible?'

'God yes. It's a bloody miracle nobody's gone down this route already. There have been a few minor attacks, like they're testing the water, but nothing as focussed as what Kraush's suggesting.'

'All right. I'll pass it on. For now-'

'Are you being paid for this job?'

The question came out of left field, and Harry let it pass. Rik was angry and resentful, undoubtedly frightened and ready to lash out at anyone, himself most of all. What he couldn't figure out was why. Was it guilt?

'You know how it works,' he said. 'If I hadn't agreed to do it, they'd have called in someone else; someone with no personal interest and paid to follow orders. They won't worry too much about protocol, either. To them you're a legitimate target who's gone off-piste.'

'But I haven't. I've kept my nose clean since leaving Five – you know that.'

A noise sounded from nearby and Rik jump to his feet and began another circuit of the park. It wasn't the guards but two dogs scrapping over the torn remains of a carcass which might have once been a fox.

'I know you're clean,' Harry assured him when Rik stopped next time. 'But someone in London must have different ideas. Something's happened to rattle their cage and they think you've jumped ship.'

'I haven't!'

'Maybe not. But you bunking off over here doesn't help.'

Rik rolled his shoulders. 'Man, what a nightmare. Do they know where I am?'

'Not yet. But give it time and they will.'

'This is crazy! London thinks I've bunked off with state secrets or whatever, and Kraush wants me to spill something I don't have.'

He rubbed his face. 'Jesus, my head's in a mess. Kraush hit me with a taser. I reckon it must have fried something.'

'Try not to worry,' Harry told him. 'The effects are temporary. Did he give a hint about what he's after?'

'He said it was something I saw when I was nosing through the archives.'

Harry wondered how Kraush would know that. The same with the search-and-detain order. It wasn't the kind of thing stuck on lamp-posts around London, and led to the uneasy suggestion that he must have inside information. He decided to leave it; it was a whole new can of worms and right now wasn't the time to go into it.

He glanced towards the road. He could just about make out if anyone approached the area. 'Where are the guards?'

'The two heavies are always on the perimeter, keeping the local drifters out of the way.'

'Yes, I saw them. Not the kind to be running a food bank.'

'The other two are busy setting up the cyber project in the next building. They said they'd let me come out and run solo if I behaved myself.' Rik gave a harsh laugh. 'What a joke.'

'How long?' Harry asked.

'What?'

'How long before they reel you back in?'

'I don't know . . . ten minutes, maybe longer. It depends on what else they're doing.'

It wasn't long to talk someone round in this kind of state. What Harry needed was time to get into Rik's head and put him in a positive state of mind. But he wasn't underestimating what being snatched, kept locked up and effectively tortured could do to a person's thinking.

'I want to get you out of this,' he said, 'but you're going to have to help me. If we make a break for it, can you keep going until we're good and clear?'

But Rik appeared to have gone in on himself, his head down and shoulders slumped. He took so long to reply that Harry began to worry. If Rik was traumatized by his treatment, possibly with the addition of drugs administered by his captors, he might not be in any fit state to cut and run if the opportunity presented itself.

'Rik.'

'Cicada,' Rik said at last.

'What?'

'Kraush asked if I'd heard of Cicada. I haven't . . . at least, I don't think so.'

'What does that mean?'

'It sounded familiar, that's all. He said it was a code or a name. When he said it I got a bit of flash, like something hovering in the background.'

'And?'

Another shrug. 'There was so much stuff in the archives . . . it was overwhelming. He gave me a notepad to write down anything I can remember, to start a train of thought.'

'And?'

'Christ, you name it, I saw it. Mission reports, updates, risk analysis checks, contacts and team names, headings, map coordinates, codes . . . I was skimming while listening for the supervisor. There were audio and video files, too: phone calls and comms, asset meetings, field briefings, debrief and psych assessments and post-mission summaries.'

Harry knew what it was like. Outsiders tended to forget that the security and intelligence services were, at heart, bureaucrats with a default position of writing things down. Dismissed by some as the dark art of arse-covering, it was the meat of covert assignments and missions. To those on the top floors and the drones lower down, it signalled success or failure.

'If Cicada was there,' Rik continued, 'I probably saw it but it didn't sink in.' He turned his head to scan their surroundings. It was then that Harry saw a nasty cut to his face. It looked livid and bruised around the edges, scabbing over to near-black in colour.

'Who did that?' Harry asked.

'Irina. The resident psycho. My face got in the way of her fist.'

Harry felt for him. This wasn't the Rik he'd known before, but someone in a darker place, more morose and inward-looking.

'This stuff never goes away, does it?' Rik continued. 'It's there forever.'

'It doesn't have to be. We can sort it out.' Harry hesitated. 'You definitely haven't poked your nose anywhere you shouldn't, have you?'

'No!' Rik's reply carried the fierce heat of conviction. 'Why doesn't anyone believe that?' With that he jumped up and began running again.

THIRTY-THREE

Harry felt a surge of impatience. He could understand Rik's attitude, but going off half-cocked wasn't helping. Somehow, he had to break whatever was keeping Rik here, even if it was his state of mind.

When Rik came back to land he was breathing heavily, his face pinched by the cold but flushed. Harry said, 'We need to leave right now.'

'Good luck with that. You think I like this shit-hole, with eyeballs on me all the time?' He looked around, his eyes flickering unhealthily. 'I think they killed a hacker friend of mine.' The words came out in a disorderly stream, a verbal dam unblocked. 'She's why I came over here, not the other stuff.'

'Girlfriend?'

'Not really. I mean, I've never met her but we've been in touch for a couple of years. We shared some work on a couple of small projects and seemed to click.'

'Go on.' Harry stood up so he could keep a better eye on the road. His nerves were beginning to shred at the possibility of being interrupted.

'She contacted me a while back, said she'd heard about my mother. She was sweet. She understood because she'd lost her mother not long ago, too. She wanted to meet.'

'Where?'

'In London. She moves around, like a lot of them. She told me the name of a hotel in Westminster, but then suggested a club near Leicester Square.' His shoulders dropped. 'She wanted somewhere busy. Fun, she said . . . I think she meant safe. She sounded worried.'

She had good cause, Harry thought sombrely. She was being followed . . . which must have ultimately led them to Rik. 'Did she say why?'

'No. She sounded like she was trying to say something but couldn't.'

'And?'

'I asked what was wrong, and to phone me. She did and said she had a problem. I asked what it was and she said she'd got into a fix with some serious people.'

'Drugs?'

'No, not that.' He looked at Harry. 'She'd been recruited to do some coding a while back. Sales and marketing stuff, she thought, the kind they send out over the internet with links to buy. Low level but paid pretty good. It was good to begin with, she said, pretty soon that began to change. The stuff she was asked to do started to get deep.'

'Deep?'

'They told her to hack into a water utility in Germany. They said it was a contract to test security systems to find any weak points.'

'Isn't that normal?'

'Sure. If hackers can find a way in, the utility can block them.' He gave a shrug. 'But she got a bad vibe about the people she was working with. She'd heard of one or two of them before.'

'In what way?'

'Offensive hacking, mostly. Breaking into systems for a laugh, then leaving malware and bots designed to bring it down. People like that don't give a shit about the effects of what they do, they just want to show off. Then the people running it said they wanted to investigate bringing a utility system to a standstill. Short term to begin with, like thirty minutes or so, to show they could. When they began talking longer term and more destructive, she figured it was time to get out.'

'When was this?'

'A week ago, maybe more. We were going to meet the following night at the club, but she didn't make it.'

Harry didn't want to ask the next question, but he had to. 'Does this friend have a name?'

Rik looked at him, and Harry recalled the obsessive secrecy in the hacking community. It was all part of the absurd mystique. 'Why do you want to know that?'

'It's not a big deal, if you don't want to tell me.'

'Nathalie,' Rik said at last. 'Nathalie Baier.'

Harry kept his face blank. Baier would have been on her way to Leicester Square to meet him.

'There's something else.' Rik spoke softly. 'Something I haven't mentioned.'

'Go on.'

'Apart from the one phone call we were using a messaging service to talk. Just before we were due to meet she said she was in danger and needed to speak to someone high-up.'

'Where?'

'Someone on the inside. In Five . . . in cyber security.'

Harry waited, wondering why Nathalie had assumed Rik would be able to help her. Then it hit him.

'Did you tell her what you used to do?'

Rik nodded. 'Not everything . . . just that I'd been on attachment to the government. She wanted to know where. I let slip once about testing firewalls in government systems. It was just talk, you know? Showing off, I suppose.'

'No shit. What the hell were you thinking?'

'Everyone does it, bigging themselves up . . . making out they know stuff, that they've got contacts nobody else has got. She was smart; she made the connection and I didn't bother correcting her.'

Harry rubbed his eyes. It wasn't a huge mistake – as long as that was as far as it had gone. Rik wouldn't be the first former intelligence and security officer to have talked about his former job. But it was no wonder that the guns were out for him. 'Did you give her anything that could have helped her penetrate our systems?'

'No!' Rik looked affronted. 'Christ, Harry – what do you think I am?'

'You ask a question like that after what you've just told me?'

'Yeah, OK. But I didn't tell her anything. All I said was that I'd got canned for nosing into classified files. That's it, I promise!'

Harry held up a hand. Rik's response carried the ring of truth. 'I believe you. What did she want to speak to Five about?'

'She said she'd been assigned to a project. A major one.'

'Doing what?'

'A cyber attack on the UK.'

Before Harry could respond to that they heard voices and Rik was up and running. Instead of returning to the bench, though, he continued out of the entrance and disappeared down the road.

THIRTY-FOUR

It was a long thirty minutes before Rik returned. Harry had decided to risk staying where he was, confident that Rik would return. Bunking off now would leave Rik feeling even more isolated than he was.

When he finally came back he was looking brighter. 'I told Kraush the running was helping me remember some snatches. I gave him a couple of file references to keep him happy, but said I needed more time. He's busy with the project so he seemed satisfied.'

'This cyber hit . . . why are they doing it?'

'Nat didn't say. She'd heard one of the organizers say it would be revenge for smears against Moscow, and for giving sanctuary to traitors who'd betrayed the *Rodina* – the motherland.'

'You believed her?'

'Not at first. It sounded crazy. I mean, why would they? But after everything that's happened recently I'm not so sure.'

'What brought you here?' Harry asked. Now wasn't the time to tell Rik what had happened to his friend Nathalie; there was too much riding on getting out of here in one piece.

'Nathalie sent me the address of an apartment here in Minsk, so I got a flight out hoping to see her. But it was a bust. The place was a derelict rat-hole. I couldn't figure out why she'd sent me there.'

'Perhaps she didn't.' It was as close as he dared come to saying Nathalie was dead.

Rik nodded but didn't react. 'As I was waiting someone hit me and threw me into the back of a vehicle. That's when I must have sent you the messages. I remember somebody sitting on me and feeling a pain in my arm, but that was it. When I woke up I was in the building down the road and my phone and laptop were gone.' He shivered with the memory. 'That's all I can remember.'

'Then what?'

'They started asking questions. It was slow at first but I knew it wasn't going to last. Then Kraush used the taser and Irina hit me. I think it was a taste of what was to come.'

'How come they allowed you out?'

'I said I needed exercise, so they suggested a run twice a day. They also let me have my iPod back. But only because they think I've got something they want.'

Harry didn't say anything. Whatever they were doing so far, they hadn't seemed ready to apply too much pressure on Rik to remember what he'd seen in the files. A favour here and there, maybe it was worth it to get him to spill. Most debriefings of informants took a long time, sometimes weeks if the end prize was considered worthwhile. The idea was to build up trust while gently pushing for more information until the subject didn't realize how much they were giving away.

'And Kraush's in charge?'

'Yes. He looks and acts tough but it's Irina I worry about.' He pointed to the cut on his cheek. 'I didn't see this coming. She's unpredictable. That was something you taught me, remember? Know who the dangerous ones are.'

'I'm glad you retained something useful. Do they have surnames?'

'Not that I've heard.'

'How many more are involved?'

'There were three originally. There was the FSB gofer I told you about . . . he'd got like a battle scar on his head and I think he had memory problems, maybe PTSD. He spoke good English and told me the others were GRU. He said he'd worked in London. I didn't see him after a while, then I found his body in a side room. He'd been shot. I reckon that was Irina.'

'Any more?'

'After he died they got a couple of heavies in to guard the buildings.'

'What's in the other building?'

'The talent – the hacking team. They arrived on a coach the other night.'

'For this cyber hit.'

'Yes. I've seen it before. It's a warehouse operation, always ready to move around to avoid detection. They crunch data and numbers, source targets and work on projects designed by whoever's running it. I'm guessing GRU in Moscow.'

'Can you prove it?'

'No, of course not.' He stared hard at Harry. 'This is so different to everything I used to work on in Five. Back then, with a bit of work you knew where everybody was because they were ground-based and left footprints. You could find them by following their contacts and building a visible network. This isn't the same at all. It's like there are no limits any more. These people are . . . they're totally off the grid. They don't have home bases, they don't leave normal footprints and they don't have contacts you can latch onto. But they're tight. It's all done in the ether and if you catch one of them it's because they made a mistake or somebody dobbed them in.'

'Why would that happen if they're all so tight?'

Rik shrugged. 'Jealousy . . . carelessness. Resentment because some hacker's got a bigger name and reputation and is picking up all the work and rewards. Or someone thinks they're a threat.'

Like Nathalie, Harry thought. 'What happens then?'

'They disappear.' Rik's thoughts were clear to read: he knew what had happened to his friend. He then confirmed it. 'Kraush told me she'd died in a traffic accident, but I think it was deliberate.'

'To stop her talking.'

'Yes. Sooner or later the people they used to work for see them as a threat.'

Harry thought about how Rik had hovered on the periphery of the hacking community as part of his work. 'But you've scraped through.'

'Only because I'm not part of it. I know a few people by their tags, but that's all.'

'Until now.'

'Yeah. Until now.'

Harry stood up and walked around, one eye out for signs of Rik's guards. His leg muscles were cold and stiff and he could feel the chill from the ground working its way into his bones. How the hell the locals stood it he couldn't even begin to guess.

He re-joined Rik, who was staring at the ground as if mesmerized. He wanted to tell him that the message to meet Nathalie at the apartment block hadn't come from her; to confirm that she'd been killed in London and her laptop and possessions stolen. But that would have to wait. If Rik knew Kraush and Irina had killed her, there was every danger he might betray what he knew and end up with the same fate.

Instead he said, 'We have to get you away from here.'

'What's the point?' Rik countered. 'If the S and D order's real, I'll end up dead or locked up . . . like Red Station only worse.'

'I don't get it. If you want to get out of here, let's do it. Now. Before they send a team after you.'

'I can't.' Rik tugged at his left trouser leg, lifting the fabric above his ankle. It revealed a heavy-duty grey plastic strap drilled with holes and fitted with a small box-like object. 'Say hello to my ball-and-chain.'

Harry recognized the device. 'A tracker? We can deal with that.'

Rik shook his head. 'No, you can't. See the box? It contains a small charge of explosive.'

'What?'

'If I go beyond a certain radius from the base unit, the signal gets cut off. They said I wouldn't get to hear the bang before it takes my legs off below the knees. Same if I try cutting the strap or opening the box. The only way of disarming it is by a coded radio signal which only they know.'

Harry felt himself go hot and cold. He'd been around explosive devices like this. Their sole aim was to kill or maim – as Cramer had discovered. And they were often unpredictable in nature.

'What if they have to move you in a hurry?'

'As long as I stay within range of the base unit transmitter, it's fine.'

'Where do they keep that?'

'In the warehouse somewhere. As long as I don't get picked up and taken beyond the signal limit, everything's sweet. Otherwise, kaboom.'

Harry's mind was in a whirl. This was beyond crazy. He couldn't accomplish anything here; he needed specialist help and only Cramer could deliver it. 'What if,' he said slowly, his thoughts going at high speed, 'I can get that thing off you?'

'Do it and I'll marry you.'

'Let's not get carried away.' He stopped speaking when he saw movement out of the corner of his eye, near the entrance. He was surprised at how much darker it had become. A woman was looking into the park and he felt a sense of alarm. Innocent passer-by or another of Rik's watchers? She was short and stocky but with dark hair under a scarf. Then she moved into view and he saw she was pushing an ancient pram loaded with scrap wood.

'How much longer have you got?'

Rik shrugged. 'Not long. They're busy working in the unit next door, which is probably why I'm not being pushed harder to remember what I saw. But I don't know how much longer they'll wait before they lose patience.'

'Whatever you've got they must think it's important. Keep them talking as long as you can.' He paused. 'This cyber hit – is anything going to happen in the next twenty-four hours?'

'I don't think so. They're still setting up.' He looked worried. 'What are you going to do?'

'I need to ring London and get some help. But I'll be back in the morning.'

'OK. What if they move me?'

'I'll find you.' He was about to go when something occurred to him. He took out the key to Rik's flat which he'd been carrying. 'Why did you leave this with your neighbour?'

Rik looked blank for a moment. Then something changed in his expression and he looked almost sad. 'I'm not sure. Instinct, maybe? It wasn't a clue, if that's what you thought . . . at least, I don't think so.' He frowned. 'Sorry. I don't think I was in a good place, you know? Too much going on and . . . perhaps I knew I was going to need your help.'

Harry said nothing; anything he did say would be meaningless. He felt for his friend and had a sense of how lonely he must have been after his mother's death.

'Can you hold onto it for now?' Rik added. 'They might search me.'

'Sure.' Harry put the key away. 'I'll give it back when we're in London.'

Rik gave a nearly-normal smile. 'Thanks, Harry. I should have called you.'

'Yes, you should. You're an idiot. Why didn't you?'

'Because I'm an idiot.'

'Good. Glad we got that straight.' He clapped him on the shoulder. 'Stay with it, OK? We'll get through this.'

THIRTY-FIVE

As soon as he got back to his hotel, courtesy of Clare, who was full of questions, Harry called Cramer.

'I hope you've got some good news.' Cramer sounded ready to burst. 'Like where the hell you've been and why you didn't call.'

'I've been a bit busy. I found Rik, but there's a problem.' He explained about Rik's captors and the tracker. 'If he tries to walk away or remove it, it goes off.'

Cramer was silent, and Harry wondered if he was remembering his own life-changing confrontation with an IED.

'They're definitely GRU?'

'That's what they said. The man's name is Kraush – no first name – and the woman's called Irina.' Harry also relayed the threatened cyber attack, but was careful not to suggest there might be any terrorist element. If that suspicion was raised Cramer would be under pressure to spread the word to other international authorities. It would, if they believed it was serious, start a chain-reaction of defence measures and word would soon get out.

'You'd better tell me where these people are,' Cramer said. 'Where Ferris is, too. We need to act quickly.'

'I'll do that,' Harry told him. 'But I need to know I can get Rik out first. How fast can you get me some help?'

'That depends. If it's anything armed and military forget it. I'd never get it past the gatekeepers; they have this weird resistance to starting another global war.'

'One person is all I need.'

'One? You know Iron Man is made up, don't you?' Dark army humour.

'Someone with electronic and bomb-disposal experience. If I'm going to bring Rik out I need to get that thing off his leg. But it can't be done with an audience.'

'I can arrange that.' Then there was a long pause. Too long.

'What's going on?' said Harry. He sensed trouble in the background. Cramer sounded as if he'd had a wad of stuffing punched up his nose.

'Sorry. Just had an internal message from Hough, my controller on this assignment.'

'Is it relevant?'

'Yes. A new name is taking over the JIO – *has* taken over. It's not official yet but the previous head is seriously ill and a man named Colmyer has stepped into his shoes.'

'How does that affect my situation?' Harry had lost interest in the movements of politicians and civil servants around Whitehall a long time ago. But whoever this Colmyer was, by Cramer's muted reaction he wasn't good news.

'Colmyer's put someone else on locating Ferris,' Cramer said. 'An outside contractor with direct access to him and him only.'

'Is he allowed to do that?'

'Legally? Search me. But it's too late to stop him.'

It didn't take rocket science to figure out the likely outcome if Harry got in the way. Contractors were not bound by the same rules and regulations as others. The outcome was obvious. He wondered if this person was already on his trail.

'Why would Colmyer be doing this? You had this organized.'

'I thought so, too. There's likely to be a shit-storm brewing in the back rooms and corridors of Whitehall, but my guess is he'll weather it and hang the consequences. I reckon he's trying to make a good impression, get himself a name early on. He's been making noises about shaking up the security and intelligence agencies for a long time, so this could be the first salvo, God help us.'

'And getting Rik killed is a way to do that?' Harry wondered what on earth Rik could possibly know that made this search so important.

'Colmyer must think so. If it is and it works, he'll be covered in glory.' Cramer sounded glum at the prospect.

'Do you have any details on the contractor?'

'Hang on, I'm just reading a summary. His name's Garth Perry . . . ex-Military Intelligence . . . pulled out of Afghan after a series of brutality accusations . . . and later diagnosed with PTSD, although that's moot and he might just be fucking nuts. He was under close observation after mixing with a violent far-right group threatening extreme action . . . and dropped off the radar a couple of weeks ago. He's thought to have similar contacts with groups throughout Europe.'

'So he might not be operating solo.'

'Probably not. If I find anything else I'll let you know.'

Harry swore silently. This wasn't good. 'The people holding Rik are jumpy already. Rik says they're a GRU direct action unit. If they get wind of Perry or anyone else in the area they might just cut their losses and press the button.'

'I guess.'

'But you won't know what's behind this then, will you? Won't that cause you sleepless nights?'

A pause. 'What are you saying?'

'Whatever it is he's supposed to know must be important to someone. Otherwise why all the fuss? Now might be a good time to tell me what you think it is.'

'I can't.'

'Why not?'

'Because I don't know!' The response was too genuinely angry to be anything but the truth. And Harry knew why: it was the field operative's dislike of being kept out of the loop by those higher on the ladder, when every instinct screamed for more background intel. But he wasn't going to let Cramer off that easily.

'So I'm out here in the wind on your behalf, with a potentially serious cyber threat on the way, and being treated like an idiot. Rik says he hasn't been doing anything, and I believe him. He's an open book, not a cyber spy.'

A few seconds ticked by, then Cramer said, 'All I've been told is, he's believed to possess information picked up during his time on loan with Six, but he didn't disclose it during his debriefing.'

'That's what his captors are saying.'

A pause. 'How the hell would they know that?'

'My question, too. But that's for the mole hunters to work out.'

'Don't even joke about it,' Cramer breathed. But he sounded predictably horrified at the idea of an internal leak.

Harry decided to give him a push. 'It wouldn't be about someone or something called Cicada, would it?'

'Come again?'

'Cicada. One of Rik's interrogators mentioned the name.'

'In what connection?'

'It may have been a name or a reference in one of the files. Rik told them he couldn't remember. In any case, if it was special forces stuff, which is what he was into, it wouldn't be of any use to a foreign power, not after all this time.'

'I agree. But that presupposes he saw something he hasn't admitted to . . . and maybe the GRU goons think the same. Ask him again.'

Harry let it go. He was sure Rik was genuinely unable to remember the name. The main thing was to get him out of there; the recriminations could come later. 'Get me a technical bod,' he said, 'and we'll see. I get the feeling they won't hold off much longer. They've already killed one of their own group, and if they get really desperate Rik will be toast . . . and then if they're really serious they'll go on the offensive.'

'All right, I'm on it.'

'Are you sure? Only there's no time for committee meetings to get it signed off.'

'Don't worry. I'm switching to army rules. Where does this person need to head for?'

'Send me a name first and I'll text the details. Use WhatsApp. The location's a major airport in eastern Europe. I suggest you get a plane on standby with special aid-emergency clearance.'

Two hours later, having briefed Clare about Rik's situation, he received a text message from Cramer.

Sally Mitchell, Chief Tech, RAF. Name the RV and time.

Harry responded. He hesitated over specifying the airport, but he had to trust Cramer would use whatever secure channels were open to him and to keep that information to himself. If it got out right away, he'd have company coming over the hill before he could get Rik out of here.

Minsk Int. Soonest.

THIRTY-SIX

'**A**re we on a fool's mission?'

Ben Cramer asked the question as soon as he saw Richard Hough. They were walking around the outskirts of Trafalgar Square, which neither man considered the correct place for a strategy meeting. But they had used worse.

Hough didn't respond immediately. Out of habit he was checking the immediate area for signs of listeners. Although it was early the square was busy with tourists, mostly Japanese and Chinese by the looks of them, all eager to take as many selfies as they could before being hustled back into line for the next visitor attraction on the itinerary. The roads around the square were thick with commuter traffic, adding layers of noise to the atmosphere along with a growing smell of exhaust fumes.

'Nobody can hear us,' Cramer assured his colleague. 'I checked.'

Hough looked surprised. 'You did? How?'

'I had a couple of techs come here yesterday with the latest in laser microphones. There's too much interference to pick up complete strings of conversation.' He smiled. 'Mind you, what they did hear was pretty hair-raising. I've got the goods on at least two back-benchers and a very senior civil servant. Also,' he pulled a device from his pocket, 'this is a sound disrupter. It kills our voices at anything over two metres.'

'Seriously?' Hough stared at it. 'It looks like a mobile phone.'

Cramer put it away. 'It is. I'm kidding.'

'Thank you.' Hough looked puzzled. 'You're not having a mental breakdown, are you? Only I can get you some counselling if you need it. Might bugger up this operation, though.'

Cramer grunted. 'No need. I'm fine.'

'Glad to hear it. You said you wanted to talk. Urgent, too, you said. You sounded like my wife when I've forgotten to do something important. And what do you mean a fool's mission?'

'Call it a soldier's instinct. I've been in this position before.' Cramer reached down and tapped his absent leg. It made a dull sound. 'Only back then I didn't listen to the warning bells. Now I am.'

Hough glanced at Cramer's leg, where the ridge of the prosthetic showed faintly beneath the movement of the cloth of his trousers. 'Does it hurt? Sorry – that's insensitive of me.'

'No problem. It used to. I try not to think about it any more.' He waved a hand to dismiss the subject. 'Something isn't right about this operation. Don't you feel that?'

Hough opened his mouth, then closed it again, so Cramer continued, 'You and I have been tasked to find a former MI5 technical officer accused of having accessed restricted files some ten years ago. Files you said had been archived or rendered inactive. I haven't seen any of them because they're too sensitive for a simple ex-squaddie like me.'

'Don't feel too hard done-by,' Hough said dryly. 'I've only been allowed a peep at a summary report and I've been around a lot longer than you.'

Cramer shrugged. 'The said techie was debriefed, kicked out of the service and sent to some remote shit-hole in Georgia—' He lifted his hand. 'Forgive my language but I've been there; it is a shit-hole.'

'I know. A dumping ground for certain people to disappear and to forget. Only some things can't be forgotten. What's your point?'

'It sounded pretty basic stuff at first: man goes missing, possibly holding sensitive information. The thing is, Tate says the accusations against Ferris are rubbish.'

'Well, he would. He's another Red Station graduate and Ferris's mate. So?'

'He also said Ferris isn't working with anyone; he's being held by a GRU active service team and they aren't being nice about it. They've already used a taser on him and killed one of their own – an FSB helper.'

'Any names for these people?'

Cramer told him, adding, 'Kraush is the one calling the shots.'

Hough nodded. 'I'll get someone on that. Anything else?'

Cramer took a deep breath. 'Yes. They're planning a top-level cyber offensive against the UK if they don't get what they want from Ferris.'

Hough's head snapped round. 'You wait until now to tell me that? I need details, Ben.'

'It's a threat aimed at Ferris to get his cooperation. We have no proof it goes beyond that. And anyway, what would you do about it? You can't send in a strike force and knock them out.'

'Maybe not, but we could at least warn Cheltenham to put some extra measures in place.'

'That would alert whoever's doing this and they'd go to ground.' Cramer laid a hand on his colleague's arm. 'We have to wait for more information.'

The two men drifted apart to make way for a gaggle of women in chadors and accompanying children, then moved back together. 'Tate strikes me as a square peg in a round hole,' said Cramer. 'But so am I, if you believe the conditioning-by-experience theory.' He gave Hough a direct look. 'Like you, if my instincts are correct.'

Hough said, 'What's your point?' He was watching a tiny Japanese woman covertly drop breadcrumbs from her coat pocket while being photographed by a giggling companion. The dead giveaway was that she was the only person within fifty yards surrounded by the birds.

'I could frighten the shit out of her,' he commented mildly, 'by showing her my card. That would ruin the local tourist trade for all of a nano-second.' He turned back to Cramer. 'Let me play the supposing game here for a minute, Ben. Back to Ferris: that seems to be the nub of the question here, otherwise why all this charade? What could possibly be so important to merit his kidnapping – if that's what it is – and a threat to bring the UK to a stand-still?'

'I don't know.'

Hough chewed his lip. 'What if the debrief wasn't as thorough as the psych team thought? What if he actually saw a file, maybe a summary or even a header, but didn't disclose it?'

Cramer shook his head. 'But why wouldn't he have mentioned it? He had nothing to lose by coming clean – he'd been caught with his hand in the cookie jar so his career was a bust anyway.'

'Unless what he saw was so toxic he didn't know what to say.'

'Possibly.'

'There is another explanation,' Hough suggested after several moments. 'What if he actually didn't *know* what he saw because it was . . . I don't know, too complex or remote?'

'Is that likely? He's no idiot.'

'Didn't you ever question an order because the details weren't clear?'

Cramer chewed that over. 'If you're talking about my last fracas in Afghan you'd be right on the nail, which makes me an idiot. But I didn't question it because I trusted the intelligence and the head sheds to have got it right.' He looked around. 'I suppose if I had I'd be walking on both original legs God gave me but out of a job.'

'But that aside.'

'No, not every time. Most were battle orders given by people who understood the situation and didn't use convoluted language. Being sent on some hair-brained op by a bunch of desk jockeys was different.' He waved a hand. 'No offence.'

'None taken. In my defence I've only been a desk jockey for a couple of years. Before that . . . well, let's just say I was following orders in the field, same as you.'

'Really?'

'Sure. Different fields but the game was essentially the same.'

There was a lull in the conversation while Cramer assessed that for what it was. Hough was somebody he could respect because he'd been out there over many years where there were more shadows than light and enemies were even harder to recognize than in the dusty environs of Afghanistan or Iraq. 'You don't like it, either, do you – this op?'

Hough tilted his head a fraction. It wasn't a yes but was hardly a denial. 'I feel . . . uncomfortable with certain aspects.'

Cramer grunted. 'And there speaks a civil servant. A "no" would have done.'

'No, then. I don't like it.'

'So what can we do about it?'

Hough squinted at him. 'What's on your mind?'

'Tate put an interesting question to me earlier. He asked who was driving this operation from our side. And why now?'

'That's two questions. What did you tell him?'

'I didn't. I couldn't.'

'And you want me to tell you.'

'I think it's time, don't you? Before we go much further.'

'Cards on the table?'

'Why not? I'm grown-up – I can handle it.'

'God help us. This is the intelligence world. If we start putting cards on tables it'll cause chaos and kingdoms will fall.'

'Humour me. If not with a name, at least why now after all this time?'

Hough looked doubtful so Cramer continued, 'I think Tate's right: most of the material Ferris got a look at is out of date by now. It's dead information. The question I keep asking myself, as the lowest rung on this particular ladder – Tate and Ferris notwithstanding – is, what's behind it?'

Hough pulled a face. 'I'm going to play dumber a little longer.'

'All right. What – or should I say who – decided that after all this time, an IT tyke like Ferris needed investigating all over again.' He waved a hand. 'So he drops off the radar, does a bunk without asking permission of the watchdogs – who, incidentally, don't have a right to know. He's ten years out of touch, so why are they getting their balls in a twist? Or was he already under surveillance?'

'Not as far as I know – at least, not by me. His name might have surfaced for some other reason and it triggered an alarm. It happens.' He paused. 'Like you, I'm operating with partial data.'

'But it was put to bed years ago, supposedly with the help of the psych wallahs, who we know rarely fail to dig out every tiny little secret people are harbouring, even if they don't know what they're harbouring.'

'True.'

'So why all this? Tate says Ferris told him he was looking at field reports on special forces assignments allied to intelligence operations. Probably like the last one I was on. They might be classified but they're hardly the kind of stuff to get the GRU excited. According to Tate, Ferris was an SAS fan-boy. It doesn't make him unique or suspect – and unlikely to be a traitor.'

'Possibly.' Hough pursed his lips. 'Say I agree with you. What makes you think there's one person driving it?'

'Because there's always one. Every proposal ever made since God was in shorts began that way. It would have been a suggestion, a question, whatever; but no proposal gets to be a decisive course of action without being originally pushed by one decider – even if a committee gives the final nod.'

'You don't believe in collective responsibility, then? That's odd, coming from a military man.'

'Hardly,' Cramer grunted. 'At the top of every plan, every campaign, every mission, there has to be someone pushing it; one person who was the originator. Work your way up the line from ground level and you'll eventually come to that one person.'

Hough didn't argue. His expression was grim.

'You're unnervingly silent,' Cramer prompted him.

Hough shrugged. 'Maybe because I've been on the arse end of bad decisions myself more than once. Soldiers aren't the only ones sent out to do things on the back of faulty thinking and a lack of preparation.' He stopped walking and straightened his coat. 'Are you actually going to tell me where Tate is right now?'

'In Belarus. Minsk. But that's not for general release. He's found Ferris but there's a specific problem not of Ferris's doing.'

'Is it solvable?'

'I hope so, otherwise neither of them will be coming home.' He stamped his foot, flexing his good leg. 'I've used contacts to get a rescue plan in place but it needs Tate to run it on the ground. He can't do that with everybody and their brother breathing down his neck.'

'I understand,' Hough said, and made a zipper gesture across his mouth. 'Scout's honour.'

Cramer gave a lopsided smile. 'I won't embarrass you with the details but you might have to field a few complaints later about the misuse of military personnel – namely one technical bod – and muscling up a seat on an aid-related flight out of Frankfurt.'

Hough lifted his eyebrows in surprise. 'You're bloody enjoying this, aren't you? What other little gems can I expect to hear about?'

'None . . . unless it all goes tits up. Better you don't know.'

'I appreciate your consideration,' Hough murmured. 'Actually, I wish I was in on it . . . but maybe you're right. If I don't know squat they can't nail my fingers to the table and get anything out of me.'

'Exactly. What about this Garth Perry. Any news?'

'Off and running, I'm afraid.' Hough looked sombre. 'A sub-contract job. It was taken out of my hands so I haven't been able to stop it.'

'And it was Colmyer's doing?'

Yes.'

Cramer looked sour. 'Well, fuck a duck,' he breathed. 'So polit-icos are running ops now.' He checked the buttons on his coat. 'Here's something to think about – something I can't check but you might be able to. Does the name Cicada mean anything to you?'

Hough's face didn't change, but there was a momentary shift there, deep in his eyes. 'Cicada? The insect?'

Cramer said mildly, 'I think you know it's not. One of Ferris's interrogators mentioned it in relation to the files he was alleged to have seen. It sounded too specific to Tate – and I agree. Someone's been prompted.' He waited for Hough to say something, but the older man looked blank.

'Sorry. Doesn't mean anything. I'll ask around, see if it raises any eyebrows.'

Cramer turned to leave, then paused. 'You know what we say in the military when you can't see an obvious enemy?'

'Surprise me.'

'Look behind you.'

THIRTY-SEVEN

Hough watched Cramer walk away across the Square, silhouetted against the low sunlight, the limp evident but not slowing him down. It made him realize that by comparison he'd been very lucky in his professional life. One or two close scrapes here and there, some uncomfortable periods where daily life had bordered on the bleak, being forced to live undercover while every hand around was guaranteed to be against him. There was a brief spell in an Egyptian prison cell once, when he'd been scooped up by pure chance during an operation. They'd let him go, choosing to believe his cover story of a visiting professor on a study visit. Worse had been the loss of a couple of colleagues and the end of his marriage, each victims of the job in different ways. But he hadn't lost a limb or come even close. The advantage of living in the shadows was, if you were sufficiently good at it, you got by with more psychological stress lines than physical ones. And he'd been very good.

He glanced around, eyeing the tourists, the birds, the passers-by. Nothing out of the ordinary, although he'd always relied on passing as ordinary when his life had depended on it, so what did he know?

Sir Geoffrey Bull, he was thinking bleakly. The buck began and stopped right there. He was still the nominal head of the JIO, sick or not, and a man whose history of the secret world was even longer than his own. He felt a twinge of sadness at the thought, and wondered what other details he hadn't been briefed on.

Like Cicada.

He checked his phone for any urgent messages but there were none. He dialled a number for a researcher in the Russian section and gave her the names of the two GRU members, then considered the quickest route to Bull's location in a private hospital near the British Museum. A taxi would be best. It was time to get some answers instead of blindly following orders.

He arrived at the hospital and checked in. Private it might be and a touch more select in décor compared to public units, but it still wore the aura of a place people came to die. At least it was quieter,

Hough reflected; more like an upmarket hotel than the hectic bustle of an NHS institution, which was probably where he'd end up when mind or body decided to give up the fight.

He found Bull lying back against his pillows, attached to tubes and wires leading to an impossibly complex-looking monitor Hough neither recognized nor cared about. The man looked like shit, he thought sombrely. A book on Roman history lay across his belly and looked heavy in content and size. Bull opened his eyes as the door squeaked and marked his page with a slip of paper. He snapped it shut and dropped it on the bed beside him with a sigh. Hough got the impression his boss wasn't too pleased to see him. The skin on his face and throat looked loose, devoid of colour, and the area round his eyes had deepened since Hough had last seen him.

Hough used the action of placing a small box of Medjool dates on the bedside cabinet to mask his shock at Bull's appearance.

'I recall you once expressed a fondness,' he explained vaguely. 'You probably need the sugar, anyway.'

'How kind.' Bull's voice had none of its customary authority, as if it had been drained away by being confined in this place, and his eyes looked a little unfocussed. 'What brings you here, Richard?'

At least he hadn't lost his ability to get to the point, Hough thought, and drew up a chair. 'Well, first of all, how are you? I'm sorry I haven't been before, but things have been a little hectic.'

'Things are always hectic. You don't have to make excuses. As for me, I'm trying to read this bloody book in the faint hope that I might finish it before it finishes me. I don't think my consultant rates my chances, though. Get to the point, old chap.'

Hough nodded. 'I have a question. Well, probably more than one.'

'If it's about your retirement party, you'll have to excuse me but I don't feel in the mood for drinks and nibbles.'

'No. Not that.' Hough had been rehearsing his words all the way across town, but now found it oddly difficult to begin, like explaining to his headmaster why his academic performance during the term hadn't been better.

'You have too many questions,' Bull said, appearing not to have heard him, 'which I do not have time to answer. Have you seen Colmyer's file? No, of course you haven't. Silly of me.' He hitched one shoulder up and said, 'I'm only going to tell you this once, then I'm going to forget it so listen carefully.'

Hough nodded. *Was this going to be easier than he'd thought?*

'What do you know about Colmyer?'

'Only what's in the press. The son of an investment banker and industrialist, but that's about it.'

Bull smiled dryly and closed his eyes. 'Well, just so you know, I am very familiar with his record. It makes interesting reading. You're correct, he's from a wealthy background, a good education and on his way up in the government. He has lots of important connections. Not all of them in this country.'

Hough found himself holding his breath. *Where was this going?*

'His father had leftist leanings, although his son claims his own are more centrist. He's made a substantial fortune based on his inheritance, which came mostly from Colmyer senior's successful investments many years ago . . . mainly in Russia and the surrounding territories.'

'Russia?' Out of all the words, that one seemed to drop into the room and hang there, oddly out of place in this medicated atmosphere.

'His father saw opportunities where others did not. Mining, oil, energy . . . in other words, industries which friend Putin has since taken on wholeheartedly with his close friends, the oligarchs, and moulded into a vast gift that keeps on giving.'

'And it was never questioned?'

Bull moved his thin shoulders in what might have been a shrug. 'He wasn't the only one. Canadians, Americans, Scandinavians . . . all blue-sky thinkers with a long-term view. In Colmyer's case, all he did was inherit, so no fault, no penalty. However, there have been questions over a sudden influx of money attached to a holding company in Ukraine. Colmyer claims he's not a controlling partner, merely a recipient of his father's investments. It seemed to satisfy those in the know and allowed him to escape any accusations of conflicts of interest.'

'Lucky for him.'

'Almost. However, he has other sources of income which he does control and which in some quarters are rumoured to be in breach of international sanctions led by the US . . .'

'So he's a player.'

'Oh, yes. And we're not talking piggy-bank cash. This is millions, paid into an account held by his eighteen-year-old son, Mark . . . who has no investment links whatsoever and as far as I can tell has the financial acumen of a rabbit.'

'So, money from the east and the west. Clever.'

'Clever but dangerous. I'm not sure he sees it.'

'I'm surprised none of this has come out,' said Hough, 'in view of his next job.'

Bull gave a faint splutter of mirth, or maybe cynicism. He coughed slightly, the effort overcoming him. 'Sorry. Can't seem to get any vitality back.' He pawed at the bed cover in a vague way and said, 'What was I saying?'

'Colmyer. No scandal.'

'Ah. Yes. That.'

Hough's ears prickled. 'Do tell.'

'Someone was shielding Colmyer from investigation for a long time – and his father before him. That shield was removed a few years ago. But back then it didn't matter because Colmyer was on his way through the system. He had momentum and credibility and nobody was going to stop him. And it was only money.'

Hough felt sure there was a message behind Bull's words, as if the older man couldn't quite bring himself to get to the point, a legacy of his training. All he had to do was tease it out. 'Legally?'

'It's only illegal if someone can prove it. The morality, however, is certainly questionable.'

Hough set that aside. Penetrating the financial history of someone like Colmyer wasn't something he could even begin to attempt. That was down to experts capable of peeling away the layers of his life like an onion. Instead he asked, 'This shield. Do you have a name?'

There was a long silence, and he thought he'd blown it. Bull's eyes closed again for a moment, and the older man uttered a lengthy sigh. Then he cleared his throat as if he'd come to a decision.

'It won't do you any good,' he murmured. 'He's dead.'

'I'd still like to hear it.'

'Persistent little bugger, aren't you?'

'I try.'

'Anthony Bellingham.'

Hough felt his mouth drop open. He couldn't help it. That name again. The former MI6 Operations Director who'd met a nasty end at the hands of Clare Jardine, the Red Station bounce-back.

'That's some shield.' Then he said with an awful feeling of apprehension, 'Who is Cicada?'

Bull didn't answer. But he seemed to sink back on the pillow with a lengthy sigh.

'Cicada,' Hough repeated. 'One of Ferris's captors appears to be GRU and mentioned the name.'

'I'm afraid I have no idea,' Bull said.

'Really? You mean you never heard the rumours? I gather it was generally regarded as a scam . . . a disinformation exercise coming out of Moscow.'

Bull remained silent so Hough continued. 'I later heard that it was attributed to a long-term mole aimed at gaining high-level access to the security and intelligence services. It was aborted when an attaché from the Russian embassy was caught handing a large amount of money to a mid-level official in the MOD. The attaché was expelled along with half a dozen others and the official sentenced to a hefty jail term. There were questions in the House for a while. Then silence.'

'What's your point, Richard?'

'Maybe Cicada wasn't aborted after all. Maybe,' he added heavily, 'there was a disinformation exercise to make us all look the wrong way.'

Still no response, so he said, 'Is there something in the files Ferris accessed that might throw some light on the subject?'

'You're like a bloody mongoose going after a snake, d'you know that?' Bull reached for his book and took out the slip of paper marking his page. 'There's an oddly thin line between loyalty and treachery. So thin you can easily step over it without realizing. Before you know it, it's too late.' He held the piece of paper out. 'I've been wanting to do this for a long time, Richard, but lacked . . . well, something meaningful in the way of courage. Now it no longer matters . . . to me, at least. But I think the time has come to do something. And maybe this Ferris thing is the ideal catalyst.'

Hough turned over the slip of paper. It held a single word in a shaky scrawl.

Colmyer.

Hough looked at his boss, waiting for more and wondering if he was in danger of over-reaching. *Did this mean what he thought?* But Bull seemed to have run dry.

'Can I get you some water?' he asked.

No response.

He flapped the piece of paper. 'Is this him? Cicada?' Hough's voice was a whisper, layered with expectation and insistence.

Nothing. Just the sound of the older man's breathing, light as butterfly wings.

'Which one is Cicada?' he insisted. 'Bellingham or Colmyer?'

But Bull was no longer listening. With morbid timing, the book on Roman history, as if finding its hold on the reader lost, slid off the bed and hit the floor with a loud smack. Simultaneously the screen on the monitor lit up and an electronic alarm began bleeping urgently, followed by voices and hurrying footsteps.

Hough turned and walked out, his presence no longer required, his head in a spin. He was relieved to be out in the fresh air and away from the aura of impending death. He had to speak to Cramer again – and soon. But first he needed to take a look at some files.

Gaining access to the archives proved tougher than he'd expected, involving a number of sign-offs. But given that he was already involved in the search for Ferris, there was little the gatekeepers could do to resist his demands. And faced by a former field officer with a reputation who suspected there was a rotten apple in the barrel, most gave their signature and beat a hasty retreat, uneasy at being too close to the whiff of treason.

He travelled down to the basement archives and opened up the digital files. It didn't take long, now he knew where to look. Joining up dots was always simpler once you had a start and a finish point.

With a faint sense of nausea on seeing the clarity of the picture before him, he closed the files and signed out, not relishing the report he was going to have to make. It would end one person's job for certain, which was only to be expected. But the seismic shock waves felt throughout the intelligence and security communities would be profound.

Locking himself away, he wrote up his findings in triplicate complete with copies of documentary evidence, sealed three envelopes addressed to the heads of MI5, MI6 and GCHQ and sent them out.

If that didn't cause stuff to hit the fan, he'd eat his copy of *Civil Service World*.

Then he cleared his desk of all non-essentials, aware that the one maxim not always observed by the civil service was that one should not shoot the messenger of bad news.

That done, he picked up the phone and rang Ben Cramer.

THIRTY-EIGHT

Harry woke early and went out in search of breakfast. It promised to be a long day and he wanted to get a decent meal inside him before he returned to the industrial zone. He was carrying his cover outfit in a large plastic laundry bag, and found a café which opened early where he wouldn't attract attention and could eat with one eye on his phone. Nothing from Cramer yet about Mitchell's arrival time and flight number, but that was likely down to military systems grinding slow.

After an hour he got tired of waiting and tapped out a message. *Sitrep on Mitchell?*

The response was swift. *Soon. Waiting conf. Comms problem.*

He went for a walk. He was resisting the temptation to go back to the zone; balanced against the desire to keep an eye on Rik and his guards was the danger of being seen in the area too often and opening up the possibility of someone taking a closer look at him.

It was close to eight-thirty when his phone beeped.

Mitchl on BRU893, ETA 11.30 a.m. Minsk. Blonde, 30's. Red rucksack. She will call U on arr.

There was a second message, this one with a photo attachment. But it wasn't of Mitchell; it was a head-and-shoulders shot of a man with short-cut hair and a thin face, and the blank stare of a file photo. Probably taken from his military record, Harry reasoned.

The text read simply, *Garth Perry. Treat as hostile.*

Things were moving, but not all of them good. If he didn't get a handle on this situation Rik would be finished. It meant he had to prepare a plan of attack – and soon. In the meantime he had to hope that Cramer's lines of communication were secure. If this Garth Perry was plugged in to the same lines as Cramer – and the likelihood was fairly high – then he wouldn't be long in arriving in Minsk, eager to complete the job. If he wasn't here already.

He rang Clare and told her the location and name of the café.

'I'll be there in ten.'

She was as good as her word and slid into the chair across from him just as a fresh coffee arrived. 'Thanks. So what's the situation with Ferris?' She poured sugar into the mug and stirred it. 'I don't normally use this stuff but I reckon I'm going to need the energy.' She took a mouthful, then said, 'Did I dream what you told me yesterday? GRU and a bloody *bomb*? For some crap information off an archive? Are they for real?'

'Rik believes it. As for the device we won't know if that's real until we get it looked at.'

'How will you do that?'

'That's what I've been working on. There's also another problem – potentially bigger. I didn't mention it before but if Rik doesn't come clean they've threatened to launch a cyber hit on the UK.'

Her mouth dropped open. 'No way.'

'I don't know whether they mean it but I believe they have the capability.'

'But why? Christ, what *is* this information they're after?'

'I don't know. But if we wait too long to find out they might just run out of patience.'

'All right. What do you intend to do?'

'Can you do a pick-up at the airport?'

'It's what I do most. Who and when?'

He gave her Mitchell's flight details and description. 'She's probably expecting me to meet her, so if there's a problem call me.'

Clare smirked. 'Who is she – a girlfriend over for a romantic getaway?'

'She's a bomb-disposal tech.'

The smirk disappeared. 'Sorry. Bad joke.' She was silent for a moment, then said, 'Where do I take her?'

'For now, take her to the hotel and wait for my call.'

She looked askance at him. 'You're going to break him out.'

'I can't. It's too risky. All they need to do if they hear me coming is press a button and he'll be toast. But I'm working on a plan.'

'Would they really do that if this thing he knows is so important to them? They seem to have invested a lot in trying to get hold of it . . . whatever it is.'

'I can't count on them not doing it, that's the problem. If I can force them into a position where moving Rik is the only option, it might give us an opportunity to get at him.'

'Great. Are you going to tell me where that is?'

Harry wagged a hand in the air. 'I haven't firmed that up yet. But that's where your local knowledge will help. Where's the nearest

A&E to the industrial zone? Somewhere not too busy, maybe on the outskirts of the city.'

Clare thought about it, her brow furrowed. 'The main A&E units are close to the centre, at Kizhevatova and Kiseleva streets. But I don't think they would risk taking him to either of those – and not with a bomb strapped to him.'

'I'm hoping they'll get rid of that before they take him in. But there's no way I can control that.'

'There's too much security in the city centre and they have police units based on the premises to prevent incidents, and scanners on the doors. Why would they need to take him to hospital?'

'That doesn't matter. If I can make it happen, it's our one chance to get Rik out of danger. But I agree the central units increase the risk of something going wrong. Where else?'

She didn't look sure and said, 'I've got an idea, but I'll need you to go with me on this.' She took out a mobile phone.

Harry said, 'What are you doing?'

'I'm calling Katya. She knows the city's emergency units better than I do – and she knows the GRU.'

'Won't she blow the whistle as soon as we tell her?'

'No. She's here to provide training and assistance to the locals. She also hates the way Moscow treats Belarus.' Clare leaned forward. 'Harry, she's our best hope to get this sorted out. Believe me – I trust her.'

He relented. 'All right – call her. But only because you called me Harry.'

She grinned. 'Yeah, but don't get used to it.' She touched a speed dial key and waited.

Katya arrived within fifteen minutes. She was blonde and slim and appeared small under a heavy coat. Harry could just see the edge of her uniform collar underneath.

'I won't take this off,' she said, indicating the coat. 'Some of the locals don't appreciate seeing Russian uniforms on the street.' Her English was excellent and fluid. She shook hands with Harry and took a seat while Clare ordered coffee.

Harry gave her a potted version of Rik's situation and the threat of the cyber attack. She listened without comment, and when the coffee arrived she took a few sips.

'If this is true,' she said carefully, 'then you are right to want to move your friend first. I can help with that. But—'

'But what?' said Harry. 'You don't believe the cyber threat?'

She put her cup down. 'I can believe it might have been said, but as a genuine threat, it seems heavy-handed. And why would they do it?'

'Why wouldn't they?' Harry countered. 'We're talking about Putin; he throws his weight around all the time.'

'Maybe. But the GRU would not be authorized to make a threat of such magnitude to gain the cooperation of just one man. It's unreasonable. Illogical.' She leaned forward and tapped the table in front of her. 'If what you say is true, your country would be brought to a standstill by this. There would be riots and looting and armed insurrection. The effects would be disastrous and the economy ruined. But Putin has no use for dead economies. How would he benefit from that? You think he wants to invade? Why? It would be crazy. He would be overstretching himself.'

'So what does he want?' said Harry.

Katya shrugged. 'I don't know. If he wants to do anything it's to control economies through the supply of oil and gas – and gaining dependency on Russia. He wants to compete with the US and have countries reliant on Moscow's support. He is already supplying the EU with a third of their imports of natural gas and wants to do more. A broken country would not be able to use such things effectively.' She sat back and declared, 'I'm not defending him, but I cannot see what he would gain by such an attack.'

'Then who would?'

'I don't know. There are people around him . . . maybe some who want to gain influence or power or maybe even take over. But Putin? I cannot see it.'

'You sound very sure.'

She nodded. 'Before coming here I was a high-level officer in our Federal Protective Service – the FSO. I was close enough to hear many conversations among senior ministers around Putin – and these are the things I heard talked about.' She gave a cool smile. 'Strategies, they called them. Tactics . . . war games. They liked to quote famous Russian tacticians like Slashchov and Suvorov and even the Chinese General Sun Tzu. It was to show how well-read they were but in the end they are men: they want to show how big their dicks are and how close to the centre of power they might be.'

Harry let that one slide. 'And this was with you right there?'

'I was rated at the highest level of security, so why should they care what I heard? In fact, I think some of them got off on it.'

'So it's a bluff?' Clare said. 'Scare tactics.'

Katya nodded. 'I'm sure of it. But you would be unwise to ignore the possibility.' She looked sombre. 'One day, maybe . . .'

'Would the locals know they were here?'

'Unlikely. But all it would need is an agreement from one official.' She looked uncomfortable. 'I know at least three senior ministers here in Minsk who would do anything to gain favours from Moscow. A nod from any one of them would be enough to allow the GRU in and for a blind eye to be turned by the police and security services.'

'Fine.' Harry put his hand on the table. 'For now, how about Rik?' He outlined his plan to get Rik away from Kraush.

Katya thought it over. 'The only other place I can think of is a small satellite unit just off the M4. It's not far from the industrial zone. I accompanied two ministers from Moscow there once to study the facilities. They treat victims of road traffic accidents on the outer city and regional roads and only send them on to the main hospitals for more serious injuries.' She took out her phone and tapped in the name. When a map image came up she showed Harry where the clinic was located. It wasn't far, which suited him fine.

'Could we get inside without too many problems?' he asked.

'I think so. There are emergency vehicles coming and going all the time; the place is a beehive because the local drivers are crazy and accidents happen all the time.'

'Then that's where we'll do it.'

'What is your plan of action?'

'If I can get Rik taken to this unit for examination, and the device is not attached, it's all to the good. If it's still in place we need to get a specialist in long enough to disable it. Once that's done we're away and clear.'

'As simple as that?' Clare looked sceptical. 'There's a lot of "ifs" in there.'

'I know. But I can't think of anything better. Hopefully the people holding him won't be expecting such a move.'

Clare said, 'What do you need from me – apart from getting Mitchell inside the unit?'

He looked at her in surprise. He wanted to say nothing at all, that she'd done more than enough already. But he knew he was in dangerous territory here, and another pair of experienced eyes would make what he was about to do much easier. 'Some back-up would be good,' he said.

'People or mechanical?'

'You, if you're serious.'

'I wouldn't have offered if I didn't mean it.' She stood up, but Katya held up a hand.

'I will help, too,' she said.

Harry was surprised, as was Clare, who plainly hadn't expected it.

'I can assist with getting you past any authority in the unit,' she explained. 'But that might be all I can do. Being compromised further would mean the end of my career.' She stood up and checked her watch. 'I must return to my office for a meeting. Clare can keep me informed from here on.' She nodded at Harry and touched Clare briefly on the shoulder, then walked out.

'We'd better be moving, too,' Clare said. 'I'll drop you back at the zone then collect your techie girlfriend and head for somewhere close to the accident unit. It'll be quicker than driving all the way out of the city. I'll text you when we're in place.'

He thanked her, the logistics of his plan with the addition of Katya whirling through his mind and beginning to settle. 'Actually, I need to hire a car. Something with a bit of beef, but looks like a clunker.'

'Where will I be?'

'You'll be looking after Mitchell.'

She chewed her lip. 'Right. I know a place. I'll take you there now and make the arrangements.'

'Great. Just one thing: if you receive a text from me saying "abort", I want you to get Mitchell back to the airport, then bug out and resume normal duties without asking questions. I mean it. No heroics.'

She gave him a level gaze. 'I hear you. It doesn't sound very promising.'

'Doesn't matter. If it comes to it I don't want to compromise you and Katya. I'd rather leave you out of it.'

'Fat chance, Tate. We're in. To be honest I could do with the distraction. As for Katya she'll be fine. What will you be doing in the meantime?'

'Keeping an eye on things and hoping Rik can keep them from pressing the button.'

They walked out to Clare's car. It was parked between two bulky SUVs with consecutive numbers and a driver-bodyguard standing by each vehicle, eyes on the street. They stiffened as Harry and Clare approached, but one of the men lifted his hand to his mouth and muttered a few words into a sleeve mic, and they relaxed.

Clare ignored them and gestured for Harry to climb aboard and signalled to pull out into the traffic. 'They belong to a private security company,' she explained. 'I see them a lot about town and they know what I do. The company they work for has the monopoly on providing transport and minders to senior government ministers. Some reckon the company is Russian-owned and the ministers don't have much say in the matter. Neat way of getting government contracts, huh?'

'And listening into official business, I bet.'

'Yeah, that, too.' She looked at him, picking up on his tone of distraction. 'Are you all right?'

Harry was only half listening, his attention focussed on another vehicle just pulling into the kerb on the opposite side of the street. Black like these two, it was coated in a layer of dirt and had a dent in the driver's door. Two men were sitting inside, the passenger with his head turned. He was looking right at Harry.

It was Garth Perry.

'Get us out of here,' said Harry. 'We've got company.'

Clare didn't argue but pulled out and put her foot down, leaving behind car horns and a screech of brakes. Harry watched in the side mirror and saw the black SUV attempt to muscle its way out but it was blocked by a heavy truck.

'Who was that?' Clare asked.

'His name's Perry,' he told her. 'Ex-military intelligence, now freelance contractor. He's after Rik and probably doesn't care who gets in the way.'

'Good to have the heads-up, Tate. When were you going to tell me?'

'I only just found out myself.'

She drove skilfully and smoothly, one eye on her rear-view mirror and slipping through the traffic with ease, using side streets and back-doubles. From the more elegant area where the hotel was located, she brought them to a more industrialized district of houses, small businesses and scruffy commercial units, until she pulled into the side of a street near a used car lot.

'It doesn't look much,' she admitted, turning off the engine, 'but the woman running it owes me a big favour and won't stiff me with a wreck. You stay here while I do the deal. You look too much like a cop even in this country.' She smiled and climbed out and disappeared inside. When she emerged ten minutes later she was in an old Nissan Pathfinder 4WD with mismatched panels and a general air of tiredness. But the engine sounded good.

'It's not pretty,' she admitted, 'but it's been tuned up. Yulia says if you have to leave it somewhere, put the keys on the front tyre and call the number on the dash and she'll get it picked it up.'

'I'm impressed,' Harry said, and meant it. But something was worrying him. 'I think you should lose this car for a while. Perry will have the number and he's got contacts in the city, probably in the police, too.'

'Got it. I'll leave it with Yulia and swap it for something else. I'm not rostered on to do a pick-up for a while now.'

Harry grabbed his cover outfit, then left her to it and drove back out to the industrial zone, one eye on the other traffic for prowling SUVs taking an interest. It was beginning to snow, with tiny flecks spitting against the windscreen and sliding down to form a small drift under the wipers, and he turned up the heater. Like the car it wasn't in the first flush of youth and rattled like a string of tin cans on a wedding car, but it gave out a welcome measure of heat.

He parked the Nissan nose-outwards in some trees out of sight of the entrance to the industrial zone and threw some branches on top of the bonnet and roof. The scratched and weather-beaten panels would make it more difficult to see here than if it had been highly polished, and if he had to leave in a hurry he'd be lined up and ready to go.

He changed into his old clothes and was about to move when he heard the sound of another engine approaching. He ducked back into cover and waited.

It was a black SUV like the ones he'd seen earlier. Idling along the road, its exhaust was burbling away with the steady beat of something with muscle. It slowed before pulling into the side and stopped.

A man stepped out from the passenger side while the driver remained in the car, the engine rumbling. The passenger stood for a moment, back turned, scanning the trees on both sides of the road. When he stepped clear of the car Harry saw his face full on.

It was Perry.

Harry remained absolutely still, although he was positive Perry couldn't see him. The man was of medium height and slim, with short hair and an angular face. He was dressed in a heavy bush-jacket style anorak, hiking trousers and boots, and had the upright stance of a military man. A hunter, not a tourist out here to appreciate the scenery.

Perry eventually got back in the car and it drove away, performing a neat u-turn and heading back towards the city, the hum of the powerful engine drifting back towards Harry until it disappeared from view.

Harry felt frustrated knowing that Perry was already in the area and had narrowed down his whereabouts to this particular spot. The fact that he had a driver indicated local help, and that meant he would be plugged into the local network with the means to have put out feelers looking for non-local visitors. And that had already led him right here. Taxi drivers, Harry decided; they talked because there was no profit in staying silent and they had no allegiance to people passing through.

He pushed it out of his mind. His primary job was to scout the industrial zone to make sure Rik and his guards were still in place. Then it would be down to time, place and circumstance. He looked up at the sky, noting the heavy cloud cover rolling in and a chill of ice water on his cheek. The weather might give him a slight edge; his presence would be more likely to go unnoticed as long as he didn't make any stupid mistakes.

THIRTY-NINE

'Sorry to hear about Bull,' Cramer murmured. The two men were back in Trafalgar Square, navigating their way through the crowds. The news of Bull's passing had trickled down the wires while Hough was on his way to meet him.

Hough gave him a summary of his talk with Bull, adding a little of the man's history and the connection with Colmyer.

Cramer's response was blunt. 'I may be a simple soldier, but no wonder it stinks. You don't get the Chief of the General Staff setting off a paper chase when a squaddie bunks off with some mess funds.'

Hough shook his head. 'Maybe not. But civil service and politicians . . . it's another kind of army with paper generals and cardboard squaddies. Different rules and outcomes.'

Cramer blew out a puff of air. 'Bollocks. There are lines of responsibility. It doesn't make any difference whether you're in uniform or pin-striped kecks. Why would Colmyer get involved?'

'He's about to be king of this particular heap; he can ask any questions he likes.' He looked steely but was sounding less sure of himself. 'However, all that's by the by. I'm going to give you the heads up because I trust you not to run to the *Daily Express* with it.'

'Why would I?'

'Yeah, well . . . some would.' He coughed and said, 'Tate asked who was driving this. I think we both know that now. But there's a much bigger question: how would Colmyer have heard about Ferris's breach of the files in the first place?'

'Quite. You said the archives were closed.'

They didn't speak as a clutch of schoolchildren in the care of at least four adults streamed by, chattering like a crowd of penguins.

Hough looked at him and said, 'This is depressing me, you know that? I'm supposed to be retiring soon and here I am knowing that the current and incoming heads of the JIO are as rotten as month-old eggs.' He stopped long enough to dig out a handkerchief and blow his nose, then said, 'Well, I wish I didn't.'

'Go on.'

'Bull gave Colmyer access . . . but much more than that. He told him precisely where to look.'

Cramer scowled. 'So is this about Bull or Colmyer?'

'Both . . . but mostly Colmyer. Bull kept secrets he shouldn't have and Colmyer's desperately trying to do the same but for different, purely selfish reasons.'

Cramer said, 'You said his father was in bed with the Russians years ago and made a fortune from it. Is that what this is about?'

Hough pulled a face. 'Colmyer senior wasn't the only westerner to have made a mint out of the old Soviet empire. Where do you think all those oligarchs got their taste for football clubs, yachts and buckets of money?'

'So what is it?'

'Junior's got money, but it only buys the same stuff other rich men can buy. Power's different. It's leverage.' He stopped behind one of the plinths and looked squarely at his colleague. 'But that can go both ways.'

Cramer nodded. Now they were getting somewhere. It felt like a gate being unlocked.

'A man like Colmyer has influence over a lot of people just down the street from here,' Hough continued, 'and along the river. He exercises it and enjoys doing so.'

Cramer nodded. 'So what's his end game?'

'Influence. But not in this neck of the woods.' Hough looked bleak at Cramer's puzzled look. 'What if someone else has got power over *him* – the kind that threatens everything he holds dear? It didn't matter when he was a low-grade politico. But now he's high on the totem pole and doesn't want anyone rocking the glory boat. He'd want to make sure they couldn't use it against him.'

'Who?'

'Think degrees. Fifty-five-point-seven north by thirty-seven-point six east. Give or take. That's—'

'I know where that is.' The map coordinates for Moscow.

They walked on, nearing the south side of the square.

'With what Bull showed him, Junior must know there's a strong possibility that Ferris saw and remembered what was in one file. Knowing that, he pulled every file reference to himself to check.'

'How do you know that?'

'I've seen the files and the audit trails. It's all there . . . along with some crucial evidence.'

Cramer was impressed. 'He really got under your skin, didn't he?'

'And some. It had to be something he was desperate to keep quiet about. Something about his past . . . or his father's. When you're as ambitious as he is, dirt's dirt and can't be ignored. It leaves a mark.'

Cramer looked up at the sky and shivered. 'Why didn't he delete it?'

'That requires input clearance and would have rung alarm bells. As long as it's locked away in the vaults there's a very good chance nobody else will ever set eyes on it.'

Cramer raised an eyebrow. 'More old stuff?'

'Oldish.'

'Couldn't he weather that? He's unlikely to be held to account for what Daddy did.'

'Not quite. He's already having to answer questions about some of his father's investments that are still active. My guess is someone – Bellingham, perhaps – saw information on a file which wasn't meant to be seen but he couldn't wipe it out. Bull would have been in the same position. Unfortunately for them all, cross-referencing files is what civil servants do best. It's in their DNA, like a spider's web stretching across the database and connecting all manner of nasty little secrets.'

'So where's the biggest threat to Junior?'

'The boys in Moscow. You know how they work: get someone on the ladder and bide their time. Wait for them to reach a height where they'll be most effective . . . then down comes the hammer.'

'That means it's current information. Including contacts?'

'Yes. He's probably known certain names all along . . . people his father was close to.'

'But can they use it?'

'Sure. He's been Junior in more ways than one so far. Now he's right where they want him, and he must know they can drop a sucker punch on him any time they choose. If they got the evidence he'd be under their thumb for ever. Play ball or we ruin your career.'

'But they'd lose everything he could tell them.'

'It's a numbers game; they'll have someone else along sooner or later.'

'But why wait for Ferris to get taken to where the GRU can pick his brains?'

Hough shrugged. 'He didn't. I think the timing was against him. He saw what was in the files about him, and when he looked for Ferris he found he'd gone awol. Two and two make five; he panicked and here we are.'

'So who told Moscow about Ferris?'

'I think Colmyer did . . . or he told someone he trusted who had access to Moscow. He's arrogant enough to think he can play them. He was probably hoping they would deal with Ferris and close the door on that nasty little secret . . . which shows how little he understands what he's got into.'

'So why couldn't you have said any of this before? You're closer to these people; you know how they think.'

'Right. Of course. And you're just a simple foot-soldier who knows nuffink.' Hough gave a hint of a smile. 'I've been out in the field until recently. It's not the best way of keeping up with internal gossip.'

They walked on a little more, and were about to part company when Hough stopped and said, *'I've given him a briefing about current activities and access to the archives for background at his request.'*

Cramer looked startled. The words sounded oddly out of character. 'What the hell was that?'

Hough looked glum. 'It's something Bull said to me one day after he dumped this Ferris thing on me. I've only just realized what it meant. Bull would have known all about Ferris, Tate and the Red Station fiasco; it was one of those events that many in the community heard about but few would have known the full details.' He pulled a face. 'We never have been good at airing our laundry beyond a very tight circle.'

'So?'

'Bull probably told Colmyer about it over sherry one day. It's what some of the big pooh-bahs like to do: sharing some of the intelligence world's lesser-known dramas to show how much in the know they are.'

Cramer was frowning. 'But didn't Ferris cough all this during his debriefing?'

Hough gave him a weary look. 'A question I asked myself. When I checked the audit trails into the files he'd looked at, there was a summary and a codename but I don't suppose Ferris gave it more than a glance because it wasn't what he was looking for. But I recognized the codename.'

'Go on.'

'It was in a field report submitted by a retiring agent handler in Berlin the year before Ferris was canned. It was submitted as part of a batch meant for further action by his replacement, and for reasons I can only guess at, was filed and forgotten.'

'Deliberately?'

'No idea. Mistakes happen, so who knows? The important thing is, it names an individual who attended at least three undisclosed meetings with Russians known to have very close links with the Kremlin.'

'Close as in . . .?'

'Decision influencers. Prominent individuals close to Putin. There are times and dates and, according to the asset, a security guard present in the meeting, details of certain favourable trade and investment guarantees made to that individual.' He flicked his toe at a piece of gravel, sending it skittering into the gutter. 'The codename was Cicada.'

'The name Ferris's kidnapper mentioned.'

'Yes. It hung around for a while years ago, the way these things do, then ran out of steam. Now we know why. But it was a time-bomb Colmyer wouldn't have wanted seen . . . especially as the file included a photo of him at one of the meetings and another, more recent one, of him glad-handing with individuals in the US Intelligence community. Bull claimed they smoothed his investment path over there in return for information on certain Russians they went on to subvert.'

'Ouch.'

'Quite. But what interested me was the names in the audit trail leading to it. There was Ferris, of course . . . and Bull.'

'And Bull told Colmyer.'

'Better than that. The trail shows Colmyer made not one but three subsequent visits to that file . . . and made two attempts to delete the photographs. If an alarm did go off, Bull must have covered for him – but we'll never know.'

A few more paces on, Cramer asked if there was any information about the names of the GRU officers.

'As a matter of fact, there is – on one of them, at least.' Hough stopped and looked around. 'One of our researchers got it within a few minutes, courtesy of Bellingcat, would you believe?' Bellingcat was the investigative website that had discovered and released the names of the suspected Skripal poisoners, along with a few other

Russians involved in clandestine operations. 'Kraush is thought to be Colonel Gleb Kraush. One of their bright sparks, apparently, on his way to the top.'

'Does that help us?'

'Not really . . . unless we drop a word in their ear so they can release it to the public. But that might be counter-productive at the moment.'

Cramer grunted. 'It would be for Ferris.'

FORTY

'I hope you've got good news,' said Rik. 'I get the feeling I'm running out of time.' He'd made a slow circuit of the park shortly after Harry had arrived, and was now watching the road. He looked drawn and was shuffling from foot to foot and puffing out vapour into the air, shoulders hunched against the cold.

'Some, yes. Where are the guards?'

'Kraush said the hackers are set up and ready to roll out their offensive and I should stay out here. '

Harry wondered how much of a threat it really was. Hitting the UK with a cyber attack was a world away from trying to get information from an intelligence file. Somehow the two didn't match up. But trying to second-guess these people was something he didn't dare risk. 'I have a plan,' he said. 'But you might not like it.'

'More or less than the shit I'm in already, you mean? Just get me out of here, Harry. I think Irina's wetting herself to use the taser. Kraush's keeping a lid on her but I don't know how much longer that will last. Kraush said they know from the audit trail which files I looked at, and he mentioned Cicada again, but it doesn't help me remember anything.'

Harry opened his mouth to reassure him, then stopped. 'The audit trail's an internal thing.'

Rik nodded. 'Sure. It's common to most systems. So?'

'But specifically, how could he know details of an audit trail in MI6?'

'There's only one way: they must have someone on the inside.'

Harry wanted to deny it but could not. If true, the enormity was mind-blowing. Did it mean someone had been feeding information out . . . possibly for years? Then logic told him there was something wrong with that line of reasoning.

'If they have a mole with access to the database,' he said slowly, 'why would they go to all this trouble to get you over here to corroborate something like a name or a code? If a mole saw the audit trail, surely he or she would be able to follow it and see exactly what you saw.'

'Unless the mole has limited access,' Rik countered, his voice dull. 'Maybe they've been told there's something in the files but they don't have specifics.' He rubbed his face. 'This is doing my head in.'

Harry pushed it aside. Rik was right. There were any number of ways this could have begun. But a mole was something for Cramer and his bosses to worry about. Right now there was too much to do. If Rik was correct about the hackers being ready, the clock was running down. Kraush and his bosses would be getting impatient. 'Right, it's action time,' he said. 'I've got an idea to get you out of this but it can't be done here; disarming that thing on your leg is too delicate an operation.'

Rik looked worried. 'What are you saying? There is nowhere else! Take a look around you.'

Across the way a figure entered the park and stumbled to a bench, where he sat staring about him as if dazed. It was one of the old men he'd seen arguing over a bottle. It gave Harry an idea. He checked his watch. Less than a couple of hours before Mitchell arrived and Clare got her close to the accident unit. But that time would slip away fast once things got moving. He said, 'Sit down.'

'What?'

'Sit, for Christ's sake, and don't ask questions.' Rik sat and Harry continued, 'Remember this: once they get here, you've been hit and you've got a pain deep in your abdomen. It would help if you could throw up.'

'Wha- how do I do that?'

'Stick your fingers down your throat, play half-dead . . . bite your lip and spit out some blood if you have to, act concussed and confused. Somehow you need to convince them to get you checked out in a hospital. And mention the Cicada word. Got it?'

Rik didn't look as if he fully understood but he nodded anyway. 'Right. Hospital and check-up, throw up, play half-dead. Drop a hint. Got it. But what are you going to be doing? You can't do all this by yourself.'

'That's something I've been meaning to tell you. I've got some local help. Someone you know.'

'Local? I don't know anybody lo—'

'Clare Jardine.'

'What?' Rik looked stunned. 'That crazy bi—'

Before he could finish Harry hit him, once in the face and once in the stomach, the second punch knocking him off the bench. The moment Rik hit the ground Harry snatched the iPod out of his pocket and pulled the wired buds from his ears. He heard a shout in the background. It was the old man – his witness. He snatched one of the ear buds from Rik's head and ripped it free of the wire, then pressed it into his hand.

'*What the fu—?*' Rik spluttered, his nose streaming blood.

Harry bent close to Rik's ear and said urgently, 'Put the ear-piece back in. You were mugged for the iPod, got it? Mugged. Play concussed, you don't know where you are and I'll see you in the hospital.' He gave Rik an encouraging pat on the face, then took off, walking as fast as he could into the trees behind the park. He made his way parallel to the road back towards the main entrance, but still within sight of the building where Rik was being held. Moments later he saw Kraush and Irina jog out of the front door and turn towards the park. They didn't seem in a hurry and he hoped it was a good sign. Hopefully as soon as they saw Rik a sense of panic would set in and they'd weigh up the best course of action against what they stood to lose if they didn't get him checked out . . . hopefully without the deadly bracelet on his leg. And Sally Mitchell could go back home again without getting out her box of tools.

FORTY-ONE

'We have to get him to a hospital.' Kraush was staring down at Ferris, who was spitting out blood and rolling around with his eyes glazed. An ear bud from his iPod lay on the ground near his head.

As soon as they had entered the park and seen Ferris on the ground, Kraush had looked around and seen the old tramp standing nearby. 'What happened?' he demanded. He stepped across before the old man could move and grabbed hold of him. It was like grasping a sack of bones and instinct told him this reject couldn't be responsible for what had happened. How he hadn't blown away in the wind was a miracle. 'Tell me what you saw.'

'They were talking,' the old man said, trying to wrench himself free but failing. Kraush's grip was like a vice, fuelled by his anger and desperation. 'The young man had been running . . . like I'd seen him before . . . and they were talking. Suddenly the other man hit him . . . twice . . . and ran off. He . . . he took something from him but I couldn't see what it was. My eyes aren't so good.'

'Who was this man?' Kraush produced a pistol and laid the end of the barrel against the old man's cheek. 'What did he look like and where did he go? *Quickly!*'

'Through the trees!' The old man pointed to the rear of the park where the bushes melted into the treeline. His hand was trembling uncontrollably and his voice weak with fear. 'I don't know who he was . . . I'd never seen him before. Understand, new faces come through here all the time. I can't tell you what he looked like, though . . . it was all so quick.'

Kraush felt like pulling the trigger and putting the old goat out of his misery, but restrained himself. A gunshot was unlikely to be noticed here but he didn't want to take the risk. If the police decided to investigate reports of shooting they might well arrive in force. That left no time to dismantle the hacking operation and clear out the people and equipment. The operation was too far advanced to allow that to happen.

He stood up and gave a double whistle, and seconds later they heard footsteps as the two security guards came racing across the road. Kraush returned to where Ferris was lying on the ground with Irina standing over him.

'I think he's playing us,' she announced coolly, and stubbed the toe of her boot into his side. There was a grunt but no other response.

'Help him up!' Kraush snapped, irritated by Irina's reaction. The bloody woman had the common sense of a brick. 'We need to get him talking, otherwise this entire project fails.' He turned to the two guards. 'While we get back inside, you go and secure the area. The man who did this might still be nearby. Find him!'

The guards hurried away while Irina grabbed hold of Ferris by his arm and virtually hoisted him to his feet. She and Kraush carried him out of the park and into the building and laid him on the mattress.

Kraush began to check him over for broken bones and shone a torch into his eyes. He was more concerned about Ferris's mental state than physical; if he'd been hit hard enough or had banged his head on the ground, it was possible he had concussion. Setting broken bones could wait but injury to the mind was altogether different.

'Not much reaction,' he announced, watching Ferris's head loll to one side. A line of drool ran down the side of his chin and his breathing seemed unnaturally fast. The situation looked bad. If they didn't get this thing cleared up, the shit-storm from Komsomolsky Prospekt would finish him forever.

'Cic . . . Cicada . . .' Rik murmured, his voice drifting off. 'The . . . name.' He slumped back and his eyes rolled.

Kraush reacted as if he'd been given an electric shock. He jumped up. 'We have to get him checked over,' he said urgently. 'There's too much riding on this to leave him.'

Irina scowled. 'Really? You're going to take him to a doctor? What if he's fooling us? How will you stop him from talking once he's out of here? And there's the device on his leg . . .'

Kraush stood up, a sense of rage building in his gut. He was fast coming to the conclusion that Irina should have turned the gun on herself instead of Alex, for all the use she was being.

'Don't argue with me,' he snarled. 'Turn off the transmitter.'

She grudgingly did as she was told, running back to the building. By the time she returned and removed the bracelet, the two guards had come back and Ferris was busy vomiting noisily down his front.

'Nothing,' the lead man explained. 'He could be anywhere. Searching every building would take too long and we'd need a small army to do it. What do you want us to do?'

'Secure the building next door and make sure everybody stays in place,' Kraush replied. 'And check that their escorts are armed and ready.' The temptation to dismantle the operation was strong, but if he did that he might as well shoot himself; going back to Moscow as a failure wasn't an option. He indicated Ferris. 'When you've done that we're taking him to a hospital. We'll say he's a prisoner in our charge. What are you doing?'

He was looking at the second guard who was bending over Ferris, moving his head gently from side to side and pulling back his eyelids.

'I was a battlefield medic in Ukraine,' the man explained without looking up. He used his finger to pull back Ferris's lip and scoop blood from the side of his mouth, then checked his ears. 'He's got a head injury. His eyes are unfocussed . . . and being sick is not a good sign.'

'That's enough,' Kraush said. 'We take him in.'

'You want us to come with you?' said the first guard.

'Yes. But stay on the outside and watch for signs of anyone taking too close an interest. But no assault rifles; side-arms only but concealed. We don't want to start a shooting war.'

FORTY-TWO

Harry watched from his hide in the loft at the flurry of activity when Kraush and his crew found Rik. In spite of the cold he felt a sheen of sweat on his forehead brought on by a circuitous dash away from the park. It had been a close-run thing when the two armed guards had arrived on the run and had split up, moving into the trees with practised precision and making very little sound, relying on hand signals to communicate. It had proved that they were not merely heavies drafted in for guard duties, but were trained and accustomed to working as a team. Luckily for him, they had reached a point in the trees not far from where he'd dived beneath a heavy patch of undergrowth, before they'd veered back towards the industrial buildings. As soon as they had gone he'd made his way back to the loft.

All he could do now was wait to see if Kraush did what he'd hoped and took Rik for medical help. While he was waiting he changed back into his normal clothes. It was a gamble but better than having to change later and risk losing sight of them.

Ten minutes later he heard a shutter door clatter open and the sound of a vehicle engine burst into life. A big 4WD pulled out from inside the first building with one of the guards at the wheel. It stopped on the edge of the road and Kraush and the other guard, with Rik slumped between them, came out and got in, followed by Irina.

No sign of anything resembling a transmitter, he noted. Was that good news or was it already on board? There was no way of checking.

He dialled Clare's number. 'They're off,' he said. 'I'll follow and keep you informed of where they're going.'

'Got it,' she responded.

Harry paused to scatter some dust on the stair treads to the loft, then hurried to his car and jumped in, sweeping away most of the camouflage branches. The engine started on the first try and ran sweetly, just as Kraush's 4WD burst out of the gates and headed towards the Beltway at speed.

Harry felt a punch of elation in his chest. As long as they didn't turn off and head towards the city, there was only one place near enough that they could be going.

He set off in their wake, losing more of the branches in the slipstream and calling Clare's number again. When she answered he told her to get to the accident unit and wait for him, and gave her Kraush's car registration. She confirmed without questions and clicked off.

The accident unit was a modern, two-storey block of glass, pale concrete and brick, surrounded by a car park and sparse, frost-covered gardens. The front of the building held a set of double doors, with several bays at one side reserved for ambulances, leading to ramps and three sets of swing doors for easy access to the building. It was evident that it had been built for function and fast turnover rather than long stays and bed rest.

Harry found a space and checked he looked half-way respectable before getting out of the car. He noted several police patrol cars parked up on the verges, with officers walking back and forth carrying clipboards. They showed no interest in him and he guessed they had come in to interview accident victims off the motorway and gather evidence. Some had cameras and he assumed these were part of traffic investigation teams.

He also spotted the two heavies from the industrial zone, sitting on a low wall by the main entrance doors watching the world go by. It was an added complication having them present but he was sure they wouldn't have got a clear sight of him in his earlier disguise.

He saw Clare approaching. She was accompanied by a young woman in tan cargo pants, a blue Puffa jacket and carrying a holdall.

'What kept you?' said Clare, with a wry grin. 'We were about to go for coffee. We got here just as the bad guys and Ferris were going in. I hope he was only acting half-dead because they were almost carrying him.' She had a certain bounce about her and seemed to be enjoying herself, which made Harry wonder if she'd been missing her old life and was being carried along by a sudden buzz of activity and the whiff of danger.

'Sally Mitchell?' he said, and shook the other woman's hand. 'Harry Tate. Glad you could make it. Sorry if this tore you away from anything important.'

Mitchell shook her head. Her hand grip was firm, dry and brief.

'Nothing that couldn't wait,' she said, with a slight Scottish accent. 'I gather we have a small device strapped to a colleague's leg, is that correct? He's being held by hostiles, according to my briefing from London, although it was light on details.'

Harry nodded, appreciating her business-like attitude. He described the tracker and the size of the box attached to Rik's ankle, and mentioned the transmitter. 'There's every possibility it might not be in place,' he continued, 'with them having to bring him here. But I couldn't afford to take the chance.'

Mitchell absorbed the facts without fuss or surprise. 'Not a problem. It won't be the first one I've come across, although they're all different in the tech used. If it's what I think it is it should be easy to deal with as long as I have no interruptions and there's no incoming.' She smiled and explained, 'With most of my jobs there's usually a bit of ordnance being tossed about by hostiles. It can make things a little hairy.'

'We'll see if we can keep that to a minimum,' Harry said, and found himself warming to her. He gestured to her holdall. 'Is that your kit?'

'Yes. But don't worry, if I get stopped by security it doesn't look much different to an electrician's tool bag to an outsider. If anyone asks, I'm staying with Clare who's looking for a friend who got caught up in a shunt, and no way am I leaving this in the car – it's too valuable.'

Clare asked, 'How long will it take?'

'I'm not sure until I see the device. Less than thirty minutes if all goes well.'

'And if it doesn't?'

Mitchell gave her a cool look. 'Then they might be picking bits of us out of the walls.'

Harry intervened. 'Thirty's good,' he said. 'Anything under would be better.'

Even without the busy surroundings of an accident unit, having Kraush and his crew and Garth Perry and his friends on the prowl, they'd be lucky to get anywhere near that amount of time before they were blown by the security guards or the opposition came storming in to find out what was going on.

Clare's phone buzzed and she checked the screen. 'You'll get your thirty,' she said, and gave Harry a look. 'Katya's on her way. Just don't let on when you see her.'

Mitchell looked between the two of them. 'Am I missing some-thing? Who's Katya?'

'A local helper,' Harry told her. 'The plan's still evolving, but Clare's right – you'll get your time.'

They walked through the front entrance, passing the two heavies outside who gave them no more than a glance; a man and two women didn't fit the profile they were looking for.

Inside they were met by a wall of warm air and two security guards who asked Mitchell to open her bag. One of them rummaged through it and gave Mitchell a surprised grin and made a comment before waving her through.

'What did he say?' asked Mitchell.

'He said he hoped you weren't a visiting surgeon,' Clare told her, and led the way through swing doors into a long corridor with bench seats either side and a handful of visitors looking by turn concerned or dulled by shock. The triage section, she whispered, was through another set of swing doors at the end.

Kraush and Irina were standing just outside the doors.

'It's them,' Clare breathed, leaning into Harry's shoulder. 'The two tailing Ferris at the airport. I'd recognize the woman's skanky hair anywhere.'

'Well spotted,' Harry replied, eyeing the two Russians. 'They're called Kraush and Irina, according to Rik, and both GRU. He's the boss and she likes hurting people.'

'Great. I'll bear that in mind.'

Kraush and the woman eventually made to walk into the triage unit but were stopped at the door by a young orderly.

'They're being told they can't go in,' Clare translated. 'Kraush's pissed and saying that's unacceptable because the injured man is a foreign criminal under their supervision and if he escapes or hurts anyone the hospital will be held responsible.'

The orderly, a hefty young man with the look of a rugby player, looked mildly interested by this but held up a large hand and stood his ground. He looked as if he were used to being confronted and didn't give a damn.

'He's saying,' Clare said, 'that they have security guards on perma-nent call because many accident victims are highly intoxicated and in shock and often threaten violence. They're sometimes found to be armed. He says they must wait in the corridor until the doctor has assessed the patient's injuries because staff have to move very quickly to perform their duties.' She hesitated until Kraush had spoken again. 'Kraush's not happy but I don't think he has any authority here. If he pushes it too far they'll have him arrested, Russian or not.' She looked at Harry. 'They're not that popular at the moment and they know it, even though they think they can act superior.'

Harry turned away as Kraush approached in case the GRU man eyeballed him and saw something he recognized. But he stormed by without looking and stopped several yards away, taking out a mobile phone and stabbing at the keys with a display of annoyance.

The two of them being so close was going to be a complication. They needed to be out of the way while Mitchell did her bit on Rik's tracker, and there was also the question of trying to get past that orderly on the door.

The doors at the far end of the corridor flapped open and footsteps approached at a brisk pace. Harry turned and saw a slim, blonde woman in a white doctor's coat. She had a stethoscope swinging from one hand and was carrying a small aluminium case and looked like she meant business.

Katya.

'Yay,' Clare murmured softly. 'The cavalry's arrived.' She turned towards Harry and said, 'We wait here until she calls us in.'

'Fine by me,' Harry said, and thought of how much of a risk Katya was taking by being here and undergoing this pretence. She might be wearing a white coat but he imagined it only took one person to recognize her and she'd be blown.

Clare must have sensed his concern, because she said, 'Just go with the flow, Tate. I know it's against your big-dog instincts, but go with the flow.'

Katya strode by without acknowledging them and disappeared through the double doors. The minutes ticked by, accompanied by the to-and-fro bustle of staff, patients and an occasional uniformed cop sticking close to a gurney. Gradually the number of people in the corridor diminished until only Harry, Clare and Mitchell, and further down, Kraush and Irina, remained.

Then the doors opened again and Katya stepped out, followed by the orderly. She walked up to Kraush, who looked instantly confrontational, with the orderly nearby, while Irina circled in the background like a pit-bull looking for someone to bite.

After a tense exchange, Kraush's jaw clenched but he was clearly outmanoeuvred and outgunned. White coats here carried the greater weight and he knew it. Any attempt at pushing past them would result in a noisy stand-off. With an obvious lack of grace he turned his back on her and began talking to Irina, who was tossing her hair in a strop. Katya shrugged at them both and returned to the triage section.

The minutes ticked away with agonising slowness, and Harry could see Kraush was becoming more and more agitated. He was pacing up and down and throwing furious glances at the closed doors as if he wanted to charge through them.

Katya returned, this time looking sombre. She walked over to Kraush and there was a muted conversation, during which Kraush looked stunned, then sceptical and finally annoyed.

Clare said softly, 'She's just informed them that their friend has taken a turn for the worse and is unconscious. She thinks there might be some mild pressure on the brain from his head injury and they need to monitor him closely for at least an hour before deciding whether to operate or send him to another unit in the city. She suggested they get something to eat in the canteen and she will call them as soon as she has any news.' She gave Harry a faint smile, her eyes twinkling. 'She's good, isn't she? I told you.'

With a final protest Kraush walked away, followed by Irina. When they had gone Katya turned to them and said in perfect English, 'Come with me. I told the other two that they have to wait but I'm not sure they will. In fact I think the man is probably calling someone in authority – maybe at the interior ministry.' She looked at Harry and Clare in turn, then at Mitchell. 'Can I speak freely?'

Harry nodded and introduced Sally Mitchell. 'She's our technical help.'

Katya gave Mitchell a look of respect. 'We have female bomb disposal technicians, too. They are often superior to men. But your expertise won't be needed here.'

'Why not?' Harry asked.

'I was able to stand by while the triage team examined your friend's legs. There is nothing there. He's clean. I could see where the strap has marked the skin, but that is all. The team are just checking him for signs of concussion but I think he will be cleared to leave. I told them I am responsible for him but I can't just take him out until they've done their job. It would be noticed and reported.'

Harry was surprised but relieved that the tracker had been removed. Kraush had evidently decided it was too risky to leave it in place. 'That's good news. How did you manage that?'

For the first time she smiled openly. It changed her face dramatically. She peeled back her white coat to reveal a dark blue uniform underneath. 'There are two things built into their DNA here,' she explained. 'Outside it is a uniform, in here it's a white coat. However, we should leave as soon as possible. And your friend is in danger of over-playing his part.'

'Understood,' Harry said. 'And thank you. I appreciate your help. I hope it doesn't cause you any problems.'

She shrugged. 'It won't. I'll make sure of it.' She added, 'I hope you can guarantee that there is no threat to the integrity of the Belarus government. The relations between our two countries are currently not so good and I don't want to make things worse.'

'Nobody apart from us knows of your involvement,' he assured her. 'Is there a back door we can use?'

Katya nodded. 'Of course. I just checked.' She turned to Clare and said, 'Bring your car to the rear of this block and wait by the entrance. It's alongside a bicycle rack. I'll meet you there.'

'We'll use mine,' said Harry, handing her his keys. 'Keep yours off their radar.'

Clare nodded then touched Katya's arm. 'Thank you. This is above and beyond.'

Katya shrugged. 'I don't like bullies and I especially don't like what those two are doing here in Minsk. The situation between our governments is tense enough; we don't need to be part of a cyber conspiracy against the UK.'

Harry and Mitchell walked down the corridor and into the main reception area just as Kraush and Irina stalked back towards the triage unit. They looked ready for a fight and Harry wasn't the only one to notice; one of the security guards on the entrance was watching them, and murmured into a radio attached to his collar.

He just hoped the young orderly was still on duty and stopped them going inside the triage unit before Clare got Rik out of the rear door.

'Let's get round the back,' he said to Mitchell. 'This place is about to go ballistic.'

The first thing he spotted outside was Kraush's car parked on a verge in a restricted zone. It was being inspected by a security guard.

Further back parked near the exit was a dirty black SUV with four men on board.

Garth Perry was one of them.

FORTY-THREE

'Where to now?' Clare asked. They were all in Harry's car. She looked in the mirror and pulled a face. 'God Almighty, Ferris, I hate to say this but you smell.'

'Yeah, I love you, too,' he countered. 'My cell didn't come with much in the way of toilet facilities.' He was looking almost chipper apart from the bruise to his face where Harry had punched him.

They had finally got Rik into the car without incident after the staff had cleared him to leave. It had been a tense wait but Clare had eventually pushed the rear door open and Rik had emerged looking slightly bewildered.

They were now heading back down the side of the building towards the exit road, expecting at any second to find Kraush standing in their way.

Harry asked, 'Is there a back way out of here?'

Clare shook her head. 'No. I checked with Katya. The site's on a virtual island between the motorway and thick trees, so there's only one way in and one out.'

That was an added complication. 'Fine. Let's take it easy.' He could see all the way down the side of the building to where Kraush's car was parked. 'Drive out as if we belong,' he said. 'If Perry's still there we need to lose him before taking Sally to the airport. I haven't worked out the rest just yet.'

'Don't worry about me,' Mitchell breathed, her faced flushed. 'Compared with what I usually have to put up with, this is fun.'

'How did this Perry bloke know where to come?' said Rik.

'According to London he's got local contacts,' Harry said. 'They didn't follow me here, so I'm guessing they must have latched onto Kraush and his crew, who haven't exactly been trying too hard to cover their tracks.'

Clare said, 'Par for the course for Russians here. They treat the country like their own back yard.'

Then, as they neared the front corner of the building, she stamped on the brakes. Two men appeared by the side of the road in front of them, arguing loudly. One was a security guard, who was being forced backwards by one of Kraush's men. The security guard seemed to be trying to take the heat out of the discussion by making calming gestures, but Kraush's man was clearly spoiling for a fight and stiff-armed him away before making a vicious fingertip strike at his throat. The guard barely managed to brush it away and reached for his side, where he carried a pistol and a short baton.

'Go left,' said Harry, pointing to a parking lane to avoid the two men. Another guard had appeared and was hurrying to support his colleague, while a couple of cops standing by a squad car were also on the move. The last thing Harry needed was to get caught up in the middle of an argument. With Kraush's men ready for a fight and the number of armed officers around, this had the potential to go badly wrong.

Which it quickly did.

Before Clare could get moving again, Kraush's man drew a pistol and fired two shots in the air. The sounds drew screams of alarm from people in the entrance and across the car park. Both security guards reacted instantly by holding out their hands to their sides and making gestures for the man to lay down his gun. There were too many people about for this to escalate without incurring innocent casualties. But the two police officers had different ideas and began running off to each side to draw the man's fire while reaching for their side-arms.

Kraush's man reacted instantly. He calmly shot the nearest officer, hitting him in the shoulder, then swivelled and shot his colleague before turning to aim his weapon at the two security guards.

Just then a slim figure in a blue uniform appeared out of the hospital entrance. She walked at a fast pace towards the men, arm extended, and shouted a warning, her voice clear and steady.

It was Katya.

'No,' Clare breathed desperately. 'Don't . . .'

Both Kraush's men saw her coming, and the one who had fired the shots turned his weapon on her. Before he could pull the trigger Katya dropped to a crouch and fired twice, the reports so close they rolled into one. As he fell back, his colleague also began to reach for his weapon. But he was too late. One of the wounded policemen and a security guard fired together, their combined shots knocking him off his feet.

In the ensuing silence, Katya turned and checked the car park for other attackers, before going across to the two aggressors and kicking their guns away.

Harry glanced towards the entrance, where he had spotted Perry's car.

It was no longer there, just a wisp of grey exhaust smoke lingering in the air where it had been parked.

'Go,' said Harry. 'Before they close the area down.'

Clare looked at him, then towards Katya, who was directing two more police officers who'd come running from the building to investigate. She was clearly torn between concern for her partner and getting away from here before the republic's *militsiya* – police force – descended in a heavy show of force and corralled everyone and began demanding documents.

'She's fine,' Harry said. 'You'd only be in the way.'

She nodded and hit the accelerator, taking them up to the exit road and out. When they reached the main road there was no sign of Perry's car. But there was a cluster of blue and white lights approaching in the distance accompanied by the mournful wail of sirens.

'You did well to convince Kraush to bring you to the hospital,' Harry said to break the silence, glancing at Rik in the visor mirror. They hadn't manged to talk yet and he wasn't sure what kind of reaction he'd get after knocking Rik off the bench.

But Rik seemed fairly cheerful, and rubbed at the side of his face with a wry smile. 'Simple, I did what you told me and played the victim. As they were picking me off the ground I mentioned the name Cicada and threw up. Not sure in which order but it did the trick, especially when one of the guards examined me and said something. After that it was all systems go.' He grinned, which was more like the old Rik Harry remembered. 'Perhaps I should train as an actor.'

'Best not,' Clare muttered. 'Katya said you were crap.'

Harry didn't join in; he'd been watching his side mirror and now saw a familiar shape a long way back, peeling out of a side road.

Perry.

'Head for the airport,' he told Clare, 'and make it quick. We've got company.'

Clare drove fast, weaving through the traffic and regaining the motorway. Perry's car was still there, but being held up by other vehicles.

'What do they want?' Clare asked.

'If London was right, Perry has orders to stop us.' He looked across at her. 'If you can, stop tight in front of departures.' He turned to Mitchell and said, 'Sorry – this is going to be fast dismount.'

She gave him a smirk and said, 'I bet you say that to all the girls.' When Harry failed to come up with a response she hefted her holdall. 'Everything's good, don't worry. Fast dismounts are par for the course where I work, although not always this close to the ground.'

They hit the approach road into the airport at speed. Clare didn't bother signalling, hoping to throw the following vehicle off balance with a late manoeuvre. It didn't quite work but there was no time for anything fancier. All she could hope for was that other traffic would act as spoilers. She followed the road up to the terminal building, the car's tyres squealing on the smooth surface, and stopped in front of the doors to departures, where security guards were on patrol and watching the vehicle arriving.

Mitchell jumped out and slapped the roof and was gone before Perry's car came into view. Clare pulled away and headed for the exit, waving gratefully at a couple of other vehicles both heading for the space left and ended up blocking the road behind them.

'I think you pulled there, Tate,' she commented, and took the road curving round the other side of the parking area towards the motorway.

Harry grunted but said nothing. He was studying the road leading to the terminal building and saw Perry's vehicle storm into view and come to a stop behind traffic. He figured they had a couple of minute's grace before Perry worked out what had happened and set off in pursuit.

'Motorway coming up,' Clare announced. 'Where to?'

'Where they won't expect us to go,' Harry replied. 'Back to the zone.'

She looked at him. 'But that's a dead end.'

'That's exactly why they won't expect us to go there. They'll expect us to go to ground in the city until we can arrange evacuation to London. The city is where Perry has his contacts; they'd find us in no time. He'll also have this car's number by now so we might as well go where we can do the most good.'

'I don't get it.'

Rik leaned forward from the rear seat. He was grinning and said, 'He's got a plan. And it's probably going to get noisy.'

FORTY-FOUR

The industrial zone wore a heavy layer of silence, as if every living creature was aware that danger was on the loose. The desolate atmosphere was helped by the first signs of a thin fall of snow, although it hadn't settled yet, adding to the muffling of sound as if a blanket had been thrown across the landscape.

Harry directed Clare to the same spot in the trees he'd used before and made sure the car was well camouflaged before leading her and Rik through to the building containing the loft space he'd found earlier. 'Wait here until I give you the all-clear,' he said softly, and disappeared inside, listening for any sounds to betray the presence of unwanted visitors. He climbed the steps to the loft and found the sleeping bag and rations undisturbed, with no trace of footprints in the thin layer of dust he'd scattered when leaving last time.

Harry left Rik to point out to Clare the building where he'd been held, then the three of them made themselves as comfortable as they could and settled down to wait for Katya to call.

When she did so, it was to say she had got away from the accident unit without a problem.

'She's clear,' Clare relayed to Harry and Rik with evident relief. 'The two security guards backed her up and said they'd be dead like one of the cops if it wasn't for her intervention. One of them used to be in the Presidential Security Service – the SBP – and recognized her. The surviving cop also swore she saved their lives. She made a report to her boss and he said he'll make sure she doesn't face charges.'

'Good,' said Harry. 'Where is she now?'

'On her way here. I'll go and wait for her by the car.'

'All right. But keep your head down. We don't know if Perry's in the area. If he sees you he won't bother asking questions.'

'No worries.' She gave him a sideways look and drew a semi-automatic from her jacket, then disappeared down the steps.

'She hasn't changed much,' said Rik. 'Still bolshie.'

Harry couldn't disagree. 'We might need that before this business is over.'

They sat in near silence while they waited for Clare and Katya. Rik had turned in on himself, which Harry assigned to the after-effects of his capture and release. In normal times he'd have spent time talking him round, but this wasn't a normal situation. Whatever Rik was dwelling on wouldn't be solved in this cold and alien space, and he just had to hope the younger man would respond well when the time came to act.

A scrape of sound signalled Clare and Katya's arrival, and they were soon up the steps and sitting down. Katya was carrying a dark blue canvas sports bag which she put to one side. She wore a tense look on her face but seemed fairly relaxed, although Harry had seen those conflicting signs before on faces following a firefight. You went over the event time and time again because you couldn't help it, reliving each frame in turn and wondering if you couldn't have done something different.

'You OK?' he asked. 'You did well back there.'

She nodded. 'I'm fine. It all happened too fast to think of anything but reacting, the way I was trained to do.'

He nodded. As a professional government bodyguard she would have been schooled to the highest standards. The Russians were no more interested than anyone else in having their personal safety guaranteed by amateurs. He didn't entirely believe she was fine and, by the concerned expression on Clare's face, neither did she. But it was something he would have to accept.

'What do you know of these hackers?' Katya asked Rik.

'I haven't seen them up close,' he replied. 'They're in a building across the road from here.' Rik gestured in that direction and looked at Harry with a question.

'Tell her,' Harry said. 'But keep it short and sweet.' He stood up and went over to a peephole in the structure from where he'd been able to keep an eye on the central road through the zone and the two main buildings where the opposition were holed up. The air was filling with swirling snow, making observation difficult, but that went both ways and the opposition would find it just as hard to keep watch on their perimeter.

Rik nodded. 'Kraush and the woman named Irina are both GRU. They drew me out of London and the two men you shot are all part of an active service unit. They told me they had two assignments: one was to find out what I'd seen in the MI6 files and second, if I didn't talk, it was to mount a three-tier offensive cyber attack on the UK.'

There was a brief silence, during which nobody reacted. Harry still thought it sounded crazy, but he knew as well as any of them that times were changing and nothing was guaranteed any more.

'They've assembled a team of outsiders,' Rik continued. 'It's not the way they normally operate, but this is different.'

'What do you mean?' Katya wasn't being openly sceptical, merely seeking clarification.

'The GRU is military and hierarchical. They have their own experts and trawl their universities for candidates and train them up. It's the way they're structured.' He looked at Katya. 'You know that, right?'

Katya looked uncomfortable. 'I know it but I find it difficult to believe that Moscow would do such a thing,' she said. 'Wanting to see inside your MI6 files, of course that would be normal. You do the same back. But a cyber attack?' She shook her head, clearly conflicted at the idea. 'Why would they?'

'What else did Kraush say about the attack?' Harry put in. He had to get this out rather than being side-tracked in supposition and doubt.

'Random Cyber Disruption is the first level. They use malware to target companies, public utilities, local authorities, distribution chains – but that's small-scale, designed to be a short-term nuisance.'

'And the second?'

'It's called Strategic Cyber Disruption, or SCD. It's a step-up and targeted against government installations, major utilities and transport systems.'

'What about our military?' Harry said, keeping his eyes on the buildings opposite.

'They'd be affected. They already rely on rail and road distribution for everything from personnel movements to weapons, munitions and equipment. Shut down the rail transport operations alone and they'd be unable to shift a thing. They've got their own haulage, but so what? SDC would also target traffic light systems. Imagine the area around any of the big cities if all the lights went to green: the chaos would be massive. Further out wouldn't be any better, and trying to get around gridlocks for distribution purposes would be a nightmare.'

'Go on.'

'Then there's the big one.' He hesitated and stared at the floor as if looking into a deep, dark well.

'Keep us waiting much longer,' Harry murmured, 'and I might just shoot you.'

'I'm sorry, all right!' Rik almost yelped. 'This is hard for me; I was dragged into the middle of this . . . shit.'

Harry turned and held up a hand in apology. 'I'm sorry. What's level three?'

Rik hesitated as if he didn't want to put voice to it. 'Total Cyber Disruption, or TCD. Kraush used the word 'Terminal', like it was a computer game.'

Harry felt a chill around his neck.

'It does what it says on the box. Everything would stop. No food, no water, no travel, no phones, no fuel, no communications. Nothing.'

'Did you believe him?' Clare asked. She looked in deep shock. 'He might have been trying to frighten you.'

'Well, he fucking well succeeded,' he replied shortly. He looked at Harry. 'Something I didn't mention before: he told me if I didn't talk they'd go after you . . . and anyone close to you. He showed me a picture of you in the street, taken a few days ago.'

'Well?' Katya said.

Rik nodded. 'It could be done, yes. But whether it would . . . I don't know.'

Harry didn't want to believe it was that simple, but logic told him it was. Enter the new era of warfare. Disrupting a nation's ability to feed and heal itself was damaging enough; kill communications and travel and absolute panic would follow. It didn't take much to produce a tiny fraction of the chaos Rik was suggesting with snow on power lines and the wrong kind of leaves on the rail tracks; a targeted assault would be far worse.

'How many?' Katya said. 'The hackers.'

'Close on twenty.'

'Why so many?' Harry asked.

'Burn-out. The work's intense; not everyone can stand the pace. When they launch an offensive they go in fast and have to be ready to move on when they're blown. It's brutal.'

'Where will the other groups be located?'

'Central and eastern Europe mostly, because they're easier to hide and control, like here. And they keep moving them around. They can uplift an entire group complete with hardware within a couple of hours, probably less, and put them on board a couple of trucks or modified coaches and take them to a new location. Another couple of hours and they're up and running again.'

'Like plug-and-play,' Clare commented sourly.

'Pretty much. Replicate that over the countries involved and they'd always have a group – several groups – operating with nobody knowing where they were.'

'But they do get caught, don't they?' Clare asked. 'We've heard about them.'

Rik looked sombre. 'Some, sure. But they work on the basis that a few losses here and there is to be expected.'

Harry turned from his survey of the other buildings. Rik was right: it was based on an old military methodology more common to eastern nations than the west. Why invent a new system when the old tried and tested template worked so well?

'It doesn't matter what it is.' He'd heard enough. This was talk for another time. Right now he couldn't sit here chewing over the maybes and maybe nots. A coach had just pulled up outside the building opposite and was reversing into the compound at the front.

'What's happening?' Rik asked, noting Harry's sudden air of tension. He climbed to his feet and glanced out of the peephole, and swore softly. 'That's not good.'

Harry agreed. If they packed up and left now they'd simply set up somewhere else. It was time to do something before they disappeared.

'They and their equipment are a threat. I want to end it. Now.'

FORTY-FIVE

Katya stood up and looked, too. 'If it is as Rik says, they are just one of many groups, what will it achieve? They will switch to another one.'

Harry nodded. 'You're probably right. But if it hurts them just a little, I'll feel a lot better. I can't just walk away and hope for the best.' He looked at the sports bag Katya had brought with her. 'What's in there?'

'I thought you might need some extra supplies. They're all untraceable, confiscated from extremists. But that's all I can do. I cannot be seen to go against them, no matter what they are doing here. I might not like it but they must have some authorization locally as well as in Moscow. It would mean instant recall if I was identified and seen to have interfered. I do not like to think what would happen . . . not just to me but to Clare.'

'That's not a problem,' said Harry. 'Rik and I can handle it.' He went over to the bag and opened it. It contained a selection of semi-automatics and clips of ammunition. He was hoping they wouldn't have to use any of the guns. Otherwise, as Rik had said, this was going to get noisy.

'Don't forget,' Katya warned, 'they are GRU. They have trained as hard as special forces; they will not be easy to take down.'

Clare was on her feet, a cold look of determination on her face. 'You're not leaving me out.' She glanced at Katya who nodded before the two of them turned and went down the steps together.

'Almost the old team,' Rik commented. 'She's not so bad, is she? Clare, I mean.'

'She never has been. Underneath that grumpy exterior she's still one of us.'

Rik dipped into the bag and came up with a pistol and extra clips. 'She has a weird way of showing it.'

Harry checked his gun had a full load. 'You remember that pink powder compact you gave her in hospital?'

'Sure. What about it?'

'She keeps it in her car. What does that tell you?'

Harry led the way downstairs where Clare and Katya were talking in subdued tones. Clare broke off and Katya turned and hurried away into the trees behind the lot.

'What's the plan?' Clare queried. She sounded relaxed but Harry saw the tension in her face. He guessed she hadn't had to consider this kind of action for some time, and would be feeling rusty. At the same time, he knew from experience that she was quite capable of handling herself in the toughest of situations.

'We'll check the buildings before we go in,' he replied. 'But keep an eye out for Perry and his crew just in case. They won't be far away.'

They left the building and reached the road, where they ducked behind a pile of rusting wire-and-metal stillages once used for storage. From there they had a closer view of the coach and the area around it. It was deserted save for the driver, who was standing by the open baggage bay, smoking. He appeared to be taking no part in whatever was going on inside the building, but the gun on his hip showed that his function was unlikely to be benign.

'What's the likely plan for them packing up?' Harry asked. He didn't want to get any of the hackers between him and Kraush and his people, otherwise they'd be in a no-win situation. Hackers weren't fighters but he wouldn't put it past Kraush to use them as a very effective shield.

'If they're leaving,' Rik said, 'they'll be unplugging laptops, servers and power lines, and any other electricals like fans and heaters. It'll take time but they'll have practised this before. If they have any programs running they might not want to do it too quickly.'

Harry nodded. Moving that amount of equipment couldn't be done in five minutes, no matter how practised they were. It was too valuable to risk any damage and neither would they want to leave their servers and computers behind in a rush to escape.

'What's the worst we can do to their stuff?' he asked.

'Depends what you want to achieve,' Rik replied. 'Smashing it up would be good, although it would take a while. Unless . . .'

'Unless what?'

'We could always leave it so that they can't use it again . . . but they won't know it until they try.' He grinned. 'You get us into the building and I'll deal with it.'

Harry didn't bother asking. He knew instinctively that Rik was thinking of planting a virus. 'How long will that take?'

'Depends. If I can use one of their computers to download a virus onto the servers, it shouldn't take long. Once it's down and in place, the first time they hook up it'll be inside their system and running.'

'Will they be able to tell?'

'Not unless they have some top-level detection software in place and someone thinks to check. With a bit of luck one of them will try to communicate with another group or their controllers and it'll spread from there.'

'Where is Kraush likely to be?'

'In the building on the right, where I was kept. The other one's for the hacking operation.'

Harry thought about it. He doubted Kraush would risk finding himself isolated in the first building. Even with Irina it would be too large an area to defend and he'd be vulnerable. Ten to one they'd be in the second building using the hackers as cover. But they would have to check first. As Katya had warned, they were GRU and military trained.

'Will the hackers be guarded?'

Rik nodded towards the driver. 'Probably. If he's out here it means they've likely got a couple inside making sure the hackers get on with their job. It depends what their orders are.'

'Let's go.' Harry led the way across the road. A glance each way revealed the area was deserted, with no signs of movement either way along the central road. If there were any of the locals about they were probably keeping their heads down until the weather improved. He briefly considered the tracks they'd leave in the layer of snow. They'd be all too visible if anyone cared to look, but there was no way of avoiding it and taking a detour would use up valuable time they didn't have.

'Follow me,' Rik said, and headed along the side of the building.

Harry and Clare followed, trusting in his confidence that he knew where he was going. He stopped at the rear corner of the building and peered round, then stepped out and slid along the back wall. There was a soft scraping sound and he said, 'Come on. We're in.'

It was a single door opening into a small room. The air was damp and dead. Harry took out a small torch and flicked it on at ground level, shielding it with his hand. The floor was concrete, littered with rodent and bird droppings, and with small puddles of water forming where snow-melt was dripping from the roof. It was cold and unwelcoming.

Harry stepped over to the inner door and peered out. The silence was intense. But it was the silence of a dead building, with no other presence nearby.

Rik tapped him on the arm and whispered, 'Follow me. We need to check out where they kept me first. It's the biggest space. They might be there.' He was holding his pistol ready, finger along the trigger-guard.

Harry nodded. It made sense and Rik already had a rough idea of the building's layout. He also had unfinished business here and needed to take the lead for his own peace of mind.

Two turns down a long corridor, checking locked doors as they went, and they reached a large sliding door, standing partly open. Rik signalled them to stop before peering through the gap, then stepping through.

'Torch,' said Rik, and Harry switched on the light and played it over the room; at least, as much as he could see. It was an immense area with a cavernous space above them and, after the narrow confines they'd just come through, a sense of openness where the night's chill seemed to hang in the air like a dry mist.

The oil-stained and puddled concrete floor showed traces where machinery had once been bolted down, with regular areas in between worn down by the passage of who knew what kind of wheeled trolleys and the innumerable tread of feet in rough boots. Elsewhere, just visible in the torchlight, they caught glimpses of unnameable nests of foliage and dried-out scraps of paper and cardboard tucked into corners, and a few skeletal remains of small animals that had not been quick enough or strong enough to fight off the predators that haunted this vast deserted night-time world.

And, standing in the centre of the floor was a hard-backed chair.

The sight of that single piece of furniture, held to the floor by brackets and bolts in such a miserable place, and clearly meant for one thing and one thing only, seemed to dominate everything.

'God Almighty,' Clare breathed, softly, as if in deep shock at the tableau before them. 'This is where they had you?'

'Yeah,' Rik replied. 'A regular home from home.' He reached out and directed Harry's arm so that the torchlight came to rest on a mattress and blankets in one corner and, further over, a plastic bucket and a partly-used toilet roll rippled with damp. 'And all mod cons provided.'

Seconds later they moved as one to step back through the door, glad to be out of there. Taking the lead again, Rik lead them along the corridor and stopped outside another door.

'I don't need to see this again,' he said. 'Against the back wall. Alex.'

Harry went inside with Clare on his heels. They saw immediately what Rik had meant. A shape lay under a bundle of cloth against the wall. Harry lifted it to one side and saw the dead FBS man, a single bullet wound to his forehead.

Beside him Clare gave a soft murmur.

'Come on,' he said, and turned and went back out of the room. He wanted to be out of this dead space and on the move, somewhere where there might be the promise of light and fresh air.

'Where else?' he said to Rik. The building was still silent but he was getting a prickly feeling across the back of his neck. Probably because of seeing the body. But they had to make sure it was clear before tackling the one next door.

Rik set off into the gloom, sure of himself this time, and stopped at another room.

'This is the store-room where they kept supplies,' he whispered, his breath warm on Harry's neck. 'Nothing much worth seeing, though.'

Harry moved past him, holding the torch with one hand and his gun with the other, side by side. A store-room would be a natural place to come back to if Kraush or Irina needed anything. It would also be an ideal spot to lie in wait if they'd heard Harry and the others coming. He stepped inside with a swift movement and flicked the torch on. But there was nothing save for a few cardboard boxes, a sink and the plink-plink of water pooling on the floor. Beneath the overriding smell of damp he detected the familiar aroma of garlic. And something else. Gun oil.

He was standing next to a pile of boxes at shoulder height. A hole ripped in the side of the top-most box showed tins of something inside. But that wasn't what caught his attention, or explained the smell of gun oil. That came from a pair of assault rifles perched on the top, side by side.

'Cool,' said Claire, and moved up alongside him. 'AK-Nines. I've seen one before but not up close.'

'Special forces?'

Clare nodded. 'I heard they were on a limited-use only list.'

For GRU operatives in other words. The guns were short, with detachable stocks and the bulbous shapes of suppressors on the barrels. They held curved magazines with a likely capacity of twenty rounds. Enough to start a short but fairly quiet war. Ideal for close-quarter combat where space would be restricted and stealth a necessity. He passed one to Clare and took the other himself, shoving the pistol inside his coat. If they were forced to engage, it would be better to keep the noise down.

'What's in there?' Clare asked, and pointed to a military-style backpack on the floor.

Harry bent and flipped open the top. Inside was nestled a transmitter with a display window, a small covered keyboard and a telescopic aerial. Next to it was the bracelet he'd last seen on Rik's leg. Harry left it where it was. Maybe they could find a use for it later.

'Nice,' Rik commented, eyeing the weapons. 'Can we get out of here? It's giving me the chills.'

'Good idea. Out the back way then round to the left.'

They hurried through to the back door where they'd come in. Harry checked the outside first, then eased through the gap with Rik on his heels. Clare was behind him but had stopped further back to pull her jacket closer around her shoulders.

The wind had picked up since they had come inside, with snow swirling through the air around them and snapping off the skin of their faces like a million cold, angry insects. Oddly, it brought with it an improvement in visibility, showing the immediate area of fencing, grass and rubbish in a faint but ghostly detail.

They had only taken a few steps away from the building when they heard a metallic rattle. It was familiar and shocking, a sound they had all heard many times before. It was followed by a slim figure appearing from behind a pile of metal crates.

'Well, well,' said a man's voice, reaching them through the wind noise. 'If it isn't Mr Tate and his little friend.'

FORTY-SIX

It was Garth Perry, dusted with snow across the top of his head and the shoulders of his heavy coat. The hems of his trousers were as dark with damp from the snowy overgrowth of grass around the deserted factory units. If he was feeling the cold he didn't show it, but grinned in triumph, his stance relaxed.

Harry didn't move, his brain careering into overdrive. Perry was holding a machine pistol which he recognized as a Czech-made Skorpion. It was short and ugly and he knew it possessed a high rate of deadly fire.

'Life's shit, isn't it, Tate?' Perry said coolly. 'You come all this way to help out a traitor and it's all been a waste of time.'

'What do you want?' Harry said, inching up the muzzle of the assault rifle. He carried on talking to slow the man down. 'In case you hadn't heard, this is my assignment. You don't get a look-in.'

Playing the part of someone defending his turf wouldn't come as a surprise to this man; theirs was a crowded field and contractors like him were paid by results. Someone horning in on their action was a threat to their income and reputation. He hoped Perry didn't take the short cut to completion by pulling the trigger and sending them all into the unknown.

'Is that a Skorpion?' he continued, edging his voice with surprise. 'I thought they were old hat by now.' And, he wanted to add, used by second-rate gang-banger types who relied on a spray-and-pray use in the knowledge that they'd have to hit something eventually, even if by accident. But he guessed Perry might take offence at that.

Perry sniffed. 'Doesn't matter. It does the job. And the rules of this job have changed. This is now my game. You're out of it.' He pointed the weapon towards Rik, who had emerged from the doorway partly behind Harry. 'Is that Ferris? I believe it is. If you could stand aside I'll complete my assignment and get the hell out of here. No hurt, no harm.' He used the machine pistol's barrel to indicate which way Harry should move. 'Of course if you don't want to play it makes no difference to me. What say you? Oh, and if you lift that AK-Nine another millimetre, you'll be dead.'

Harry froze. His head was telling him what to do but with Perry standing so close with that murderous little gun in his hand, one false move and they'd all be caught in a withering blast of rounds. Then he heard the tiniest scuff of movement in the background. He thought it was Rik about to step out from behind him and opened his mouth to stop him. But then he saw Perry stiffen, and realized the contractor wasn't looking at either of them, but further back.

Clare.

The report from the AK-9 she was holding was little more than a damp paper bag popping, and Harry swore he felt the round go past his ear. But it found its target somewhere in Perry's shoulder and spun him around, his momentary expression one of open-mouthed shock. Amazingly, he didn't try to fight it but used the momentum to keep turning and launch himself behind the metal crates. One second he was there, the next he was gone.

Clare stepped past Harry looking as if she was about to give chase, but he grabbed her arm. 'Leave it,' he said. 'The others won't be far away.'

She didn't resist, but turned back. It was true: going out into the dark after a fleeing killer would be suicide.

'What now?' said Rik. 'It's going to be harder to deal with the hackers with Perry and his men here.'

'But easier than going looking for them. Clare and I will watch your back while you deal with the technical stuff.' Turning his back on the direction Perry had taken took an extreme effort of will, but there was no alternative. If Kraush got even the first level of their planned cyber assault off, it would be disastrous. They had to stop it now. Perry would have to wait.

He led the way along the rear of the first building and into the yard around the next one, stepping through a large hole in the rotting wire fence. He stopped on the other side and waited, listening to the sighing of wind as it flowed through the trees and coursed around the structure, setting up a low, mournful moan from holes in the fabric like some enormous low-level orchestral instrument. If there were any guards stationed around here, he couldn't see them, and hearing any movement over the wind noise was impossible.

He stepped forward and saw a faint glimmer of light through a window, where the paint he'd noticed on his first recce must have fallen or been scraped away. He gestured for Rik to take a look while he stood with his back to the building, watching for any signs of attack.

Rik studied the inside for a few moments, then said, 'I can see fifteen, maybe twenty in all . . . and a couple of guards with hand-guns on watch. There's no sign of Kraush or Irina.' He turned back to Harry. 'What do you want to do?'

'Get them all out of there.' Harry checked out the window. It was big enough to get through but too high to make it easy. If the guards inside knew their job, they'd be able to pick them off one by one. Unless they could find a back door, that left a frontal assault. And he didn't like the odds.

Then he remembered the power line from the sub-station. It wasn't the original, he was certain of that, which meant it had been laid recently. And no way would Kraush have risked relying on using the original connectors.

But Rik was ahead of him. 'We disrupt the power,' he said, 'disrupt the hackers to put them off, and it'll bring the guards out to see what's wrong.'

They moved across the rear of the building and found where the power line approached the building. Rik pointed to a large box structure against the rear wall of the building.

'It's a transformer,' he said. 'But it's not big enough. They're probably using it for basic lights and power points, but the supply wouldn't be constant enough for a bunch of servers and computers.' He ducked his head to one side, closer to the building. 'Hear that?'

Harry listened and picked up a low-level rumble emerging over the wind noise. A vehicle engine? He glanced up at a window above them. It had a crack in the glass revealing a jagged line of light.

'They've got a generator on the inside,' said Rik. 'Probably brought in on a truck.'

'Great,' said Clare. 'How do we deal with it?'

'Easy.' Rik grinned and reached round to a square section on the side and flipped it open. 'Ready?' There was a click and the light in the window went out.

FORTY-SEVEN

Harry led the way to the far side of the building and edged along the wall. Rik followed with Clare bringing up the rear. The relative quiet here was almost a shock. Sheltered by the building, the wind noise had dropped and the snow was falling in a gentle, near-serene pattern.

Harry stopped and held up his hand. There was the outline shape of a side door just ahead, and he could hear voices coming through the fabric of the building. It sounded as if someone was panicking while another voice was telling everyone in a shut-the-fuck-up voice to calm down.

Looking beyond the door to the front of the compound Harry could see the rear end of the coach. The lights were off, but even as he noted this a beam of torchlight played momentarily over the vehicle from the front door.

The three of them sank to their heels, waiting to see if anyone was going to look down the side of the building. But nobody did and the torchlight went off.

Harry turned and said, 'Clare, you're with me. We go inside and chase everyone out, loud and fast. When they're clear you stay near the door to deal with opposition and Rik, you get to work on the servers. I'll watch the back.'

He waited for them to acknowledge, then stepped forward and tried the door handle. It turned without a sound and the rumble of a generator turned into a steady roar. The voices must be coming from the next room over.

The open door emitted a heavy smell of diesel and oil, and a rush of warm air like a working garage. The room was in darkness save for the flicker of red and green LED warning lights on a panel. Harry switched on his torch, shielding the lens with his fingers. He was looking at a space of about fifty feet long and twenty wide, with a shutter door at the front end. A large yellow generator sat squarely in the middle of the floor with cables running to the far side and through a crude hole that had been knocked through the adjoining wall. Heavy sacking had been jammed around the cables in the hole, no doubt to guard against the intrusion of diesel fumes. Elsewhere the remains of rotting work benches sagged against the walls and electric sockets hung from the ceiling, and everything was covered in bird droppings and grime.

Harry walked across to a narrow door in the opposite wall and listened. Voices, louder now but still muffled. Order was being restored. He motioned for Rik and Clare to approach the door, signalling that they would all go in and fan out.

The door swung open smoothly on oiled hinges. Another empty space. But this one had trestle tables with bottles of drinking water and fruit juice, biscuits and other assorted snacks. Nerd food, he thought; but no sign of proper meals . . . until he spotted a pile of crushed pizza boxes in one corner. And further back were piles of sleeping bags and backpacks.

This was where the hackers bedded down and ate between work sessions. He turned to Rik and whispered, 'Does this look real?'

Rik peered past him and nodded. 'I guess. They normally work them in short bursts to avoid burn-out.'

Directly across from them was another door, with a faint light showing around the edges. The voices were louder now. Harry moved across the room and hoped nobody chose this moment to come for a bag of Pringles or whatever the local snacks were called.

This door opened to reveal an almost demonic scene from a sci-fi movie. Blue-ish light from many screens pulsed up to the rafters, lighting up the faces of the hackers, most of them bending to their task and seated in two rows at trestle tables. Cables snaked like spaghetti across the floor in the gloom, and two figures were moving about behind the operators with hand-held torches, stopping occasionally to look down at a monitor and murmur instructions. Harry thought at first that they were guards but realized they were more likely to be supervisors.

Nearly all the hackers were young and most were male, with a handful of women. There was little about them to stand out, and they would have passed by in the street without being noticed, dressed in heavy jumpers, trousers and boots.

They were so intent on their work that none of them noticed the newcomers enter the room.

Harry went left towards the rear, while Clare went right, sliding along the wall, the pallor of her face picking up the nearest bank of blue-tinged light. Rik waited by the door, checking out the servers and monitors.

Something immediately struck Harry as wrong about this scene: hackers and equipment as expected, but no guards. It wasn't right.

Then he realized someone was watching him. It was a man seated three places in from the end, facing him, eyes wide open at the intrusion. He wasn't at a keyboard or monitor, but sitting at a blank space on a table with his hands resting on the surface.

A guard. A gun lay in front of him.

Before Harry could react a single gunshot rang out, the sound shocking in its intensity. Everything stopped instantly, with screams taking over amid the thud and clatter of chairs falling over as people jumped to their feet.

Rik had stepped into the centre of the room, his gun held high. He looked wild and almost other-worldly in the reflected light, and shouted, '*Quiet!*'

To emphasize the order, he fired directly into an unused monitor on a side table, blowing it apart. More screams, but this time quickly silenced.

The guard hadn't made any move towards his gun, but stayed absolutely still. Harry motioned him to get up and move away from the table, which he did in slow motion, holding his hands out to the side. Trained to a point but not to the point of suicide.

'Outside,' Harry said calmly in the silence, stepping over and retrieving the man's gun. 'Leave your places and go. Sit in the coach.' Amid a volley of queries and objections, a few who understood him began heading towards the door, scrambling past others who didn't. To encourage them Harry raised the assault rifle. The remainder quickly got the message and began to move.

Clare followed, then kept watch at the door as the last one left. Rik, meanwhile, was already at work at one of the laptops.

'How long, Ferris?' Clare called out. 'Only there are some bodies out there not on the bus. I think they're armed.'

'How many?' Harry queried. It couldn't be Perry's men, not up this close . . . unless they'd joined forces with Kraush.

'Three at least, possibly more. One woman.'

Irina, Harry thought. Hooray for equality. Kraush would be around somewhere, too.

'Give me a couple of minutes,' Rik replied. 'The signal's not great.' He'd barely finished speaking when a shot came through the front door and slammed into a keyboard, scattering the pieces into the air. Simultaneously, a window near where Harry was standing shattered and an object hit the floor and rolled, leaving a trail of heavy smoke behind.

Harry swore. Smoke grenade. Next they'd come in all guns blazing. It depended how serious they were. Kraush must have decided it wasn't worth trying to save anything and simply wanted to close them down, maybe grab the equipment.

As if to confirm it he heard a heavy motor burst into life outside. The coach; the hackers were abandoning ship.

But not everyone was leaving. A window along the side wall smashed and another smoke grenade bounced in, coming to rest under one of the trestle tables and leaking a malevolent plume of thick, acrid smoke.

Harry went over and kicked it into a corner. 'Rik?'

'I'm getting there,' Rik said calmly. 'Can't you fight them off or something? I need more time.'

Up by the front door Clare was trying to get a clear view of the numbers outside, but finding it hard. It was snowing more heavily now, carpeting the front yard and beginning to fill in the tyre tracks left by the coach, and whoever was out there had picked their positions carefully. There was some movement across the road but it was indistinct and she didn't want to risk hitting an innocent drawn by the excitement.

She moved back just as a round snapped through the door at floor level. Someone hoping for a ricochet. She didn't bother returning fire; it would only draw a response and without a decent target she'd be wasting rounds on snowy air.

Harry appeared across the doorway. He had a wet handkerchief clamped over his mouth and passed her a scarf left by one of the hackers and a plastic bottle of water. She soaked the scarf and wrapped it around her face. It wouldn't help much but it was better than sucking in smoke.

Harry ducked back across the room and through the side door into the generator room. They needed a way out and couldn't afford anyone getting inside. He peered through the outside door just as a figure ran into view, backlit by a careless torch from the front of the compound.

Harry fired twice, the sound of the suppressed shots lost under the chugging of the generator. The figure yelled and rolled before disappearing into the dark. Hit or miss, he couldn't tell.

He slipped outside and closed the door behind him, listening to the sighing of the wind. Snowflakes splattered across his face, heavier now and colder with a sharp touch of ice. This was going to be both a help and a hindrance.

He saw another figure towards the rear and turned, ready to fire.

'*Tate – it's me!*' Katya's voice, urgent but surprisingly calm.

Harry took his finger off the trigger and moved to meet her. 'Why are you still here?' he said. 'You should be miles away.'

She shook her head. 'They found my car and disabled it. I only just avoided them. One of them has been injured – an Englishman. But I don't think seriously.'

That had to be Perry. 'We've cleared the building and Rik's working on the servers.'

'How long?'

'No idea. It'll be done soon and we can get out of here. Are you armed?'

'Yes, but I don't have many shots left.'

He handed her the gun he'd taken from the guard inside, then turned and scanned the darkness. Unless they were equipped with night vision goggles, the opposition would be finding it just as tough operating in this kind of weather. But they had the advantage of knowing where everyone was, right inside the building. Even as he thought it they heard the rattle of gunfire coming from the front and far side of the building, and the tinkle of breaking glass. Kraush and Perry alike must have decided to ignore the possibility of attracting attention in favour of ending this in a fusillade of fire. He hoped Clare and Rik were keeping their heads down.

'Come with me,' he said, and began moving towards the rear.

'Where are we going?'

'We need to put them off before they storm the building.'

They made their way to the side, expecting some opposition, but all was quiet except for the continuing sound of shots at the front. Harry moved quickly and came to a stop near the front corner. Gun flashes were coming from at least four points in the darkness, and he realized why: they were concentrating their fire on the front door and raking the building in a sustained fashion, laying down a withering curtain of lead that would soon kill anyone inside. There was no response from Clare and he hoped she was safe.

Harry waited for a heavy flurry of snow, then moved out towards the road through a gap in the fence. Katya was right behind him. This put him almost at right-angles to the line of guns. Katya saw what he was doing and moved across the road, hunkering down by a tangle of fencing on the far side.

A gun opened up close by, the flare off an assault rifle lighting up the man's face. It was all Harry needed and he squeezed his trigger, the two suppressed shots lost in the wind. The other gun fell silent and Harry was on the move before the other side found his position.

One down.

Katya, meanwhile, had disappeared into the darkness to await the same opportunity. Seconds later, after another burst of fire from near the road, two unsilenced shots sounded, drawing a scream of pain and a rattle of fire which arched into the air as the gunman lost control of his weapon.

Two down.

There was a shout, followed by silence.

'Katya?' Harry risked a call but knew it was pointless.

He heard a click and turned. Two figures were standing a few yards away. In the flare from another burst of fire from behind Harry they were just visible, dressed in winter jackets and boots, with ski hats pulled down low. Both were armed with semi-automatics. One was tall, the other shorter and stocky.

Kraush and Irina.

Then Kraush moved to reveal that he was holding someone by the scruff of their jacket, slumped against his leg.

It was Katya.

FORTY-EIGHT

arry swore. He'd been careless, assuming it was Kraush storming the building. Instead it must have been Perry and his team . . . with Kraush in the background quite happy to step back a pace and let them reduce the odds so he could move in afterwards and mop up.

'Put down your weapon, Mr Tate.' Kraush was pointing his gun at Katya's head. 'Or I'll kill her.' His English was near perfect, the accent there but his delivery measured and calm.

'What do you want?' Harry asked, desperately thinking of a way out of this mess and wondering if Katya was even still alive. He bent and placed the AK-9 on the ground.

'Call on your friends to come out with their hands up and we'll talk.' Even as he finished speaking Kraush's gun hand swept up and he fired without warning, the bullet crackling through the air past Harry. There was the thump of a body hitting the ground. 'Local gangsters,' he explained casually. 'We offered them a deal to help us but they are also taking your countryman's money. So greedy.' He pointed with his gun across the road. 'Call your friends.'

'And get myself shot by whoever else is out there?' Harry said. 'How will that help you get Cicada's details? That's what you want, isn't it?'

Kraush stiffened, his reaction telling Harry that he'd surprised the man. It was obvious he still needed that information badly to take back with him to his masters.

'He's bluffing.' The woman, Irina, her voice sharply sceptical. 'Don't listen to him.' She raised her gun towards Harry.

'No!' Kraush's voice cut through the wind, stopping her. 'We need confirmation from Ferris. Go and find the others and call them in . . . and the Englishman. Tell them to wait for us before going in.'

Harry was surprised. So Kraush and Perry were working together. It was unexpected but maybe Perry's local contacts had no choice: stay friendly with the GRU team or suffer the consequences from their bigger neighbour. Perry must have swallowed it for the sake of convenience. Either way he would accomplish what he'd been sent out here to do. Unfortunately, it looked like Kraush was already going against that agreement.

For a moment it looked as if Irina was going to argue, but she held her tongue and stormed away into the darkness, calling out in Russian.

The silence after all the gunfire was intense, save for the hiss of wind through the trees.

When Irina returned it was with just one man. He was dressed like the guard Harry had disarmed inside the building and looked scared, as if he knew he might be facing an uncertain future.

'I couldn't find the Englishman.' Irina sounded almost petulant. 'But I know he's out there.'

'No matter.' Kraush looked at Harry. 'Perhaps you could prevail on your friend Mr Perry to join us?'

'He's not my friend. He has orders to kill Rik Ferris . . . and me.'

'Really? How very un-British. Almost Russian, in fact.' Kraush gave a bark of laughter. 'So now we will have to protect Ferris from him? Ironic, no?' He pointed towards the building. 'After you. And take this woman with you.' He released Katya, who slumped to the ground. 'Don't think I won't shoot you both if you do anything stupid. We do not have much time.'

Harry bent and picked Katya up. She was light and easy to carry, and he was relieved to hear her breathing. He walked across the road, slipping on the icy surface, and stopped a few yards back from the front door. As he did so a light came on overhead, bathing them all in a yellow glow.

Harry felt Katya move against him and gently set her on her feet. She turned to face him and slumped against his chest, her legs almost giving way and grabbing at his waist to hold herself up.

'Clare – it's Harry,' he called out, praying she was alive to answer. Silence.

'Clare. I've got Katya. She's hurt.'

The door moved and Clare appeared, her face a pale oval against the dark. She stepped further into view, her face a mix of horror and concern. She was unarmed.

Garth Perry was standing behind her. He was holding a gun to her head. His other arm was held in a rough sling, and he didn't look happy.

'This is getting silly, Tate,' he said. 'Where's Ferris?'

Harry didn't have to act surprised. 'I have no idea.' He gestured with his head at Kraush and Irina. 'You think I'm in charge here?'

Perry chuckled. 'Oops. Got yourself in a tangle there, haven't you?' He raised his voice. '*Come out, Ferris, or your friends are all dead. I'm not kidding!*'

But the wind was the only response, raising a rattle from some cladding over their heads and a flurry of snow falling from the roof.

'*I mean it! Five seconds and I start shooting!*'

Nothing.

'*Five.*'

Harry wondered where Rik was.

'*Four.*'

If he had any sense he'd be somewhere safe because the moment he showed up Perry would make sure he was the first to be killed.

'*Three.*'

Perry's gun swung round to point at Harry.

'*Two.*'

'Rik.' Clare shouted, and moved her arm.

There was a crackle of electricity and Garth Perry went rigid as Clare jammed her hand into his groin. She was holding a taser.

Perry lost his hold on his gun and followed it to the ground, unable to stop himself falling.

At the same time, Rik Ferris stepped out from the side of the building and shot Kraush in the throat, dropping him to the snow-covered yard.

Stepping up alongside Harry, Irina snarled and lifted her gun. Unable to get a line on Rik she aimed instead at Clare, an easy target.

Then Katya moved. Pulling her hand from Harry's coat pocket, she lifted out the gun he'd taken from the sports bag she'd brought with her, and in a fluid movement pressed the barrel into Irina's side and squeezed the trigger.

'Damn,' said Rik Ferris, looking down at Perry, who was still trembling with shock. 'I wanted to do that.'

Clare smiled and handed him the taser. 'If he tries to get up be my guest.' Then she hurried over to Katya and wrapped her in her arms.

Forty minutes later they had finished clearing the building. Rik had made sure the computers and servers were connected before feeding out loaded emails to every address he could find on the laptops left by the hackers. When that was done he disconnected everything, then left the building, returning two minutes later with the backpack containing the transmitter and bracelet and a fuel can from the generator next door.

'What are you doing?' Harry asked.

'We can't leave the bracelet here,' Rik replied. 'The locals are like jackdaws. The moment we leave they'll be in here seeing what they can get.' He took the cap off the fuel can and began splashing the contents over the servers and laptops, then placed the bracelet in the middle. 'I've set it so I can just press a button once we're clear. The signal will do the rest.'

Harry's phone had rung several times but he'd ignored it. Cramer, probably, chasing news. There would be time enough to answer it when he was certain they were all going to get out of here in one piece without being arrested or shot. He hadn't figured that bit out yet.

It was Katya who came up with a solution to explaining away the scenario. She had made calls to check local police and anti-terrorist activity, and found that snow on the approach roads to the industrial zone had caused multiple pile-ups, meaning there would be no sudden arrival of more guns to add to the chaos of the night.

'I'll stay here and wait for the police,' she said. 'I can say my car broke down near the road and I heard gunfire, so I came to investigate and found that a fight had gone on between opposing gangs.'

'Gangs?' Rik asked.

'Well, I can't say they are GRU or contractors for the British Intelligence agencies. How would I know that? I checked the bodies and they are all carrying false documentation. I will say I heard Russian so I assumed they were *Mafyia*. It would be reasonable to suspect them, since they are everywhere.'

'What about Perry?' He wasn't sure how his presence here would pan out, and he was likely to talk if faced with a lengthy prison sentence.

'He's dead,' said Katya. 'His heart, I think.'

Harry felt a rush of relief. 'And the guard Irina brought in?'

'I let him go. He won't want to stay here anyway. There are too many questions he cannot answer. I'll say others escaped in the confusion, too.'

'Will they believe you?'

She nodded. 'Sure. The government here won't want the truth to come out – that their territory was being used for a hacking drive against a foreign sovereign state. You'll see, in forty-eight hours it will be as if nothing happened here.'

They left the building and made their way to their vehicles. Just before leaving, Rik flicked open the control panel on the transmitter and pressed a button. For a moment there was utter silence, then the crump of a small explosion followed by a flicker of bright light coming through the trees as the diesel fumes in the hackers' room ignited.

'Kismet,' said Rik with a smile.

Harry flopped onto his hotel bed near the airport and stared at the ceiling. He was bone tired and had a phone call to make which he wasn't relishing. There would be questions and objections, most of which would be unanswerable, but he didn't care. All he wanted to do was to make sure Rik wasn't going to end up in the pokey.

Earlier he'd said a grateful goodbye to Katya and Clare, promising never to call them again, and hoping they would be safe. Katya had been confident that they would be. But in an aside to Harry she'd assured him that if they needed to move on at short notice, they would.

'You'd do that?'

'Coming here after Moscow,' she said, 'means I already have. Another country, another job . . . we'll be fine, Clare and me. We're a team.' She smiled. 'I hear New Zealand is nice most times of the year.'

When Harry dialled Cramer he answered as if his feet were on fire. 'Where the hell have you been? I've been trying to get hold of you.'

'Sorry,' Harry replied. 'Got a little bogged down here. There was a sharp exchange of views and the man from *Despicable Me*.'

'*Who*?'

'It's a film. His name is Gru. GRU – geddit? You should take some time out and see it – you'd like it.'

There was a strangled sound from Cramer. '*What happened, dammit?*'

'I'd rather not talk about it right now. Walls have ears and all that.'

'But everything went well?' Cramer, desperately trying for calmer while equally desperate to know what had gone down.

'I'll ring you when I get back to London.'

'Christ, Harry, give me *something*. I'm being leaned on here.'

'Tell 'em there'll be no come-backs. Everything's been taken care of.'

'Really? What about Perry?'

'His heart wasn't in it.' He cut the call with Cramer's voice echoing in his ear. He really was very tired.

FORTY-NINE

Two days later.

This time Cramer had left his minder behind. He looked as if he was desperate to break into a sprint as he crossed the floor of the restaurant but was holding himself in. He sat down after scoping the room and stared at Harry in expectation.

'The coffee and chocolate cake here are excellent,' Harry said lightly, deliberately drawing out the news. 'I've already ordered for you.' He gave a nod to the waitress, who smiled and disappeared into the kitchen.

Cramer ground a fist into the palm of his hand. 'Enough with the games, Harry. Give. What the fuck happened over there? It's like there's a total news blackout. We haven't heard a whisper and our sources in Belarus are wondering what we're talking about. Aside from a gun battle at a hospital they—' He stopped, eyes wide. 'Bugger. Was that you? The embassy said it was gang-related.'

'So it was. Just not the usual gangs. What did you expect – a media briefing on Sky News?'

'All right . . . fine.' He raised both hands. 'So tell. I promise, no recording. But it would help if you could come in for a debrief.'

Harry shook his head. 'That's not going to happen. Your man Perry was going to knock Rik off – and me if I'd got in the way – so I don't owe your bosses anything, least of all a little get-together over tea and biscuits.' He tapped the table. 'This is as much of a debrief as you get.'

Cramer relented but added forcefully, 'Perry wasn't my man.'

'I believe you. He had a bunch of friends with him, by the way. Local recruits.'

'What happened?'

'We dealt with them, too.'

Cramer listened while Harry gave him a summary of what had gone on in the hospital and the industrial zone, and who were the key players. It would be enough for Cramer to make a connection with the events in London and Nathalie's murder, so that the pen-pushers and file holders wouldn't be able to find holes in the story. He made no mention of Clare or Katya, but admitted only to some local help. One mention of Clare and someone higher up the totem pole of MI6 might be tempted to send a team over to hunt her down.

'What about Ferris?'

'He's fine, thanks for asking. He didn't spill any beans because he couldn't remember any worth spilling.'

'I meant is he all right?' Cramer sounded faintly embarrassed. 'But, since you mention it, no loss of . . . information?'

'I know what you meant. He's all good, as da kids say. And the information is in safe hands. So don't go looking.'

The waitress appeared with a loaded tray, interrupting Cramer's next question, and departed with a flutter of her eyebrows at Harry.

'I'm not sure I like the sound of that,' Cramer said. 'What do you mean, safe hands?'

Harry kept his voice casual while helping himself to cake. 'Cicada. Before Kraush and his friends departed, they confirmed the name.' They hadn't, on grounds of being dead, but Cramer and his bosses would never know that. As bluffs went, Harry was taking a huge risk, but the bigger the lie the more likely it was to be believed.

'Jesus.' Cramer sounded impressed. 'You know who it is, then?'

'Yep.' The cake really was excellent and Harry had some more, nodding at Cramer to eat. 'But don't worry – he's your problem to deal with. My lips are sealed.'

'That sounds . . . ominous.'

Harry didn't answer, and Cramer sat back, a crumb of cake on his lip. 'Don't tell me: you've left full details with a third party in case anything should happen.' He looked as if he was trying not to smile. 'Bit of a cliché, isn't it?'

'Second, third and fourth, actually.' Harry drank some coffee, wishing it was Jean sitting across from him. Maybe tomorrow. His treat. He couldn't wait.

Cramer shrugged. 'Fair enough. Makes me wish I'd been there.'

'You'd have liked it. *Will* the problem be dealt with?' He stared hard at him.

'Already done. Heads have rolled. Talking of which, will there be any local fall-out from Minsk?'

'No. It's being handled.'

'How? Who by?'

'By whom. None of your business. Interested parties. And it's a group of hackers out of action.' He didn't want to go into how Katya was going to work things out, but she had suggested her Belarus contacts would be grateful to find a way to use the situation for their own ends while keeping it firmly under wraps.

'Good. Anything else? Only I can't believe this is all we're here for. You want reimbursing with expenses, maybe even a fee, that's fine. Agreed.'

Harry smiled. 'Oh, I definitely want that . . . and more.'

'Dear God, I knew it. I'm listening.'

'I want written guarantees, signed by the Attorney General or the PM or whoever handles these things, that Rik's in the clear.'

'Wait, I—'

'No argument. Clear and free.'

'Of course, but—'

'And no dropping him into some black hole the moment he comes back.'

'We don't do that kind of thing.' Cramer's reply was automatic. Then he remembered who he was talking to. 'Sorry . . . I'm talking bollocks. He'll have to go through a debriefing, of course. Where are you hiding him, by the way?'

'I put him on a flight from Minsk to foreign parts, just in case your bosses came up with the kind of duplicitous response for which they're renowned. He won't come back until he has those guarantees. Oh, and remind the gatekeepers that he did save the country from an all-out cyber attack.' He forked up more cake.

'I'd give you the guarantees here and now,' Cramer replied. 'But they're not mine to give. But I know somebody who'll get it moving. He's retiring soon and knows where all the skeletons are, so he won't give a rat's arse about upsetting anyone.' He put his fork down and stood up. 'Will that do for now?'

'I'll take it,' Harry said. Sometimes you had to negotiate in good faith. And he had a good feeling about Cramer.

Cramer nodded and held out a hand. 'Good work, Harry. And please thank your . . . friends, for their help.' He smiled knowingly, then turned and walked away.

Harry watched him disappear through the door, and wondered how much he could be trusted. Had he spoken to Sally Mitchell and got a description of Clare and Katya? If so, it wouldn't take much to put together a team and go looking in Minsk. It would take one name off the bulletin board and earn someone some brownie points.

He put it out of his mind. Cramer was solid, he was certain. Not like some of the schemers and movers who'd turn someone in for a step up the ladder. He was more concerned that the person who had started all this would be signed off and would quietly disappear into the background, no doubt using friends of friends to diminish the risk of a public scandal.

He scraped up a last smear of chocolate cream, images in his mind of grey faces in grey suits in the grey buildings along the Thames, doing their best to be seen to be doing something while ushering some innocent sucker to the stocks and claiming they'd made the world a safer place.

They didn't deserve chocolate cake.